The Mandela Project

Gordon Henderson

T **AUP** **UK**
Terrestrial And Universal
Publications

ISBN: 978 0 9955713-9-6

Published in the United Kingdom

TAUP UK
Sheerness
Kent

enquiries@taup.uk

PREFACE

My name is David Statton. I am employed by the British Government to do the dirty work that ministers don't like talking about. My job is to kill people for them. What follows is my story.

Chapter 1

As the red sun sank slowly into Abhainn Loch a' Bhraoin, the surface of the long, sausage shaped stretch of water was filled with an orange glow that lent it an inviting warmth but it was a chilly illusion.

The water was cold enough to remind me that winter's frosty fingers had not yet loosened their grip on the narrow throat of the mountain stream that fed a constant supply of fresh, icy water into a loch teeming with salmon and trout.

I had just spent the afternoon standing up to my waist in the shallows, casting out into deeper water in the hope of tempting the huge salmon I had been pursuing for many months.

I knew the fish was out there somewhere. On several occasions, I had seen it leaping majestically out of the water, as if flaunting its size, and then disappearing beneath the surface. The fish looked at least four feet long and well over twenty pounds in weight, but despite all my angling skills it had eluded me.

The warmth from the bright spring sunshine, bolstered by thick woollen underwear and heavy rubber waders, protected me from the worst effects of the cold water but, with the approach of night, any heat generated by the sun soon disappeared. It was replaced by a bitter coldness that quickly penetrated both garments, driving me out of the loch to seek refuge on its gorse and heather covered bank.

It didn't take long to pack up my equipment and soon I was trudging down the hill with a rod bag slung across one shoulder. In one hand I carried a bag of fishing tackle and in the other a basket containing half a dozen goodish sized trout. My fishing trip had not been entirely unsuccessful.

My dinner that night would consist of trout, fried in garlic butter and served with spinach and mashed swede, washed down with half a bottle of South African pinotage.

I know some food snobs would sniff at my choice. They insist fish should be accompanied by white wine. However, I believe people should drink the wine they enjoy, whatever food they are eating. For me, that is pinotage.

The fast-approaching night was already throwing a cloak of darkness across the eastern horizon and occasionally a set of headlights cut through the gathering gloom as a vehicle headed along the A832.

This road bisects the Corrieshalloc Gorge National Nature Reserve and usually is deserted, but not this evening. The Easter weekend was fast approaching and the next day was Good Friday. This heralded the traditional start of the tourist season and visitors were already making their way north towards Dundonell.

Despite the darkness, I made good progress down the rutted hillside track and soon reached the dry-stone wall marking the boundary of my property. I pushed open the gates and walked along the wide gravel drive leading to the parking area at the front of the small, comfortable cottage in which I lived.

Halfway along the drive I stopped at the cairn Freddie and I had built. I put down the basket of fish and ran my hand across the slate plaque that was attached to the front of the cairn. It was too dark to see the inscription, but that didn't matter because I knew it read: *In Memory of Andrew Hamish Macmillan. A true friend.*

I looked across my neat front garden and smiled sadly as I remembered the tough little Scotsman, known to everybody as Mr Mac. He had died tragically during our attempt to rescue a Soviet scientist from the high security prison on Robben Island five years before.

As he passed away, Mr Mac made me promise to use the fee for the South African operation to buy the dream cottage in the Scottish Highlands on which he had set his heart.

So, that's exactly what I did, and then moved into the cottage with Freddie Carlse, the young Cape Coloured girl with whom I fell in love during our ill-fated Robben Island operation.

Freddie felt the same way as me, but love was not enough. Despite our best efforts, our feelings for each other could not counteract the weather and homesickness.

After two harsh Scottish winters, Freddie became increasingly unsettled. I could see she pined for South Africa's wonderful climate and its way of life. *Die lekker lewe.* I knew also how much she missed her family and friends. So, it came as no surprise when one day she announced tearfully that she was leaving me and moving back to Cape Town.

I didn't want to live without Freddie and didn't want her to go, but pride stopped me pleading with her to stay. It was a wrench seeing her leave, but at least we parted on the best of terms. We were friends and lovers to the very end.

After Freddie's return to South Africa I thought of her a lot, but my damn pride prevented me from contacting her. That same perverse cussedness made me convince myself I was content with my solitary life in Abhainn Loch a' Bhraoin.

But it was now three years since Freddie returned to South Africa and I could no longer pretend I was happy living on my own. The truth was that I missed her vibrant and sometimes feisty presence.

Suddenly, as I caressed the cold stone reminder of my past, a wave of loneliness swept over me. I shrugged the feeling off, picked up the basket and made my way quickly to the cottage.

As I unlocked the kitchen door a set of headlights flared brightly on the dark horizon as a vehicle turned off the A832 onto the side-track that spurred from it. I paused, with the key still in the lock, and watched the lights for a few seconds.

The vehicle came towards me, bobbing up and down as it navigated the track's bumpy surface. I opened the backdoor and stepped inside. I made sure the door was locked properly and then drew the kitchen curtains.

I put the basket of fish on the roughly hewn kitchen table-top, then made my way through to the utility room, where I stored my fishing equipment. I stripped off my waders and woollen underwear and slipped on a pair of denim jeans and a heavy fisherman's jumper.

I reached up and pulled a wooden box from the top shelf of the tall Welsh dresser that stood against one wall of the utility room. I removed a Smith & Wesson .44 Magnum revolver and put the box back on the shelf. I slipped the pistol into the waistband of my jeans and pulled the baggy jumper over it.

I went through to the front door and unlocked it before making my way to the lounge. I closed the curtains and waited for my visitor to arrive. Five minutes later I heard a vehicle crunch across the gravel car-park before stopping. There was silence.

I peeked through a gap in the curtains. The security light that was fitted to the front of my cottage came on as two men got out of a black Range Rover. There was something vaguely familiar about them, but I couldn't put a name to either face.

The driver wore a uniform with a peaked cap. I was not expecting visitors, let alone somebody important enough to warrant his own chauffeur. I touched the handle of my Smith & Wesson. The big pistol felt comforting in the small of my back.

The passenger wore a trilby hat and an expensive covert coat with a silk collar, beneath which was a yellow paisley scarf. He wore black leather gloves and shoes polished to such a shine it hinted at either an obsession with spit and polish, or enough wealth to be able to employ somebody else to clean them for him. He carried a slim attaché case.

The man in the trilby walked purposefully to the cottage. He knocked on my front door with the self-assurance that comes to those who have risen to a position in which their power over the lives of lesser mortals is unquestioned and unquestionable. His driver stood in the shadows a couple of feet behind him.

I made my way to the doorway that led to the entrance hall, but didn't go through it. I took the revolver from my waistband. 'The door is open,' I shouted and heard the grating of metal as the door-handle was twisted. The door swung open. 'Turn on the light as you come in,' I called out. 'The switch is on your left.'

There was a click and the hall was filled with bright light.

'It's poor security to leave your front door open at night, Mister Statton,' the man in the trilby said as he stepped into the hall. His mouth twitched, but there was no danger of the slight movement disturbing the neatly trimmed moustache that nestled against his top lip. It was an apology for a smile.

'Not when you're holding one of these it isn't.' I pointed my Smith & Wesson at him.

'We come in peace,' the man in the trilby hat assured me. As he spoke his driver stepped into the hall behind him. Now he was standing in the light, I could see he was not wearing a chauffeur's uniform, but that of a staff officer in the British Army.

The soldier was tall with a demeanour that showed the confidence of a man who has managed to reach the rank of colonel. He had a lean, handsome, face that was marred only by a vivid white scar that ran across his tanned cheek.

'We just want to talk to you,' the man in the trilby said.

'Is that so?'

'Yes,' he replied.

4

'Who is we?' I studied him carefully, trying to put a name to his face. 'I can see your friend is a colonel in the Intelligence Corps, but I have no idea who you are.'

'Do you really need to point that thing at me?' The man in the trilby asked. 'Guns make me very nervous.'

'They're meant to,' I said, but I lowered the pistol and slipped it back into my waistband.

He stepped towards me, removing his glove from the right hand he offered me. 'Toby Smithers,' he introduced himself and attempted another smile, but again he didn't endow it with enthusiasm or sincerity.

I shook his hand anyway.

'I'm Minister of State at the Cabinet Office,' Smithers added, as if this was sufficient explanation for his uninvited presence in my home. It wasn't, but it did remind me where I had seen him before. He was a Member of Parliament who was often on television defending government policy.

I ushered both men into my lounge and sat down in my only armchair. I indicated that my visitors should share the small settee opposite. There was only just room for them sitting side by side, but they didn't seem to mind the tight squeeze. Smithers took off his trilby and laid it with his attaché case on the low coffee table that stood on the floor between us.

There was no room left on the table for anything else, so the soldier balanced his cap on his knees. He studied me with sharp blue eyes. 'Don't you think the pistol was slightly melodramatic, Mister Statton?' He asked as he ran his finger along the scar on his cheek as if checking it was still there. The gesture could have betrayed a touch of nerves, but the man didn't strike me as being the nervous kind.

'You might be right,' I agreed. 'But my old granddad told me it's better to be safe than sorry.'

'I noticed you left the front door unlocked and then made us let ourselves in,' the soldier said. 'Was that a precaution?'

'Yes. It's standard procedure when strangers turn up on your doorstep unannounced. I'm surprised an Intelligence Corps colonel doesn't know that.'

'I'm not a field agent,' the army officer said by way of explanation. 'I'm just a policy wonk. My job is to analyse the intelligence information collected by you spooks.'

5

'I'm no longer an intelligence agent.'

'In my experience; once a spook, always a spook,' the colonel said with a smile. Unlike Smithers, at least his smile looked genuine.

'I take it you don't get many visitors, Mister Statton?' Smithers interjected.

'Just the occasional tourist who gets lost. However, you're obviously not a tourist and you don't look lost. You know my name, so you must have tracked me down for a purpose. So, tell me, Mister Smithers; why is a minister from the Cabinet Office visiting me in the wilds of Scotland accompanied by an Intelligence Corps officer?'

Smithers reached down to his attaché case. There were a couple of clicks and the lid sprang open. He took a thick file from the case and closed it again. 'The Prime Minister has set up a Cabinet committee of inquiry and she has asked me to chair it.'

'An inquiry into what?' I asked.

'To investigate the circumstances surrounding the death of Dermot O'Neill,' Smithers replied.

'Dermot O'Neill?'

'Yes. Do you remember him?'

'How could I ever forget?' I tried to keep the bitterness from my voice. He had hit a raw nerve.

'With difficulty, I should imagine,' Smithers said as he flicked through a bundle of papers he had removed from the file. 'After all, it was you who killed him.' A frown of concentration furrowed his brow, as if he was trying to make sense of what he was reading.

Smithers didn't fool me. I guessed he knew the contents of the papers inside out.

'Ah, yes,' he murmured eventually, as if he had discovered some forgotten fact. He pointed with his finger to a section of text that had been highlighted with a yellow marker pen. 'You shot him in the chest.'

'That's true,' I said. 'It was either him or me.'

'Well, that was certainly your claim at the time,' Smithers said. He tapped the page. 'However, it says in this report that no weapon was found on O'Neill's body.'

'What's this all about?' I asked. 'The incident with O'Neill happened seventeen years ago. I thought the matter was dead and buried.'

'The only thing dead and buried is Dermot O'Neill,' he said

solemnly.

'I have no regrets,' I said.

'Maybe not, but his family does. They are still very unhappy about the manner of his death and they want answers.'

'They got answers back in Nineteen-Seventy. There was an Inquiry into what happened then and a report was released. The family received a copy. Why has another inquiry been set up now?'

Smithers ignored my question, instead he said: 'Yes Dermot O'Neill's family did get a copy of the original Inquiry report, but they have always maintained you assassinated him on the orders of the British Government.'

'I know what they maintain.'

'Is it true?'

'The Inquiry didn't think so.'

'Ah, yes. Let's consider that Inquiry.' Smithers pulled another sheet of paper from his file. 'This is the executive summary of its findings.' He waved the document in front of my face, but not for so long that I had time to read any of the notes scrawled on it.

'The Inquiry concluded you acted alone and killed O'Neill in self-defence because you thought he was armed,' he said.

'He was armed,' I insisted.

'That's not what the report says,' he tapped the file again. 'The investigating officer was quite clear on that point. He said you were mistaken about seeing O'Neill with a gun.'

'He was wrong.'

'Are you suggesting he was not telling the truth?'

I smiled. 'Let's just say that truth is somewhat overrated. Sometimes it does more harm than good.'

'But surely O'Neill's family deserves to know the truth?' He pressed.

'Knowing the truth won't bring him back to life,' I pointed out.

'That's as maybe,' he said. 'But if the Government did order his assassination then the public has a right to know.'

I raised an eyebrow. 'Since when did the Government consider the rights of the public?'

Smithers bristled at that. He chose to take the criticism personally. 'I think you do my colleagues and me a disservice.' He looked at me earnestly. 'All members of Parliament, including ministers, are answerable to their constituents. That is why we only ever pursue policies that are in the best interests of those we serve.'

I tried not to laugh. Only a career politician could make such a claim whilst keeping a straight face. 'You members of Parliament can live in cloud-cuckoo-land if you like,' I said. 'But in the real world out there,' I pointed towards the window, 'field agents have to make life and death decisions.'

'And in O'Neill's case you decided it was death,' Smithers said coldly.

'Yes I did,' I admitted. 'But it wasn't my decision to go after O'Neill in the first place.'

'So whose decision was it?' He asked.

I stared at him. Suddenly a sixth sense warned me that all was not as it seemed. Smithers was up to something, but I had no idea what. I decided to tread carefully. 'It might be better if I tell you about the events leading up to Dermot O'Neill's death.'

'I'm listening.'

'You will remember that in June, Nineteen-Seventy the Conservatives won the General Election and Ted Heath became Prime Minister.'

'I do indeed,' Smithers said. 'It was the year I was elected to Parliament for the first time.'

'As I recall the Tories won that election against all the odds,' the soldier interjected.

'Yes,' Smithers said. 'A couple of days before polling took place we were way behind the Labour Party in the opinion polls. It was a real shock when we won.' He looked at me. 'So what point are you making, Mister Statton?'

'That shock election result was symptomatic of the unstable political situation at that time. Public opinion swung one way and another almost on a daily basis.'

'Tell me about it,' Smithers said with feeling. 'I was there, remember. There was great deal of political uncertainty.'

'Well, you will remember also that the uncertainty put the government under almost constant pressure. I don't think Ted Heath would have stayed in power if some of the events leading up to what happened to O'Neill had been made public.'

'What did happen, Mister Statton? What is the truth?'

'The truth? The truth is, Dermot O'Neill was an Irish Republican Army thug who personally murdered a dozen Protestants and at least six British soldiers. He was also responsible for executing several members of the Catholic community in Belfast who were accused by the IRA of collaborating with the British.'

'He was a murderer?'

'He was a murderer and a psychopath. He happened to be a member of the IRA, but if he had been a Loyalist he would have still been a psycho.'

'Is that why you killed him?'

'Not exactly,' I said.

'Not exactly?' Smithers repeated. 'What does that mean?'

I didn't answer him straight away, instead I stood up and walked over to the sideboard that stood in the corner of the lounge. I picked up a bottle of Islay single malt whisky and waved it at my visitors.

'Drink?' I asked.

Both men recognised the *Laphroaig* label on the bottle and accepted my invitation. I poured a couple of fingers of whisky each into three glasses and passed one to each of them. I didn't offer them water, they both looked like men who would not want to dilute good malt. I sat back down and sipped my drink.

'To understand why O'Neill was killed you need to know a little more about him,' I said eventually.

'I have his file.' Smithers picked up another sheaf of papers.

'Not everything is in that file,' I said.

'For instance?'

'For instance, O'Neill was part of an IRA cell in Glasgow that planned to blow up a city pub called *Annie Millers*, which was used by Rangers football supporters.'

Smithers flicked through the file.

'Special Branch were tipped off about the plan and O'Neill was picked up and held in custody,' I explained. 'He was interrogated by an MI5 specialist unit and eventually admitted his involvement in the conspiracy. He agreed to turn Queen's evidence in exchange for his release from custody, twenty-five thousand pounds and...'

'There is nothing about any of that here,' Smithers interrupted me. He waved the file at me.

I resisted the urge to tell the politician that's what I had told him.

'Why is it not included?' He demanded.

'Don't be so naïve. It was deliberately left out.'

'Why?'

'If you let me finish, you'll find out.'

Smithers' face flushed and his mouth pinched with displeasure, but he let me continue.

'As I was saying,' I went on, 'in return for information, O'Neill demanded his release from custody, twenty-five grand and a new identity.'

'Such an arrangement would have required ministerial approval,' Smithers pointed out, perhaps to demonstrate his knowledge and reassert his authority.

'Quite so, Mister Smithers, which is why the demand was referred to the relevant minister,' I explained patiently. 'He sanctioned the deal and O'Neill made a statement to MI5. He gave them chapter and verse about the planned IRA attack on *Annie Millers*, after which he was escorted back to Northern Ireland and handed over to the Royal Ulster Constabulary for safe keeping.'

'What happened?' The Army colonel asked.

'On the day that O'Neill claimed the IRA would be planting their bomb, the security forces set up an ambush in *Annie Millers*.'

'I vaguely remember reading about a pub frequented by Glasgow Rangers fans being blown up,' the soldier said. 'But I don't recall it was called *Annie Millers*.'

'It wasn't,' I said. 'Unfortunately, O'Neill told the truth about the day and time, but lied about the target. While the Special Branch were staking out *Annie Millers*, a bomb went off in a pub called *The Flower of Scotland* that was located a few streets away.'

'You mean O'Neill deliberately sent the police to the wrong pub?' Smithers asked.

'Yeah.'

'Surely MI5 or Special Branch should have doubled checked his story?' the colonel said.

'Hindsight is a wonderful thing,' the MP said in a superior tone.

The man's pomposity was getting right up my nose. 'That might be your opinion, Mister Smithers,' I snapped. 'However, on this occasion a more wonderful thing would have been a little foresight.'

I glared at him and then took a sip of whisky. I counted to ten. It didn't make me feel much better about the politician, but I was able to keep my voice calm when next I spoke. 'Look, in my book there was no excuse for what happened. MI5 should not have been taken in by O'Neill. As the colonel has rightly observed, any half-competent intelligence officer would have checked out his story before passing any information over to Special Branch.'

The colonel nodded. 'And Special Branch must share some of the blame,' he said. 'At the very least they should have taken the precaution of sealing off all the streets in the immediate area round *Annie Millers*,' he said. 'It sounds as if the whole episode was a massive cock-up on behalf of our internal security agencies.'

'It was,' I agreed, 'and that cock-up resulted in the deaths of nineteen innocent people, whose only crime was that they went out for a drink to celebrate their football team's win. In addition, dozens of soccer fans were seriously injured in the blast.'

'Jesus Christ,' the Army officer swore.

'Sadly, he wasn't around to help the poor sods who were blown up. You can add them to the list of O'Neill's victims.'

'What happened to O'Neill?' Smithers asked.

'He disappeared.'

'How on earth did that happen?'

'Well, he was supposed to have been kept under lock and key by the RUC, but somehow he managed to escape. That's when the Department for Covert Operations became involved. We were tasked with finding him.'

I took another sip of my *Laphroaig* and savoured the peaty, iodine taste that was the result of the malt being stored on the Isle of Islay in casks that were open to the elements.

'We eventually tracked O'Neill down to an IRA safe-house in Londonderry, which was placed under twenty-four-seven surveillance.' I paused again as my mind went back over the years.

'As you can imagine, when the bomb went off in The Flower of Scotland, all hell broke out. The security services went into panic mode, whilst you politicians went into cover our arses mode.'

Smithers looked affronted again. He took my words as a personal insult, but I didn't care. He was typical of the career politicians for whom I had little respect.

'Ministers decided the best way of covering up the mess was to eliminate the only external witness who knew the truth about the fiasco.'

'O'Neill?' The colonel asked.

'Exactly.'

'What happened?'

'Section Two was issued with an XPD order to take him out.'

The army officer looked puzzled 'I've never heard of XPD orders,' he said. 'What are they?'

'XPD stands for Expedient Demise,' Smithers explained as he took a pen from his pocket and made a note on a sheet of paper.

'Is that the fancy name for a death warrant?' The soldier asked.

Smithers said nothing, but his tight little smile was answer enough. He turned to me. 'I'm beginning to understand,' he said. 'You were assigned to carry out the XPD order?'

'Yes. I broke into the IRA safe-house and discovered O'Neill in the lounge. He was on the telephone calling up help. However, when I pushed open the door he slammed the phone down and pointed a gun at me.'

'You're still here,' the army man said. 'So, what happened?'

'I was ready for him. I shot him in the chest.'

'How many times did you shoot him?' Smithers asked.

'I used my Smith and Wesson point four-four Magnum.'

'What sort of answer is that?' The MP asked impatiently.

'Have you ever seen what happens when a point four-four Magnum bullet hits its target?' I asked.

'Firearms are not one of my specialities,' he admitted. 'Is it relevant?'

'Very relevant,' his companion answered for me. 'If you hit your target, one shot from a Smith and Wesson point four-four is all you need to blow somebody apart.'

'And I hit my target,' I confirmed.

Smithers looked at me steadily. He used the tip of his little finger to brush his moustache, pursed his lips and then asked: 'Tell me, Statton. Would you have shot O'Neill even if he hadn't been carrying a gun?'

'Yes,' I said without hesitation. 'It was my job. It's what Section Two does. They do the dirty work for politicians like you, Mister Smithers. They kill people.' I knocked back the last of my whisky. I stood up and walked over to the drinks cabinet.

'Another?' I asked. Smithers turned down my offer but the Intelligence Corps officer held his empty glass up for me to take. That earned him a few brownie points in my eyes. I poured us both a *Laphroaig*.

'So what's this all about?' I asked as I resumed my seat.

For the second time that evening, Smithers ignored my question. 'Who issued the XPD order to kill O'Neill?' He asked.

'The Director-General of the Department for Covert Operations, Sir Bertie Reynolds,' I replied.

'I thought XPDs needed political authority.' It was not a question and it confirmed that Smithers was somebody who knew his way round the corridors of power. I decided he was not to be underestimated.

'They do. They have to be signed off by a minister from the Cabinet Office.'

'So who signed off that particular XPD order?'

'The same minister who sanctioned the deal with O'Neill. James Hamilton-Browne.'

'Jim? The current Home Secretary?'

'Yes.'

Smithers sucked in his cheeks. 'Why is none of this in the file?' He asked again. He sounded cross, as if the omission was my fault.

'I told you earlier. It was deliberately left out,' I said. 'Do you really think that Ted Heath would have wanted the shortcomings of the security services committed to paper?'

Smithers did not respond.

'You of all people should know there is no parliamentary scrutiny of security matters,' I went on. 'So when the security services overstep the mark, or screw up, it's the PM who is covered in smelly, brown stuff when the shit hits the fan.' I paused and sipped my drink.

'I don't understand,' Smithers said. 'You said it was Jim who took the decision, not Ted Heath.'

'No, I said it was Hamilton-Browne who sanctioned the deal with O'Neill and signed the XPD order. However, I know for a fact he was operating on orders from Heath. That's why I said earlier that if the truth had come out, it might well have brought down the Government. Harold Wilson would have had a field day.'

'I think you're exaggerating somewhat,' Smithers said. 'It is very unlikely the Government would have been brought down. We had a majority of thirty-one.'

'True, but Heath wasn't universally loved by his backbenchers,' I responded. 'It only needed sixteen rebels to go against him in a vote of confidence and he would have been toast.'

Smithers nodded. He understood the capricious nature of

backbench MPs. He was a right-wing Thatcherite and had been one of Ted Heath's biggest critics. 'Let me get this straight,' he said. 'Rather than admit culpability Ted decided to divert attention by blaming O'Neill's death on the Department for Covert Operations?'

'It happens,' I said.

'And Sir Bertie blamed you.'

'Yeah. I became the department's sacrificial lamb.'

'You seem fairly philosophical about what happened.'

'It could have been worse. At least the department tried to help me by making sure the result of the Inquiry was ambivalent. As you can see for yourself, the final report left some doubt as to my motive.'

'I noticed that,' Smithers said.

'And the Inquiry concluded also that there was insufficient evidence to warrant a criminal charge. Instead, it was recommended I be subject to the department's own internal disciplinary procedures.'

'What did the department decide?' The soldier asked.

'I was found guilty of poor judgement; failing to inform my superiors of my intention to kill O'Neill; and bringing the Department for Covert Operations into disrepute.'

'It looks as if the department came down on you pretty hard,' Smithers said, referring to the executive summary again. 'It says here your contract was terminated.'

'Yeah. Instant dismissal, without back-pay or a reference. Now, will you please tell me what this is all about? Why is the Government conducting another inquiry?'

Smithers stared at me. 'Can I be honest with you?'

'Well, honesty is not something I have come to expect from MPs, let alone ministers of the Crown,' I replied. 'But go ahead and I'll try to reign in my natural scepticism.'

Smithers gave me another of his non-smiles. 'In three weeks' time the Prime Minister will be calling a General Election. It will take place on Thursday, June 11th. Mrs Thatcher is convinced that one of the big issues at that election will be the continuing violence in Northern Ireland. She is determined to show that she is committed to completing the peace process, which started with the Anglo-Irish Agreement two years ago.'

'There hasn't been much peace recently,' I pointed out. 'As I recall the agreement didn't go down well with the UDA and the UVF.'

'The PM thinks she can get the Loyalist para-militaries to buy into the peace process as long as she can get the Republicans to sign up first.'

'She does, does she?' I wasn't convinced.

'Yes. Mrs Thatcher believes the key will be countering the distrust of the Catholics towards the Government and the security forces. She thinks having a new Inquiry to investigate properly the death of Dermot O'Neill will demonstrate our determination to be even-handed and appease the IRA.'

I looked at him dispassionately. It all sounded very odd. The idea of Margaret Thatcher trying to appease the IRA was hard to believe. 'What exactly do you think the Inquiry will achieve?' I asked.

'Well, from what I've read in this file, and having listened to your side of the story, I think the conclusion drawn by the Inquiry will endorse the original finding. O'Neill was killed by you in self-defence. However, there are aspects of the case that still cause us grave concerns.'

I continued to look at Smithers and wondered where this was going. 'What exactly are those concerns?'

'For a start, you have confirmed that the killing of O'Neill was sanctioned by a Cabinet Office minister.'

I could hardly deny it.

'In addition,' Smithers went on, 'there is clear evidence that ministers did not undertake a sufficiently robust investigation into the circumstances of his death.'

'Is that it?' I asked.

'No. There is evidence also that ministers covered up their action by pinning all the blame on you.'

'You seem to have decided the conclusion of the Inquiry already,' I said. This did not come as a big surprise. I can see a stitch up when I see it.

'I am the Committee of Inquiry Chairman,' Smithers tried yet another of his smiles. It was no warmer. 'Once the Inquiry's conclusions have been circulated, the Prime Minister will apologise to O'Neill's family.'

Margaret Thatcher apologising? I just didn't believe it. This was getting odder and odder.

'And she will ask the Home Secretary to resign.'

Now that sounded more like it. That I could believe. 'Didn't I read in the Daily Telegraph that Hamilton-Browne was threatening to challenge the Prime Minister in a leadership contest?' I asked.

'That was pure speculation on behalf of the press.'

'And a potential challenge has nothing whatsoever to do with her asking him to resign?'

'Any such suggestion is speculation as well.'

'I'll take that as a yes, then.'

Smithers made no effort to deny my accusation, instead he said: 'Of course, you will need to appear before the Committee of Inquiry. You will make a formal statement setting out exactly what you have told us, including about the XPD order and who signed it.'

I shook my head.

'I don't understand,' Smithers said. 'What are you saying?'

'I'm saying: No way, Jose.'

'You mean you refuse to provide us with a statement?'

'That's exactly what I mean.'

'That is most unfortunate, Mister Statton,' he said. 'Without your evidence we will not be able to force Hamilton-Browne to resign.'

'If you're so keen to get rid of Hamilton-Browne why don't you get the Director-General to give evidence? After all, he was the one who actually issued the XPD order.'

'We can't do that, because Sir Bertie has resigned,' Smithers explained, 'and is refusing to co-operate.'

'I don't blame him.' The old boy was doing the right thing for once.

'That's why we need your evidence, Statton. Will you reconsider?'

'No,' I replied.

'Why?'

I thought about that for a few moments. 'I did what I did because it was my job. Like it or not, I believe taking out O'Neill was the right thing to do. He was a murdering thug who was an enemy of the United Kingdom.'

I took another sip of my whisky and then said: 'Look, gentlemen, although I am an unreconstructed cynic, I happen to love my country.'

The colonel and Smithers looked at each other, but they said nothing.

'I know Sir Bertie and his henchmen screwed me,' I went on, 'and I have no reason to show any loyalty to them.'

'I can understand that,' the soldier said.

'But, as it happens, I do feel some loyalty,' I said. 'I don't blame them for what happened. At the end of the day they were just doing what their political masters wanted.'

Smithers nodded, as if accepting his share of my criticism.

'There is something else,' I said. 'I also have loyalty to my ex-colleagues. I don't want to see the DFCO dragged through the mud again and it will be if another investigation is launched. So, no, Mister Smithers, I won't help you.'

Once again my two visitors exchanged glances. The soldier nodded slightly and then studied me carefully.

'Exactly who are you, colonel?' I asked him.

'Sorry, I should have introduced myself earlier.' He offered me his hand. 'Rupert Disraeli-Astor.'

That's when I realised why his face was familiar to me. 'Weren't you called Dizz in your regiment?' I asked as I shook his hand.

'A carry-over from my school days,' the soldier smiled.

'And you were with Herbie Jones at Goose Green?'

Disraeli-Astor nodded again, but this time he didn't smile. The Falklands War in 1982 had seen the death of many good men, including Lieutenant-Colonel Herbert "H" Jones, who was commanding officer of the 2nd Battalion of the Parachute Regiment. He was slain as he led an attack on an Argentinian trench. 'Yes,' he said quietly. 'I was with "H".'

'But you weren't in the paras?'

'No, I was a captain in the Intelligence Corps at the time. But I was seconded to Phil Neame's D Company.'

'Is it true that after the war you were promoted straight from captain to colonel because the Ministry of Defence brass-hats didn't want a Major Dizz-Astor on their hands? Or is that an urban myth?'

'I like to think it's a myth,' Disraeli-Astor said with a modest smile. 'I prefer to believe my double promotion had more to do with my war record.'

I nodded as I remembered his exploits during the battle of Goose Green. After the victory on Darwin Ridge, D Company made its way to a small airfield that was close by. The platoon that Disraeli-Astor led was ambushed by an Argentinian machine gun team. Half his men were killed instantly and the remainder were wounded.

Disraeli-Astor managed to carry three of the wounded soldiers to safety before he was shot in his right leg and shoulder when successfully rescuing a fourth para. His bravery saw him awarded the Distinguished Service Order. Perhaps he was right, and the escapade did result also in him being promoted straight to colonel.

'What's your involvement with this lot?' I asked, nodding towards the minister.

'Colonel Disraeli-Astor is taking over as Director-General at the Department for Covert Operations,' Smithers answered for the soldier. 'The PM wants the department shaken up and believes the Colonel is the best person to achieve that.'

'The DFCO has become moribund,' Disraeli-Astor explained as he touched his scar again. 'It has lost some very good people during the past twenty years, particularly field agents. People with experience and integrity. People like you, Statton.'

I said nothing.

'What the Colonel is saying, Mister Statton, is that we would like you to come back.'

'Come back?'

'Yes, we need people of your calibre,' Disraeli-Astor said. 'Currently the department is full of ageing time-servers and wet behind the ears university graduates with more qualifications than common sense.'

'It's been a long time since I left the department. I'm not sure I'd fit in. I'm completely out of touch with procedures.'

'I've had a look through your department file,' Dizz-Astor said. 'It doesn't look as if you took much notice of procedures when you worked for the department before.'

I shrugged. 'When Intelligence agents are in the field they often have to act quickly and sometimes that means they have to cut corners. They don't have much time for procedures.'

'I accept what you say,' the soldier said. 'The problem is that our existing procedures are outdated and do not recognise the realities faced by field agents in today's world. I have to change the way the department operates. That's one of the reasons I need you back. I want you to help me.'

'In what capacity?'

It was Smithers who answered my question. He didn't like to be side-lined for too long. 'The head of Section Two has just retired and we would like you to replace him.'

'Why me?' I asked.

Disraeli-Astor leaned forward. 'I'll be straight with you, Statton.'

'I always welcome straight talking.'

'The truth is that I know how to run a regiment and I'm comfortable I can take over management of the Department for Covert Operations. However, as I said before, I'm no spook. I need somebody who knows about field work and can teach me the ropes. That person must be somebody I can trust. Somebody who is loyal and has integrity.' He stared at me intently. 'You have just proven you have both those qualities in abundance.'

'Are you telling me that little charade was a test?'

'Yes,' Disraeli-Astor admitted.

'So there is to be no new committee of inquiry?'

'No,' Smithers said. 'An inquiry was mooted by the Foreign Office, which is why we have all this paperwork on file. However, the PM vetoed the idea because she refuses to make any concessions to the IRA. She has not forgotten what they did in 1984 when they blew up the Grand Hotel in Brighton. She lost some very close friends that night.'

That sounded more like the uncompromising Maggie Thatcher Britain had come to love or hate. 'What about Hamilton-Browne?' I asked.

'Oh, Jim has decided not to stand at the next General Election. No doubt he will end up in the House of Lords.'

'He's no longer a threat to the PM?'

This time the smile Smithers gave me was wider and warmer. He was happy. 'No,' he said simply.

I turned back to Disraeli-Astor. 'What I don't understand is why you travelled all the way to the Highlands of Scotland. I appreciate your little pantomime was designed to find out whether you could trust me. However, there must be plenty of people in the department with the loyalty and integrity you are looking for.'

'Yes, there are,' Disraeli-Astor said. 'But none of them has your other qualities. I need an experienced field agent. Somebody who is resolute, ruthless and resourceful. I think you fit the bill. They don't.'

'I'm flattered,' I said. 'But I'm not as young as I was when I tackled Dermot O'Neill.'

'You are too modest, Statton,' the colonel said. 'I've checked your record since leaving the DFCO and it's impressive. For instance, that operation you put together back in Eighty-Two, when you managed to get the Russian scientist off Robben Island was pretty impressive. Our American cousins were very complimentary.'

'I don't know why. That operation was hardly an unqualified success. Gregori Zamyatin was dead when I handed him over to the Russians.'

'But at least you got him out of the hands of the South Africans. That in itself was a success.'

'Success is relative,' I said. 'I lost some good friends in that operation.'

'You're not the only one who lost friends in Eighty-Two,' Astor said. 'I lost my share in the Falklands. But life goes on.'

I felt a worm of excitement in my stomach that I hadn't felt for some time. My life was drifting and I was getting bored. It was lonely in the Highlands without Freddie and the idea of moving back to London suddenly seemed very attractive.

'Do you really want me in the department?' I asked Disraeli-Astor.

'Yes,' he replied.

'In that case I'll think about it and get back to you.'

'That won't be necessary, Statton. If you want to join us, just report for duty at the beginning of next month. You know where we are. If you don't turn up I'll know you're not interested.'

He raised his glass in a salute and I reciprocated. We both knew I would turn up.

Chapter 2

Café Adler was almost full but we found a table by the window that allowed us to look out at the small booth from which uniformed policemen monitored traffic using Checkpoint Charlie.

For decades the Berlin Wall had imprisoned half the population of the city in the Soviet Empire. Now people from East Berlin could cross into the non-communist West without fear of being shot at by border guards.

However, despite the relaxation in travel, the control booth was still manned. This was because the checkpoint was an official crossing between East and West Germany and would remain so until the planned reunification of the two countries.

'He's late,' Disraeli-Astor said as he fiddled with his coffee cup using one hand, whilst stroking the scar on his cheek with the finger of his other. I knew he often did this when he was impatient or irritated.

I checked my watch. 'Only five minutes, that's nothing in this city.'

'Late is late in my book,' he moaned.

I had worked with Disraeli-Astor for three years now. Although he was head of one of Britain's most secret intelligence agencies, at heart he would always be a soldier for whom punctuality is often the difference between life and death.

He had told me on more than one occasion that he would never get used to being part of a civil service culture where time frames are flexible and deadlines are extendable.

I sipped my espresso and stared out into Friedrichstraße. Being Friday it was a busy night with a constant stream of pedestrians walking in both directions, many of whom were tourists with cameras slung round their necks to take photographs of the Berlin Wall before it was demolished.

On the opposite side of the street a group of young men had congregated by the concrete fortification from which chunks had been hacked by people looking for souvenirs. Several of the youngsters were drinking beer from cans. Judging by their boisterous behaviour these were not the first drinks they had consumed that night.

One member of the group was carrying a pickaxe. He was a big, brawny fellow with broad shoulders who looked as if he belonged behind an anvil or a plough. The youth swung the pickaxe and its pointed end struck the wall with a loud cracking sound. A fist sized chunk of cement was chipped away and fell to the ground.

There was a loud cheer from the group. A youngster leapt forward and picked up the chunk of cement. He held it above his head with a wide grin on his face.

The brawny youth swung the pickaxe again and another chunk was ripped from the wall. He struck several times, until each member of the group had a souvenir, then, with another cheer, the group made its way along Friedrichstraße and disappeared into the night.

We sat in silence for a while, drinking our coffees and watching as a line of cars made its way from the Soviet Sector into the American Sector. Very few vehicles travelled in the opposite direction, but that was hardly surprising because there was little nightlife in drab and dreary East Berlin to attract westerners.

A long black ZiL came slowly through the border crossing and then veered towards us to park in the restricted area outside the Café Adler. The car carried Russian diplomatic plates, so it was unlikely the driver was worried about picking up a parking ticket. The rear passenger door opened and a man got out. I recognised him immediately. I was sure he wouldn't be worried about traffic cops either.

'Here comes our man,' I said.

'Are you sure?' Disraeli-Astor asked.

'Yes, I've met him before.'

The Russian looked through the window and saw me. I raised my hand to acknowledge him and he nodded in return. He turned back to the ZiL and said something to his driver, then came into the café.

There was a spare seat at our table and by the time the man had joined us his car had disappeared. Perhaps the driver was worried about the West German cops after all.

No sooner had the Russian sat down than a waiter appeared with a white napkin over his arm and an order pad in his hand. Our man ordered a large schnapps, but Astor and I passed on the alcohol and instead settled for more coffee.

'Good evening, Mister Statton.' The man exuded as much warmth as the Russian Steppes in winter.

'Good evening, General Urinoff.' I held out a hand, which he shook without much enthusiasm.

'Long time no see, old chap,' Urinoff said in the cut-glass English accent he had affected when first we met at a riverside pub in Kent. That day he was masquerading as a retired major in the British Army and wore a smart blazer, cream slacks, a crisp white shirt and a cravat decorated with the Mercury emblem of the Royal Signals.

'Eight years to be precise,' I reminded him. The last time we met was on a windswept beach near Cape Town, when I handed a dead scientist, Gregori Zamyatin, over to him. By then Urinoff had abandoned his assumed identity, fake accent and expensive clothes. Instead, he was dressed in a cheap Soviet made grey two-piece suit, tie-less shirt buttoned to the neck, scuffed leather shoes, and a leather worker's cap.

'We gave Comrade Zamyatin a proper state funeral,' Urinoff said. He now wore the dress uniform of a Russian General, complete with a chest full of medal ribbons. 'What happened to the CIA deputy-director who died?'

'He missed out on a state funeral,' I said. 'He had to make do with a beach barbeque.'

'I saw the fire from the submarine,' Urinoff said. 'It looked like quite a blaze.'

'It was,' I said. I did not explain that the fierce flames were caused because we placed the body of the rogue CIA agent in the cab of a Mercedes van and used special incendiary grenades to set light to it. Somehow, the why and how seemed irrelevant. Gavin Rogers II was dead and that was all that mattered.

'I never did thank you for distracting Rogers,' I said. 'If you hadn't made him look over his shoulder, I wouldn't have been able to shoot him.'

Urinoff shrugged. 'As I said at the time, killing him saved me a job.'

'I didn't kill him,' I pointed out. 'I only wounded him. He would have killed me if he hadn't been shot in the back by somebody else.'

'That is true,' Urinoff conceded. 'So, who was that somebody who suddenly appeared from nowhere?'

23

'I have no idea,' I lied. 'He disappeared before I could thank him.' As it happens, the man who saved my life that day was a CIA agent called Hank Graham, but I decided that some things are best kept a secret.

My boss coughed politely. I took the hint. 'Sorry. This is Colonel Disraeli-Astor.' The two men shook hands.

'I am most honoured that the Director-General of the Department for Covert Operations took the trouble to come all the way to Berlin to meet me personally,' Urinoff said stiffly.

Perhaps this slightly stilted show of gratitude was simply for show. However, I couldn't tell, one way or the other, because his immobile face gave nothing away.

'Your presence here makes me feel important,' he went on, then paused for effect before adding: 'But of course that is exactly what you intend, Colonel. Is it not?'

'Yes, but only because you are important,' Disraeli-Astor insisted, adopting the sincere look he sometimes practiced on me when he wanted something. This ploy was wasted on me and it didn't seem to work much better on the Russian.

'I am grateful for your reassurance,' Urinoff said in a neutral voice.

It was too neutral for Disraeli-Astor. 'Very important,' he emphasised. 'It is not every day that a KGB General defects to the West.'

'I have spent a lot of time in the West,' Urinoff said with a shrug of his shoulders. 'I found it very much to my taste. I particularly like the British way of life, which is why I contacted you, rather than the Yankees.'

The waiter returned with our drinks so we lapsed into silence. He put them in front of us and then deftly tucked the bill next to our earlier one in the small plastic container that stood in middle of the table. He did this without saying a word and then wandered off to serve a table on the far side of the room.

'We are delighted you chose to approach us first,' Disraeli-Astor said in a low voice. 'However, I do have one question for you, General Urinoff.'

'Which is?' The Russian asked.

'Why do you want to defect?'

At first Urinoff didn't answer, instead he picked up his schnapps and knocked it back in one gulp. He waved a hand to catch the waiter's eye and held his glass aloft to order a replacement.

'Things are not as they were in my country,' he said eventually. 'The writing has been on the wall for people like me ever since Gorbachev took over as leader and started his programme of perestroika and glasnost.'

'By people like you, I assume you mean the KGB?' I asked.

He nodded. 'The Union of Soviet Socialist Republics is breaking up and by next year will have disappeared. When that happens Mother Russia will stand alone and the KGB will be finished.'

Disraeli-Astor and I exchanged glances. We knew the Soviet empire was on the verge of collapse, but we had no idea it was that close.

'Of course, Russia will still have need of a security service,' Urinoff went on. 'However, the likes of me will no longer be welcome. I will be forever tainted by association with those whose mistakes brought about the downfall of the Soviet Union. I want to get out now, before I'm pushed.'

'But if the picture you paint is a true reflection of the state of your country, why should we help you defect?' Disraeli-Astor asked. 'Putting it bluntly; what's in it for us?'

'That is easy, Director-General. I know where the bodies are buried,' Urinoff said immediately, 'and I know who put them there. For instance, I am sure you would love to know who has been feeding us secret documents from your GCHQ.' He picked up his schnapps glass and then, remembering it was empty, he looked round for the waiter, but he had disappeared.

'What makes you think we don't know already?' Disraeli-Astor said.

'Don't treat me like a fool, Colonel,' the Russian said, slamming his glass down on the table. 'We both know your Secret Intelligence Service is not as efficient as it once was. Is that not so?' He paused, as if challenging my boss to contradict or agree with him.

Disraeli-Astor did not rise to the bait. He could have repeated the criticism he had made to me, on more than one occasion, about the quality of intelligence information MI6 had provided in recent months. Instead, he said nothing.

Urinoff shrugged. 'Very well, let us just say that I will either be providing you with useful information, or confirming something you already know,' he said.

'We never turn down information,' Disraeli-Astor said with a smile.

'There is much more that I can tell you,' the Russian said. He did not return the smile.

'Such as?'

'The Cold War might almost be over, Colonel, but the West faces danger from other quarters, not least from Islamic fundamentalism.'

Disraeli-Astor nodded his agreement. The rise in Islamic fanaticism was becoming a real worry for Western governments.

'Then there is Afghanistan, which is in turmoil, with its government fighting off attacks from the mujahideen,' Urinoff said.

'You would know all about the Afghan turmoil,' Disraeli-Astor said waspishly. 'Most of the current problem in Afghanistan was caused by the Soviet invasion in nineteen-seventy-nine and the withdrawal of your troops last year.'

'Invading Afghanistan was a big mistake,' Urinoff said. 'I warned against it at the time. I told the Politburo that it would become our Vietnam and I was right.'

The waiter finally turned up with the Russian's drink. He put it on the table, picked up the empty glass and slipped yet another bill into the plastic container. I had no idea why he couldn't just have added our drinks up at the end and given us one bill.

'But Afghanistan is not the only Moslem country which is a threat to you,' Urinoff said as he picked up his drink. 'Iraq and Iran are still at each other's throats,' he paused and took a delicate sip of his schnapps, rather than downing it in one go. 'Then there is Syria and Libya, both of which are becoming increasingly unstable.' He took a second sip of his schnapps.

'It is true that the British Government is concerned about the Middle East,' Disraeli-Astor admitted.

'But the Middle East should not be your only concern,' Urinoff said. 'There are other problems brewing in the world.'

I could sense he was holding something back. 'Such as?' I asked.

'Such as in South Africa.'

'What about it?'

'It is on the brink of a revolution that will not only destabilise the whole of Southern Africa, but will have a major impact on those countries that have investments in South Africa. Particularly your country.'

'Thank you for sharing that information with us, General,' Disraeli-Astor said. His tone was patronising.

I gave him a warning glance. That attitude was not the way to win friends and influence people. Certainly, not somebody as prickly as Urinoff, who already looked irritated, but my boss ignored my look and ploughed on regardless. 'However, we are fully au fait with the situation in South Africa. Indeed, I have been assured that the South African Government is taking steps to address the problems facing the country.'

'I suppose it was your Foreign Office who gave you that assurance?' The Russian asked. 'Or was it MI6?'

'It was the Foreign Office,' Disraeli-Astor said. 'They believe the decision by President F.W. de Klerk earlier this year to unban the African National Congress, and release Nelson Mandela from prison, will help reduce discontent amongst the black population in South Africa.'

'How exactly will those things bring that about?' Urinoff asked gently.

'Because they are the first tentative steps towards a deal between the South African government and the African National Congress that will lead to new elections.'

'Where blacks will have the vote?'

'Yes, everybody will be franchised, irrespective of colour.'

'Which would lead to an ANC government?'

'That would be the obvious outcome.'

'And the white population would accept that result?'

'The advice I have been given by the Foreign Office is that there will be some Afrikaners who will be unhappy at that outcome. However, a clear majority of the white population would go along with de Klerk, and accept a Nelson Mandela led government.'

You had to hand it to my boss. He had the Government line off pat.

'So you think there will be a peaceful transition?'

'Yes. The Foreign Office has been assured by the ANC that if it wins the election it will invite the Nation Party to help form an interim Government of National Unity. It will start the process of correcting social and economic injustices left by the legacy of Apartheid.'

'That is all very laudable, Director-General, but such an outcome depends on the ANC winning that election, does it not?'

'Of course, but in the circumstances, any other result is unthinkable.'

'Unthinkable, but possible,' Urinoff said. 'Particularly when you consider there is a secret multi-national network of wealthy businessmen plotting to make sure the unthinkable happens.'

Disraeli-Astor could not hide his surprise at this bombshell.

'Judging by the look on your face, I take it your Foreign Office did not advise you of that particular development?' Urinoff asked a rhetorical question. He already knew the answer. 'Well, that's because they know nothing about it.'

'And you do?'

'Of course. Once again the KGB is one step ahead of your Secret Intelligence Service.'

Disraeli-Astor was silent for a while and I imagined he was cursing MI6 for putting him in an uncomfortable position. Eventually he asked: 'In that case, what can you tell us about this plot?'

'I can tell you a lot,' Urinoff said. 'But I'm not going to. Not yet anyway. You will hear all about it once I am safely in your country.'

'How do I know the information is worth waiting for?'

'Oh, I think you will find you will get good value for your money. For instance, I know what the group is called, I know the name of its members, I know its leaders, I know who they are working with in South Africa and I know their objective.' He gave another of his tight, cold smiles. 'Which, you must admit, is much more than you know. Is it not, colonel?'

Disraeli-Astor went red in the face at this obvious put down.

I knew my boss well enough to know he has a very short fuse and was likely to say something we would come to regret. I stepped in smartly to ease the tension. 'What else do you know, General?'

'Well I know that the group is supported by certain people in my country who, for their own reasons, are set on undermining Gorbachev.'

'People like you?' Disraeli-Astor asked.

'No. The people of whom I speak are thugs and criminals. They say they hanker after the old ways, but in fact their only motivation is to line their own pockets.'

'You know who these people are?'

'Of course. They are being supported by some misguided people in my own organisation.'

'The KGB?'

'Yes, but I want nothing to do with them.'

'So, what do you want, General?' I asked.

'That is simple. I want a new life and I want a new identity.'

'I suppose your new identity would be that of Major Percival Carsons?' I smiled at him. This was the alias Urinoff used when I first met him at the pub in Kent.

He shrugged. 'Why not? It's as good a name as any.'

'What else?' Disraeli-Astor asked.

'I want a nice house in which to live in peace and quiet, preferably surrounded by green fields. I want a decent car and enough money with which to enjoy a comfortable retirement.'

'Is that all?' I asked. 'What about a gold Rolex watch, your own personal jet plane and a hundred feet long motor yacht?'

'Those things would be nice,' he said. 'However, I do not wish to be greedy and I sense you feel I am asking for too much already.'

'Really? What gives you that impression?'

'Because I lived in England long enough to understand the way you Brits use irony and sarcasm to hide your concerns. You seem incapable of being blunt.'

'I can do blunt if you want blunt,' I said.

Urinoff shrugged. 'I'll be blunt for you,' he said. 'You think I ask for too much, Mister Statton.'

I said nothing.

'I think my demands are very little for which to ask,' he went on. 'When you consider your money will be exchanged for all the information I have up here,' he tapped his temple.

'Don't worry, General Urinoff, *I* appreciate what you have to offer,' Disraeli-Astor interjected softly. 'And I think the things for which you ask can be arranged. However, I will need to discuss your request with my Prime Minister.'

'I would expect nothing else, Colonel Disraeli-Astor,' Urinoff said and lapsed into silence as he sipped his drink. 'There is one final condition,' he said eventually.

'You want the yacht after all,' I said.

The Russian smiled at me. We understood each other. Our

exchange had been part of the usual sparring between experienced field agents.

My boss just gave me a glare. 'Go on, General,' he said.

'My defection must remain a secret. It cannot be used by your Government for propaganda purposes.'

'How can we keep your defection a secret from the Kremlin?' Disraeli-Astor asked.

Urinoff glanced at me and raised an eyebrow as if to ask: Is this guy for real?

It was my turn to shrug. My boss might have been a damn fine soldier in his time, but he would never make a field agent in a million years. 'That's easy,' I said. 'The General will have to die.' I turned to the Russian. 'I take it you have a plan?'

'Of course,' he replied. 'This is what I have in mind.'

'Sounds good,' Disraeli-Astor said when Urinoff had finished setting out his plan.

'Thank you, colonel,' the KGB man said. 'I'm delighted you approve.'

My boss didn't pick up on the hint of sarcasm in the Russian's voice. I did, but then I'm an expert. 'Of course, we will do everything we can to help you,' he said. 'If you are agreeable, Statton will be your contact.'

'That is fine with me,' the Russian said. 'It will be good to work with at least one professional.' Again the man's scorn went over my boss's head.

'There is one other thing,' Urinoff went on, 'I want to be out by the end of the month. If I detect any delay, I will contact the Americans. I'm sure they would welcome me with open arms.'

'Don't worry. There will be no delay, General,' Disraeli-Astor assured him confidently. 'I will be working very hard to make it happen.'

I sighed inwardly. What my boss meant, was that it would be me working hard to make all the arrangements needed to bring Urinoff to the West, but I didn't say anything.

After three years working for Disraeli-Astor I knew he would take the credit if the operation was a success and I would be blamed if it went tits up.

Chapter 3

Boizenburg is a small town set on the right bank of the Elbe and was one of the most westerly communities in the German Democratic Republic. The town is surrounded by fields and sits astride a highway that links it to Berlin and Hamburg.

My meeting with General Alexei Urinoff took place on the highway out of Boizenburg.

I had travelled down from Hamburg earlier that day in a car bearing diplomatic plates loaned to me by the British Consulate. When I crossed into communist East Germany, the guards only took a cursory glance at my forged passport. Perhaps they realised that within a few months they would be relying on the forces of western capitalism for a job.

This close to the border, the Ministry of State Security had maintained a heavy presence in Boizenburg. Following East Germany's first free elections, held two weeks earlier, which paved the way for German reunification, a large border garrison was no longer needed.

I parked in a clearing on the fringes of a forest that grew on the outskirts of Boizenburg and through which the highway headed west towards the Federal Republic of Germany. Now I was sitting in the dark waiting for something to happen.

I tensed as I saw headlights coming along the highway from the direction of Boizenburg. I eased open the driver's door, but the lights swept past without stopping. I relaxed again, but decided to get out of the car anyway and wait in the trees.

There was a sharp chill to the night air and I wished I had worn a hat. I pulled the collar of my sheepskin coat up round my ears. That helped, but not much. I had a pair of leather gloves in the car but I chose not to wear them. They would make it more difficult to fire the 9 mm Browning semi-automatic pistol that was stuffed in one pocket of my coat along with my right hand. The other pocket contained only my left hand.

I would have preferred my trusty Smith & Wesson but getting the big pistol aboard the BA plane that flew me from Gatwick to Hamburg would have been complicated. I could have taken my gun through security in a diplomatic bag, but the Foreign Office would only have co-operated under protest, and anyway, it would have blown my cover.

I did send through a request to the British Embassy to provide me with a Magnum revolver. However, the young consular officer who met me at Hamburg Airport, with a surly look and a small brown cardboard box containing the Browning, insisted it was that or nothing. I knew better than to argue.

A dog barked somewhere in the distance and this set off a chain-reaction that filled the night air with a variety of howls and yelps. These slowly died away, leaving the only sound that of the leaves of the trees, which surrounded me on three sides, as they were rustled by a light wind.

The moon came out from behind a cloud, sending shadows across the clearing where my car was parked and at the back of which I now stood, stamping my feet occasionally in an effort to keep the circulation flowing.

Suddenly another set of headlights headed in my direction from the direction of the town, lighting up the tarmac surface of the highway with dipped yellow beams. I sensed this was the car for which I was waiting. This time I was right.

The headlights soon reached the clearing in the forest where I waited. As they drew level the car slowed and came to a halt. It was a black ZiL and in the bright moonlight I could see two men sitting in the front seats. The men were of the same height and size. That made sense.

General Urinoff got out of the car and looked around. He was dressed in smart western style clothes. He wore a dark suit, white button-down shirt and a striped club tie. He wore no overcoat, but didn't appear to be affected by the cold. I suppose that comes with growing up in a part of the world where winter temperatures regularly dip to 40 degrees below.

I walked out of the shelter of the trees and across the clearing towards the road. Urinoff saw me coming and waved a greeting.

'Help me,' he said when I arrived at the car. 'We must be quick. Somebody might come.' He opened the passenger door and now I could see that the other man was dressed in Urinoff's KGB military uniform.

The man looked as if he was sleeping, but as the Russian unclipped the man's seat belt he flopped forward. He looked drugged or dead. I knew it was the latter.

I went to the driver's side of the car, opened the door and leant in to help the Russian. We manhandled the uniform clad body into the driver's seat where we propped him up behind the steering wheel and strapped him into position with the seat belt.

Urinoff took his peaked cap from the backseat and perched it on the dead man's head. On the backseat there was also a holdall, a briefcase and a camel-hair overcoat, which he put on before lifting the luggage out of the car and placing it on the ground.

We slammed shut both doors, sealing the dead driver into his tomb. I took the Browning from my pocket and fired at the driver's window, blowing a large hole in the glass. I then shot half a dozen bullets into the head of the dead body making a real mess of its face. I stepped back and let Urinoff take over.

He took something from the pocket of his overcoat and held it up for me to see. It was marked with writing I recognized as Hebrew. It was an Israeli made incendiary grenade. He withdrew the pin, dropped the grenade through the hole in the window and snatched up his two bags from the ground.

We ran quickly into the shelter of the trees and were already safely in my car when the grenade went off filling the ZiL with a bright light. Soon the inside of the limousine was consumed by flames.

'They will blame it on the Jews,' Urinoff said dispassionately as he threw his holdall onto the backseat. However, I noticed he kept the briefcase on his knees where he could guard it.

'Did you sort out his teeth?' I asked as I started the car and drove quickly out of the woods and onto the highway in the direction of Hamburg.

'Of course,' Urinoff sounded affronted that I had even asked the question. 'It was no problem. I know a dentist in Potsdam who owed me a favour. I gave him my dental records and he replicated on our friend all the work I have had done on my teeth.'

We had travelled several hundred yards along the highway when the ZiL's petrol tank exploded and a ball of fire lit the sky behind us.

'So who was he?' I asked.

'Just somebody from the morgue who happened to be about my age and roughly my build,' Urinoff replied. 'He didn't bear much of a resemblance to me facially, but your bullets and the fire will ensure that the only way he can be identified is by his teeth.'

'Won't the body be missed?'

'No, I smuggled it out without being seen. I removed all the paperwork and got rid of it. The morgue is full of bodies and none of the staff will notice there's one body less in the storage area.'

'What about family?'

'The dead man had no family. There is nobody to claim his body or mourn his death. Trust me, he will not be missed.'

'What a way to go; missed by nobody and with nothing to show for your life except some paperwork that no longer exists.'

'Well at least he will get a proper funeral in the Moscow military cemetery and be buried with some nice new gold caps on his teeth.' Urinoff smiled mirthlessly and pointed at his mouth. Then he closed his eyes, fell asleep and slept until we reached Hamburg Airport.

At the airport I hid the Browning pistol in a concealed cavity in the boot, locked the car and put the keys on top of its front nearside wheel. Somebody from the British Consulate would collect the car and within 24 hours the pistol would be on its way to West Berlin where an Intelligence Corps armourer would destroy it.

Our plane was on time. Urinoff and I arrived at Heathrow well before the Browning reached Helmstedt. We were met by two cars, one to ferry me home and the other to take the Russian to a secluded country house just outside Windsor, used by the DFCO as a safe-house.

Over the next few weeks, experienced Home Office interrogators would debrief Urinoff in comfortable surroundings befitting a man holding the rank of a KGB General.

The Russian defector would probably spend a few hours each day being interviewed; the rest of the time was his own. In some ways I envied him the peace and quiet he was going to enjoy.

All I could look forward to was my small apartment in Shepherds Bush and the battle through heavy traffic that my daily commute to the DFCO offices in Central London entailed.

I decided the time had come to visit my Highland cottage, which I still used as an occasional bolt-hole. I resolved to submit a holiday requisition when I got back to my office.

Chapter 4

DFCO offices, Whitehall, London, Thursday 29th March

The Department for Covert Operations is housed in offices tucked away on the ground floor of the Treasury. Section Two has a couple of offices in the basement of the same building.

Nobody had ever explained satisfactorily to me why we were located in the Treasury, rather than any other ministry. Perhaps nobody knew the answer. There was some speculation that the reason was because we reported direct to the Prime Minister, who was the First Lord of the Treasury, and our offices were within easy reach of Downing Street. However, this seemed an unlikely explanation because there was plenty of government office space available closer to Number 10.

One of the Section Two offices was mine. It was just large enough to fit in a desk, two chairs, a filing cabinet and a radiator as temperamental as my secretary, Poppy Fotheringay-Evans.

The door to my office led to a much larger open-plan office in which there were half a dozen desks and a table on which stood basic beverage making equipment and assorted crockery.

Three of the desks in the main office were not currently being used, except as somewhere to keep a collection of potted plants that Poppy was supposed to look after. Unfortunately, because she often forgot to water them, they were permanently on the verge of death.

Of the remaining desks, the one closest to my office door belonged to my secretary. The other two desks were used by my deputy, Timothy Fraser, and Melissa Messenger.

Melissa had recently graduated from Oxford with a first-class honours degree in political science and was working in the department as part of the Civil Service Fast Stream Internship Programme. In the autumn, she would be moving to the Foreign Office to undertake training to become a diplomat.

I was in the middle of filling in a holiday requisition form when Poppy sidled into my office.

'Morning, boss,' she said with a wide smile. That was always a good sign. My secretary blew hot and cold, depending upon the state of her current romantic relationship. Judging from her mood that morning her present beau must be keeping her satisfied.

'Where's my coffee?' I asked. 'It's almost twenty to ten.'

'On its way,' she replied. 'I missed my train this morning and was late getting to the office, so Melissa said she would make the coffee. She's gone to fill up the kettle with water.'

'Well, when she gets back, tell her to hurry up. I need an intake of caffeine urgently.'

'OK, but you won't have long to drink it because Rupert wants to see you in his office at ten o'clock.'

Poppy Fotheringay-Evans was the only person in the department who could get away with referring to our boss by his first name. When I asked her about this she explained that her older half-brother and Disraeli-Astor were at the same public school together.

I suppose having known somebody since their schooldays, and having a double-barrelled name, gives you the self-confidence to be on first name terms with the Director-General.

'I won't bother to ask why you missed your train,' I said. 'I've heard all your excuses and I don't want you to become repetitive.'

'Roger decided to stay the night,' she said with a suggestive wink.

'Over indulging in sex is not an excuse, Poppy, it's a lifestyle choice.'

'Don't be an old fuddy-duddy,' she said before disappearing.

I called her back. 'Tell Melissa to forget my drink. I'm not sure I can face one of her coffees this morning. She might be the most intelligent person in this department, but she's the only woman I know who can make instant coffee taste like mud. Anyway, I'm off to meet the D-G and I'm sure his personal assistant will offer me a cup of his special Blue Mountain coffee.

'Of course she will,' she said archly. 'She has the hots for you.'

'Don't be ridiculous,' I said. 'Colleen Masters is only a child.'

'She's the same age as me.'

'Well, I'm old enough to be your father, which makes her a child in my eyes.'

'You don't fancy her then?'

'There is no denying Miss Masters is a very attractive young lady,' I said, dodging her question.

'In that case, why don't you ask her out?' She persisted, putting her own spin on my reply.

'When I need advice about my love life, Poppy, I will ask

somebody with more experience than you.' I realised immediately this was the wrong thing to say.

She raised an eyebrow and giggled. 'Don't worry. I've had plenty of experience. Just ask Roger.'

I shook my head in despair. 'You're shameless,' I said.

'I might be shameless, but I'm right. Admit it, you fancy Colleen.'

'I'm not looking for a relationship,' I said firmly. 'But if I did want one, I would have no problem finding a woman of my own age. I certainly wouldn't resort to cradle snatching.'

'I don't believe you,' she said with a wicked grin and then disappeared before I could respond.

I stared at the door and wondered if I was really that easy to read.

Ten minutes later I was reminded of my conversation with Poppy because when I walked into the Director-General's suite of offices his PA looked up at me and greeted me with a wide smile. 'Good morning, David,' she said. I imagined there was an invitation in her brown eyes, but that could have been just wishful thinking on my part.

She leaned back in her chair and used both hands to tuck her long dark hair behind her ears. As she moved, her shapely breasts pushed against the front of her silk blouse. Despite my earlier comments I had to admit that Colleen Masters was certainly no child.

'You can go straight in,' she said. 'The D-G is expecting you. I was about to make coffee for him. Would you like one?'

'That would be lovely. Poppy was late this morning and she never got around to making me one.'

'What was it this time?' She asked.

'A night of sexual gymnastics with her latest boyfriend,' I replied.

'That must be Roger. I hear he is something of a ram. I'm surprised she managed to stagger in at all.'

'You sound jealous,' I said as I headed for the D-G's door.

'Far from it,' she said with another smile. 'Roger is far too young for me. I prefer older men.'

As I entered Disraeli-Astor's office and closed the door behind me, I wondered whether there was any significance in her words.

'What's this?' My boss asked when I handed him my holiday requisition form.

'You'll find a clue printed at the top in capital letters,' I replied.

'ANNUAL LEAVE REQUEST,' he read slowly and loudly.

'Well done,' I said, clapping my hands gently. 'Teacher will be pleased.'

'You want a holiday?'

'That's what submitting a leave request usually means.'

'But you want a two-week holiday?' He tapped the form as if he could not believe his eyes.

'Yes. I've not had a proper break since I re-joined the department three years ago.'

'But now is not a good time, Statton. There's a lot going on.'

'When is there not a lot going on?'

'Workloads are relative. We are particularly busy currently. For instance, there's the Russian chappie's defection.'

'You mean General Alexei Urinoff,' I reminded him. Disraeli-Astor was the world's worst at remembering names.

'Yes, that's his name. Well, liaising with the Home Office and the Cabinet Office is going to take a lot of time and energy.'

'I'm sure the department can manage to expend the necessary time and energy without me. Reacting to workloads is relative as well.'

'But Urinoff's defection is something you've been handling,' Disraeli-Astor insisted.

'That's not a problem. Timmy Fraser has been kept in the loop and should be able to handle things in my absence.'

'Fraser?' the D-G said scornfully.

'Yes. He's my deputy.'

'I know who Fraser is,' he said.

'So what's the problem?' I asked.

'He's an idiot.'

'You employed him,' I pointed out.

There was a knock on the door and Colleen Masters came in carrying a tray on which stood cups, saucers, a cafetière, sugar and a small jug that I knew would contain cream. Disraeli-Astor knew how to live well. I guess it was spending so many years dining in an officers' mess.

Colleen poured us both a cup of coffee, but left us to put in our own cream and sugar.

Disraeli-Astor waited until Colleen had left the office and closed the door before speaking again. 'Where was I?'

'You were saying that the young man you employed as my deputy is an idiot.'

'So I was,' he said and then sniffed his coffee as if it was a fine wine and then sighed with satisfaction.

'Personally, I think you are being a little harsh on Timmy,' I added quietly.

Disraeli-Astor nodded sagely. 'Perhaps you're right.' He put a spoonful of demerara sugar in his coffee. 'Look, Fraser is a bright enough lad,' he said, waving his spoon at me. 'But he is more than a little wet behind the ears. I'm not sure he's up to handling something as big as the Urinoff business on his own.'

'I seem to recall telling you I needed somebody more experienced as my deputy,' I said. 'But you insisted on recruiting Timmy.'

'Fraser came highly recommended by Toby Smithers,' he said defensively.

'Is it supposed to make me feel better having as my deputy somebody who doesn't know his Argentina from his Armenia, just because he was recommended by a minister of the Crown?' I paused, before adding: 'Somebody, who I might add, has never had a proper job and whose only apparent qualification for public life is that he went to an expensive public school?'

'I went to an expensive public school,' Disraeli-Astor pointed out quietly before adding a dash of cream to his coffee.

'So my secretary keeps reminding me.' I sipped my coffee. I took it black and without sugar.

'Poppy is a good girl,' Disraeli-Astor's voice softened. 'I went to school with her half-brother Giles Fotheringay-Evans.'

'I know,' I said. 'She keeps reminding me of that as well.'

He studied my holiday request form again then threw it into an in-tray on his desk that was already full to overflowing. He had complained repeatedly about how much he hated paperwork. 'OK, I'll consider your application later.'

'I know what that means,' I mumbled. I knew his "later" could well mean two months' time.

'Don't mumble,' he said.

I sighed heavily. 'So what did you want to see me about?'

'A couple of things,' he replied. 'But connected.'

'Connected to what?'

'Don't be difficult, Statton. You know what I mean. Connected to each other.'

'Sorry, I'm feeling tired and irritable. It's why I need a holiday.'

'Don't keep on about your damn holiday. I told you before, I will look at your leave application as a matter of urgency.'

It wasn't what he had said, but I let it pass. 'So what do you want to discuss and what's the connection?'

'South Africa,' he said.

'What about it?'

'Do you remember what Urine-off told us when we met him in Berlin?

'It's Urinoff, and yes I do remember. It was about some secret group plotting to prevent the ANC from taking power in South Africa?'

'Yes,' he said. 'Well during his initial debrief Urinoff revealed more information about the group.'

'What sort of information?'

Disraeli-Astor opened a buff file that lay on his desk and took out a computer printout. He handed it to me. I recognised the printout immediately. It was a standard transcript of a Home Office foreign-alien debriefing session. On this occasion, the printout detailed an initial statement made by Urinoff.

'I suppose it's too early for this to have been verified?' I asked when I had finished reading the transcript.

'I only received the printout first thing this morning,' he explained.

'So Urinoff is claiming that a group of businessmen is working with the Afrikaner Broederbond and the Pan Africanist Congress to take control of South Africa?'

'Yes. As you can see the Russians believe an election in South Africa is inevitable. The Phoenix Group will help the Broederbond and PAC win that election by providing them with unlimited funds.'

'I agree an election is inevitable,' I said. 'However, a link-up between the Boers and the PAC seems pretty far-fetched. It's like the British National Front going into coalition with the Socialist Workers Party.'

'But far-fetched or not, what if it happens?'

My immediate thought was about what might happen to Freddie in those circumstances. 'I'd sooner not think about it,' I said. 'Look what happened in Zimbabwe.'

'I know,' he agreed. 'It's an economic basket case; the Shona and Matabele hate each other with a vengeance; and civil unrest is rife.'

'Exactly, well multiply those problems by a factor of ten and that's what South Africa would turn into.'

'If South Africa goes the same way as Zimbabwe it would have a massive knock-on effect across the whole of Southern Africa,' Disraeli-Astor said. 'And that would have major implications for our country.'

I thought again about the dangers Freddie might face if violence broke out in South Africa. 'Let's hope Urinoff's information is wrong.'

'Amen to that,' my boss said. 'However, let's not be overly pessimistic until we have investigated his claims. I think it is important we do that straight away.'

'I take it that when you say *we*, it means you want me to check up on Urinoff's story.'

He smiled. 'Well, I think this is something you should follow up personally. I sense at some stage your special talents might be needed.'

'What leads you to that conclusion?'

'A soldier's gut instinct.'

'Would that be the same soldier's gut instinct that led you to recruit Timmy Fraser?'

'Regrettably, that decision might have been ill-judged,' he admitted, without showing any sign of regret. 'But we are where we are.'

'Yes, we are where I can't take leave because there is no one in the section with enough experience to cover for me.'

Disraeli-Astor shook his head as if in despair. 'I thought we had agreed to drop that subject,' he said as he picked up the cafetière.

'Not that I remember.'

'Have some more coffee,' he said in a conciliatory tone. 'Perhaps it will put you in a better mood.'

'There's nothing wrong with my mood that a holiday won't cure,' I insisted. 'But, since you ask, I will have another coffee. Those fancy cups you use are very small.'

He picked up his own cup and looked at it. 'Are they really?' He seemed genuinely surprised at my complaint. 'Perhaps it's because you're more used to a mug.'

'I sometimes think that's what you take me for.'

'What a mug?' He looked confused and then the penny dropped. 'Is that what you think?'

'Yes, and the problem is that I let you get away with it. Anybody else would insist on taking their leave.'

'I'm not preventing you from taking leave, it's just the timing that is awkward. Only you can check out the Russian, because you understand each other. I saw that in Berlin.'

I was surprised. 'You noticed?'

'Of course I did. You're both professional spooks.'

'I'll take that as a compliment,' I said. 'However, it still doesn't make me feel any happier about losing out on my leave.'

'Look, Statton, I am genuinely sorry about having to put your application on the back burner, but I'm being put under a lot of pressure from on high and I would be very grateful for your co-operation and understanding.'

'How high is *on high*?'

'Number Ten,' he said.

'That high?'

'Yes, The Prime Minister has already seen a copy of the transcript of the interview with our Russian guest and she rang me personally to express her concern.'

Disraeli-Astor stared at me over the rim of his coffee cup for a few moments before continuing. 'Mrs T is worried about British commercial interests in Southern Africa and wants us to find out more about the threat. She insists it takes top priority.'

He drank the rest of his coffee and put his cup down. 'Her exact words were: "I didn't go out on a limb to protect British investments in South Africa by opposing sanctions, only to see a bunch of fascists and communists put those investments at risk."' He said this in a passable imitation of Margaret Thatcher's voice, '"I want you to find out who is behind this group, Director-General, and I want you to stop them."'

That scuppered any lingering hopes I might have had of an immediate holiday. If the Iron Lady was on his case, then Disraeli-Astor wouldn't be digging my leave application out of his in-tray anytime soon.

I scanned the printout again and found the name for which I was looking. 'Urinoff mentions a Sir Reginald Wren in his statement.

What do you know about him?' I asked. 'He's not somebody I know.'

'I know him well enough to call him Sir Reggie without being punched on the nose,' Disraeli-Astor said. 'He is Chairman and major shareholder of Afro Mining Corporation, which has widespread interests across Africa, but mainly in South Africa. AMC mines and trades in a range of commodities from coal to gold. The company also has a stake in other sectors including retail, brewing and transport.'

'So he's a real business heavyweight?'

'Yes, and one of Britain's richest men. However, some of Sir Reggie's business deals have been distinctly shady. Word has it that he is something of a spiv.'

'Not somebody you would invite to join your gentlemen's club then?'

'Certainly not.'

'So how did he get his knighthood?'

'He was a generous donor to the Labour Party when it was in power in the Seventies.'

'What's a capitalist doing making donations to the Labour Party?'

'Because he's a clever capitalist. He hedged his bets by donating large sums to both Labour and the Conservatives before the nineteen-seventy-four general election. Labour won, but if the election had gone the other way Sir Reggie would still have got his gong.'

'So, because of his business interests, Wren has a vested interest in ensuring there is a government in South Africa over which he and his mates have some influence.'

'Exactly.'

'But if a Broederbond-PAC coalition government would be as pro-business as Wren believes, why is Mrs T so concerned?' I asked.

'Because the Foreign Office has convinced her that the ANC will start a civil war in South Africa if it is denied power.'

'Much as it grieves me to say so; on this occasion the FO is probably right. A civil war would be inevitable,' I said. 'Not only that, but in such circumstances, opposition from the ANC would be very violent. In addition, the Cape Coloureds and many English-speaking whites would oppose a Broederbond-PAC government.'

'It could turn into a real problem,' he announced portentously.

'That, boss, is the understatement of the year. It would be a disaster,' I said. 'So what do you want me to do?'

'Go down to Windsor and talk to Urinoff.'

'That makes sense,' I agreed. The Home Office interrogators were good at their job, but only a field agent can truly understand the mind of another field agent. 'We need to find out if Urinoff's claims about this group hold water and, if so, whether Wren really is involved.'

Disraeli-Astor looked puzzled. 'Why do you say that?'

'Because, pointing the finger at Wren might be a KGB stitch up.'

'You mean the Russian's defection might be a ruse? Would he really do that?'

'I wouldn't put anything past him. He's a devious bastard.'

'If Urinoff is that clever, won't it be difficult to find out whether he's telling the truth about Sir Reggie?'

'Don't worry, I have other ways of finding out if Wren *is* up to something, but talking to the Russian is a good start. I'll go down to Windsor first thing in the morning.'

'Could you leave your visit until Saturday?'

I looked at him silently. I wondered whether *he* would be working at the weekend. I doubted it. '*I could,*' I said eventually. 'But whether *I will* depends on your reason for asking.'

'I have something else lined up for you tomorrow.' He probably sensed what I was thinking, because the scar on his cheek was accentuated by a blush that made his face pink. 'More coffee?' he added quickly.

'How can I resist,' I replied in a resigned voice. I watched as he poured more coffee for me. 'So what joys await me tomorrow?'

'The Joint Security Operations Liaison Committee is due to meet in the morning,' he replied as he drained the remnants of coffee from the cafetière into his own cup. 'I would like you there with me.'

'You want me to attend a JSOLC meeting?'

'Yes.'

'The other members won't like that,' I pointed out.

'They have no choice. I have cleared your attendance with the Prime Minister.'

'Have you, by God?'

'Yes.'

'But why?'

'I suggested to the PM that we set up a special Active Operations

Sub-committee of the JSOLC to oversee the South African business…'

'That doesn't answer my question,' I interrupted him in full flow.

'Patience my dear boy,' he said in the patronising tone he knew I hated. 'I will come to that in a moment.'

I hid my irritation by sipping my coffee.

'Mrs Thatcher thought a sub-committee was a good idea. I told her I was assigning the department's best field agent to investigate the Phoenix Group and wanted to co-opt him onto the AOSC so we could be better kept up to date.'

It started to dawn on me what my boss was up to.

He smiled at me. 'The PM thought that was a good idea as well.'

'So, exactly how many people are going to sit on this AOSC?' I asked.

'I was thinking five, including you and me.'

'I see. And I don't suppose one of the other three members will be a sympathetic representative from the Cabinet Office?'

He didn't need to answer, the smug look on his face told me all I needed to know. I had to hand it to my boss. He might not cut the mustard as a spy-master, and he might be overly influenced by his network of public school friends, but when it came to inter-departmental politics he was in a league of his own.

'You crafty sod,' I said. Disraeli-Astor seemed to take this as a compliment and his smile widened.

It was clear he intended to ensure all the operational decisions relating to the operation, including agreeing any expenditure, were made by the AOSC, on which he controlled a majority of the votes. I suspect he saw this as a way of supplementing the department's budget.

Of course, involving me in his little scheme also served another purpose. It gave him leverage when it came to my leave application. My request would be granted, but only if I was a good boy and voted with him whenever called upon so to do.

I was tempted to tell Disraeli-Astor that he couldn't take my vote for granted, but my cottage in the Scottish Highlands beckoned, so I kept my mouth shut.

Chapter 5

Where is young master Fraser?' I asked Melissa.

I had tasked my deputy with putting together a briefing paper on Sir Reginald Wren. Although I was trying to keep an open mind about the businessman, I thought it was better to be prepared.

'He's at the British Library doing some research,' she told me.

'Research that should have been finished by last night,' I said tetchily. 'I told Timmy that I wanted something by first thing this morning, but the top of my desk is currently a brief free zone.'

'He spent all yesterday at the library, but there was a problem.'

'There always is with him. What was it this time?'

'During the afternoon a fire alarm went off and the place had to be evacuated. By the time the fire brigade turned up, checked the building and gave the all clear, it was closing time. That's why he went back this morning.'

I closed my eyes and shook my head in exasperation. My deputy seemed to attract problems the way jam attracts wasps.

'Right, get over to Euston Road straight away and help Timmy to complete his research. I'm off to the Cabinet Office for a meeting and I want that briefing note on my desk by the time I get back.'

'OK, I'll grab a cup of tea and then go find him.'

'Melissa, you're not at university now. When I say straight away, that means immediately. Go!'

She grabbed her handbag and stomped out of the office with her bottom lip leading the way.

I looked at my watch. It was gone half past nine. I heard feet clomping down the stairs that led from the floor above.

'Morning, boss,' Poppy said as she dashed into the office. 'What's wrong with Melissa? I passed her in the upstairs corridor and she had a face like thunder.'

'I had to lay down the law to her.'

'What about?'

'Let's just say that, in common with certain other members of my staff, urgency and time management appear to be alien concepts to her.'

'I saw Colleen Masters last night,' she neatly changed the subject, a knack that formed a natural part of her gene pool.

'You're late,' I said, not letting her get away with her ploy.

'Roger stayed over again,' she explained, as if this made everything alright. 'Aren't you interested in what Colleen and I talked about?'

I was determined not to be diverted. 'If Roger is going to stay with you regularly, either sleep in separate bedrooms, or buy yourself a decent alarm clock.'

'I have an alarm clock, but I always forget to switch it on.' She shrugged out of her coat and sat down behind her desk. 'You didn't answer my question,' she added.

'What question would that be?'

'I asked if you were interested in what Colleen and I were talking about last night.'

'I suspect my answer is irrelevant, because, from the look on your face, you're going to tell me anyway.'

'It was you,' she said with a giggle.

'Is that so?'

'Yes. Colleen asked me why you hadn't asked her out on a date yet.'

'And what was your reply?'

'I told her you were shy.'

'Shy?'

'Yes. I said you were a bit nervous and would probably ask her out once you had built up your courage.'

'Do you know something Poppy?'

'What's that, boss?'

'You're a bloody nightmare.'

She gave me one of her best toothy smiles. 'I know, but how would you manage without me?'

'I'm sure I'd find a way,' I said and went into my office to collect my briefcase.

'Do you want a coffee?' Poppy called out.

'Your offer is half an hour too late, because I'm on my way to Downing Street,' I told her as I returned to the outer office.

'Give Maggie my love,' Poppy said.

'I'm not going to Number Ten. It's the Cabinet Office for me today. I'm off to a meeting with your mate the D-G.'

47

'But Rupert's office is upstairs, not at the Cabinet Office.'

'Are you being deliberately provocative, Poppy?'

'Yes,' she said with an impish grin

I managed not to return her grin, but it was difficult because I could never stay cross with my secretary for long, particularly when she was in one of her better moods.

'OK. Let me make myself clear,' I said patiently. 'I'm going with the D-G for a meeting in the Cabinet Office. Unfortunately, we won't be seeing Mrs Thatcher so I won't be able to pass on your expressions of devotion. However, I'm sure she'll be able to contain her disappointment.'

The Cabinet Office is housed in 12 Downing Street and it took me no longer than five minutes to walk the short distance there from my office in the basement of the Treasury. When I reached the conference centre I found Disraeli-Astor standing on his own at one end. He was drinking coffee from a cup on the side of which was printed the Government's coat of arms.

'Grab a cup,' he said as I joined him. He pointed towards a side table on which a couple of plastic flasks stood next to cups and saucers. 'But be warned, it's barely warm and it tastes like that instant stuff.'

'Not instant coffee! How common!' I exclaimed in a whisper, but on this occasion my sarcasm was lost on him. I pumped coffee out of a flask into a cup. As he had warned, it was not very hot, but it tasted no worse than the coffee that Melissa inflicted on me when I gave her the chance.

'So what do you want me to do?' I asked.

Disraeli-Astor looked around to make sure that nobody was listening. They weren't. 'Do nothing and say nothing unless I nudge you and then all I want you to do is back me up.'

'Back you up how?'

'I don't know,' he said. 'Play it by ear.' With that he was off to chat to a smartly dressed man who had just come striding into the room, closely followed by Roland Lafarge.

Roly, was Disraeli-Astor's deputy. He was a dour Yorkshireman who had worked for the department since the end of the Korean War and was due to retire the following year. He saw me and wandered over to join me.

I poured him a coffee. He took a sip and grimaced.

'The boss says it tastes like instant coffee,' I said.

'Instant crap, more like,' Roly said, putting his almost full cup down. 'Come on, Dave, let's sit down.'

We took our seats round the long oval conference table that stretched from one end of the room to the other. On the table in front of me was an agenda, a pad of lined paper, a pencil, a small bottle of mineral water, a glass and a folded piece of white card bearing my name. I knew who I was, but it was probably of use to those attendees who didn't know me from a bar of soap.

There were seventeen people present, including me, all men except for one woman, wearing horn-rimmed spectacles, who was one of two representatives from the Foreign Office.

The other government departments and agencies represented were the Home Office, the Cabinet Office, the Joint Intelligence Committee, MI5, MI6, and the Metropolitan Police Special Branch.

Roly sat on Disraeli-Astor's left hand and I to his right. My boss introduced me and explained that I was attending the meeting at the behest of the Prime Minister, which was bending the truth somewhat, but nobody took issue with him.

By tradition JSOLC meetings were chaired by one of the representatives from the Cabinet Office. One was a minister of state, who turned out to be the smartly dressed man who Disraeli-Astor had greeted when he came into the room.

The man's name plaque identified him as Jeffery Johnson MP. He was accompanied by a senior executive officer, whose name was obscured by a bottle of water. Not surprisingly it was the politician who took the chair. He tapped a teaspoon against his coffee cup and brought the meeting to order.

'Thank you gentlemen and lady. Let's get started, because we have a full agenda today. I have an important engagement in my constituency this afternoon and would like to get the meeting wrapped up by lunchtime.'

Johnson was right about the agenda. It had a long list of security related items including: the execution in Iraq of British journalist Farzad Bazoft for alleged spying. The introduction of the Official Secrets Act 1989 was raised together with its implications for security and there was the preparations for the Poll Tax protest march in London that was planned for the following Sunday. Finally we came to the operation to bring General Urinoff to Britain.

Throughout the meeting, the chairman tapped the desk impatiently with his pencil whenever somebody spoke for too long. He regularly made a point of looking ostentatiously at his watch to remind us that he wanted the meeting finished by lunchtime.

By the time we reached the last item on the agenda, the hands on the ornate wall clock were fast approaching 1 pm.

'Our final piece of business was tabled by Colonel Disraeli-Astor, so I will let him explain what it is about. Over to you Director-General.'

'Thank you, Mister Chairman. I won't keep you long on this item,' Disraeli-Astor said. 'In fact, it is really a continuation of agenda Item Eight.'

'The defection of the Russian?'

'Yes. During his initial debrief interview, General Urinoff provided certain information that is very worrying. It relates to a multinational group that is planning action in South Africa. Action that could have wide-ranging implications for British investment in the region.'

'Mister Chairman, I think Colonel Disraeli-Astor is perhaps giving the Russian defector's claim more credence than it warrants.' The intervention came from one of the people from the Home Office. His name plaque showed he was the Rt. Hon. Douglas Campbell MP.

I recognised him as the minister responsible for home security, in which capacity he was the only attendee, apart from Disraeli-Astor, Roly and me, who had seen a copy of the initial debrief transcript. This was because the staff who were debriefing Urinoff were employed by the Home Office and reported to Campbell.

This Home Office involvement was an historic arrangement that rankled with the D-G, who was manoeuvring to cut them out of the security loop by getting permission to recruit the department's own interrogators. I suspected his proposal to set up a sub-committee of the JSOLC was part of his long-term strategy to achieve that.

'Having read the transcript of the interview with General Urinoff.' Campbell paused to ensure that everybody understood he had access to information unavailable to most of the other people sitting at the table. 'There was a distinct lack of evidence to back up his claim that any such group exists. And if it does exist, I could see nothing in the transcript that proved the group is a threat to Britain's interests in

South Africa.'

'It is certainly true that Urinoff gave few details about the group,' Disraeli-Astor agreed. 'But this was only his initial debrief session and we need to find out urgently more about them. Which is why Mister Statton is going down to Windsor tomorrow to interview Urinoff personally and find out exactly what he knows about the conspiracy.'

'I'm not sure conspiracy is the right word to use,' Campbell objected. He was being a real pain.

'So what word would you use to describe a plot to destabilise a sovereign nation?' My boss asked calmly.

'I am not convinced there is any such plot. Remember, I have read Urinoff's statement and that is not what he said at all,' Campbell insisted.

'You are entitled to your opinion, minister,' Disraeli-Astor said in a tone that made clear he thought the politician was wrong.

'And I stand by my opinion. I suggest you read the transcript again, Director-General. Perhaps then you will understand what I am saying.' Campbell said this with a patronising smile.

If he thought Disraeli-Astor would take this lying down he was wrong. When it comes to patronising people, my boss is a past master. 'Oh, I understand exactly what you are saying, minister and I am sure you *think* you are right,' he said, with extra emphasis on the word think. 'However, since you have no intelligence experience, I'm surprised you feel qualified to interpret a debrief transcript with such certainty.'

Campbell's face went red at this put down.

'But I am happy to read the transcript again, as you suggest, in fact I have it here.' My boss took a sheet of paper from his pocket and laid it on the table in front of him. 'Let me begin by quoting Urinoff: "We have received information from a reliable source that elections are inevitable in South Africa and could take place sometime in the next couple of years.".' He looked up from the paper. 'This is backed up by certain intelligence we had already received from another source.' He paused and kicked me gently on the shin.

This was my cue, although I had no idea why my boss wanted me to interrupt at that particular juncture. However, I did as I was told and played it by ear.

51

'That is correct, Mister Chairman,' I chipped in. 'General Urinoff's statement confirmed information shared with us by another Government department.' I looked up the table at the woman in the horn-rimmed spectacles. 'As I am sure our colleague from the Foreign Office can verify.'

The woman looked startled and exchanged glances with the representative from MI6, who looked equally nonplussed. However, there was no way she was going to admit to not knowing what I was talking about. She was probably cursing her colleagues back in the FO for not having briefed her properly.

'That is perfectly true, Mister Chairman,' she said smoothly. 'The Foreign Office has been monitoring the situation very carefully and I would agree that it is our expectation that elections will be held in South Africa in the near future.'

Disraeli-Astor gave me a strange look and then continued: 'Urinoff went on to say, and I quote: "Our assessment is that those elections almost certainly will lead to a win for the African National Congress."'

'That too was the assessment of our intelligence source,' I interjected. I was really getting into this backing-up-the-boss lark.

'That is our assessment also,' the Foreign Office woman said.

'That is good to know,' Disraeli-Astor said quickly. He did not look happy at being interrupted again. 'May I continue? Thank you. Urinoff went on to say, and again I am reading his words verbatim: "However, we have evidence of a multinational group of businessmen that is drawing up plans to prevent such an outcome." Note those words, Mister Chairman: "drawing up plans".' Disraeli-Astor looked at Campbell without blinking.

The politician was unmoved. 'Well that still does not constitute a conspiracy,' he insisted.

'Conspiracy was not my description of the group's actions. It was that of the Prime Minister.' Disraeli-Astor said. This immediately shut up Campbell on that subject. 'Our Russian friend also mentioned the name of a British subject as being involved,' my boss added, although he was careful to not mention Sir Reginald Wren by name.

'Yes, I noticed that too,' said Campbell, who also didn't reveal Wren's identity. 'However, I think the Soviets are playing games.' He looked round the table as if expecting to be contradicted. 'I happen to know the person in question and he is an upright member of society. I am just not convinced the Russian defector is telling the truth.'

'Convinced or not, you must agree that we have a duty to investigate Urinoff's claims,' Disraeli-Astor said. 'For instance, his allegation that the Afrikaans Broederbond and the Pan Africanist Congress are working together to take control of South Africa is deeply worrying.'

'It would be worrying if it was true,' Campbell said. 'But remember the Russian is a KGB General. He could be making it all up to mislead us.'

'It is certainly possible Urinoff is feeding us misinformation,' Disraeli-Astor agreed. 'But what if he is telling the truth? Can we take that risk?'

'Look, I'm not sure...' Campbell started, but was cut off by Jeffery Johnson, who tapped his spoon against the side of his coffee cup again to bring the meeting to order.

'Gentlemen, gentlemen,' he said. 'This is getting us nowhere. Have you anything further to add, Colonel Disraeli-Astor?'

'Yes, Mister Chairman, I have a message from the Prime Minister.' These words triggered a shuffling of papers amongst the civil servants round the table and the backs of the politicians present stiffened visibly.

'Mrs Thatcher wants this matter dealt with as a matter of urgency,' Disraeli-Astor explained, 'and she doesn't want its resolution held back by bureaucratic formalities, or inter-agency rivalry,' he looked directly at Campbell. 'And before you ask; they were her exact words, not mine.'

The politician said nothing.

'To ensure departments co-operate,' Disraeli-Astor went on, 'the Prime Minister supports the setting up of an Active Operations Sub-committee to co-ordinate any action taken to defeat this group.'

'That sounds a good idea,' Johnson said. 'What sort of format does the PM have in mind for such a sub-committee?'

'Well she believes the AOSC should be kept small. Five members was mentioned,' Disraeli-Astor said with a straight face. 'It was suggested that there be one representative each from the Department for Covert Operations, the Cabinet Office, the Home Office and the Foreign Office.'

There was a general nodding of agreement round the table.

'In addition, because Section Two will be taking the lead in the operation, the PM thinks the fifth member of the sub-committee should come from there and has approved Mister Statton as that member.'

I saw Campbell was about to say something, but, thought better of it.

'In addition, it was suggested that the AOSC Chairman should be elected at its first meeting.' Disraeli-Astor sat back in his chair.

'I assume the AOSC will report back regularly to this committee?' Johnson asked.

'I am sure that will be the Chairman's intention,' the D-G assured him, before adding quickly: 'Whoever that person might be.'

'Splendid,' Johnson said. He looked round the table. 'Are there any objections to the setting up of this sub-committee? No? That's agreed then. Colonel Disraeli-Astor, perhaps you would like to call the first meeting when you think the time is right. Now, if there are no other comments I declare the meeting closed.'

When we left Downing Street Roland Lafarge headed up Whitehall. He had an appointment with his doctor. Disraeli-Astor and I made our way back to the Treasury.

'That went well,' I said.

'Yes, except one thing puzzles me,' Disraeli-Astor replied.

'What's that?'

'Why did you keep interrupting me?'

'You're exaggerating. It was only twice and I did it to back you up.'

'I said I would nudge you if I needed your help.'

'You did nudge me.'

'What are you talking about?'

'You kicked me under the table.'

'That was an accident. I was crossing my legs.'

'How was I supposed to know that?' I asked. 'Anyway, there was no harm done, was there?'

'No, except you inferred the Foreign Office had passed information to us. How are we going to explain that away?'

'I'm sure you'll think of something.'

We walked on in silence for a while. 'It was lucky our item was so close to lunch,' I said eventually. 'The Chairman rushed it through and didn't leave time for too many awkward questions.'

'The timing was by design,' Disraeli-Astor said smugly. 'I asked Jeffery to make ours the last item on the agenda.'

'You spoke to Johnson before the meeting?'

'Yesterday,' he said with a smile. 'I know him well. We went to the same school, although he was a year ahead of me.'

'I should have guessed,' I said. 'Is there anybody in the Government you didn't go to school with?'

'Let me see,' he said and looked at me thoughtfully. 'Yes,' he replied finally. 'I don't recall seeing Margaret Thatcher at Eton.'

That made me laugh out loud. It was the first time I had heard my boss crack a joke. 'And I take it you had already briefed your pal on your proposal for a sub-committee and its make up?'

'Yes, Jeffery was very supportive, particularly when he found out that Mrs T endorsed the plan and was going to be keeping a close eye on things.'

'So I take it Mister Johnson will be sitting on the AOSC supporting your bid to become chairman?'

'Goodness, no, Jeffery is much too canny for that. He wouldn't want to be involved with the day to day monitoring of the operation. He has delegated the senior executive officer who was with him at the meeting to attend on his behalf and report back to him.'

'I hope the SEO is house trained,' I said.

'Oh, very much so. He will do the right thing when it comes to a vote.'

'I see, so if things go well your friend Johnson will be able to share the glory, but if things go tits up he can blame it on his official.'

'We'll make a politician of you yet, Statton!'

'Over my dead body,' I said. We walked on in silence for a few minutes and then I added: 'Talking of politicians, you'll have to watch that prat from the Home Office.'

'You mean Dougie?'

'Dougie? Don't tell me you went to school with the Right Honourable Douglas Campbell as well!'

He smiled. 'Not exactly, Dougie is a few years older than me, but he was at Eton before going up to Oxford.'

'From where, no doubt, he graduated with a first class honours degree in political back stabbing.'

Disraeli-Astor smiled. 'Fear not, Statton. Dougie might be a sharp operator, but I have his measure.'

I made no comment. I just hoped he was right.

When I got back to my office there was a file on my desk containing a report on Sir Reginald Wren and a note from my secretary asking me to ring Colleen Masters. I stared at the note for a while and wondered what she wanted. I decided to ring her later.

I opened the Wren file and started to read. Twenty minutes later I wandered through to the outer office carrying the file.

'Have you rung Colleen yet?' Poppy whispered as I passed her desk.

'I've been busy,' I replied.

'Well she told me what she wants to talk to you about,' she said knowingly, 'and it's your loss.'

I ignored her and headed for Timothy Fraser's desk.

'Good work, Timmy,' I said holding the file aloft. 'Very comprehensive.'

He blushed and refused to meet my eyes. 'Thanks, Mister Statton, but it was Melissa who dug out most of the information. To be honest I was struggling before she joined me this morning.'

I looked down at him. Although he had graduated from Oxford with an upper 2:1 degree in Ancient History, he was a plodder with little imagination and a total lack of common sense. However, he did have a couple of positive attributes. One was that he followed orders without question and the other was that he was honest to the point of being naïve.

'I'm sure you did your bit, Timmy,' I assured him. I turned to Melissa, who had been watching the exchange. 'Well done Melissa. You get today's gold star.'

At first, she hesitated and I could see that she was deciding whether to still be angry at me, or forgive me. Eventually she set aside her pout and allowed her face to break into a smile. 'Thanks, but it was no problem. I have always enjoyed research work. Would you like a cup of coffee?'

'No thanks, but I would love a cup of tea.' I decided to settle for the safer option. There was little that even Melissa could mess up pouring hot water over a tea bag and adding milk and sugar.

I turned back to Timmy. 'I'm visiting the Windsor safe-house tomorrow to talk to Urinoff and I'd like you to come with me. Are you free?'

'Of course, sir, I'd like that. I've never visited the safe-house. What time are we leaving?'

'I want to get down there early, so I'll pick you up at oh-seven-hundred hours.'

'I'll be ready.' He gave me a shy smile. I had made his day.

'I want to tape our conversation with General Urinoff,' I told him, 'so, pop down to the equipment stores and book out a recorder.'

'Can't we use the Home Office recording equipment?'

'No. For security reasons they take it back to Marsham Street with them each night.'

'Okay I'll go down to the stores now.' He sprang to his feet and headed for the door.

'Whoa!' I stopped him in his tracks. 'I'm going out shortly, and won't be coming back today, so I'd like you to take the recorder home with you.'

'No problem! I'm on my way!' He said and almost ran out of the door. I shook my head. Enthusiasm was fine, but sometimes Timmy's desire to please sat ill with my own cynicism.

When I got back to my office I rang the Blue Oyster, a jazz club owned by an acquaintance of mine, Manny Silver, which was located in one of the less salubrious side roads in Soho.

Manny's club was not as well-known as Ronnie Scott's, and didn't attract the high-profile jazz performers his arch rival did. However, it also avoided many of the pseuds, celebrities, and punters who only frequented the larger club because they thought it was cool to be seen in Ronnie Scott's.

Me? I preferred the Blue Oyster's understated simplicity, range of speciality beers, unpretentious decor and the raw talent of the unknown, and often brilliant, jazz musicians that Manny Silver seemed to unearth on a regular basis.

When I finished my telephone call to Manny I sat and stared at the telephone for an age. I was torn. I wanted to ring Colleen Masters, but something held me back. I sensed my next conversation with her would lead me down a road towards emotional challenges I wasn't sure I was ready to face. Perhaps it was a man thing. A fear that I would be putting myself into a situation over which I had no control.

But, despite my reservations, there was something about Colleen Masters that sent my pulses racing. I picked up the telephone and dialled her number.

Colleen answered the phone with a professional briskness. 'Good afternoon. This is the Director-General's office. How can I help you?'

'I had a message to ring you.'

'Is that you, David?'

'I hope so, if not, I'm having an identity crisis.'

She laughed lightly. It was a pleasant sound.

'What's the problem?' I asked. 'Is it something the D-G wants?'

'No, it was a personal call from me.'

'You?'

'Yes. I have two tickets for *Les Misérables*. I was supposed to be going with a girlfriend, but she has gone down with the flu and can't make it. I wondered if you'd like to join me.' I detected a hint of nervousness in her voice. 'Of course, I'll understand if you're busy or it's not your cup of tea.'

Les Misérables was a show I'd been meaning to see for ages. Colleen's invitation was all that was needed for me to set aside my earlier reservations. 'I'd be happy to join you,' I said without hesitation. 'When are the tickets for?'

'Tomorrow night,' she replied. 'Sorry it's such short notice.'

'Let me check my diary,' I said and waited for a few seconds as I stared at the bare top of my desk. 'Okay, I have a free evening tomorrow.' I made it sound as if my social life was full. I should be so lucky.

'So we're on?' Colleen asked.

'Yes,' I replied. 'But only if you let me treat you to dinner first.'

'That sounds good,' she said.

'Do you like Chinese food?'

'Who doesn't?'

'Then I know just the place. Would you like me to pick you up?'

'If that won't be putting you out.'

'Where do you live?'

'Bayswater.'

'Not a problem. It's on my way from Shepherd's Bush. What's your address?'

She gave it to me. I knew the road in which she lived. It was in a nice area full of expensive properties. She either had independent wealth, or the department was paying her more than I thought.

'Will six o'clock be OK?' I asked.

'Fine,' she said. 'See you then.'

I put down the phone and sat staring into space. I wondered if I was doing the right thing.

Soho, London

The Blue Oyster club was buzzing and the air was full of jazz music and cigarette smoke. In the basement a quartet was laying down a tight rhythm that flowed through the building. It had a beat that couldn't fail to get the feet tapping of the couple of dozen or so people who had bagged seats in front of the tiny stage on which they performed.

On the ground floor the chairs at the plain wooden tables were occupied by more people who were out for a good time on a Friday night. I was one of them and knew we had come to the right place.

'So how are you, David?' Asked Manny Silver. He inhaled deeply on a cigarette and blew smoke out to join the blue fug hanging over the tables like a toxic London smog.

'All the better for being here. I've missed the Blue Oyster.'

'And we've missed you, my friend,' he said. 'Can I offer you a drink?'

'A beer would be great,' I said. 'Do you still stock Bishop's Finger?'

'Of course,' he replied. 'The people who frequent my club have an eclectic taste in clothes, footwear, lovers and beer.' He called a waitress over and ordered me an ale and himself a bottle of lager, which he called real beer. He had an odd idea of taste. It was probably all the Turkish cigarettes he chain-smoked.

'You're still discovering some decent talent I see.' I drummed my finger tips on the table in time to the beat. We lapsed into silence as the combo's horn player started into a solo that made the hairs on the back of my neck prickle. 'Those boys are good,' I said when the solo had finished.

'Yeah, they're not bad for *shegetzs*. I'm lucky to have them. They auditioned at Ronnie Scott's and were promised a gig this week, but their slot was cancelled because Johnny Dankworth wanted to record

59

a live album in the club.

'My boys were told they could perform next week instead, but they told the *schmuck* to piss off.' Manny looked pleased with himself. There was no love lost between the two jazz club owners.

'It's Ronnie's loss,' I said.

The waitress turned up carrying a small round tray on which was balanced our bottled beers and two glasses. She put a couple of coasters on the table in front of us and stood the glasses on them before carefully pouring our beers into them. The head on my beer was perfect. She was an expert that girl.

'Thanks, Ruby,' I said and took an inch off my beer and enjoyed its hoppy bitter taste. Bishop's Finger is brewed in Faversham and was my drink of choice when I was a young man growing up in Kent. I still loved it.

'My pleasure, Mister Statton,' she replied and managed to sound sincere.

'So, David, to what do I owe this pleasure?' Manny asked once the waitress had disappeared. Somehow he managed to sip his lager and smoke a cigarette at the same time. 'I haven't seen you for months and suddenly you ring me and ask to meet as a matter of urgency.'

'Are you still involved in your other little venture?' I asked. 'Or is this joint making you so much money you no longer need side lines?'

Manny laughed and almost choked on a combination of smoke and beer. 'Come on, David. I'm a Jew. I never turn down the chance to make more money when the opportunity arises.'

'And have you kept your safe breaking skills honed?'

He looked hurt. 'Listen, my friend, it's like riding a bike,' he said, leaning towards me and lowering his voice. 'Once you are able to break the code on a peter, it's not a skill you lose.'

'And have you kept up to date with the latest burglar alarm technology?'

'Of course,' Manny assured me as he lit yet another cigarette from the butt of his last one. He waved it round the room. 'This building is fitted with the very latest alarm system. There is nobody in England who could break into my joint – except me!'

'That's good, because the house I want you to break into has one of the most modern burglar alarms on the market.

'Where is this house?'

'Belgravia,' I replied.

'*Oy vey!*' Manny exclaimed. 'Belgravia! Now he tells me! Now that will be a challenge.'

'Too much of a challenge for you, Manny?'

'You know me better than that, David,' he sounded offended. 'I have always relished a challenge, no matter how difficult. Listen, I might spend a lot of my time running this club, but I haven't forgotten how to disarm a burglar alarm and I am still the best peter-man in London.'

'I wasn't questioning your ability, Manny,' I said. 'I just wondered about your motivation now that you own the Blue Oyster. It must be bringing you in a steady income.'

'The club is doing well enough, David, there's no denying that. It certainly keeps my bank manager happy. And I have to admit that running it gives me a great deal of pleasure. However, it doesn't provide me with the same buzz as blowing a peter.'

'I don't want the safe blown, Manny,' I said. 'In fact, I don't want the owner to know that it has been opened. That is very important.'

'You don't want me to nick nothing?'

'No. I just want you to take photographs of everything in the safe, including any documents.' I slid a khaki coloured cardboard box across the table to him. The box was about 6 inch cubed and stamped on its lid was the legend: MOD Property.

Manny looked at the package in alarm.

'Don't worry it doesn't contain a bomb,' I assured him. 'It's a special camera that has been developed in America for use by the US Army. The camera is digital and has no film, instead it stores images on a memory card that can then be downloaded onto a computer. It also has an automatic flash and focus. Basically, all you have to do is point the camera at what you want to photograph and press a button.'

Manny lifted the lid and peered inside the box. 'It looks complicated, David. All those buttons and levers.'

'It's very simple,' I assured him. I slid a brown envelope towards him.

'Like me,' he said in his most lugubrious manner. 'What's in there?' He nodded at the envelope, but didn't touch it.

'An instruction booklet.'

'I hope the bloody thing works. I don't want to do the job only to

61

find that none of the photos come out.'

'That won't be a problem. This is the latest technology. The beauty of a digital camera is that you can check photos as they are taken.'

'Are you having me on?'

'No, there's a little screen on the back of the camera that shows each photo as you take it. If you're not happy with the result you can delete the photo and take another.'

He shook his head in amazement. 'Oy vey! Whatever will they invent next? I can't keep up with all these gadgets and gismos.'

I tapped the envelope. 'Also in there is the address of the mark and diagrams of the electrical circuit and alarm system in his home.'

Manny looked happier at this news. 'That will make the job much easier,' he said as he finally picked up the envelope and slipped it into his jacket pocket.

I pointed at the box. 'There are only a handful of those cameras in the country. They all belong to the Ministry of Defence. I had to call in a few favours to borrow one, so don't break it.'

'Don't worry, I'll be careful,' he paused as he finished off his lager and lit yet another cigarette. 'How did you get hold of the specification for the alarm?' He asked eventually.

'You know better than to ask, Manny.'

He smiled. 'The alarm company?'

I didn't answer.

He nodded knowingly. 'When do you want the photos?'

'Monday.'

'Next Monday?'

'Yes.'

'That doesn't leave me much time to prepare?'

'I appreciate that. However, our mark is flying to Zurich early tomorrow morning and isn't due back until Monday evening. You'll have the whole weekend to get the job done.'

'How do you know the geezer is going away?'

'Because he's flying himself to Switzerland and has filed flight plans with the Civil Aviation Authority. All flight plans submitted are automatically reported to the Government Communications HQ in Cheltenham, where the information is fed into the central computer. If the pilot is registered as an active target then it is immediately flagged up with the relevant agency. In this case my department.'

'Bleeding computers are taking over the world.' He didn't sound impressed.

'They are, Manny. Knowledge is power and computers provide us with knowledge.'

'Problem is, the old bill has computers too,' he said miserably. What chance do old lags like me have against them?'

'You're no old lag, Manny,' I said with a laugh. 'You've never been inside. You've managed to keep one step ahead of the police.'

'It's getting tougher all the time.'

'It's called progress.'

'Well progress puts the fear of God up me.'

'You have nothing to fear, because on this occasion you're on the side of the angels.'

Manny laughed loudly and emitted a mouthful of smoke to further thicken the smoky atmosphere.

'What's so amusing? The idea that you have nothing to fear?'

'No, the thought of you as the Archangel Gabriel.'

Chapter 6

Kingsbury House was located in the countryside on the outskirts of Windsor. Its Georgian style façade betrayed pretensions of a grandeur that were not quite realised. The Edwardian industrialist who built Kingsbury House dreamed of turning it into his own stately home, but he went bankrupt before the last of the building's four wings was started.

The house stood empty for decades, before being taken over by the Government during the Second World War. The Ministry of Works eventually finished off the building, but abandoned the industrialist's original grand plan and instead gave the last wing a more modest look that befitted wartime austerity.

Kingsbury House was now used by Government departments to hold discreet internal conferences and as a safe-house for defectors and other people who the authorities wanted to keep away from the public gaze.

Located just off the A308 and close to Windsor Racecourse, the building stood in ample grounds surrounded by high hedges. It was reached by a gravel drive that ran through extensive gardens, most of which were laid to lawn. It was all protected by a discreet security fence and electronically operated metal gates.

Timmy was waiting at the front door of his apartment when I arrived to pick him up. He was carrying a large black bag containing a tape recorder. He placed it carefully on the back seat of my car and jumped into the passenger seat.

The early Saturday morning traffic was light as we made our way out of London on the M4 under a leaden sky that suggested rain was not far away. We made good time and reached the outskirts of Windsor well before 9 o'clock, just as the first spots of rain on my windscreen forced me to switch on my wipers.

By the time we drew up outside the gates of Kingsbury House rain was hammering down on the car roof with a rhythmic rattle that would have done justice to a washboard player in a skiffle group.

Timmy got out of the car and spoke into the intercom positioned on one of the pillars from which the imposing metal gates hung.

There was a delay of a few minutes before the gates swung open and when he clambered back in the car he was soaked through. It was another of my deputy's more positive qualities that he never complained about being cold and wet.

I drove through the gate and up the drive to the house. To one side of the building was a small car-park, in which the only vehicle to be seen was a small van belonging to the private security company contracted to provide guards for the house.

I knew there would be no Home Office interrogation staff on duty today, because they had weekends off and were probably spending time with their loved ones, or braving the weather on a golf course. Not for the first time I wondered whether I was in the right job, then I remembered I had no loved ones with whom to spend time and I didn't play golf.

Kingsbury House had impressive double front doors, which provided access into and out of the building. All the other external doors were locked and bolted, as were all the downstairs windows. These security measures were designed to prevent intruders, rather than imprison anybody who happened to be in residence. They were able to leave the house whenever they chose.

However, although guests could wander at will round the extensive grounds, they were not permitted to venture out into the wider world beyond the security fences without supervision.

Timmy and I got out of the car and headed up the flight of granite steps leading to the front doors, one of which was open. We were about to step inside when I realised he wasn't carrying the black bag.

'Where's the tape recorder?' I asked.

'Oh, bother! Sorry, sir, it's still on the back seat.' He looked back at the car and hesitated. The rain had increased in tempo.

'It's no good to us there, Timmy. Is it?'

'No, sir,' he said. He pulled up the collar of his wet jacket and headed off towards the car-park, just as another security van came through the main gates and down the drive.

I sighed and stepped inside the building and found myself in a lobby, the back wall of which was a glass partition stretching from floor to ceiling. Set into the partition was a door with no handles.

To my right was an office with a toughened glass screen behind which a security guard sat at a desk reading a football magazine. On its front cover was a photograph of a soccer player in a green and white hooped jersey. At the far end of the office was a door and next to it a dark jacket hung on a coat rack.

The guard looked up at me, closed his magazine and laid it carefully on the desk. He rose slowly to his feet and ambled over to the window.

'Good morning, sir,' he said in a broad Northern Irish accent. His voice sounded tinny as it came through the small intercom system that was set into the glass screen. 'Please identify yourself.'

'Police,' I said simply. 'I thought my colleague explained that earlier at the gate.'

The guard made a point of looking for Timmy. 'You seem to have lost your colleague,' he said.

'He forgot something and had to pop back to the car,' I explained.

'Well he's probably a very wet colleague now,' he said with a smirk.

Wet was exactly the word that described my deputy, drenched by rain or not, but I felt the need to defend him. 'He was already wet because you took so long to open the gate,' I pointed out.

'I'm sorry about that,' the guard said, but he didn't sound very sympathetic. 'But it's not my fault it's raining.'

'Wet or not, he told you who we were.'

'Aye, he said you were the police, but that proves nothing. You could be anybody. So I repeat; please identify yourself.'

'I'm Inspector Statton,' I said, trying to hide my irritation at the man's attitude. 'And my colleague is Sergeant Fraser.'

'Proof of identity,' the guard said shortly.

For obvious reasons an organisation as secretive as the Department for Covert Operations, which part of the British Secret Service, does not issue its agents with identity cards. However, the warrant card I passed through the narrow slot that ran along the bottom of the screen had been specially issued to me by the Metropolitan Police.

As I watched the guard study my warrant cards, I mourned the passing of the in-house staff who used to look after security for the department. I was on first name terms with them all and they always recognised me immediately, despite my visits to Kingsbury House being few and far between.

However, following the sub-contracting out of security to the private sector, the guards were never in post long enough to build up a personal relationship with even regular visitors. It was therefore no surprise to me I had never seen this guard before.

The man had long black hair that covered his ears and a bushy, full beard of the same colour. His dark brown eyes stared intently at me from beneath thick eyebrows. They were angry eyes and they combined with his thin, cruel lips to give him the look of somebody who was easily provoked.

The guard looked as if he had seen his fair share of fights. He had a small scar across the bridge of his nose and another that ran across the back of a right hand from which one finger was missing.

He wore a white uniform blouse with short sleeves and a high collar, above which I could just see the top of a tattoo on the side of his neck. It looked like a flag of some sort.

He was probably typical of the unemployed, and often unemployable, who were the only people desperate enough to accept the very low wages that private security companies were prepared to pay.

Such low wages was one of the side-effects of contracting out public services to private sector. Cutting overheads, including wages, was the only way that firms could meet their contractual obligations, but at the same time make a healthy profit.

Satisfied my face matched that shown on the warrant card, the guard slowly and painstakingly notated my name and number into the register that lay open on the counter behind the screen.

'You're not from round here,' I said.

'No, I'm from Derry,' the man replied, but he didn't elaborate.

The door to the office opened and another guard entered. He wore a raincoat from which water dripped onto the floor. The man took off his coat, shook it and hung it on the coat rack. He was older than the first guard, and had cropped, white hair. He was tall and had an upright bearing that hinted at a military background.

'Morning, Billy,' he greeted his Irish colleague.

The first guard looked at his watch. 'You're late,' he complained without returning the greeting. He passed my warrant cards to me.

'Sorry,' the new arrival said as he joined his colleague at the counter. 'My van wouldn't start, but I'm here now, so I'll take over. You get away.'

He studied the register and then me. 'Morning, Inspector. I guess you're here to see Major Carsons.' He used the name under which

Urinoff was registered in the safe-house. He guessed right, but that wasn't a surprise because the Russian was currently the only resident.

The first guard put on the jacket that was hanging on the coat rack, picked up the football magazine, stuffed it into his pocket and disappeared out of the door. He had no raincoat and I hoped it was still raining. It would serve the surly bastard right if he got soaked.

'Yes,' I confirmed as Timmy came into the lobby and stood at my side. He was even wetter than before. 'This is my colleague, Sergeant Fraser,' I explained to the guard.

'I have to see some form of identification,' the guard explained to me apologetically. 'It's not that I don't believe you, Inspector.'

I shrugged and watched as Timmy produced his warrant card and slipped it under the glass screen. The security guard gave the card a cursory glance, entered Timmy's details in the register underneath mine, and handed it back.

'Major Carsons is in the Stuart Suite, Inspector,' the guard explained. 'D'you know where that is?'

'I've visited Kingsbury House several times before,' I explained.

'Major Carsons usually makes himself a very early breakfast before going for a stroll round the garden,' the guard said as he pressed a button. The door in the glass petition opened silently. 'However, I expect the bad weather put him off his walk today, so you'll find him in his apartment. No doubt he'll be waiting for his newspaper; would you mind taking it up to him?'

'Of course not,' I said.

'Thank you, sir.' The guard pushed a copy of *The Times* under the screen. I picked it up and stepped through the door, closely followed by Timmy whose wet hair was pasted to his head. He left a trail of water in his wake as he squelched across the floor.

Once through the door, we were in a hallway that led to a wide staircase. Timmy looked like an overawed schoolboy as he stared up at the huge gilt framed portraits that decorated the walls and the huge cut glass chandelier that hung from the ceiling.

All he could say was: 'Wow!'

'Come on,' I said striding towards the staircase. 'The Stuart Suite is upstairs in the North Wing.'

'How many suites are there?' Timmy asked.

'Four in all,' I replied as we reached the landing at the top of the staircase. 'One in each wing.' I added as we walked down a wide corridor. 'We're currently in the South Wing and this is the entrance to the Tudor Suite,' I pointed to a heavy oak door on our right. 'In addition, each wing has several other rooms, including a conference suite.'

'Was this place a hotel at one time?' Timmy said.

'No, it was a private home until World War Two,' I explained. 'Then it was requisitioned by the Government for use as a convalescent home for wounded officers.'

When we reached the end of the corridor we turned left into a narrower passageway which led us to the North Wing.

'Here's the Stuart Suite,' I said as we arrived at a door on the left-hand side of the corridor. I knocked on the door. There was no answer, so I tried again. Once more, I was met only by silence. I turned the gleaming gold-plated handle and the catch clicked. I pushed open the door.

I stepped through the door, with Timmy at my heels. We found ourselves in a spacious sitting room that contained a floral-patterned settee and matching arm-chairs. Behind one of the chairs was a standard lamp, the shade of which was decorated with the same pink flowers as the covers on the furniture.

Between settee and chairs was positioned a long coffee table on which were several magazines and a neat pile of newspapers to which I added that day's edition.

Set into the wall opposite was a long window that looked out onto a large courtyard, in the centre of which was a flower bed full of daffodils. The yellow blooms had been battered and flattened by the driving rain, which now seemed to have eased off.

Against one of the sitting-room walls stood a bookcase and alongside another stood a cocktail cabinet. Set into both walls was a door. The one on our left led to the bedroom and the other to a kitchen-diner. It was to the latter that we headed first.

It was another good-sized room, one end of which was the cooking area. It contained a stove, a fridge and a work surface on which stood an electric kettle, toaster and microwave oven.

Underneath the work surface were two large cupboards, and there were two more storage units fitted to the wall above the work area. Against the wall to our left was a sink unit and washing machine. Above the sink was a window that looked out onto the courtyard.

At the dining end of the room was a small square table and a single chair. On the table was a dinner plate, in the centre of which sat a double eggcup, complete with eggs, and a tea spoon with yolk stuck to it. One of the eggs was whole, but the top of the other one had been removed and had been placed on the side of the plate. The rest of the shell was empty. I touched the unused egg with the tip of my finger. It was cold.

Next to the dinner plate was an empty mug and a small plate on which was a knife and half a slice of equally cold toast. In the middle of the table stood a coffee pot, which was no warmer than the food.

The only other item on the table was an upturned glass that had once contained orange juice. The remnants of the drink flowed in a sticky stream across the table and dripped slowly onto the floor.

Timmy wrinkled his nose. 'What a mess,' he said.

I grunted non-committally.

We made our way back to the sitting-room and headed for the door leading to the bedroom.

'It's very quiet,' Timmy said. 'Perhaps he's still asleep.

I said nothing. Cautiously I turned the handle, not sure what to expect. I nudged open the bedroom door with my foot. Like the rest of the suite the bedroom was a generous size. It contained a double wardrobe, a long dressing table, an easy chair, a small coffee table and a large four-poster bed that looked as if it might be made from oak.

'Check out the bathroom,' I said pointing to another door. 'And while you're in there, dry yourself off.'

Timmy headed for the bathroom and I heard a click as he turned on the light. 'He's not in here, sir,' he shouted.

That's when I noticed the rope.

It was tied around the heavy, solid leg of the bed and stretched across the room and out of a window, which looked out onto the courtyard. The window was open and a breeze rustled the heavy brocade curtains. I looked out onto the courtyard.

I heard Timmy come back into the bedroom. 'I've found him,' I said, glancing over my shoulder.

Timmy was vigorously rubbing his hair with a towel. He dropped the wet towel onto the easy chair and walked over to stand next to me. His hair now stood up like porcupine quills.

'He's out there.' I nodded towards the window where Alexei

Urinoff was hanging from the end of the rope.

Together we pulled the dead Russian through the window and carried him over to the bed.

'Shall I call the police?' Timmy asked as he nervously smoothed his tousled hair down with a hand. His face was as white as the sheet with which he watched me cover the body.

'Not on your life,' I said. 'This is department business. We'll handle this ourselves. The last thing we need is the local plod poking its nose in.'

'But doesn't the Cabinet Office procedures manual say that any suspicious death has to be reported to the police.' My deputy must be the only member of the DFCO to have read the manual from cover to cover.

'It does, but that manual was drafted by civil servants with no understanding of the real world. If we obeyed all their procedures, we would never get anything done. That's why we ignore most of them.'

'Oh, I see,' Timmy said. He looked at me, crestfallen. 'I have a lot to learn, don't I?'

'Don't worry, son,' I assured him. 'You'll get there someday.'

'Thank you, sir. I'll try to follow your example.'

'I'm not sure that will guarantee you a successful career, Timmy, but I wish you luck. Now, getting back to the business in hand, I want to have a proper look round here. While I'm doing that, I'd like you to contact the department's duty officer.'

Timmy looked around the room. 'I don't remember seeing a telephone anywhere in the apartment,' he said.

'That's because there isn't one,' I told him. 'But there's an office at the end of this corridor with a telephone in it. Go use that one.' I told him. 'And don't forget that you'll need to use this week's password. Do you remember what it is?'

He nodded. 'Fleet Street,' he whispered and glanced at the bed as if the dead Russian was going to overhear him.

I was relieved he knew the password and hadn't asked me. It changes every week and I could never remember what it was.

'Tell the duty officer that we need a clean-up unit down here pronto. They are to remove Urinoff's body and make sure there is no sign left of his presence in the safe-house.'

Timmy looked at me quizzically.

'As far as the Soviets are concerned, the man on that bed died in East Germany three days ago,' I explained, 'and that's exactly what we want them to carry on believing.'

He headed for the door, but I called him back.

'And, Timmy, tell duty I want a post-mortem carried out on the body and the results faxed through to my office as soon as possible, but no later than Monday. Make sure he understands this is a priority job.'

'Righto, sir.'

'He'll probably complain that it's the weekend and none of the government pathologists are on duty. Suggest he contacts Doctor James Knowles at the Met Police Forensic Science Lab. Tell him to use my name. Jim owes me a favour.'

'Why a post-mortem?' He asked. 'Surely it's obvious that Urinoff committed suicide.'

'Timmy, in our game nothing is ever obvious,' I replied. 'An important thing to remember about intelligence work is that you should view everything through sceptical eyes, particularly when there are things that don't make sense.'

'What things don't make sense, sir?'

'Several things. For a start, ask yourself, this question. Why did General Urinoff cook himself a breakfast, eat half of it and then commit suicide? Does that make sense?'

Timmy looked at me blankly and said nothing.

'Look, I can't imagine that Urinoff topped himself because he was unhappy with the quality of his eggs. So why did he kill himself?'

He shook his head.

'Exactly. We don't know. That's why I want a post-mortem carried out. Perhaps it will provide us with a clue to what happened. Now on your way, we're wasting time.'

When Timmy had disappeared, I had a good look round the rooms that made up the suite, starting with the bathroom. I discovered nothing new about Urinoff in the bathroom, except that he was a tidy person.

There were no bottles standing on the edge of the sink or bath, as is the case in many bathrooms, and the towels were folded carefully over the heated towel rail that was attached to one wall. All the usual things found in a bathroom were stored away neatly in the large bathroom cabinet that was attached to the wall above the sink.

In addition to toiletries, such as shaving equipment, shower gel, shampoo and toothpaste, there were various packs of pills, laxatives and some indigestion tablets, but nothing that suggested that Urinoff might have been in any way depressed.

I made my way back to the bedroom, but found little of interest. Half the double wardrobe was made up of shelves on which were neatly stacked the clothes Urinoff had brought with him from East Germany in his holdall, which now lay empty underneath the bottom shelf.

Hanging in the other half of the wardrobe was the dark suit, shirt and camel-hair overcoat worn by the Russian when he left East Germany. I checked all the pockets of the suit and coat, but found nothing more interesting than a used ticket for Berlin's S-Bahn and a small ball of fluff.

There were also some new clothes that had been purchased for him in the UK since his arrival, including a silk dressing gown, which he told the interrogators was something he had always wanted, and a pair of slippers.

I turned to the dressing table, which at first yielded nothing of interest. On its polished wooden top was a lace runner, on which were carefully positioned three bottles of aftershave, a manicure set, a hair brush and comb, and a tin of pomade, something I hadn't seen for years.

The dresser had four drawers, the top one of which contained underwear. The next drawer down was full of neatly folded and matched socks. The bottom two drawers were empty.

Instinctively I pulled out the first of the empty drawers and discovered taped to its back a small, flat key, which seemed familiar. I pulled the key away from the drawer and slipped it in my pocket.

I looked under the bed, but found nothing there except more fluff. I stood up and stared round the room, looking for potential hiding places, but there were none. Finished in the bedroom I headed for the sitting room. It looked even less promising than the bedroom. As far as I could see, there were no potential hiding places.

I walked over to the cocktail cabinet. It contained glasses and half a dozen bottles of spirit, of which only the Royal Dragon vodka had been opened. It was half empty.

I turned my attention to the bookcase. I took each book out in turn and flicked through to see if it had been hollowed out to hide something.

I was not sure what I was looking for, but it didn't matter much because the books were just that; books. I sighed in frustration. There was nothing in the sitting room that would provide a hint as to why the dead Russian might have killed himself.

There were no clues in the kitchen either. I searched through all the cupboards, but all I found was an assortment of tins, packets, pots and pans. In the bread bin I found half a sliced loaf and in the waste bin there was nothing more interesting than an empty baked bean tin and some dirty paper towels.

Timmy re-appeared just as I finished searching the kitchen. 'The clean-up unit is on its way,' he said.

'OK. There's nothing more we can do here. Let's get back to town and leave the experts to sort out this mess.'

'Some of our colleagues will be arriving shortly,' I told the grey-haired security guard once he had let us through the glass door and we were standing in the lobby. 'They will be taking Major Carsons to a different location in London and will be using the back entrance.'

'The rain has stopped. Will the Major be coming down for a walk before he leaves?' The guard asked as he entered our time of departure in the register.

'No,' I replied. 'He's not feeling his best at the moment.'

'That's a shame. I would have liked to say goodbye to him. He's a real gentleman.'

'I'll pass that on to him,' I said. 'It will please him.'

'Thank you, sir. Have a good day.'

It was on the drive back to London that I remembered why the key I found in Urinoff's bedroom looked familiar. It was identical to one I had at home. It was the key to my rarely used briefcase, which was currently stashed away in a cupboard.

The Russian had been carrying a similar briefcase when he travelled to London, but I didn't find it when I searched his suite. So, where was it?

Chapter 7

The Golden Dragon restaurant was in the heart of London's Chinatown. It was not as plush as some of the more up-market restaurants in neighbouring Gerrard Street, but the Dragon's less pretentious decor and relaxed style suited me. It also had great food. It was my favourite eatery and I was a frequent visitor.

'Mister Statton, what a pleasure to see you again,' said the restaurant's owner, Jian Ming, as Colleen and I walked through the door into the reception area. 'And you have brought such a pretty lady with you to grace my restaurant.'

Jian Ming bowed politely at my companion, who beamed in pleasure. 'I have your usual table waiting for you, Mister Statton,' he led us the length of the dining area and showed us to a table tucked away in the back corner.

We sat down and a waitress appeared with menus and handed them to us. 'Would you like to order drinks?' She asked.

'Wine?' I asked Colleen.

'Red please,' she replied.

'We'll have a bottle of South African Shiraz,' I told the waitress.

'Very good, sir,' she said and disappeared.

Colleen flicked through the extensive menu and then closed it. 'I like it all. I'll let you order for both of us,' she said with a smile. Jian Ming was right; my companion was very pretty.

'OK. How about starting with crispy duck and pancakes, followed by mixed hors d'oeuvres, and for the main meal kung-po king prawns and special chow mien?'

'That sounds wonderful.'

The waitress came back with our bottle of Shiraz and I had to go through the ritual of tasting the wine to ensure it wasn't corked. It was fine, so I indicated she should pour two glasses.

'Are you ready to order your meal, sir?'

'Yes,' I replied and gave her our order. I waited until she had left us and was out of earshot. 'I tried to contact your boss at home today,' I said, 'but he didn't answer his telephone.'

'He's out of circulation,' Colleen replied and then lowered her voice to add: 'It's his wedding anniversary tomorrow and he's taken his wife to Paris for the weekend.'

'Did he give you a contact telephone number?'

She didn't reply at first.

'It's standard procedure,' I pointed out.

She looked slightly uncomfortable. 'Well, yes, he did leave me the telephone number for his hotel, but said I was to give it to nobody else and that I should only ring him in an emergency. Is it an emergency?'

I thought about that for a moment. My abortive call to the D-G was to report Alexei Urinoff's death, but was there anything Disraeli-Astor could do over the weekend? The answer was no. Urinoff was dead and he would be just as dead on Monday.

'No, it's not an emergency. It can wait. What's the boss's timetable like on Monday?'

'He has a full day. Back to back meetings from nine o'clock until five.'

'Can you squeeze me in before nine, or after five?'

She gave me her best harassed personal assistant frown. 'It depends on how long you need with him. Is it important?'

'I think the boss will consider it very important, and as for how long we need, the meeting will only last as long as he wants it to last.'

Colleen picked up her wine and held it towards me. I touched it with my own glass. 'Cheers!' I said.

'Cheers!' She responded and then sipped her wine thoughtfully. 'Well, the D-G's last meeting is with the Security Minister, Douglas Campbell,' she said eventually. 'Then he has a dinner engagement in the City of London at seven-thirty and he won't be going home first. I suppose I could fit you in at about five thirty. But he must change into his dinner suit, and then get to the Guildhall, so your meeting can't take any longer than half an hour.'

'That should be ample time,' I assured her.

'In that case I'll book you in,' she said.

'Why is the boss meeting Campbell?' I asked.

'I'm not sure. The minister asked for a meeting, but he didn't say why. If the D-G wants you to know, then I'm sure he'll tell you.'

The waitress appeared carrying a plate of shredded crispy duck, a bamboo container of pancakes, a bowl of hoisin sauce and a plate of sliced cucumber and spring onions. She set the dishes on the table-top and took the lid off the bamboo container. 'Enjoy,' she said with a bow.

'How can she do that?' Colleen asked, after the waitress had left.

'Do what?'

'Carry so much with one pair of hands without dropping anything?'

'Practice,' I said. 'A bit like my job.'

I offered Colleen the bamboo container and she took a pancake and put it on her plate. Quickly she spread hoisin sauce across the pancake, laid spring onions and cucumber on it, added crispy duck and expertly rolled it into a tube. She was tucking into her starter even before I had lifted my own pancake out of the container.

I smiled to myself as I loaded up my pancake. It was good to have a female dinner guest with a healthy appetite who ate with gusto and no airs and graces. My mind went back to the first time I had taken Freddie for a meal in South Africa. We ate in a small restaurant in Fishoek and she had been a hearty eater. But now she was gone and suddenly I realised how much I missed a woman's company in my life.

A couple came into the restaurant and were shown to a table. The woman was shorter than the man, but not by much. She had long blonde hair, a shapely figure and an attractive face with high cheek bones that hinted at a Scandinavian heritage.

The man was dark and handsome in a way that melts the heart of a certain type of woman. He wore his stylish clothes with an effortless panache that only continental men seem able to achieve. He moved with a feline grace and his mannerisms were almost feminine. I guessed he was gay, which made them an odd couple.

'She's beautiful,' Colleen said between mouthfuls. She had seen the couple come in too.

'So is he,' I said.

'I see what you mean. He's certainly not my type. I prefer my men to be men,' she said, before finishing off her pancake roll. She sipped her wine appreciatively and then helped herself to some more duck. When her second pancake was prepared she placed it in the centre of her plate and looked up at me.

'The thing you wanted to speak to the D-G about, does it have anything to do with our guest in the safe-house?' She asked in a whisper.

'You know about him?'

'Of course, I know everything that goes on in the department.'

'Does the boss tell you everything?'

'When he remembers,' she said. 'However, I always know what's going on anyway, because I read everything that ends up in his in-tray.'

She said nothing more for a while, instead she concentrated all her attention on her second crispy duck pancake. When she had finished, she looked up at me. 'You didn't answer my question.'

'That's because I try to avoid talking business when I'm having dinner with a pretty lady.'

'Thanks, but I know your game. You're using flattery to avoid answering me.'

'I was diplomatically telling you to drop the subject,' I said quietly. 'One can't be too careful.'

She bristled. 'I'm cleared up to top secret level.'

'I wasn't thinking of you, Colleen. One of the first lessons taught to field agents is never discuss sensitive business in public.'

She looked around the restaurant. 'Nobody is taking any interest in us,' she insisted.

'Another lesson is to always remember that walls have ears.'

'Can we talk about it later then?' She asked. 'When we're alone?'

'Pass the hoisin sauce,' I said, ignoring her question.

'Was everything satisfactory, Mister Statton?' Jian Ming asked as I settled the bill.

'It was up to your restaurant's usual excellent standard, Mister Ming.'

'And were you happy, pretty lady?' He asked Colleen.

'Yes. The food was fantastic,' she said. 'And the service was exemplary. It was a special evening. Thank you, Mister Ming.'

Jian Ming beamed. He loved being praised, particularly by a woman. He opened the door and bowed as Colleen made her way outside.

'Thank you for taking me there, David,' she said as we headed up Macclesfield Street towards Shaftsbury Avenue, in which the Palace Theatre was located. 'That's one of the best Chinese meals I've ever eaten.'

'I'm pleased you enjoyed it.'

'And what a lovely man,' she added.

'Thank you. I don't often get compliments like that.'

She punched me lightly on the arm. 'Idiot! I was talking about Mister Ming,' she said sternly. She softened her words by briefly resting her head on my shoulder, then we walked arm in arm the rest of the way to the theatre. It felt good.

It was during the intermission that I noticed the man and woman from the Golden Dragon, or rather it was Colleen who saw them first.

We were standing in the dress circle bar during the intermission, when she nudged me. 'Over by the door,' she whispered. 'It looks as if we weren't alone in deciding to have a Chinese before coming to the show,' she said.

The man was standing with his back against the wall looking towards the bar counter where people were queuing four deep to get drinks. He held a glass in his hand but he wasn't drinking from it.

A large mirror filled the wall behind the bar counter and when I looked in that direction I could see the reflection of the faces of the people who were waiting to be served. They didn't look happy.

I could clearly see also the man by the door. He looked unhappy too. I don't know why. At least he had a drink.

The woman stood at the man's side and sipped occasionally from a wine glass. She had her back turned slightly away from her companion and was staring in the opposite direction. She looked bored.

I studied them carefully, but discreetly. Judging from their body language, I concluded that although they were together, they were not a couple. I was even more convinced that if the pair were in a relationship, it was of a purely platonic nature.

I could see that Colleen was staring at the woman with a thoughtful look on her face. 'What is it?' I whispered?

She shook her head. 'It's nothing,' she said. 'It's just that she reminds me of a girl I once knew.'

After the show finished we left the theatre and headed for the car-park that was located near the Golden Dragon.

'Now we're on our own, will you tell me what you want to see the D-G about on Monday?' Colleen asked as we strolled arm in arm up Shaftesbury Avenue.

'Well done,' I said.

'What for?'

'You managed to keep your curiosity in check for well over three hours.'

'Pig!' she said, pulling her arm away from me long enough to punch me playfully again.

'That's twice you've thumped me tonight,' I scolded her.

'Well you really are a tease,' she said, grabbing hold of my arm again.

'Who's teasing?'

'You are. Why else would you not tell me?'

'Perhaps it's because we're still surrounded by walls.' I pointed at the shop we were passing.

'That's daft and you know it. How could anybody hear us from inside an empty shop?'

'How do you know it's empty?'

'Because it's Saturday night and Arthur Beale closes at seven o'clock, which is why the windows are in darkness and all the lights are off. Look, you might as well tell me, because I will find out anyway on Monday.'

She was right of course and I was about to admit as much when I heard behind us two pairs of footsteps, one lighter than the other.

We were now passing a health food shop and I pulled Colleen into its darkened doorway.

'What the hell?' she gasped but I cut off the rest of her protest by hugging her tightly. I pulled her face towards me, leaned down and kissed her on the lips, but not so passionately that I could not keep track of the footsteps as they grew closer.

Whoever was following us paused briefly when they reached the doorway in which we stood. I could imagine two pairs of eyes glancing at us to see what we were doing. Then the footsteps resumed their progress.

I waited for a few seconds, savouring the last of our kiss, then I pulled away and stepped out of the doorway in time to see two people turn the corner into Macclesfield Street. Before they disappeared, I recognised them as the couple who had been in the Chinese restaurant and the theatre.

'That was nice,' Colleen said. 'Unexpected, but nice.'

'Did you see them?' I asked as we turned into Macclesfield Street. I pointed at the couple who had almost reached the other end of the road.

'Yes,' she replied. 'They were the couple we saw earlier. They're probably in the same car-park as us. Isn't that a coincidence?'

'Maybe,' I answered cautiously, 'and maybe not.'

'Are you always so paranoid?'

'Yes. Paranoia comes with my job. It's what keeps me alive.'

When we reached the underground car-park there was no sign of the couple and mine was the only car to be seen.

'Is it the Russian you want to talk to the D-G about?' Colleen asked as I opened her door for her.

'You're persistent, I give that to you.'

'Persistence, comes with my job,' she said with a light laugh. 'So, answer my question.'

'OK. The answer is yes. I want to talk to the boss about Urinoff.'

'What about him? Has he revealed something important during his stay in Windsor?' She might be super professional but she was still a woman and it was obvious she was determined to wheedle more information out of me.

'He's no longer in Windsor,' I said.

She looked at me sharply. 'Not in the safe-house?'

I shook my head.

'Where is he?' She asked.

'Right now, he's probably on a slab in a mortuary waiting to be cut open by a pathologist.' I drove up the ramp and out into the street.

'He's dead?' She sounded shocked.

'Very.'

'What happened?'

I told her how I had found Urinoff hanging from a rope.

'He committed suicide?'

'I won't know that until I receive the autopsy report.'

'You must contact the D-G and tell him,' she said.

'If you recall, that's exactly what I wanted to do.'

'That's different. I didn't know what had happened then. You must ring him as soon as you get home. I'll give you his number.'

'Think it through, Colleen. I won't get home until gone midnight, which will be after one o'clock in Paris. Do you really think the boss will welcome a call from me at that time of the morning? Anyway, what can he do about the situation? The D-G might be powerful, but he's not Jesus Christ. He can't bring Urinoff back to life.'

'I suppose that's true,' she conceded. 'I could fit in an early morning meeting for you on Monday,' she said.

'I thought the boss was tied up all day.'

'He is, but I'm sure he will want to see you early. I can juggle his diary. Can you make 8.30 am?'

'Yes, but I'm not sure you will get the boss in that early.'

'Don't worry,' she said. 'He'll be there.'

I saw the steely look in Colleen's eyes and believed her.

It was almost midnight by the time we reached Bayswater. The traffic was still heavy and there was a queue of cars behind me when I stopped at a red traffic light on the corner of the road in which Colleen lived.

When the lights turned green I pulled into Pembridge Street. The road was lined with parked cars on both sides, but I managed to find a space almost outside Colleen's apartment. As I signalled to pull into the space, a car drove up behind me. I was blinded momentarily as its headlights were reflected in my interior mirror.

I silently cursed the driver, but had no time to remonstrate with him because he accelerated to overtake me. I glanced across as the car sped past me. It was a BMW, with alloy wheels and go faster stripes. I could see nothing of the driver. There was a woman in the passenger seat, but I couldn't see her face because it was obscured by her hair.

'What an idiot,' I said as I manoeuvred quickly into the parking space.

'Probably one of our local boy racers,' Colleen said. 'Too many of the youngsters round here have more money than sense.'

I stared up the road where the BMW's tail lights were just disappearing into the night and wondered whether Colleen was right. I had my doubts.

'I would invite you in for a coffee,' she said, 'but I have to be up early in the morning.'

'It's not a problem,' I assured her. 'It's been a long day.'

'Perhaps next time,' she said.

'Will there be a next time?' I asked.

'I hope so.'

'What are you doing next Saturday evening?'

'I'm not sure,' she said. 'I'll check my diary and let you know on Monday. What do you have in mind?'

'Do you like jazz?'

'Yes.'

'That's what I have in mind. Dinner and then an evening of jazz. I know just the place.'

'Sounds good.' She leant over and kissed me on the cheek. 'Thanks for a nice evening.' With that she opened the passenger door and was gone.

When I arrived at my apartment I poured myself a large whisky and sat in front of the log effect electric fire I inherited from the previous tenants. I thought about the evening's events. I couldn't rid myself of the nagging suspicion that the gay man and his lady friend were following me.

I told myself I was being paranoid and there was a perfectly logical explanation for the couple being in the same place as Colleen and me on three separate occasions in one evening.

But coincidence or not, there was one simple fact that even my logic could not dispute: If I could see the man in the dress circle bar mirror, then he could just as easily have been using the mirror to watch me.

And there was something else weighing on my mind. The passenger in the BMW, which sped past me in Pembridge Street, had long blonde hair, just like the woman in the Chinese restaurant. That seemed to me one coincidence too many.

Chapter 8

Disraeli-Astor didn't even give me a chance to sit down. 'You should have contacted me about the Russian,' he said as I walked into his office.

'His name was General Urinoff,' I pointed out as I took a seat opposite him.

He frowned. 'Don't change the subject,' he said crossly.

I resisted the temptation to point out that Urinoff and his nationality were the same subject, instead I said: 'I take it that Colleen has already passed on my news to you.'

'Yes, she rang yesterday to ask me to come in early this morning.' This time he glared at me angrily. 'My PA appears to be the only person in this department who keeps me fully informed of developments.'

'That's because your PA is the only person in this department who had your weekend contact telephone number,' I countered. 'As it happens, I did ring you at home, but there was no answer. Sadly, I seem to have misplaced my crystal ball, so I had no idea you had decided to whisk your wife off to Paris.'

'It was my wedding anniversary,' he said sharply. 'Although I'm not sure it's any of your damn business.'

'Sorry, governor,' I said tugging an imaginary forelock. 'You're the Director-General, so you can do what you like. You're certainly not answerable to common oiks like me.'

He stared at me and I could see he was trying to contain his anger. 'Don't come over all working-class with me, Statton,' he said when he was calmer, 'because being a down-trodden martyr doesn't suit you.'

'Look, I don't mind not knowing what you're up to at the weekend, but I do object to receiving a bollocking for not contacting you, when I have no idea where you are.'

'OK, I'm sorry,' he apologised. 'Perhaps I should have told you where I was going.'

'Well, that's something on which we can agree.'

There was a knock at the door and Colleen appeared balancing a coffee tray on top of a pile of opened mail. She put the tray on a side table and the mail in Disraeli-Astor's already full in-tray. Neither of us spoke until she had disappeared again.

'I'm sinking in bloody paperwork,' he complained, picking up everything from his in-tray with both hands and waving it in the air. 'This pile of rubbish is my correspondence for last Friday and today.'

'That pile of rubbish includes my leave application.'

'Correspondence. Memos. Briefing notes. Leave forms. Whatever it is, it's still bloody paperwork!' He glared at me as if I was solely responsible for his workload.

He returned the papers to his in-tray and flicked through them with a disgusted look on his face. He stopped when he noticed a document near the bottom of the pile. It was marked **Secret**. He tossed it across the desk to me.

'You'd better have this,' he said. 'I think you'll find it is the transcript of the Thursday debrief session with the Russian. I'll trawl through the rest of the bumph to see if there is anything else I can offload on to you.'

'Thanks,' I said. 'I can't wait.'

'Now, getting back to the conversation we were having. I understand from Colleen that she offered to give you the telephone number for my hotel, but you refused to take it. Why was that?' Disraeli-Astor asked as he poured cream into his coffee.

'Because she only offered it to me late on Saturday evening. I took the view there was nothing you could do from Paris that would improve the situation and any decision about our next move could wait until this morning.'

'That makes sense,' he admitted and then took a sip of his coffee. 'In fact, I suppose I should thank you,' he went on. 'If you had phoned me I would have felt obliged to return to London and my wife would not have been a happy bunny.'

He lapsed into silence as he contemplated what might have happened if he had upset his spouse. He looked miserable at the prospect. This seemed to confirm the rumours about who wore the trousers in the Disraeli-Astor household.

'This really is excellent coffee.' I changed the subject.

This cheered him up as I knew it would. 'I'm pleased you like it,' he said. 'I get it from a little place in the village.' He sniffed his coffee as if to remind himself how good it was. 'So how did the

Russian chappie die?' He asked.

'We found him hanging from the leg of a four-poster bed.'

'I beg your pardon? Hanging from a what?'

I quickly explained the circumstances of the Russian's death and how Timmy and I found him.

'Are you saying he topped himself by jumping out of the window with a rope around his neck?'

'That's what it looks like.'

He must have recognised something in my voice. 'You don't sound convinced,' he said.

'I have no reason to believe anything other than that Alexei Urinoff killed himself,' I said cautiously. 'However, I have asked for an autopsy to be carried out just in case.'

'In case of what? Is there something else?'

'It could be nothing,' I said. 'But when Urinoff left East Germany he was carrying a holdall and a briefcase. I found the holdall in his bedroom at the safe-house, but there was no sign of the briefcase.'

'Perhaps he got rid of it,' Disraeli-Astor said.

'How? Flush it down the toilet?'

'Don't be sarcastic. He could have thrown it in a dustbin.'

'Difficult, because the dustbins at the safe-house are kept in a secure area to which Urinoff didn't have access.' Now it was my turn to lapse into silence.

'He could have thrown the briefcase over the perimeter fence,' he suggested.

'That's possible,' I conceded. 'However, why would he do that?'

He didn't respond.

'And if he did get rid of his briefcase,' I went on. 'Why did he keep this?' I took from my pocket the key I found in the safe-house. I laid it in on his desk in front of him. 'I found it taped to the back of a drawer in the dressing table in his bedroom.'

'Is that the key to his briefcase?'

'That's what I think.'

'Perhaps a previous occupant of the room hid the key.'

'You haven't had many dealings with the safe-house have you, boss?'

He shook his head. 'No, why?'

'Because, every time a guest of the department leaves the house, a clean-up squad moves in and gives their room the once over.'

'Perhaps the squad missed it.'

'Trust me, our clean-up squads do not miss that sort of thing.'

Disraeli-Astor stared at the key while he finished drinking his coffee.

'It's a shame about the Russian,' he said eventually. 'I rather hoped a chat with him might reveal more about what Sir Reggie and his pals are planning.'

'Well he's beyond little chats now,' I replied. 'Unless you know a decent psychic medium.'

'Does that mean we're back to square one?'

'Not necessarily. I have opened another line of enquiry.'

He raised an enquiring eyebrow. 'Am I allowed to know what this line of enquiry is?'

'Do you really want to know?'

'Well as Director-General I think I should be told what is going on, don't you?'

'That's not always been the case. There were things your predecessor preferred not to be told about.'

'Well I'm not Sir Bertie, so tell me.'

'If you insist.'

'I insist.'

'Very well. I arranged for somebody to break into Sir Reginald Wren's home over the weekend.'

He didn't look happy. 'Why did you do that?'

'Because I want to know what he keeps in his safe.'

'His safe?'

'Yes, it's where wealthy people keep their valuables.'

'I know what a safe is, but what do you expect to find in his?'

'If I knew that, there would be no need to break into it.'

'I suppose not. But …'

'Look,' I interrupted him. 'In addition to valuables, a safe is where some people hide away all their nasty little secrets.'

'But was burglary really necessary?'

'Do you want to find out what Wren is up to or not?'

He ignored my question. 'Who did you use for the job?' He asked.

'Manny Silver. Do you know him?'

He shook his head. 'Is he any good?'

'He's the best safe cracker in London,' I told him. 'Discreet, thorough and very tidy.'

'Tidy?'

'Yes, Wren will never know that his house has been burgled, his safe opened and its contents photographed.'

'So, what did your chap find?' He asked, making a point of reminding me Manny Silver was my contact. He had learned already the art of being a civil servant. He was starting to cover his backside in case anything went wrong.

'I don't know, I haven't seen him yet.'

'Well keep me fully briefed. I cannot emphasise enough how important this is, Statton. I have a meeting with the PM on Wednesday and she has demanded an update on the South African situation.'

'You will know as soon as I do,' I promised.

'How much did this Silver character cost?'

'A grand.'

'A thousand pounds?' He sounded shocked.

'Yeah. The best men don't come cheap.'

'Can he be trusted?'

'Yes. We're paying top dollar for Manny's loyalty.'

'I wish we *were* paying him in dollars,' Disraeli-Astor said as he poured himself another cup of coffee and passed the pot to me. 'At the current exchange rate, it would save us four hundred pounds.'

When I tipped the pot up, I found there was barely half a cup left. I enjoyed it anyway.

'I understand you informed my PA about the Russian's death on Saturday night at a social function.' He made it sound as if I had taken Colleen to a grand ball.

'We went for a Chinese meal and then took in a show.'

'Hmmm. Well, I am not sure I approve of you fraternising with the office staff.'

'I don't recall there being anything in my employment contract preventing me fraternising with whomsoever I choose,' I said, knowing full well my boss would have forgotten that I had no employment contract. 'I'm not sure what I do outside work is any of your damn business.'

He sniffed audibly. 'Where I come from, fraternisation with the staff was frowned on.'

'Look, boss, don't come over all upper-class twit with me,

because it doesn't suit you.'

'Touché,' he said with a good-humoured smile, accepting my dig without taking umbrage.

It just goes to show that breeding and a public-school education does help people handle difficult social situations, conflict and adversity with an equanimity that is sometimes beyond us working-class peasants.

It was just after nine thirty when I arrived in the Section Two office. Poppy was already sitting behind her desk tapping away at her word processor. She didn't acknowledge my presence.

'Morning Poppy,' I said. 'Are Timmy and Melissa not in yet?'

She glanced over at their empty desks. 'Doesn't look like it.'

'Any chance of a coffee?' I asked.

She looked at me and I saw her mascara had run and there were black marks under her tearful eyes.

'What's wrong?' I asked gently.

'Roger is a bastard,' she declared bitterly.

'Last week he was the best thing since sliced bread.'

'His dick will be sliced if he comes near me again.'

'Ouch!' I said. 'What's he done now?'

'We were supposed to be going away for the weekend, but he called me on Friday and said that he couldn't make it. He said his mother was ill and he had to visit her in Doncaster Infirmary.'

'I didn't know he came from Yorkshire.'

'He doesn't, but his mother moved up north when she split up from Roger's dad.'

'Visiting his sick mother in hospital seems a reasonable enough reason to break a date.'

'I would agree, if it had been the truth.'

'And it wasn't?'

'No,' she said as tears began to trickle down her cheeks, spreading mascara even further across her face.

'What happened?'

'I went to Camden Market on Saturday with one of my girlfriends and when we were passing that fancy restaurant on the corner by the main entrance I looked through the window and saw Roger sitting at a table with a woman, the bastard.' This all came out in a rush.

'I assume the woman wasn't his mother?'

'No, it was his wife.'

'How do you know?'

'Because I confronted them.'

'Why am I not surprised?'

'Because you know what a hardnosed bitch I can be at times.'

'What did you do?' Despite my instinctive inclination to remain detached from Poppy's problems, I couldn't resist the temptation to find out more about her confrontation with Roger.

'It was messy,' she said and smiled for the first time.

'Did you throw a drink over him?'

She shook her head. 'No, his spaghetti bolognaise.'

'What, just like that?'

'No. When I went into the restaurant I walked up to his table and asked him who his floozy was.'

'His floozy? I bet that went down well. What did he say?'

'Nothing, he just looked at me with his mouth open like a trout. That's when I realised that the rotter looks like a fish.'

'And?'

'The woman asked me who I was calling a floozy.'

'And you said?'

'If the cap fits, darling.'

'And what was her reaction to that?'

'Well, she didn't look best pleased. She went red in the face and said Roger was her husband.'

'I see.'

'Exactly. That's when I picked up his bowl of spag-bog and tipped it over his head.'

'Did that make you feel better?'

She shook her head and looked miserable. 'Not at all,' she said with a catch in her voice. 'Roger really is a bastard, but I still love him.'

That's when she lost me. I have never been able to understand female logic. I made a strategic exit and headed for my office.

'Do you really want a coffee?' Poppy called after me.

I wasn't sure I did, because nothing that she could produce out of a jar came close to the coffee Colleen made in Disraeli-Astor's office. However, I had asked her for one, so I felt duty bound to have one. 'Of course,' I answered from the doorway to my office.

'Give me five,' she said and then added. 'Oh, by the way there are a couple of telex messages on the machine for you.'

'Thanks. Any chance you could bring them to my office for me?' I shouted, making sure I was sitting behind my desk before she could respond, which she did anyway.

'But you're already on your feet.'

'No I'm not,' I shouted back.

I heard her stomp across to the telex machine, there was the sound of paper tearing and then more footsteps as she headed for my office. She slapped two telexes on my desk without a word and then disappeared back to the outer office. I could probably say goodbye to a cup of coffee, but that wasn't a prospect that disappointed me overly.

I picked up the first telex, which was from Manny Silver. It read simply: "Exercise completed successfully. No problems. Package awaiting collection. Come today. Oyster."

The second telex was longer and was from the government's duty pathologist. It set out in graphic detail the result of the autopsy on Urinoff, including the condition of all the dead man's organs.

When I finished wading through all the scientific technical information, I reached the important conclusions, which immediately blew away a creeping drowsiness that had made my eyes begin to flutter.

"There was evidence of a high level of ricin in the casualty's body." The autopsy report read. "Along with the absence of blood swellings on the neck in the vicinity of the noose, it suggests that the casualty died from poisoning before strangulation."

I read the conclusions again.

My deputy poked his head round the edge of my door. 'Morning, sir.'

'Just the person,' I replied. 'Come in.'

Timmy sat down self-consciously in the chair in front of my desk. He looked like a naughty schoolboy who has been summoned to the head master's office for a dressing down. I passed the pathologist's telex to him.

'Skip the first page,' I told him. 'Just concentrate on the conclusions.'

'What is ricin?' He asked when he had finished reading.

'It's a poison that is produced naturally in the seeds of the plant Ricinus communis, otherwise known as a castor oil plant.'

'Is it rare?'

'Not really,' I said. 'They grow in lots of gardens in England.'

'So, it's readily available.'

'Yes, but ricin is not the poison of choice in the UK. Although it's used a lot by the KGB.'

'Blimey!' Timmy said as he studied the autopsy report. 'Urinoff was a KGB general. Perhaps he killed himself with poison,' he suggested.

'Is that what you think?' I asked.

'It's possible, sir.'

'Is it? So, exactly how did he manage to jump out of that window after he had killed himself by swallowing ricin?'

Timmy thought about that. 'It's possible that his death from poison was not instantaneous,' he said. 'Perhaps he managed to climb out of the window before he died.'

'Ricin doesn't act immediately, so that certainly would be a possible theory, except for two things.'

He looked at me expectantly. I detected a look of hero worship in his eyes and I felt slightly uncomfortable.

'One,' I said gruffly. 'Why would Urinoff take poison if he planned to hang himself?'

Timmy didn't answer, but his face flushed red.

'And two. The pathologist makes clear in his report that Urinoff died from poison not strangulation.' I pointed to the sentence in the report.

Timmy's blush deepened. 'I didn't notice that bit, sir,' he said apologetically and stared at the telex. 'What *does* it mean?' He asked.

'It means, Timothy, that our Russian friend was murdered.'

'Murdered?' He repeated and looked at me in confusion. 'But by whom? He was in a safe-house.'

'Exactly. So, think about it. Who over the weekend had access to Urinoff except for us?'

He looked at me blankly and shook his head. 'Nobody had access to the safe-house except us. I know that, because I noticed on the security entry register that we were the only visitors.'

'Yes, we were the only visitors. What does that tell you?'

He looked at me and I could see I had lost him.

'Let me give you a clue. You mentioned it yourself. The security entrance register.'

Again, he looked at me blankly. Then I saw a gleam of understanding in his eyes. 'It was a security guard!'

'There is no other logical explanation,' I told him.

'Blimey!' He exclaimed again.

'I can think of stronger words to use.'

'But which guard was it?'

'Well the autopsy fixed the time of death at about 7 am, which would fit in with him not finishing his breakfast.'

'You think his egg was poisoned?'

'Unlikely, it was probably added to his orange juice. I think that sometime during the night, while Urinoff was sleeping, the guard let himself into his kitchen and doctored his drink.'

'I saw a guard arriving when I went back to the car to collect the tape recorder. Was he relieving the guy who was on the night-shift?'

'Yeah.'

'Did he have a pirate beard?'

'You saw him?'

'Yes. I noticed him as I came from the car to the safe-house.'

'Did you get a look at his face?'

'No, he had his head down against the rain. All I could see was his beard and his long hair. Is that our man?'

'It looks like it.'

'So, what are we going to do?'

'We find out who he is. Get onto admin and find out which security company has the contract for the safe-house.'

'It's Ace Security,' he replied immediately. 'They're based in Slough.'

I stared at him. I was amazed. 'How do you know that?'

'Their company name was painted on the side of the van that was parked at the safe-house when we arrived.'

'What about being based in Slough?'

'Their telephone number starts with 01753, which is the area code for Slough.'

'How do you know that's their phone number?'

'Because it was on the side of the van too.'

'And how do you know the code was for Slough?'

'I just remember things like that.'

'But surely the Slough number would cover the surrounding area, including Windsor,' I pointed out.

'Yeah, but Windsor is probably too small a town to support a security company that's large enough to win a government contract.'

I could not fault his logic. Perhaps I had misjudged him. 'Can you remember all of the telephone number?' I asked.

'Yes,' he said and told me what it was.

I was impressed. 'Well done, Timmy. Sometimes you astound me.'

'Thank you, sir,' he said with another blush, this time of pleasure. 'But it's nothing really. It's just a knack I have,' he added modestly.

'Well, knack or not, it gives us something to work on. I want you to contact Ace Security and make an appointment to see the managing director. The night-shift guard was from Northern Ireland, I want you to go down to Slough and find out everything you can about him.'

'Will do, sir,' he said, heading for the door.

'And, Timmy,' I said, calling him back. 'This business takes top priority, so I want you to go see them straight away.'

He looked crestfallen. 'That might be difficult, sir,' he said.

'Why?'

'I'm having trouble with my car and it's in the garage being fixed. Shall I catch a train?'

'No, take a government pool car.'

'The garage will want some form of authorisation before they release one,' Timmy pointed out.

I sighed. He was right. I scribbled a message on a sheet of department notepaper, signed it and handed the note to him.

'Thanks,' he said with a grin. 'I'm on my way,' he added and shot out of my office before I could change my mind.

I picked up the phone and rang Colleen Masters.

'Is that five-thirty slot with the boss still open?' I asked when she answered the phone.

'You've already seen him once today.'

'Am I being rationed?'

'The D-G is very busy. His time is precious.'

'Who says I want to see him?'

'You old smoothie. If it's me you want to see, you only have to ask.'

'As it happens, I just want some more of that posh Blue Mountain

94

coffee that the D-G gets from his village shop.'

'You really are a pig,' she said.

'Oink-oink.'

She giggled.

'Seriously, Colleen, I need to see the boss again. It's urgent.'

'Is it about the Russian?'

'Yeah,' I said

'In that case you can have the five-thirty slot. I take it you have an update on his suicide?'

'Murder,' I corrected her. 'I'll explain later, I have to dash.'

'Hang on! Before you go, David.'

'I'm still here,' I said.

'I checked and I'm free next Saturday if the invitation for dinner and jazz still stands.'

'It still stands,' I confirmed. 'I'll pick you up at seven.'

'Thanks. I'm looking forward to it.'

I returned the receiver to its cradle and smiled to myself. I could think of worse things to do on Saturday evening than spend it with Colleen Masters. Perhaps this time it would be longer than a few hours.

I picked the phone up again.

My next call was to the Blue Oyster to make sure that Manny Silver was still there. He was, so I told him I was on my way.

'I'm going out,' I said to Poppy as I left my office.

She was staring down at a celebrity magazine, but looked up at me when I spoke. She looked as if she had been crying again. She saw me look at the magazine.

'Don't worry. I've finished typing up your response to the paper from the Foreign Office setting out the economic implications to the West of the reunification of Germany.' She said. 'Gripping stuff. None of it made any sense to me.'

'Don't worry, you're not alone. The FO won't understand it either, but it will look good in their file. Put it on my desk with all the other rubbish and I will check it out for typos when I get back.'

'If its rubbish, why did you get me to type it up,' she sniffed loudly.

'Because it gave you something to do. Hopefully, it helped take your mind off Roger the Dodger.'

'My magazine does that perfectly well.'

'But the department doesn't pay you to sit at your desk reading magazines all day,' I pointed out.

'I've only been reading it for five minutes,' she said defensively. 'Anyway, I'm on my tea break.'

There was no sign of a tea mug on her desk.

'Well, if you want something to do when you've finished your tea-less break, you can type these messages onto official classified paper.' I laid the two telexes on her desk. 'In triplicate,' I added.

She looked at the slips of paper and nodded. 'Will you be back?' She asked, dabbing her nose delicately with a paper handkerchief.

'Yes, I'll only be an hour or so,' I replied. I leaned down and turned her magazine 180 degrees. 'And you might be able to read the words better if your mag was the right way up.'

'Thanks,' she said. 'You're such an understanding boss.' She tried a wan smile on me.

'Don't confuse being understanding with being gullible,' I replied.

'I meant it,' she insisted. 'You're the best boss I've ever had.'

'Poppy, as far as I remember you never had a job before you joined the department. I'm the only boss you've ever had.'

'That's true,' she said. Her smile widened into a grin.

Chapter 9

I noticed the man because he was peering into the display window of the pharmacist on Bridge Street. He wore a stylish sports jacket, Ralph Loren polo shirt, shiny black shoes, and grey slacks with a crease sharp enough to cut cheese.

I was not convinced by his expression of deep concentration as he studied the colourful sale poster in the window. He just didn't strike me as somebody who would be interested in a buy-one-get-one-free offer for packs of sanitary towels.

I made my way into Westminster Underground Station and joined a long queue at the ticket office. It took me ten minutes to buy my ticket to Piccadilly Circus and as I made my way through the ticket barrier there was no sign of the man in the sports jacket.

Perhaps I was wrong and the man was checking out the price of tampons for the blonde-haired woman who had accompanied him to see *Les Misérables* at the same time as Colleen and me.

When I arrived at the platform it was full of tourists who had already visited the Houses of Parliament and Westminster Abbey and were now heading in search of other attractions.

Eventually a District Line train came gliding into the station and its doors slid open to allow me to board. The carriage was already full to overflowing, but I managed to squeeze into a gap in the mass of people who were strap hanging.

Through the jungle of arms, I caught a glimpse of a face before it disappeared into the heaving press of humanity. It was the man from the pharmacy. This was beyond coincidence and I was convinced he was following me.

If Colleen had been with me, she probably would have taken this as more evidence of my paranoia, but as I told her, being paranoid kept me alive, not least because it made me ultra-cautious.

It took the train only a few minutes to reach Victoria, where I got off and headed for the Victoria Line north bound platform. I didn't have to look behind me to know the man was following me.

When the train arrived, there were plenty of empty seats, but I ignored them. Instead, I stood at the end of the carriage next to the door. I picked up a discarded Evening Standard from the floor and I flicked through it glancing at the headlines.

An earthquake measuring 5.1 on the Richter scale had hit Shropshire and was felt throughout much of England. The unexpected threat caused widespread anxiety. I knew the feeling.

My destination was Green Park, where I would change again for a Piccadilly Line train to Leicester Square, but the station came and went. I didn't make a move and stayed in my place until we reached Oxford Square, leaning against the side of the carriage pretending to read the newspaper.

The doors opened and a number of people got off, no doubt heading for the shops. I timed my manoeuvre to perfection. Just as the doors started to close again I straightened up and jumped onto the platform. Without stopping, I headed for the south bound platform.

Behind me I heard the train pick up speed. I glanced over my shoulder as it disappeared into the tunnel on its way to Warren Street. The man who was tailing me was still only halfway out of his seat.

Soho

The Blue Oyster Club was dark and silent and the air was heavy with the stink of smoke and stale beer. Somewhere in the distance a vacuum cleaner whined as it tried to suck up the cigarette butts and other litter left behind by the weekend's customers. Luckily for Manny, the cleaner could not suck up the takings generated by those same customers. His money was already deposited in the bank.

'So how did it go at the weekend, Manny?' I asked.

'Not bad, David,' he said as he lit another cigarette and started to fill the club with fresh smoke. 'I booked a fantastic trio and we pulled in more punters than Ronnie Scott's. I reckon we grossed over ten grand.'

'I bet you only declare half that amount to the taxman and you paid the band a tenth of the amount entered into your purchase ledger.' I knew Manny well.

He smiled at me. 'Well, the taxman has more than enough money and there were only three guys in the group.'

'I know how many players make up a trio, Manny,' I said. 'However, whilst I am always pleased to learn that business is good for you, I was actually asking about your photo session.'

He grinned. 'That went well too,' he said.

'In that case, where's the camera?' I asked.

Manny lifted the camera box from the floor and laid it on the table in front of him. He didn't offer to pass it to me. 'There is the little matter of the grand I was promised.'

'You know the rules, Manny. I check the photos and, if I'm happy with their quality, I hand over the money. The department doesn't pay for crap.'

'You supplied the equipment,' Manny said defensively. 'I aint never used a digital camera before. If the photos are crap, it's down to you.'

'Let's see them,' I said and held my hand out.

Reluctantly Manny slid the camera towards me, but I could see he was not happy. This worried me and I feared the digital photographs would be of no help to me.

'I did try to check them as I went,' he explained as he watched me take the camera from its box. 'But I aint sure I pressed the right button. All I got was a blank screen.'

This information did nothing for my confidence. I kept the envelope containing fifty used twenty-pound notes safely in my pocket. As it turned out I had nothing to fear. When I checked the digital images, I found they were as good as I could have hoped.

There were eight photos in all. They showed the contents of Wren's safe, including a couple of documents but, because of the size of the camera's screen, the text on the documents was too small for me to read.

I had been warned by my contact at the MOD that because of the low pixel resolution of the images the text would be fuzzy. However, he had assured me that once downloaded onto a computer the definition could be enhanced so it was legible. I hoped he was right.

'Good work, Manny.' I took the envelope from my pocket, slid it across the table to him and put the camera back into its box.

'It's always a pleasure doing business with you, David.'

'And you, Manny.' I stood up. 'By the way, who have you got playing next Saturday night?' I asked as I picked up the camera.

'Remember the quartet that was playing when you were here last Friday night?'

'They were good,' I said.

'Well they're doing another session on Saturday. Were you thinking of coming?'

'Yeah. I'm bringing a friend with me. Can you make sure we get a decent table?'

'Upstairs or downstairs?'

'Holding a conversation in the basement is impossible,' I said. 'Make it the ground floor. That way we'll be able to chat, but still be able to enjoy the music.'

'OK, upstairs it is. I'll ensure the best table is reserved for you. Is it a lady friend?'

'Yes.'

'In that case, I'll lay on a bottle of fizz for you. On the house.'

'Free champagne, Manny? That's not like you. Are you running a temperature?'

He waved the envelope at me. 'Don't worry, my friend. You pay for your drinks in other ways,' he said with a wink.

DFCO offices

When I arrived back in the office, Melissa was busily tapping away at her word processor. She looked up as I approached her and smiled. 'I've been doing some more research on our friend Sir Reginald Wren and I am just preparing a report for you,' she explained. 'He has some interesting business connections.'

'That doesn't surprise me,' I said. 'Rumour has it that Wren is a bit of a spiv. I look forward to seeing what you've discovered.' I put the camera box on her desk next to her keyboard.

She raised an eyebrow.

'It's a digital camera,' I explained. 'It belongs to the Ministry of Defence. They loaned it to us for a job. I'd like you to take it back to their computer department. Ask them to download the images from the disk onto a computer, increase the resolution and print them out on A4 photo paper.'

She took the camera from its box and studied it with interest. 'I've heard about digital cameras, but I've never seen one.' She stroked the camera tenderly. 'This is the future of photography,' she said with the brash certainty of youth. 'Within ten years most traditional cameras will have been replaced by these little beauties.'

I had my doubts. 'Digital cameras could be just another fad like Polaroid,' I said.

She shook her head. 'The digital revolution is well and truly underway and there is no stopping it.' She studied the camera

100

intently. 'I find new technology fascinating.'

'That's good. Since you love high tech stuff so much, you can hang around at the MOD to make sure the computer boffins download the photos straight away. If necessary, flutter your eyelashes at them. Whatever happens, don't leave the camera with them, or it will be bloody days before I get any pictures back.'

Melissa was already on her feet and was putting on her coat. She looked excited at the task I had set her. Some people are easily pleased.

'And Melissa,' I said as she went out the door. 'Make sure that once those MOD clowns have printed off the photos, they erase all the images from the camera. If possible, see if you can bring the disk back with you so that we can destroy it.'

'Sure thing, boss,' she assured me, then was gone.

Poppy had disappeared too. I could see her word processor was still switched on, so guessed she had probably popped to the toilet.

I made my way through to my office and picked up the transcript of Alexei Urinoff's debrief session that Disraeli-Astor had given me earlier. It was dated Thursday 29th March and would have been the last interview the interrogators had with the Russian. They were not at Kingsbury House on Friday 30th. I wasn't sure why. Perhaps it was a Home Office golf day.

Unlike the initial debrief interview, which was quite short, this one lasted six hours, with only a short break for lunch. The transcript ran for over fifty pages and was full of information about how the Politburo planned to cope with the fast changing collapse of the Soviet empire.

There were lots of facts and figures about the planned withdrawal by the USSR military from a number of Soviet bloc countries, including East Germany. Then there was an interesting section on the Soviet invasion of Afghanistan, with a detailed analysis of how their retreat from that country the previous year would speed up the break-up of the USSR.

There was a section also on Chechnya and lots of intelligence information about the build-up of rebel forces in that country. The Soviets were convinced there were plans afoot to declare independence. Urinoff gave some detailed information about what the Soviet military was doing to counter the Chechen threat. In his opinion the armed forces were over stretched and at breaking point. I marked this particular passage as one I should draw to the attention of Disraeli-Astor.

Finally, almost two hours after I started reading the document, I came to the first mention of South Africa. It was a very short section and it was noticeable that Urinoff's tone had changed. After almost six hours questioning he sounded fed up and irritable.

I read the transcript again:-

Interviewer 1: General Urinoff, I would now like to touch on the South African issue.

Interviewee: I'm tired. Can't it wait until tomorrow?

Interviewer 1: We will not be visiting you tomorrow. We have other departmental commitments to which we must attend.

Interviewee: Well that's not my fault. Why should I exhaust myself to suit your diary? I have given you a great deal of information today and I am tired and hungry.

Interviewer 2: Look, Alexei, we're all tired. I promise we won't keep you for much longer, but we just need to clear up a couple of things that you told us yesterday.

Interviewee: Very well. You have fifteen minutes.

Interviewer 2: Thank you. We appreciate your patience.

Interviewer 1: You claimed that Sir Reginald Wren was a member of this group that is plotting with the Broederbond and the PAC to take control of Africa...

Interviewee: It was not a claim; it was the truth.

Interviewer 2: We believe you General. However, you said there were many other businessmen involved. Can you provide us with more names?

Interviewee: Yes, but not today.

Interviewer 1: Why not?

Interviewee: Because I can't remember them right now, but I have a list and can let you have the names on Monday.

Interviewer 2: Monday will be fine, Alexei. Can you tell us anything else about this group of businessmen?

Interviewee: Yes. They call themselves the Phoenix Group.

Interviewer 2: The Phoenix Group?

Interviewee: Yes.

Interviewer 1: What proof do we have that the list is authentic?

Interviewee: One of the names on the list is that of an American businessman whose involvement in the group is currently under investigation by the CIA. That is something you can check for yourself. I am sure the British Intelligence Service will be able to obtain verification of what I say from the Yankees.

Interviewer 1: What is the man's name, General?

Interviewee: You will have to wait until Monday to find that out.

Interviewer 1: But we...

Interviewer 2: That's not a problem, Alexei. Now, about Sir Reginald. We have made enquiries and have been unable to find any evidence to show he is the type of person to become involved with this plot. He has a completely clean police record and an impeccable business record. Indeed, several very important people have vouched for his integrity.

Interviewee: There is a reason for that. There are people in your country's Establishment who share the objectives of the Phoenix Group, so have good reason to protect Wren.

Interviewer 1: That is a very serious allegation, General, do you have evidence to back up your claim?

Interviewee: Yes, I have documents that not only identifies those people, but the level of their support for the group.

Interviewer 2: Can we not see that evidence now, Alexei?

Interviewee: No, it's locked away in a briefcase in my bedroom. It will have to wait until after the weekend. Now sorry, gentlemen, but your fifteen minutes is up. Good afternoon.

Interviewee leaves the interview room at 18:06 hours.

I was just mulling over the significance of Urinoff's final comments when my phone rang.

'Timmy's on the phone for you,' Poppy said without preamble.

'OK, put him through,' I told her, but she had already gone and I heard several clicks on the line as she attempted to transfer my deputy's call. Poppy hadn't yet mastered the department's phone system and it was some time before I heard my deputy's voice.

'Are you there, Mister Statton?' He asked.

'Yes, Timmy, I'm here.'

'Sorry, I thought Poppy had lost you. She's not very good with the new phones.'

'Tell me about it,' I said. I sometimes wondered why we kept her on. 'How did you get on, Timmy?'

'I was right about the security company, they are based in Slough. I visited their office and spoke to the managing director who was very helpful. It seems the Irish guy at the safe-house was a last minute replacement for the regular guard who was taken ill.'

'Did you get his details?'

'Yes, his name is William Butler and he's supposed to live in a block of flats in Slough.'

'What do you mean "supposed"?'

'Well, when I checked out the address I was given for him, I found an old lady was living there. She had never heard of Butler.'

'Is the woman kosher?' I asked.

'She seems to be. She's lived at the address for over twenty years and her details check out with Slough Borough Council.'

'What else did the security company boss say about Butler?'

'It seems he was a temp supplied by an agency on Friday.'

'A temp as a security guard? What the hell is this country coming to?'

'The MD showed me all the paperwork from the temporary staff agency, including Butler's references and employment record. It all looked pukka.'

'The sick guard who Butler replaced. Did you get his name?'

'Yes, it was Malcolm Cole.'

'And his address?'

'He lives in Slough also, but I don't know much about him.'

'Well get round to his home as soon as possible,' I said. 'I want to know everything about him, including what was wrong with him on Friday. Find out where he banks and check out his account to see if there have been any unusual payments recently.'

'Will do.'

'And, Timmy, I want you to visit the temping agency and find out what they know about Butler, or whatever his name really is.'

'You don't think Butler is the guard's name?'

'No.'

'What makes you think that?'

'Intuition and something he told me when I spoke to him at the safe-house.'

'What did he tell you?'

'That he came from Derry. In addition, he was reading a Celtic Football Club programme.'

'Is that significant, sir?'

'Possibly. It just doesn't ring true. In Northern Ireland only a

Protestant would be named William.'

'So, he's a Protestant. What's wrong with that?'

'Nothing in itself. However, it's very unlikely that an Ulster Protestant would call his home town "Derry" and be a supporter of Celtic Football Club. He would call it "Londonderry" and support Glasgow Rangers. I'd lay odds our friend is a Catholic with an Irish first name, like Patrick or Dermot.'

'You're brilliant, sir!'

'We don't have time for the bleeding obvious, my boy. We need to act fast if we're to catch this character.'

'OK, I'll get straight onto it,' Timmy said and was gone.

I put the phone down and scratched my head. Events were moving fast, but I had no idea where they were heading, or what they meant. I walked through to the outer office. 'How are you feeling now, Poppy?'

She smiled brightly at me. 'Better than I was this morning. Roger just rang and wants to meet up to straighten things out.'

'Did you agree?'

'Of course.'

'But you said he was a rotten bastard.'

'He is, but I still want him.'

I could think of no response to this, so I gave up. 'Any chance of that cup of coffee you promised me this morning?'

'Didn't I get you one?'

'No.'

'Sorry, my mind was on other things. I'll make you one straight away.'

'Thanks,' I said as I headed back to my desk and started re-reading parts of the transcript. Ten minutes later I heard footsteps approaching my office and expected Poppy to appear with my coffee, but it was Melissa.

She was carrying a large handbag, from which poked a buff coloured envelope. She took out the envelope and offered it to me. 'The photos are inside,' she explained.

I took the envelope from her and saw it had a DFCO imprint on its back. Melissa noticed the way I looked at the envelope.

'Yeah. It's one of our envelopes,' she said. 'I thought the MOD guys might not have one large enough to hand and I didn't want to hang about too long. I guessed you'd want to see the photos as soon as possible.'

'You guessed right,' I said, as I pulled eight A4 size photographs from the envelope and laid them face up on my desk.

'I also got this for you.' She took a small object from her handbag and handed it to me. 'It's the digital disk.'

'Well done,' I said. 'I didn't think the MOD would let you have it. They're like gold dust.'

'It didn't come cheap,' she said. 'I had to agree to go on a date.'

'Good girl. It's nice to know there are still some people willing to sacrifice themselves in the line of duty.'

'It won't be too much of a sacrifice. She's very pretty with a great body. We'll get on well together.' Melissa looked at me as if expecting me to comment. When I didn't respond she headed out of my office with a half-smile on her face.

'Melissa!' I called as she disappeared through the door. She quickly returned. 'Poppy did promise to make me a coffee about ten minutes ago. Ask her where it is.'

'Don't worry, I'll make you one,' she said as she poked her head back around the doorframe. 'I was going to make myself a cup of tea anyway.'

'Tea will be fine for me too,' I said quickly.

I started looking through the photographs. The first showed a stack of £20-pound notes. There were ten bundles, each with a paper band wrapped around it with the figure £1000 printed on it. Ten grand in all.

The next three photos depicted a Glock semi-automatic pistol; a cellophane packet containing an unidentifiable white substance; and a British passport, which Manny had opened to take a snapshot of the page containing the owner's identity.

I didn't recognise the name on the passport, which was that of an "Ernest Thomas". However, the holder's photo showed a man whose face I had seen before. It was in the file put together for me by Melissa. It belonged to Sir Reginald Wren.

The next three shots showed a handsome, grey haired man in different poses. The first photo showed him standing on the foredeck of what was unmistakeably a luxury yacht with his arm round a pretty young woman with long blonde hair. She was nestled against him, with her breast pressed into his side. It was no surprise that he was smiling broadly.

In the second photo the couple were sitting on a sofa in what looked like a plush stateroom. The man was leaning forward over a low coffee table. He was holding a rolled bank note to one nostril, whilst pressing a finger against his other. The other end of the banknote rested on a line of white powder, which stood out vividly against the dark wood of the table top.

The third shot showed the man laying naked on the bed in the same stateroom. Straddling him was the pretty young woman. She was naked too and her long blonde hair hung down, hiding her face. His face was not hidden and he was clearly enjoying his sexual experience.

I stared down at the photos. I recognised both people, but, although I had seen her before, I had no idea of the woman's name. However, I knew the man's name. It was the Rt. Hon Douglas Campbell MP.

Clearly all three photographs had been taken on a yacht, with the last two probably being snapped without Campbell's knowledge, but who owned the boat and who took the photos? I thought about those questions for a while, but had no immediate answer so moved to the final photograph.

The photo depicted a single sheet of headed notepaper belonging to the American and Continental Mining Corporation, which carried a New York address. Unfortunately, the individual letters of the text were slightly fuzzy, but they were clear enough for me to read.

Beneath the company name was printed a single word in capital letters: **MEMORANDUM.**

The memo was dated Thursday, March 8th 1990 and had been circulated to "All Members of the Phoenix Group".

The memo read...

SUBJECT: THE MANDELA PROJECT

Colleagues

Please accept my apologies for the impersonal nature of this circular, but time constraints prevent me from contacting you all individually. However, I thought it was important, following our meeting in Paris last month (thanks again to HD for his hospitality), to update you on a number of matters that impact on the Mandela Project.

1)   You will recall I reported a suspicion that the CIA had infiltrated my company and were investigating my links with the Phoenix Group. I can confirm now that the CIA spy was identified by my company security officers. I can confirm also that the agent in question was this week found dead in a hotel bedroom in Nevada whilst visiting one of our quarries.

2)   I have been in touch with a number of representatives on Capitol Hill, to whom my company has made sizeable financial contributions in the run up to congressional elections later this year. They have been urged to put pressure on Bill Webster to back off.

3)   MS made contact with the contract killer recommended by BOL and he agreed to provide the Phoenix Group with exclusive use of his services until Nelson Mandela has been eliminated. The hit man's contract began on March 1st and he has already proven his worth in Nevada (as reported in Para 1 above!).

4)   As was explained at our meeting, BOL and SRW have a contact at the heart of the British Government. SRW has now confirmed he has certain sensitive material that will enable him to put pressure on the contact to influence Government policy to our advantage, should that be necessary. BOL has already started receiving useful information which has been forwarded already to MS.

5)   Finally, I can confirm that next month's meeting will take place at 10:00 hrs on Sunday, April 1, 1990, at FK's bank in Zurich.

I look forward to seeing you there.

John Derwent Engels
Phoenix Group Chairman

I read the memo a couple more times, before staring at the wall opposite. I guessed that "SRW" was Wren, but I had no idea to whom the other initials referred. I was still deep in thought when Melissa came in carrying a mug of tea in one hand and a file in the other. She put the mug on my desk and handed the file to me.

'It's the report on Sir Reginald Wren,' she explained. 'I'm off now, but if you have any questions I'll be in the office early in the morning.'

'Thanks,' I said as she left my office. I glanced at the clock. It was almost half past five.

I looked at the mug, on the side of which was printed in bright red letters: **Boss - *I can either get up bright or early. Take your pick!*** It was a Secret Santa gift given to me at the department's dinner the previous Christmas. However, I soon found out the gift was from Poppy, for whom keeping a secret, Santa or otherwise, was an alien concept.

For some reason she thought the slogan was hilarious and spent the whole evening going around all the other tables in the restaurant showing my mug to other diners.

Steam was rising from the mug and I realised with a resigned sigh that I would not have time to let the tea cool down if I was to make my meeting with Disraeli-Astor.

I swept up the photographs and the Thursday debrief transcript, slipped them into the file containing the new Wren report, with which Melissa had just presented me, and dashed for the door.

Colleen was nowhere to be seen when I arrived in her office. Her desk was clear and there was no sign of a coat or handbag. I knocked on the D-G's door and let myself in. His office was empty, so I settled into the chair that stood in front of his desk and opened the file. I removed the Wren report and started to read.

Melissa had obviously put some effort into her research. It gave me some additional background information about Wren, including his property portfolio. In addition to his London flat, he had houses in Marbella, Monaco and Cape Town. He also owned a luxury yacht.

This latter information seemed to answer the two questions I had asked myself less than an hour before. I guessed that it was on Wren's boat that the photos of Douglas Campbell and the blonde girl had been taken, and it was Wren himself who took them, probably using a hidden camera for the latter two.

I heard the door behind me open. 'Sorry to keep you waiting, Statton,' Disraeli-Astor said as he strode past me. He didn't seem too fazed that I had let myself into his office. 'I would offer you a cup of coffee, but Colleen went home early. She had some personal business to sort out.'

'It's not a problem. I've been reading a report about Sir Reginald Wren that Melissa put together. It's good stuff.'

'That girl is a star.'

'Yeah. We'll miss her when she's gone.'

'Where is she going?' Disraeli-Astor looked puzzled.

'She'll soon be heading off to the Foreign Office. She's on the Civil Service Fast Stream Programme. You knew that when you took her on.'

'Yes, of course I did,' he said, although I could tell he had forgotten. 'There's no coffee, but I can offer you something stronger,' he said, pointing towards the drinks cabinet that stood in the corner of the room.

'How much stronger?'

'Glenmorangie or Courvoisier strength,' he replied.

'A Courvoisier sounds good to me.'

He stood up and wandered over to the cabinet. 'I understand from Colleen that you believe the Russian was murdered,' he said.

'He was,' I said and then watched as he poured a generous measure of cognac into a balloon glass and handed it to me.

'How can you be so certain?' He asked as he poured himself a large malt whisky, before returning to his seat.

There was a pile of paperwork in front of me on his desk. I moved it to one side, took the pathologist's telex from the file, which now lay on my lap, and slid it across to him.

He didn't pick up the telex, instead he moved the pile of paperwork back in front of me. 'That's for you.'

'What is it?' I asked.

'Half the contents of my in-tray. This morning you seemed eager for me to share my workload with you,' he gave me an innocent smile. 'In fact, you said you couldn't wait. I didn't want to disappoint you, so here it is.'

'Someday I really must explain to you the difference between eagerness and sarcasm,' I said as I took the pile of papers and stuffed them into my empty briefcase.

'I know exactly what sarcasm is.' He picked up the telex. 'I get enough of it from you.' When he had finished reading he gave me a quizzical look. I quickly explained the implications of the autopsy report.

He nodded knowingly. 'So what else do you have for me about the South African business?' He asked.

'Well for a start I have some very interesting photographs.' I paused as I raised my glass to my lips and drank some of the honey coloured cognac. 'And I picked up some more information from the last debrief interview that Urinoff gave,' I went on eventually. 'I take it you didn't read the transcript before you gave it to me?'

'No, I ran out of time.'

'Have you heard of an outfit called the Phoenix Group?' I asked.

He shook his head.

'It's the name of the business group of which Wren is a member,' I explained and took the relevant page from the debrief transcript and passed to him.

He started to read and winced visibly when he reached the paragraph about the involvement of members of the Establishment in protecting Wren. He looked up at me and frowned. 'So Urinoff had a list of members of the Phoenix Group and details of people who allegedly have been helping Sir Reginald,' he said.

I noticed he had dropped the informal "Reggie", but obviously could not bring himself to call a knight of the realm, even a spiv knight, by his surname alone.

'Apparently so,' I agreed.

He sipped his drink as he considered this. 'Getting hold of that information seems a good reason for killing Urinoff and stealing his briefcase,' he said eventually.

'Well spotted,' I said.

He looked pleased with himself. 'What else have you got?'

'An empty brandy glass,' I replied.

'Help yourself.'

I handed him the photograph that replicated the memo from the Phoenix Group Chairman. While he studied the document I poured myself another cognac. His glass was empty so I recharged it without being asked.

'Thanks,' he murmured, 'this is dynamite.'

'It certainly looks as if Urinoff was telling the truth about a conspiracy.'

'I can't believe they plan to assassinate Nelson Mandela,' he said with a shake of his head.

'You'd better start believing,' I said. 'Those boys are serious.'

'But are they capable of carrying out their threat?' I could tell from his tone that he wanted me to say no.

I disappointed him. 'They are more than capable. Their hired gun has already killed a CIA agent in America and probably General Urinoff here in Britain.'

'You think this group was behind the Russian's death?'

'Who else would want to silence him and steal his briefcase?'

'I see what you mean,' he said and drank half his whisky in one gulp. He screwed up his face as he swallowed the fiery liquid.

'I'm not sure that Glenmorangie is meant to be treated like that,' I chided him.

He ignored me. 'One thing puzzles me,' he said.

'Only one thing? You're lucky. There are a number of things about it that puzzle me.' I sipped some of my cognac and felt its warmth slide down my throat. 'But what's your particular problem?'

'How did the Phoenix Group know the Russian was in the safe-house?'

'I don't know,' I admitted, 'but I think I know a man who does.'

'Who?'

'Wren, and I intend finding out if I'm right.'

'What else did your burglar friend find out about Sir Reginald?'

I took four more photos from the file and slid them across the desk to him. 'I think these speak volumes about the type of man Wren is,' I said.

He looked at the photos one by one, describing each in turn. 'A false passport; ten thousand pounds, which I assume is his away day money; a pistol; and a packet of powder.' He looked up at me. 'Drugs?'

'Cocaine,' I said. I didn't explain why I was so certain. He would be able to work that out for himself soon enough.

'I thought Sir Reginald might be a spiv,' he said, 'but I didn't know he was a coke-head.'

'You can never tell,' I said non-committedly. We sat in silence for a while as we savoured our drinks, each lost in thought. 'What was your meeting with Douglas Campbell about?' I asked eventually.

'He wanted to discuss the AOSC. He had lots of questions about our intentions. I think he is going to make life difficult. He wants us to fail.'

'Us?'

'The DFCO.'

'What's his motive?'

'Political manoeuvring, pure and simple. A game in which Dougie is a past master. He has his eye on becoming Home Secretary and believes he will have a better chance of success under a new Prime Minister.'

'Is there going to be a new PM?'

'That's what the Westminster rumour mill is saying. There is a lot of unrest on the Conservative backbenches.'

'What's new? Some backbenchers have nothing better to do than stir up trouble for their leader.'

'I know, but it is different this time.'

'Why?'

'Because many MPs feel they won't win the next general election with Maggie as their leader.'

'They're idiots. Most of them owe their seats to Mrs T. It was her who got them elected three years ago. Don't they realise that?'

'MPs have very short memories, they see no further than the latest newspaper headlines. And don't forget much has happened since the last election.' He held up a hand with fingers spread wide.

'The Economy is struggling, with interest rates hitting home-owners hard,' he said, folding his little finger over with his other hand. 'Many people are worried about waiting lists in the NHS; the Conservative Party is deeply divided over the issue of Europe; there is widespread opposition to the Poll Tax. Let's face it, the PM is not as popular as she used to be. An opinion poll this morning put Labour twenty-four percentage points ahead of the Conservatives.' By the time Disraeli-Astor finished listing the problems, all his fingers had been folded to leave his hand as a clenched fist. 'That is why Tory backbenchers are getting worried.'

'But Maggie has won three elections on the trot, doesn't that count for anything with her MPs?'

'A worried backbencher quickly turns into a disloyal backbencher,' he said with unaccustomed cynicism. 'And I fear that some of our elected members have the backbone of a jelly fish.'

This was one occasion on which I could not disagree with him.

'Do you remember what happened last year?' He went on. 'Some unknown donkey from the back benches was persuaded to challenge

113

Mrs Thatcher for leadership of the Conservative Party?'

'His name was Sir Anthony Meyer,' I reminded him. 'And as I recall, that unknown donkey got sixty votes.'

'Exactly! That shows how spooked the backbenchers have become.'

'But that still meant over three hundred MPs supported Maggie,' I pointed out.

'Yes, but many of that three hundred are frightened now of losing their seats and Michael Heseltine is whipping up opposition against the PM.'

'Heseltine?'

'Yes. He's making noises about challenging her and as an ex-cabinet minister, he's a far bigger political beast than Sir Anthony. Mrs Thatcher's problem is that several members of her Cabinet actively support Heseltine and are trying to undermine her authority.'

'So, the lady could be in trouble?'

'Big trouble.'

'How does your friend Dougie think all this can help him?'

'He is not my friend,' Disraeli-Astor insisted quickly. 'We just went to the same school.'

'Whatever,' I said. 'I still don't see what he gets out of Mrs T being deposed.'

'I told you, he hankers after the Home Secretary job. The current incumbent, David Waddington, is very much a Thatcher man and if she goes, he will go as well. Dougie is working closely with Michael Heseltine in his campaign to destabilise the PM.'

'And how does all this affect the DFCO?' I asked.

'Dougie is a calculating bastard,' he said with a hint of admiration. 'I suspect he thinks that if the Phoenix Group is not stopped and Mandela is assassinated, then the department will carry the can…'

'And the PM will be blamed because we report directly to her,' I interjected.

'Exactly. She is ultimately responsible for the department's actions. If we fail, the buck stops with her. It could be the straw that breaks the camel's back.'

'And breaks Mrs T.'

'Yes. Dougie reckons that if Maggie is toppled then Heseltine is the front runner to become PM and his reward for helping him will be the post of Home Secretary.'

'How do you know all this?' I asked.

'I'm the Director-General, Statton. It's my job to keep my ear to the ground. I like to think I know everything about those who govern us.'

'Not everything,' I said and took from my file the photograph of Campbell standing on the yacht with the pretty blonde woman. I handed it to him. 'Recognise them?' I asked.

He studied the photo in silence. 'That's Douglas Campbell, but I don't know who the woman is. It's definitely not his wife,' he said disapprovingly.

'You don't say.' I didn't tell him I had seen the woman before.

'But there could be a perfectly innocent explanation,' he said.

I slid another print across his desk to him, but he didn't pick it up. Instead he just stared at it, as if touching the photo would somehow contaminate him. 'I think I need another drink.' He stood up. 'You?'

'I can never say no to a decent cognac.' I handed him my glass.

'Is Dougie doing what I think he is?' He asked as he walked over to his drinks cabinet.

'If you think he's snorting cocaine, the answer is probably yes,' I said as I watched him pour our drinks. 'Of course there might be a perfectly innocent explanation,' I went on. 'For instance, perhaps he is sucking talcum powder up his nose.'

'Don't be facetious,' he said as he handed me another drink.

'If you insist, boss.' I took something else from the file. 'There is one more photo.'

'Do I want to see it?'

'Probably not, but you're going to anyway, because unlike the other two this one has no possible innocent interpretations.' I laid the print on top of the previous one.

He looked down at the photo and his face flushed a deep red that highlighted the scar on his cheek. 'I see what you mean,' he said before taking a gulp of his drink. 'You think these were taken on the same day?'

'Yes.'

'And your man found them in Sir Reginald's safe?'

'Yes again. I think they were taken on Wren's yacht.'

'I didn't know he had a yacht.'

'Well he does. It was in the report that Melissa put together.'

He picked up the photos and flicked through them. 'I wish I had seen these before my meeting with Dougie. I wouldn't have been so civil when he made a fuss about me calling a meeting for the AOSC at short notice.'

'What meeting?'

'There's one tomorrow at fourteen hundred hours.'

'I don't remember receiving notification of a meeting.'

'I'm telling you now.'

'Well I am busy tomorrow afternoon.'

He looked at me coldly. 'Tell me, Statton. Were you born insubordinate and antagonistic, or did it grow on you?'

'Oh, definitely the latter. It comes from years of being taken for granted by bosses who went to public school.'

His expression softened slightly. 'OK. I am duly admonished. I should have told you about the meeting earlier. Let me make amends by giving you advance warning of another meeting. It's at Number Ten on Wednesday.'

'You told me about it this morning.'

'I know, but the PM has now asked that you come to the meeting as well.' He looked at me and frowned. 'Although I can't imagine why she invited you, because you'll probably be bolshie with her as well.'

'Not me. I'll be on my best behaviour,' I promised. 'Anyway, I'm only bolshie with public school toffs. Mrs T went to a state grammar school.' I raised my glass to him.

He sighed deeply, but raised his glass to acknowledge my own gesture.

I knocked back the rest of my cognac, put my glass on his desk and stood up.

'Oh, and Statton,' he added. 'I don't think we need mention the Mandela Project at tomorrow's meeting. We don't want any questions being asked about how we obtained the information. Burglary is an offence and one cannot be too careful, can one?'

'Damn right, Director-General. One certainly cannot be too careful,' I agreed in an accentuated upper class voice.

'Someday you'll push me a little too hard, Statton,' he said.

'I bet you said that to all the boys at Eton.'

'Out!' He pointed to the door with a glare that would have been angry if it hadn't been for the grin he tried to hide.

Chapter 10

Melissa was as good as her word. When I walked into the office the next day she was already there, although I could see that she had only just arrived. It was raining cats and dogs outside and her long black hair hung down either side of her face in wet, lank strands.

'Good morning,' she said as she struggled out of her rain soaked coat.

'Is that some kind of joke, Melissa?' I asked. 'The weather is dreadful and you look like a drowned rat. I think you'd better go find a towel and dry your hair. I don't want my best researcher catching pneumonia.'

'I'm not sure I like being compared to a rodent, but thanks for the last bit. I take it you were happy with the Wren report?'

'It was excellent work; very informative.'

Her smile widened. 'I told you, I enjoy research work.'

'That's good, because once you've dried yourself off I'd like you to dig out some more information about Wren.'

'What do you want to know?'

'Where he has sailed his yacht in the last couple of years and where it's currently moored.'

'OK, but I'm in the middle of something else. Can I finish that first?'

'As long as it isn't going to take all week,' I said. 'The information on Wren's yacht isn't urgent, but I'd like it by Friday.'

'No problem. My job will only take about an hour to finish, but I can take time out to make you a coffee if you'd like one.'

'Don't worry, you get on with your work. I can wait until Poppy arrives.' I headed into my office, took off my own raincoat and hung it on the hook behind the door.

I sat down at my desk and listened to water drip off my raincoat onto the lino covered floor. My desk was clear except for the mug of cold tea left from the previous night. I moved it aside and emptied the contents of my briefcase onto the desk top. It looked as if Disraeli-Astor was going to off-load his paperwork onto me, so I decided I needed a set of in and out trays.

My phone rang and Melissa told me she had Timmy on the line. After a couple of clicks I heard my deputy's voice.

'Is that you, Mister Statton?'

'Yes. Where are you?'

'I'm ringing from my car,' he said with a hint of pride in his voice. For some reason he had been allocated one of the few Government pool cars fitted with a telephone. Those vehicles were usually reserved for senior staff and my deputy was lucky to have been allocated one. He was determined to make the most of it.

'I meant, where are you geographically?' I said.

'Oh! Sorry, sir. I'm at the Elephant and Castle.'

'So, why are you calling me?'

'Because I'm stuck in traffic and wanted you to know I was going to be late.'

'That was very thoughtful of you.' I tried not to sound too sarcastic. 'But don't worry, I'll still be here when you arrive. I don't suppose you have Poppy with you?'

'No. Why's that?'

'Because she's late again.'

'I think you'll find that she's back with Roger,' he said with what sounded like a snigger.

'What makes you say that?'

'She told me yesterday that he had asked her to visit his grandfather's home in County Sligo.'

'I didn't know that Roger was Irish,' I said, automatically filing the information away in my mind.

'Yes. Apparently he's a typical Irish charmer.' Timmy sounded jealous.

'Goodbye, Timmy. Get here as soon as you can.'

I picked up the first document my boss had dumped on me. It was a ten page inter-departmental memo issued by the Cabinet Office setting out a new process for submitting annual budget requisitions.

Attached to the memo was a thick form that had to be completed in triplicate. I was not sure why Disraeli-Astor had passed it to me. Putting together the DFCO's budget was one of the responsibilities of the Deputy Director-General.

I knew Roland Lafarge was starting to wind down in anticipation of his forthcoming retirement, but I didn't see why I should be lumbered with the budget. Maybe it was because I was the only other person in the department who could successfully add two and two to make four without the use of a calculator.

I spent half an hour reading through the document, after which I was even more determined to avoid having it dumped in my lap. I put it into an envelope with a compliments slip saying simply: "For your attention". I wrote Roly's name on the envelope and put it to one side on my desk.

Poppy put her head round the corner. 'Hi, Boss. Would you like a drink?' She asked.

'I'll have a coffee, if you remember how to make one.'

She came into my office. 'Why wouldn't I remember?' She asked with a frown.

'Because you keep promising me one, but it never arrives.'

'I've had things on my mind,' she said as she picked up the mug from my desk. 'It's stone cold,' she said accusingly, pointing at the tea.

'It was too hot to drink,' I said.

'You're supposed to drink it hot,' she pointed out.

'Not boiling hot. I have more respect for my tonsils,' I said. 'Where have you been, Poppy?'

'Roger stayed over,' she said.

'What about his wife?'

'She wasn't with him,' she giggled.

'You know what I mean. Is your relationship with Roger the Dodger actually going anywhere?'

'Roger says he is going to leave the old cow. He wants to marry me.'

'Of course he does,' I said. 'And I'm sure you'll live happily ever after.'

'You don't think he means it.' It was not a question.

'I'm sure he is the most loyal, honest, genuine, upright person in the world and his wife will give him a glowing reference.'

'Oh, you are an awful septic,' she said.

'You mean sceptic, Poppy. And yes, I gained a double first in cynicism at the University of Life. Now go and make me a coffee before I remember that you were late for work again and issue you with a written warning.'

She blew me a kiss and disappeared, leaving a trail of cold tea spots across my office lino to mingle with the drops of rainwater.

119

I shook my head and picked up another document from the pile on my desk. It was a briefing note from the Commissioner of the Metropolitan Police, dated 29th March, about the Poll Tax demonstration that was due to take place two days later.

The report stated confidently that the Met had liaised with the demonstration organisers; were monitoring the situation carefully; had preparations well in hand; and had formulated plans to control demonstrators, who, intelligence reports predicted, would behave peaceably.

What a load of bollocks, I thought. As planned, the demonstration took place on 31st Match, but it was taken over by left-wing militants who turned it into a riot. So much for police intelligence.

There was a knock on my open door. 'I'm here, Mister Statton,' Timmy Fraser said as he walked into my office carrying a file. 'Sorry I'm late. Westminster Bridge Road was flooded and it created chaos.'

'It doesn't take more than a shower to cause chaos on the roads in this country,' I moaned.

Timmy sat in the chair opposite my desk.

'What did Cole have to say for himself?' I asked.

'I didn't speak to him, because he wasn't in when I went to his house.'

'So he wasn't exactly on his death bed then? What was wrong with him?'

'He told his boss he had a cold.'

'A cold? Since when did a cold stop anybody from working?'

'It could have been a touch of flu,' he said.

'Do you really believe that?'

'I like to give people the benefit of the doubt.'

'Timmy, if you are going to have a long term future in Section Two then you really do have to understand that for a field agent there is no such thing as benefit of the doubt. If something smells fishy, then you have to assume it's probably a big, fat dead cod.'

'Point taken, sir.'

'I hope so.'

'But my visit to Slough wasn't a complete waste of time,' he said. 'I managed to get the security company to give me Cole's bank details and when I contacted his bank I found out that five hundred pounds was paid into his account on Friday. I got the bank to check details of the transaction and discovered it was a direct transfer from a bank account in the name of William Butler.'

'I see. Knowing that, are you still willing to give Cole the benefit of the doubt?'

'Well, I have to admit the payment does look suspicious.'

'That, my son, is like saying a billiard ball looks round.'

Timmy pulled some documents out of the file he carried. 'I got these from the temps' agency.' He passed the papers to me.

The first document was an employment application form in the name of William Butler. It listed his personal details, including his address, bank details, employment record, and passport number.

Attached to the form was a photograph of a long haired, bearded man. I recognised him immediately as the guard who was on duty when we visited the safe-house in Windsor. Safe-house? Tell that to Alexei Urinoff.

'When was this photograph taken?' I asked.

'Last week.'

'Was this the bank account from which the payment to Coles was made?' I asked, tapping the document.

'Yes.'

'Did you contact the Home Office to check Butler's passport details?' I asked.

'Not yet,' Timmy answered. 'I was going to do that later this morning.'

'Don't worry, I'll get Melissa to check it out, although I think we will find the passport is a forgery.'

The second document was a job reference from William Butler's previous employer, Securicor, for whom he claimed to have worked for ten years. I had my doubts. Nothing about Butler, or whatever his real name was, rang true.

'OK, our first priority is to find out Butler's real identity. I want you to go back down to Slough and find Cole. If he's not at home, track him down.'

'How will I...' he stopped in mid-sentence when he saw the look I gave him.

'You could try his workplace,' I suggested. 'Or a local pub, or the bookies, or the local supermarket. You could even try the local church. He might be at confession.'

'You think he's a Catholic?' He asked.

I sighed. 'It was a joke, Timmy,' I said. 'Look, don't worry. I'm sure you'll find him somewhere. When you do, take him into custody and then wait for me. I have a meeting this afternoon. As soon as it's finished I'll come and join you. I want a chat with our Mister Cole.'

He looked uncomfortable. 'I'm not sure I have the authority to arrest him,' he said anxiously. 'I'm not a policeman.'

'Cole doesn't know that, does he, son?'

He stared at me blankly. I hated that look.

'You still have the Met Police warrant card, don't you?' I asked.

He nodded.

'Well, just pretend to be a plod.'

At last he twigged. 'OK. I'll do my best.'

'I'm sure you will.'

'One other thing, sir…'

'What's that, Timmy?'

'Can I keep the pool car?' He asked hesitantly.

'Well, I don't expect you to walk to Slough,' I said. 'And it will be useful if you have a car phone so you can contact me if you have trouble finding Cole.'

He looked delighted.

'Off you go then,' I said.

He didn't need telling twice. Before I could change my mind he scuttled out with a broad smile on his face, almost barging into Poppy who was heading into my office carrying a mug of coffee.

'Thanks,' I said as she put the mug down on my desk. 'I need a couple of wire trays for my desk, Poppy. Do we have any going spare in the office?'

'Not that I know of,' she said.

'In that case, please submit a requisition form for a couple.'

'A requisition form?'

'Yes, you know what they are don't you?'

'Of course I do, it's just that I'm really busy at the moment and I'm not sure when I'll have time to fill one in.'

'It won't take long, Poppy,' I said gently.

'OK, I'll do it straight away,' she agreed reluctantly. 'But what do you want the trays for?'

'To grow plants in.'

She considered me with narrowed eyes.

'What do you think I want them for?' I asked. 'They are to help me sort out all this paperwork,' I said impatiently. 'There will be a tray on this side of the desk into which you will put all my post and any paperwork that finds its way down from the D-G's office. There will be another tray over there that you will empty daily. Look, does it matter what I want the bloody things for?'

'Yes, because I have to say on the form why we need them,' she explained.

'I don't care what you tell them. Just as long as I get my trays as soon as possible.'

'The government stationery supply department is useless,' she said as she headed out of the door. 'You'll be lucky to get them this side of Christmas.'

'Great,' I muttered. Past experience told me that on this occasion my secretary might not be exaggerating.

I started back on the paperwork that Disraeli-Astor had dumped on me and had waded through about half when Melissa rescued me from what was becoming a mind-numbing exercise.

She tapped on the open door to my office and looked in.

'Come in,' I said gratefully.

'Sorry to disturb you, boss,' she apologised.

'Don't worry. You're doing me a favour. I can only take so much paperwork before I start thinking of ways to commit suicide quickly and painlessly.'

She grinned. 'I have that information you wanted about Sir Reginald's yacht,' she said.

'And?'

'And the yacht is currently moored in Monaco.'

'How did you find that out?'

'It was easy really. I thought Sir Reginald might maintain moorings in all the places in which he owns a home. I contacted the harbour authorities in Cape Town, Marbella and Monaco. I was right, he pays an annual charge for moorings in all of them. More interestingly, the harbour master in Monaco told me that Wren's yacht has been moored there for three years and hasn't moved.'

'Good work, Melissa,' I said and passed to her Butler's employment application form. 'Your next job is to find out what you can about this goon, although you might not find that bit of research quite so easy.'

'Who is William Butler?' she asked.

'He's the guard who was on duty at the safe-house in Windsor when Timmy and I visited Urinoff. However, I don't think Butler is his real name and the passport mentioned on that form is probably a forgery, so check it out with the Home Office.'

I passed her the photograph of Butler. 'You'll need to contact Special Branch as well. Ask to look through the mugshot books they have on suspected members of republican dissident groups in Northern Ireland, such as the Provisional IRA. See if you can find a match with our hairy friend here.'

'Will there be many photos?' She asked.

'The last time I checked there were about six thousand IRA suspects on file at Scotland Yard, although many of those are probably sympathisers, rather than active members.'

'So you want me to wade through six thousand photos?' She didn't sound impressed.

'Yeah. But it could have been worse,' I assured her. 'At least it's not sixty thousand.'

'Is that supposed to make me feel better?'

'Not really, but I thought it was worth a try.'

'You'll have to try harder than that.'

'Alright, how about if I get Timmy to help you when he gets back from Slough.'

'That's no better. This is a job that needs to be done methodically, and there's only one person in this office who can do that.'

'You?'

'Yes,' she said. 'Look, don't get me wrong. I like Timmy, but for a job like this he will just get in the way.'

I smiled at her. She was probably right.

The Cabinet War Rooms are an underground complex that housed the government command centre during the Second World War. It was here that Winston Churchill held Cabinet meetings and directed the British war effort. Now a museum, the complex is located beneath the Treasury.

The museum is separated from the basement offices of Section Two by a foot thick concrete wall and a single bomb proof metal door that was secured with a combination lock. Its number was known only to the stern faced guard who sat at a desk in the room that served as the smaller of DFCO's security offices.

The main rooms of the museum are open to the public, but parts of the bunker complex are not accessible to anybody other than employees of the Imperial War Museum, of which the Cabinet War Rooms are a part.

However, there was one room into which only DFCO staff are allowed. It has two entrances, one of which is the door leading to and from the security room. The second door opens into a corridor that runs through that part of the complex to which members of the general public are excluded. The door to this entrance is also bomb proof, solid metal, double locked and sealed top and bottom.

'Morning, Joe,' I said to the guard.'

His stern face broke into a smile. 'Morning, Mister Statton. I aint seen you down 'ere in the dungeon for ages. Where's that lovely secretary of yours?'

'She's upstairs, hopefully ordering some filing trays for me.'

'You mean them things what go on your desk for paperwork?'

'That's them.'

Joe got up and walked over to the cupboard that stood in the corner of the room. He opened the door and reached inside. 'Are these any good?' He took out two wire trays and handed them to me. Each tray had a little slot on the front with a card in it. On one card the word "In" was printed and on the other "Out".

'Just the job,' I said, 'but don't you need them yourself?'

'No use to me, guv. I don't get no paperwork down 'ere. They was just cluttering up my desk so I took 'em off. You can 'ave 'em.' He walked over to the metal connecting door. Taking care to hide what he was doing, he punched numbers into the combination lock.

'Thanks,' I said and put the trays down on the edge of his desk. 'I'll leave them here until I've finished in the archives.'

Joe swung the heavy door open and flicked the light switch that was positioned on the inside wall.

I walked through the door into a long narrow room that was fitted with high shelves on which were stacked large cardboard storage boxes. This was where the Department for Covert Operations stored all its completed case files and associated documents.

The department was much less bureaucratic than any other arm of government, and, because of the nature of its business, Section Two generated less paperwork than any other section. However, the archive was crammed to the gunnels with the paperwork generated by countless pens, pencils, type writer ribbons and, in more recent

125

years, dot-matrix printers.

To my left was the door that led to the Cabinet War Rooms and at the far end of the room stood a desk and chair, next to which was a small table containing a photocopier. On top of the desk was a typewriter and a thick binder containing the index of files stored in the various boxes. Every box placed in the store was numbered and dated.

Inside each box was a contents list, a copy of which was filed in date order in the index binder. As long as you knew the year in which a particular file originated, then it was easy to find the relevant box in which it was stored. Luckily, I knew the year of the file for which I was searching.

From the ceiling hung a line of bare light bulbs. At some time the two bulbs at the end of the room had been changed for pink coloured ones. They gave that part of the archive room a somewhat eerie look.

There were four boxes containing files from 1970. That particular year was a busy time for the DFCO. I found the file I wanted in the second storage box and took it over to the desk and sat down. I opened the file and soon found the form for which I was looking. I photocopied it and put the original in the file and returned it to the storage box.

I sat back down and took a bottle of Tippex from a drawer in the desk. I blanked out some of the information on the form and then photocopied it again. I slipped the form in the typewriter and added a new name and date.

I studied the form and nodded in satisfaction. The typeface of the insertion was slightly different from the original, but I was confident that anybody giving the form a cursory examination would not notice it was a forgery, particularly if that person had never seen one before. It would certainly be good enough for what I wanted.

Downing Street, Westminster

The AOSC meeting didn't last long. Disraeli-Astor got himself elected as Chairman (with the help of my vote) without any trouble. The only person to vote against was Douglas Campbell. That was no surprise.

My boss then gave an update on the situation with regards to General Urinoff and the Phoenix Group's plans to destabilise South Africa, which wasn't much. He didn't mention the information we had obtained from Wren's safe.

Next he persuaded the committee members to support a request to the Cabinet Office for a generous budget for the Mandela Project operation. Nobody asked him to justify the bid. Over inflated budget proposals are a standard civil service practice.

Finally, Disraeli-Astor saw off an attempt by Douglas Campbell to neuter the Department. The Home Office minister argued that no action should be authorised by the AOSC without first obtaining permission from the full JSOLC committee.

Luckily we had pre-empted such an attempt and Disraeli-Astor was prepared. He pointed out that calling a meeting of the full committee would lead to a delay that might jeopardise any ensuing field operation. Instead, he moved that Jeffery Johnson be given a daily update by AOSC. It would then be for him to decide who should be informed. The motion was agreed, with only Campbell objecting.

This successful counter-manoeuvre was achieved without the necessity of using the information we had about Campbell, which, if revealed, would have forced him to resign as a minister. Our strategy was designed to keep our gunpowder dry for another day, if at all possible, and we succeeded. This was a tactic I came up with and I was pleased my boss took my advice.

The AOSC meeting was over by two thirty and shortly after that I was on a train from Paddington to Slough, where I took a taxi to the small terraced house in which Timmy was detaining Cole.

Slough, Berkshire, England
My deputy showed me into a grimy lounge in which a scruffy looking man sat in an armchair with soiled upholstery from which white stuffing was seeping from a split seam.

'Hello, Mister Cole,' I said.

The security guard looked up at me. 'Who the fuck are you?'

'Inspector Statton,' I introduced myself.

'He's my boss,' Timmy explained.

'More fucking filth,' Cole said bitterly.

'Well, at least you're used to filth,' I said looking round the room. 'This gaff is a pigsty.'

'Bollocks to you,' Cole retorted. 'You aint got no right coming into my home and insulting me like that.'

'Who says I need the right?'

'I do.'

'Is that so?'

'Yeah.'

'I see.' I stared at him in silence.

He looked uncomfortable, but still protested. 'This is harassment.'

'Who's harassing you?'

'That posh twat for a start,' he pointed at Timmy. 'He barged in here and told me that he was arresting me.'

'Did he really?'

'Yes he did.' He returned my stare defiantly. 'I want to see my solicitor,' he demanded.

'Of course you do, Mister Cole, but as Mick Jagger once sang: *You can't always get what you want.*'

'I demand to see my lawyer.'

'Sadly that won't be possible.'

'Why not?'

'Well, for a start you're not under arrest.'

'No?'

'No.'

'So I can go?'

'No.'

'I don't understand.'

'That's because you are a stupid little turd. Let me explain to you in simple words that even somebody of your limited intelligence should be able to understand.' My stare didn't waver and this time his eyes sank to the floor.

'The thing is, Malcolm, can I call you Malcolm?'

Cole didn't respond, instead he carried on staring at what looked like a coffee stain on his threadbare carpet.

'The thing is, Malcolm,' I repeated anyway, 'you haven't been arrested. You are just being detained so you can help us with our enquiries.'

'aint that the same thing?'

'Not in law.'

Finally, Cole looked up at me. 'So what do you want?' He asked.

'I want you to tell me about William Butler.'

'I don't know no William Butler.'

'Are you sure?'

'Yeah.'

'He was the agency security-guard who took your place when you phoned in sick.'

'So what? I don't employ the company's workers.'

'So are you saying that you don't know William Butler?'

'No. I mean yes, I don't know him.'

'I see.' I pulled a sheet of paper from my briefcase. I handed it to Cole, who stared at it silently. 'So how do you explain the five hundred pounds that was paid into your account last week?' I asked.

Cole shrugged. 'I don't know nothing about that,' he said.

'Don't know?' I repeated. I continued to stare at him before pulling a second sheet of paper from my case. I handed it to him. 'As you can see,' I said, 'the payment was a bank transfer from William Butler's account. Why would he do that?'

'I don't know,' he said.

'I don't believe you,' I said.

'Well, you can go fuck yourself.'

'Thank you, but I'd rather not.' I pulled a third sheet of paper from my briefcase and passed it to Cole.

The security guard stared at the paper and frowned again. 'I don't get it,' he said.

'It's simple, Malcolm,' I said. 'That form is called an expedient demise order. We call it an XPD order for short.'

'I don't know what that means,' Cole said.

'It means that I am authorised to kill you,' I said with a smile.

'You can't do that!' Cole tried to sound defiant, but it didn't quite come off.

'Unfortunately, this piece of paper says I can,' I said and tapped the form. 'As you can see it is signed by a member of the Government.'

'But why?'

'Why? Because you are a terrorist and a traitor.'

'I aint no terrorist,' Cole said angrily.

'OK,' I said. 'I'll settle for you being a traitor.'

'I aint no traitor, neither,' Cole insisted.

'Then what are you doing accepting five hundred pounds from a known IRA killer?'

'I didn't know Butler was in the IRA.'

'I thought you said you didn't know Butler?'

Cole shrugged.

'Listen, my friend, you're in big trouble.' I pulled my Smith & Wesson out of my shoulder-holster and pointed it at the guard's forehead. 'You're out of your depth. That XPD order you are holding gives me the legal right to shoot you between the eyes right now. Is that what you want?'

Cole shook his head. He could not hide his fright, and much of his belligerence had disappeared, but he still summonsed up enough defiance to insist: 'You can't frighten me. The police aint allowed to shoot people, just like that.'

'That's very true, Malcolm,' I said. 'But unfortunately for you, we're not the police.'

Cole looked from me to Timmy and back again. 'Then who are you?'

I cocked the pistol. 'It doesn't matter who we are. All you need to know is that I hate traitors and have instructions to kill you if necessary.'

'Please don't shoot me,' he pleaded. 'I told you, I aint no traitor!'

'Then tell me about Butler. Did he pay you five hundred pounds?'

Cole nodded.

'I can't hear you.'

'Yeah. He gave me the monkey.'

'What for?'

'He wanted me to pull a sickie.'

'Why?'

'I don't know.'

'You don't know?' I turned to Timmy. 'Do you believe matey here, Sergeant Fraser?'

My deputy shook his head, but said nothing. He stared wide-eyed at the XPD order Cole held in his hand.

'But it's true,' Cole wailed, all defiance had deserted him.

'How long have you known Butler?' I asked.

'Only a few days.'

'How did he make contact with you?'

'I sing in a folk group,' he said. 'We play gigs most Wednesdays and Saturdays.'

'Why Wednesdays?' I asked.

'It's my day off,' he explained.

I nodded. 'Go on.'

'Last Wednesday evening we was playing in a pub in Stoke Poges. It's a regular gig we do every month.'

'And?'

'During our performance we always ask if anyone has a request. Last week this Irish bloke put his hand up and asked if we could play *The Merry Ploughboy*.'

'Butler?'

'Yeah. We said it weren't a song we knew, but he said he would sing it, so we let him join us on the stage and he started singing. We just rode with the tune as best we could. He was a pretty good singer, and he looked the part, with his beard and pony tail.'

'Ponytail?' I asked.

'Yeah, he had long hair, but it was tied back in a ponytail.'

'When did he approach you?'

'At the end of our performance. After we loaded our equipment into the van, he insisted on buying us all a drink. We sat in the pub for ages chatting. He was good company and told us lots of stories about the troubles in Northern Ireland.

'At first he claimed he weren't involved in any of the paramilitary organisations, but, the lobe of his left ear was missing. When I asked how he had lost it, he said it was bitten off in a fight in the Maze Prison. That's when he admitted he was a member of the Ulster Volunteer Force.'

'The UVF? Do you expect me to believe that?'

'I don't understand,' Cole said. I could tell he was serious.

'*The Merry Ploughboy* is an Irish Republican song. There is no way a member of the UVF would sing it.'

'I didn't realise,' Cole said.

'Come on, Malcolm. You're a folk singer.'

'I swear I didn't realise it was an IRA song.'

'OK, let's assume that's true,' I said. 'So tell me, exactly when did Butler ask you to pull a sickie so he could take your place.'

'He rang me the next day, on the Thursday, and offered me five hundred quid.'

'How did he get your telephone number?'

'I gave it to him at the gig.'

'He asked for it?'

'Yes.'

'Didn't you find that odd?'

'No. Members of the audience often ask me for my number.'

'Get you, superstar,' I said. I was still pointing the Smith & Wesson at him, but I eased the hammer down, slipped on the safety catch and holstered it. 'OK, here's the deal. You give me back the XPD order and I'll ignore it.'

Cole handed over the sheet of paper quickly, as if holding onto it would seal his fate. 'I really aint no traitor, Inspector,' he said. 'I wish I'd never got involved with that Irish bastard.'

'Perhaps you'll be more careful who you give your telephone number to in the future,' I said. 'Now, is there anything else you remember about Butler you think I should know?' I asked.

Cole shook his head automatically, then thought better of it. 'There was something else,' he said.

'Yes?'

'He had a tattoo on his neck.'

'What did it look like?' I asked.

'It was a flag,' Cole said.

'Was it the Union flag?

'Nah, it was green, white and red,' Cole said eventually.

'Are you sure?' I asked. 'Could the red have been orange?'

Cole thought for a few seconds and then nodded slowly. 'Yeah, it could have been orange.'

'That makes sense,' I said thoughtfully.

'Was the tattoo significant?' Timmy asked as we made our way back to London in his pool car.

'Yeah. It's the flag of the Republic of Ireland,' I explained. 'That seems to confirm that our friend William Butler is probably an Irish republican masquerading as a member of a loyalist paramilitary group.'

Timmy lapsed into silence when we reached the outskirts of Slough. He navigated carefully through the heavy rush hour traffic that was heading for the motorway. 'There's something that puzzles me, boss,' he said once we were safely on the M4.

'What's that?'

'How did you manage to organise an XPD order so quickly? I thought they took ages to obtain and had to be signed off by the Cabinet Office.'

'They do,' I confirmed, 'and you have to provide concrete evidence that the person named in the order is a real, current and exceptional threat to the country's security. In addition, you have to prove also there is no alternative to an XPD order. Since the early nineteen-seventies, the burden of proof has been made so onerous that obtaining an order has become almost impossible.'

'So how did you get an order for Cole? We had no real evidence he was a threat to anybody.'

'Did you actually read the document, son?' I asked.

'No, I didn't get a chance. You gave it to Cole and then he gave it straight back to you.'

'The XPD order was signed off by Douglas Hamilton-Browne. Does that name ring any bells with you?'

'Wasn't he the Home Secretary at one time?'

'That's right.'

'Didn't he stand down at the last General Election?'

'He did. He was given a life peerage, but his father died last year and Hamilton-Browne inherited his title. He is now the Earl of Portmore.'

'Is he still in the Government?'

'No. But in Nineteen-Seventy he was a minister in the Cabinet Office.'

'I don't understand.'

'In Nineteen-Seventy Hamilton-Browne signed off an XPD order for an IRA killer called Dermot O'Neill. I dug that order out from the department's archives. I took a photocopy of the document and doctored it so the form was made out in Cole's name.'

'That's brilliant, boss!' he exclaimed.

'Maybe, but not strictly kosher. So let's keep it to ourselves?'

'Don't worry, I won't even tell my budgie.'

I glanced at him. 'What are you talking about?' I asked. At first I thought he was joking. I was wrong.

'I tell my budgie everything,' he said with a blush and I realised he was serious. 'I always talk to Mercury when I get home from work. It helps me to unwind.'

'Mercury?' I asked. 'What sort of name is that for a bloody bird?'

'I named him after Freddie Mercury.'

'You named him after Freddie Mercury?' I asked weakly.

'Yes. He's lead singer of Queen,' he explained. 'They're a pop group.'

'I know Queen, Timmy,' I said with a sigh. 'But, I sometimes wonder whether I know you.'

Chapter 11

Downing Street, London, Wednesday 4th April

Our meeting with the Prime Minister was at 11:00 hours. Margaret Thatcher was a stickler for good time keeping so we left the office at 10:45 to walk the short distance up Whitehall to Downing Street.

'Are you sure Cole was in cahoots with Butler?' Disraeli-Astor asked. My boss is the only person I know who would use the word cahoots in conversation.

'Yes. They were working together alright,' I confirmed.

'And Cole admitted the Irishman paid him five hundred pounds to pretend to be ill?'

'Well it would have been difficult for him to deny pulling a sickie for money, because we had a copy of both their bank statements,' I pointed out as we reached the security checkpoint at the entrance to Downing Street.

'So, Cole did it for money, not ideology?' He asked as he showed his government security pass to the policemen who was guarding the gate.

I had forgotten to bring my official parliamentary pass, so instead I flashed my forged Met Police warrant card and was nodded through with barely a glance at it.

'I don't believe Cole is a member of the IRA, if that's what you mean,' I said in answer to Disraeli-Astor's question.

'But you think Butler is?'

'Yes, he told Cole he was a member of the Ulster Defence Force, but I'm certain that was a lie.' I told him why. 'And I don't think William Butler is his real name.' I added.

We reached Number 10 and Disraeli-Astor knocked on the iconic shiny black painted door. 'Explain,' he said, so I did.

'I sent Melissa to Scotland Yard,' I added as the door swung open. 'She's looking through the Special Branch mugshots to see if she can find out Butler's real identity.'

'Morning, Colonel,' the policeman who was on duty in the entrance hall greeted the D-G with a friendly smile and a smart salute.

'Morning, George. How's your boy doing?'

'He's just been promoted. Three stripes now,' the policeman said.

'Does he still have his heart is set on becoming regimental sergeant major?'

'He does indeed, sir.'

'Like father, like son. Eh, George?'

'Och, aye. I'll be the proudest ex-para in the world if he makes it.'

'George was my regimental sergeant major,' Disraeli-Astor explained.

'I take it you're here to see the PM, Colonel?' The policeman asked.

'That's right. I assume the meeting is in the Green Room?'

'I haven't been told differently, sir.'

'Very well. We'll head there.'

'Of course, you'll know your way, sir?'

'Yes, George. Thank you.' We headed for the door that took us through to the inner entrance hall. 'I sometimes miss my army days,' Disraeli-Astor said nostalgically. We made our way up the Grand Staircase, the wall of which was full of pictures of past prime ministers. 'Life in the regiment was so…'

'Regimented?' I suggested.

'I was going to say orderly.'

People across the world know 10 Downing Street as the home of the British Prime Minister. What many do not appreciate is that there is much more behind that famous black front door than living accommodation.

Although it is true that most prime ministers and their families have resided in Number 10, they occupy only a relatively small apartment on the third floor. The rest of the building is taken up with a variety of offices, conference centres, including one that contains a long coffin-shaped table around which the Cabinet sit for their meetings. There are also a number of drawing rooms, which are situated on the first floor.

It was to one of these drawing rooms that we headed. At one time it had been called the "Blue drawing room", but Margaret Thatcher had it repainted green when she moved into Number 10, so its name changed accordingly.

When we reached our destination, we were met by one of the Prime Minister's aides. She was a tall girl, who wore a narrow skirt and a wide smile.

'Good morning, gentlemen,' she said. 'I'm afraid there's been a change of plan. We have a few more attendees than usual today so the meeting is taking place in the Cabinet Room.'

'It's not a problem,' Disraeli-Astor said with his usual gentlemanly good grace, but I've known him long enough to recognise his irritation at not being advised earlier of the change.

'The PM is already there if you would like to join her. The Cabinet Room is downstairs. Do you know your way?'

'Yes, thank you,' Disraeli-Astor said before turning on his heel and walking back into the White drawing room, through which entry is gained to the smaller Green Room.

'See what I mean? A total cock-up,' he muttered once we were heading back down the stairs. 'That wouldn't happen in the army.'

'Which army is that then?' I asked. 'You surely can't mean the British Army, because I saw my fair share of cock-ups when I was serving with the First Armoured Division in Germany.'

He glared at me, but said nothing.

We soon reached the ante room outside the Cabinet Room, alongside the door of which stood a tall, thick set man in a pin striped suit. He had a chubby florid face, with a mouth that turned down at the corners.

'You found us then Rupert?' He said with a slight upwards twitch of his lips. This might have been an attempt at a smile, but it was hard to tell because there was no corresponding warmth in his dark brown eyes.

'We went to the Green Room,' Disraeli-Astor explained apologetically. 'Nobody told us the venue had changed.'

'Sorry, old boy, but it was a last minute decision,' the man said. He looked at me and studied me with interest. 'You must be the chappie that the Boss asked for.' The man held out his hand. 'Peter Morrison, I'm the Boss's Parliamentary Private Secretary.'

'Pleased to meet you, Peter.' His hand was warm and clammy. I shook it without much enthusiasm. He was somebody for whom I took an instant dislike. It happens sometimes.

'Actually, it is Sir Peter,' he said stiffly.

I am not sure whether he expected me to apologise for my failure to acknowledge his knighthood, if so, he would have been disappointed. 'David Statton,' I introduced myself. 'But I'm just a common old Mister, so you can call me David.'

Morrison stared at me for a few seconds with expressionless eyes, before turning back to Disraeli-Astor. 'Follow me,' he said brusquely. 'We can go straight in.'

The D-G leaned towards me as Morrison disappeared through the door to the Cabinet Room. 'Behave yourself,' he hissed under his breath.

'I'll do my best,' I whispered back. 'But that bloke is just like your mate Dougie. He gets right up my nose.'

As we entered the Cabinet Room Big Ben struck eleven o'clock.

'Welcome gentlemen,' Margaret Thatcher said. 'Please take a seat.'

The Prime Minister was sitting in the only chair in the room with arms and was positioned half way up the left hand side of the long table. It was shaped in a way that allowed her to see everybody else who was sitting at the table, even when holding a full Cabinet meeting with over twenty of her senior ministers present.

Peter Morrison sat down directly behind the Prime Minister, in a seat positioned against the wall next to the grey-marble fire place. There were already a number of other people sitting in seats along the wall. I assumed these were either the parliamentary private secretaries for the cabinet ministers present, or officials from the Cabinet Office.

There were a dozen people sitting at the oval table, some of whom I recognised. To the left of Mrs Thatcher sat the Cabinet Secretary, Sir Robin Butler, and to her right was the Deputy Prime Minister, Sir Geoffrey Howe. Also on that side of the table sat the Chancellor, John Major; the Foreign Secretary, Douglas Hurd; the Home Secretary, David Waddington; and the Secretary of State for Trade and Industry, Nicholas Ridley.

Opposite the Prime Minister sat four people, only one of whom I recognised. That man turned to look at me as we joined them on their side of the table. A smile lit up his black face. 'Good morning, Mister Statton,' Nelson Mandela said in his distinctive deep voice. 'So we meet again.'

I smiled back at him. We had met last in 1982. On that occasion he was sitting in a dark prison cell in the high security prison on Robben Island, from which a group of mercenaries was trying to rescue him, along with a Soviet nuclear scientist, Gregori Zamyatin.

I was the leader of that group.

I wasted precious minutes trying to persuade Mandela to leave his cell and come with us, but my pleas were in vain. He maintained he was more help to the ANC's campaign for political freedom by remaining a high profile prisoner. If he escaped and was forced to flee overseas, he would become just one more exiled opponent of the South African regime. As it turned out, events proved him right.

'Good morning, Mister Mandela,' I returned his greeting. 'It's a pleasure to see you free at last.'

At this point the Prime Minister broke in. 'Down to business, gentlemen,' she said briskly. 'Let me begin by welcoming our friend the United States Ambassador to our meeting. Welcome, sir.'

The man directly to the right of Nelson Mandela nodded his head in acknowledgement, but said nothing.

'And of course, another good friend, the South African Ambassador,' Mrs Thatcher went on.

This time the man on Mandela's left nodded.

'We are pleased both of you could join us on this special occasion.' Mrs Thatcher bestowed on the two men a beaming smile before adding: 'And of course, we are delighted to welcome Mister Mandela to London.'

'I am delighted to be here, Prime Minister,' Mandela replied. 'It provides me with the opportunity to thank you personally for the efforts you took to help secure my release.' He paused and when he spoke again it was in a quieter, almost apologetic voice.

'As you know, many of my colleagues in the ANC are not happy with you because Britain vetoed the economic sanctions proposed by the United Nations. They believe sanctions would help us to defeat Apartheid and deliver justice for the black majority in our country. My colleagues would not be pleased if they knew I was meeting with you.'

'We understand the problems you face, Mister Mandela, and we appreciate the risk you are taking visiting us.'

'But you should understand also, Prime Minister, that I share the concerns of my comrades about your opposition to economic sanctions. Your stance is a great disappointment to me.'

Margaret Thatcher bristled slightly at the ANC leader's criticism. 'That is something on which we will have to disagree, Mister Mandela. Our position is that economic sanctions would hurt hardest the very people for whom you are campaigning, but perhaps it is a subject best left for discussion on another day.'

'I agree,' Mandela said. 'Today is neither the time nor the place for recriminations. Let me just say that despite my strong opposition to your position, I believe the ANC has to be pragmatic. We have to talk with everybody, even those with whom we disagree.'

'Thank you, Mister Mandela. We appreciate what a difficult balancing act it must be to reconcile the views of your more radical colleagues, with your own pragmatism,' Margaret Thatcher said.

Mandela nodded gently. 'But it is a balancing act that must succeed, because we face now yet another threat to peace in our country. That is why I agreed to attend this meeting.'

'We know your attendance here today puts you in a difficult position back home in South Africa, Mister Mandela. So, we propose this meeting remains secret and unminuted. Is that not so, gentlemen?' The PM looked at her Cabinet colleagues. Nobody seemed inclined to argue with her.

'Excellent,' she went on. 'Then it is settled. This meeting didn't take place.' She turned her gaze on Nelson Mandela and smiled at him.

The African acknowledged the PM's gesture by returning her smile with another brief nod of a head on which the crinkly black hair was turning increasingly grey.

'We would now like to welcome to our meeting Colonel Disraeli-Astor and his colleague Mister Statton, who are from the Department for Covert Operations,' Mrs Thatcher explained. 'They are joining us today to brief us on the latest situation regarding the threat to which Mister Mandela referred and which we are here to discuss.'

She turned to my boss. 'Director-General, as you know attendees at our weekly meetings are kept to a minimum, so perhaps I should explain why so many of my colleagues are present today.' She indicated the Cabinet ministers who were sitting alongside her.

'The threat faced by our South African friends is very grave. It has such serious implications for our own national interests that we decided to convene a COBRA committee and hold it at the same time as our planned meeting.'

'What is this cobra committee, Prime Minister?' Asked the South African Ambassador. I had never met the man, but I knew his name was Hendrick Meyer.

'Sorry, Mister Ambassador. I have been struck down by the acronym disease that plagues Whitehall and Westminster. The COBRA to which I refer is not a snake. The first four letters stand for Cabinet Office Briefing Room, but to be honest, I have no idea what the A stands for.'

'It stands for nothing, Prime Minister,' Sir Robin Butler explained. 'Strictly speaking the acronym should be C.O.B.R. It was the media who added the A. I suppose it helps them remember the name.'

He turned to Hendrick Meyer. 'Your Excellency, COBRA is a crisis response committee that is set up from time to time and is chaired by the Prime Minister,' he explained. 'Its purpose is to co-ordinate the actions of various Government departments and other bodies, such as the police, the army or the security services, to deal with a particular emergency situation. The committee includes those Cabinet ministers whose departments have a direct interest in that emergency.'

'Thank you for clarifying that for us, Sir Robin,' Mrs Thatcher said before addressing her wider audience. Her expression was now sombre. 'Gentlemen, what we face, is a real crisis,' she paused as if to let the importance of her words sink in.

'As some of you will know, we have received information confirming that a group of international businessmen, calling themselves the Phoenix Group, are working with the Broederbond and Pan African Council to destabilise the peace process in South Africa. For their plan to work they must first assassinate the leaders of the ANC, starting with Mister Mandela.'

I felt Disraeli-Astor stiffen at this last piece of information. He glanced at me and I gave him a discreet shake of my head. I had no idea how the PM knew about the plot to kill Mandela.

'I understand there have been some questions raised about the veracity of the information to which you refer, Prime Minister,' Douglas Hurd, said.

'What information would that be, Foreign Secretary?' Mrs Thatcher asked. There was an icy tinge to her voice.

'The information gleaned from the Soviet defector by the Home Office interrogators before he died.' Douglas Hurd seemed oblivious to the PM's tone. 'The Minister of State for Home Security briefed me personally. He does not believe there is a plot to assassinate

Mister Mandela, and is not convinced this Phoenix Group even exists. He believes the Russians were behind the defection of the KGB general so that he could supply us with false intelligence.'

David Waddington frowned at his Cabinet colleague. He seemed bemused by this revelation.

'Is that the official position of the Home Office, David?' Margaret Thatcher asked.

'No, Prime Minister. Unfortunately, Douglas Campbell has not yet had a chance to brief me on the last interview session with the Russian,' the Home Secretary said diplomatically. However, he did not look happy that his junior minister had briefed Douglas Hurd before him. 'So we have not yet formed a view as to whether the Russian's information can be trusted.'

'Well, as it happens, the information to which I was referring came not from General Urinoff, but from our American friends.' She turned to the US Ambassador, Henry E Catto Jnr.

'Mister Ambassador, you saw the transcripts from the interviews with the KGB General before he met his tragic death. Would you not agree that he appears to have backed up the information you received from your own sources?'

'He sure did ma'am,' Catto said. 'Although General Urinoff said nothing about the plan to assassinate Mister Mandela, the rest of his story stacks up.'

'Would you like to elaborate?' She invited.

'I think it might be better if I hand over to my military attaché to do that, Prime Minister,' Catto said, gesturing towards the man who sat next to him. 'He has a better grasp of the facts.'

I bet he does, I thought. With his cropped hair, broad shoulders, button down shirt and self-assured demeanour, I guessed the so called "military attaché" was based at the CIA headquarters in Langley, rather than the State Department in Washington.

'I didn't catch your name, Mister, er?' Mrs Thatcher's blue eyes drilled into the younger of the two Americans.

'Bob Fletcher, ma'am,' the attaché said, with a blush turning his cheeks red. He suddenly looked a lot less self-assured. Margaret Thatcher had that effect on some men.

'So, Mister Fletcher, what can you tell us about this business?'

'Well, ma'am, I can confirm the Phoenix Group certainly does exist and one of its leading members is an American businessman who we have been watching for some time.' Fletcher looked at the ambassador who nodded slightly. 'His name is John Engels and he's head of the American and Continental Mining Corporation.'

Disraeli-Astor glanced at me with a frown, as if warning me to say nothing, but I had no intention of confirming our knowledge of Engels. I'm not that stupid.

'Do we know anything about this company, Nicholas?' The PM asked the Trade Secretary.

'To be honest, Prime Minister, I've not heard of it, but I will have somebody put together a dossier for you.'

'We can help with that,' Henry Catto offered. 'I'll have my trade attaché liaise with you, Mister Secretary.'

'Thank you, Mister Ambassador,' Nicholas Ridley said.

'What more can you tell us about this mysterious group, Mister Fletcher?' Mrs Thatcher asked.

'For a start, we believe the Phoenix Group poses a very real threat to the interests of both your country and ours, ma'am,' the military attaché replied. 'It appears determined to achieve its aim.'

'Which is?' The PM asked.

'To take over my country.' It was the South African Ambassador who answered.

'Take over in South Africa? Is that true, Mister Fletcher?'

'It's what we believe, ma'am.'

'And they intend to assassinate Mister Mandela as part of their plan?'

'Yes, ma'am.'

'And you believe they have the means to achieve that?'

'We sure do ma'am. The businessmen behind the Phoenix Group have access to massive resources and are ruthless enough to do anything to achieve their aims. We believe they have already hired a hitman to murder a CIA agent who was embedded in Engels' company.'

'Do you have proof of that?'

'Unfortunately only circumstantial evidence, ma'am. However, we do have a photograph taken in the downstairs lobby of the hotel in which our agent was found dead. We think it's the murderer and we're confident that when we track him down he will provide us with evidence to nail Engels.'

'Can't you just haul in this Engels fellow on suspicion of

conspiracy, or something and question him?' Tom King asked.

'Unfortunately not, sir. John Engels has a lot of political clout and without concrete evidence to prosecute him he's untouchable. Sadly we don't yet have that evidence.'

'Engels has been using his political contacts to put pressure on the Director of the CIA, Bill Webster, in an effort to get the Agency to back off,' the American ambassador interjected.

'Is that political pressure working?' The PM asked.

'No, ma'am,' it was Fletcher who answered. 'But no doubt they will keep trying.'

'We think there is a possibility the killer of your CIA agent might have murdered General Urinoff also,' Disraeli-Astor told Fletcher. 'That photograph you have of the suspected murderer might be useful during our ongoing investigations. Would it be possible to get a copy?'

'No problem, Colonel. If you send somebody along to the embassy tomorrow I'll have a copy ready for you.'

'I'll come,' I offered, guessing my boss would volunteer me for the job anyway. As it happens, I wanted to talk to Fletcher on his own. 'What time would be convenient?'

'I am tied up in meetings all morning, but I'll be available any time after lunch.'

'OK. Let's say fifteen hundred hours.'

'Is there anything else, Mister Fletcher?' Mrs Thatcher asked.

'No, ma'am,' the military attaché said.

'Very well, gentlemen,' she went on. 'It seems quite clear that this Phoenix Group is planning to destabilise our friends in South Africa. Does it not, Douglas?' Mrs Thatcher stared at the Foreign Secretary, defying him to contradict her. Sensibly, he kept quiet.

She turned to my boss. 'Colonel, following detailed discussions with their Excellences we have reached a decision.'

That the Prime Minister had met already with the two ambassadors didn't come as a surprise. I guessed she knew more about the South African situation than she had let on.

'What did you decide, Prime Minister?' Disraeli-Astor asked.

'That we must defeat this Phoenix Group using whatever means are available and with whatever force is required.' She gave my boss a knowing look and repeated: 'Whatever force is required. Do I make myself clear, Colonel?'

'Very clear, Prime Minister,' he said.

'Good,' Mrs Thatcher said.

'The United States Government will offer any help needed by your security services to track down and defeat these people, Prime Minister,' Henry Catto said. 'The President has agreed to put at your disposal all of the resources of the CIA.'

'That is very reassuring, Ambassador. I am sure Colonel Disraeli-Astor will take you up on your offer should he need it. Please pass on our thanks to Mister Bush.'

'The same goes for my country, Prime Minister,' the South African ambassador assured her. 'Obviously we will do what we can to protect Mister Mandela whilst he is in South Africa, but we are somewhat hamstrung by considerable internal opposition from the Broederbond. Its tentacles stretch into every corner of our country, including our armed forces, police and security services.' Hendrick Meyer paused and looked slightly embarrassed.

'Unfortunately, it is likely any operation we launch will be compromised by those who are opposed to President De Klerk's commitment to peace and reconciliation. It grieves me to admit this, but only an outside agency can tackle that opposition effectively.

'It is for that reason my Government welcomes your involvement and commitment, Prime Minister, and, of course, that of our American friends. President De Klerk has asked me to make clear that should it be necessary for your security services to operate in South Africa, they will receive our full support and co-operation.'

'We are grateful for that reassurance, your Excellency,' Mrs Thatcher said warmly. 'In return, you can be assured the British Government will take whatever steps are needed to protect Mister Mandela and ensure peace in your beautiful country. Now Mister Statton, perhaps you would like to give us the Department for Covert Operations' perspective on this threat from the Phoenix Group.'

I spent the next few minutes explaining what Section Two had been doing and what we had discovered. It included our analysis of the information provided by Urinoff; how we suspected William Butler of murdering him; and how we thought he was operating under an assumed name. I concluded by describing our efforts to discover Butler's real identity; our belief he might be linked to the Phoenix Group; and our efforts to discover his real identity.

I said nothing about what we had found out about the Mandela

Project from John Engels' memorandum.

When I finished, Margaret Thatcher thanked me and then said: 'Mister Statton, it is very important you find out the true identity of General Urinoff's killer as soon as possible. I then want you to hunt him down and find out whether he is in any way connected to this plot to assassinate Mister Mandela.'

'Yes, Prime Minister,' I said.

'I appreciate the expertise of the DFCO, and in particular Section Two,' the Foreign Secretary said quietly. 'But would it not be better to use MI6 for this operation, Prime Minister? It has at its disposal far more resources than Colonel Disraeli-Astor.'

'The same could be said of MI5,' the Home Secretary interjected quickly. 'They could do the job. It seems obvious that much of the ground work will take place in the UK, which is our territory, rather than MI6.'

Margaret Thatcher looked from one to the other of her colleagues. 'You are quite right gentlemen. However, Mister Mandela has specifically asked that Mister Statton takes the lead role in the operation to track down those who are threatening him.'

'I have a good reason for my request, Prime Minister,' Mandela chipped in. 'Several years ago Mister Statton led a team that tried to rescue me from prison on Robben Island. He glanced at me and smiled.

'I was very impressed with the way he conducted himself that night,' he went on, 'and I took it upon myself to keep a track of him over the years since then. It will take an extraordinary man to defeat my enemies, Prime Minister. I think Mister Statton is that man.'

'Thank you, Mister Mandela,' Mrs Thatcher said and turned to her two senior Cabinet ministers. So now you understand my problem, gentlemen. Mister Statton works for the Department for Covert Operations, not MI5 or MI6.' She looked thoughtfully across the table at me and then said: 'I suppose the answer is for all three agencies to work together, with the DFCO taking the lead.'

I glanced at Disraeli-Astor, who managed to keep a straight face. 'An excellent suggestion, Prime Minister,' he said. 'It makes a lot of sense. As you know we already work together on the Joint Security Operations Liaison Committee, so I am sure we can come to an arrangement that would allow us to tap into the MI5 and MI6 resources. Perhaps, through the Active Operations Sub-committee we have set up to oversee the operation.' He smiled politely.

Douglas Hurd and David Waddington were not smiling - politely or otherwise - but there was little they could do other than to accept the inevitable. They had been outflanked by the Prime Minister, who, through the DFCO, which reported directly to her, would have sole control over the operation to defeat the Phoenix Group. I was in no doubt that this strategy had already been agreed between her and Disraeli-Astor.

'There is one further thing I have to report,' Mrs Thatcher said. 'Mister Mandela will be returning to London later this month. On that occasion his presence in our country will not be a secret. He will be attending a pop-concert being organised in his honour.

'He will be arriving in London on the fifteenth of April, which is Easter Sunday. The concert itself will take place on Easter Monday and Mister Mandela will leave Britain on Tuesday the seventeenth.'

She turned to the Home Secretary. 'David, I want the Metropolitan Police Special Branch to take the lead when it comes to protecting Mister Mandela while he is our guest. It is quite possible the Phoenix Group will use his attendance at the concert as an opportunity to assassinate him. I want the very tightest security operation to be mounted at Wembley Stadium. Is that understood?'

'Yes, Prime Minister,' David Waddington said, looking more cheerful now that Special Branch had been made the lead agency.

'Mister Statton,' Mrs Thatcher said.

'Yes, Prime Minister.'

'I am impressed with your record and have a special role for you. Although Special Branch will be in charge of security for Mister Mandela's visit, I would like you to visit Wembley on the day of the concert and check the right security measures are in place to protect him.'

'I am sure the Met Police will ensure Mister Mandela is kept safe, Prime Minister,' the Home Secretary insisted, looking less cheerful now.

'That might well be the case, David, however, it will do no harm Mister Statton double checking, will it? Belts and braces and all that.'

'Yes, Prime Minister,' Waddington said.

'Yes, Prime Minister,' I echoed and with that the meeting was over.

'**Did** you notice Geoffrey Howe and John Major kept very quiet during the meeting?' Disraeli-Astor asked as we left 10 Downing Street and headed back to the office.

'Yes, what's that all about?'

'Let's just say that Mrs T needs to watch her back,' he said.

'You think they're out to get her?'

'So rumour has it.'

'I know that Howe and the PM have had a strained relationship for years,' I said.

'Which wasn't helped when she moved him from the Foreign Office last year. He loved being Foreign Secretary and he resented being replaced by John Major, who had only been a Cabinet minister for two years, and a junior one at that.'

'So Howe is one of those plotting against the PM?'

'Yes.'

'But what about Major? He owes his current position to Mrs T? Surely he would show some sort of loyalty to her?'

'Oh, there is no doubt John Major is loyal to the PM and I don't think he would ever stand against her in an open contest. However, loyalty in politics is often only skin deep. The word in the Commons' tea rooms is that Major is lining himself up as the unity candidate should Mrs T be forced to stand down.'

He went silent as we passed a group of tourists.

'How did Hurd know about the threat to Mandela?' He asked eventually when we could no longer be overheard.

'Your mate Campbell told him.'

'I know that. But how did Dougie find out?'

'I suspect Wren tipped him off.'

'What did he promise Sir Reggie in return?'

'Your guess is as good as mine.'

'What a treacherous blighter!'

I didn't disagree.

'There is something I don't understand,' I said.

'What's that?'

'Why did Campbell brief Douglas Hurd and not his boss? It made the Home Secretary look out of touch and incompetent.'

'You have just answered your own question,' he replied. 'As I told you before, Dougie hankers after David Waddington's job. I dare say showing him up was part of his game plan.'

'And I thought being a field agent was a dirty business,' I said. 'It seems to me that politics is even dirtier.'

Disraeli-Astor didn't argue with me and we lapsed into silence again as we reached the end of Downing Street and made our way through the tall black steel gates that had been installed the previous year.

Beyond the gates, groups of tourists gawped towards 10 Downing Street where a succession of Cabinet ministers came out of the door, clambering into long black limousines that were waiting to whisk them back to their offices.

'Did you notice what Nelson Mandela called me?' I asked when we reached Whitehall and headed back to our own offices.

'I can't recall his exact words,' Disraeli-Astor lied.

'He asked for me personally and said that I'm an extraordinary man.'

'Oh, that. Don't let it go to your head. He was just being diplomatic.'

'But what about Margaret Thatcher? She said she was impressed with my record and wants me to check up on the Special Branch. That's a real compliment and she's not exactly renowned for diplomacy.'

'I think you will find that she was just re-asserting her authority over the Home Secretary,' he said. 'Anyway, what is this all about?'

'I was thinking. Don't you think having both Mandela and the PM show such confidence in my ability is worth a pay rise?'

'It would be extraordinary if somebody in your position did not have at least a modicum of ability. Perhaps that is what Mister Mandela meant when he called you an extraordinary man.'

'Is that your idea of a joke, boss?'

'Well I did think it was a rather clever play on words.'

'So I take it that your play on words was a long-winded way of saying no more money for me?'

'My dear chap, money is not everything. It's far more satisfying to have a feeling of self-worth.'

'Thanks. I'll remember to tell my bank manager that next time he complains when I exceed my overdraft limit.'

Chapter 12

DFCO offices, Thursday 5th April

When I arrived in the Section Two offices I found Timmy sitting at his desk looking through the paperwork we had for William Butler. I was not feeling at my best. I had a thumping headache and a tickle at the back of my throat that hinted a cold might be on its way.

I picked up the job application form provided by the temping agency. 'I have a question for you.' I tapped the form. 'Did you check this address was the same as the one given you by the security company?'

Timmy shook his head and blushed. 'I didn't think.'

'Do you ever?' I asked tetchily.

'Sorry, sir.'

I handed him the application form. 'So was that the address you visited?'

He glanced at the form. 'Yes,' he said immediately.

'That's a shame. I hoped there was some sort of mistake.'

'Hang on a minute,' Timmy said excitedly. 'That's not right.'

'What's not right?'

'Well it's definitely the same block of flats I went to,' he said. 'But the address I got from the security company was number twelve, this form says number twenty-one.'

'So they sent you to the wrong flat?'

'It looks like it.'

'Then you know what your job is today?'

'Go down to Slough and check out the correct address?'

'You've got it in one.'

He sprang to his feet.

'Whoa!' I said. 'Before you charge off like a bull in a china shop, let me give you a word of warning.'

He sat down again.

'OK, listen to me. I want you to be careful. No heroics. Butler didn't see you when we visited the safe-house, so he doesn't know who you are. If he answers the door pretend to be somebody else.'

'Who?'

'It doesn't matter. Use your initiative. Say you want to sell him home insurance, or that you're from the council checking up on something.'

'Checking up on what?' He asked.

'I don't know. Make it up as you go along.'

He looked troubled. 'Do you have any suggestions, sir?'

'For God's sake, Timmy. Tell him you're conducting a survey. Take a clip board with you and ask him a few questions.'

'What sort of questions?'

I shook my head in despair. Sometimes my deputy pushed my patience to its very limit. 'Ask him anything. Ask him whether he has a problem parking. Ask him whether he's happy with the rubbish collection system. Ask him how much toilet paper he uses each week. I don't care what you ask him. It doesn't matter. It's irrelevant. The important thing to remember is that the object of the exercise at this stage is to identify Butler, not arrest him. Do you at least understand that much?'

'Yes, sir, but would it be alright if I go down to Slough this afternoon?'

'Why?'

'Because I've just had a sudden thought.'

'Alleluia! So you can think for yourself. What is this thought?'

'I'm sorry, sir, but I forgot that I'm driving down to the West Country this evening to see my mother. It's her birthday tomorrow and you gave me the day off so that I could spend a long weekend with her. Remember?'

'Of course I remember,' I lied.

'The thing is, if I check out Butler's address this afternoon, I can head straight down the M4. It would save me time and hassle.'

'Alright,' I agreed. It made a lot of sense and a couple of hours would make no difference one way or another. 'Just as long as you ring me if you discover anything important,' I added, although, in truth, my expectation of him finding any sign of Butler was not very high. If the Irishman had any sense he would have done a runner as soon as he left the safe-house after killing Urinoff.

'Will do, sir,' Timmy said. 'And thank you.'

He sounded so grateful, it made me feel guilty for being irritable with him. 'Good man,' I said. 'Wish your mum a happy birthday for me.'

As soon as Timmy left my office I picked up the telephone. With a meeting at the US Embassy scheduled for 15:00 hours, I decided to kill two birds with one stone. I made a phone call and set up an early afternoon appointment at the South African Embassy in The Strand.

As I put the phone down it rang. It was Colleen Masters.

'Good morning, David.'

'Morning, Colleen. To what do I owe this pleasure?'

'I'm ringing on behalf of the boss.'

'What's wrong with him? Has his index finger dropped off?'

She laughed. 'The D-G doesn't make telephone calls himself. It's what he has a personal assistant for.'

'So what does God want now?'

'He's off soon to a meeting with Jeffery Johnson and he wondered if there was any update on the Mandela Project. He likes to offer the committee a few titbits to keep the members quiet.'

'You can tell him I think we might have located the flat where Butler lived. Timmy is going down to Slough this afternoon to check it out.'

I decided not to mention this was the second time my deputy had visited the block of flats. Disraeli-Astor already thought he was an idiot and it would only have reinforced that opinion. Although, on this occasion it wasn't Timmy's fault he went to the wrong flat. He was given duff information by the security company.

'Anything else?'

'Yes. You'd better remind the boss I'm visiting the American embassy this afternoon. No doubt he will have forgotten.'

'Will he know why you're going to the embassy, or will he have forgotten that as well?'

'Who can tell? But I'll give him the benefit of the doubt and assume he remembers the conversation we had with the American Ambassador. However, if he does look puzzled, tell him I'm meeting the Embassy's military attaché to pick up the photograph he requested.'

'Is that all?' She asked.

'No, I also intend opening up lines of communication with the CIA. In addition, you can tell the boss I've set up a meeting with the South Africans this afternoon as well.'

'Presumably to make contact with their security forces as well?'

'Correct.'

'The D-G will like that,' she said. 'It will show members of the

JSOLC that the department is on the ball.'

'Section Two might be on the ball,' I said. 'But I'm not so sure about the rest of his DFCO empire.'

'I'm sure your foresight and enthusiasm won't go unrecognised by the D-G,' she said.

'What sort of recognition do you have in mind?'

'Perhaps he'll give you a pay rise.'

'Don't make me laugh.' I thought about my conversation with Disraeli-Astor less than 24 hours before. I wondered whether he'd told her about it. He seemed to tell her about everything else. 'Trust me, you could squeeze more blood out of a stone than you can money out of the boss.'

'Sorry, I have to go now, David,' she said quickly. 'I can hear him calling me. He's probably panicking because his meeting is in half an hour and he hasn't yet prepared his brief.' She lowered her voice. 'By the way, I'm looking forward to Saturday night.'

'Me too. What could be better than a nice meal, good company and a decent jazz session?'

'I can think of at least one thing,' she whispered. 'Bring your overnight bag.'

'If you insist.'

'Oh, I do.'

The Strand, London.

It was only a ten minutes brisk walk from the DFCO offices to the Strand and I arrived with plenty of time to spare for my 14:00 hours meeting at the South African Embassy.

'Goeie middag, Meneer Ambassadeur,' I said when I was shown into Hendrick Meyer's office.

'Goeie middag, meneer,' the South African replied with a genial smile. 'En Dankie.' He was standing in the middle of his office. He held out a hand and when I reached for it he grasped it warmly in a two-handed shake. 'Waar het jy my taal geleer?'

I shook my head. 'I'm sorry, but I only understood a couple of those words,' I apologised. 'My knowledge of Afrikaans is limited. I'm afraid we'll have to speak English.'

'There is no need to apologise,' Meyer assured me in impeccable English. 'I am grateful you took the effort to use even a few Afrikaans words. 'I asked where you learned my language.'

153

'I lived with a South African girl for a couple of years.'

'I assume you are referring to Miss Brigette Carlse.'

'You have done your homework,' I said.

'I am sure you would not have expected anything less of me. Is that not so, Mister Statton?'

'It is so.' I smiled. The South African National Intelligence Service had a lengthy dossier on me. No doubt Meyer would have requested a copy of my file the moment he found out I was going to be involved in protecting Nelson Mandela against attacks by the Phoenix Group.

'However, I know Miss Carlse as Freddie,' I explained.

'Freddie?'

'Her full name is Brigette Frederika Carlse. Was that not in the file?'

Meyer shook his head. 'So it was Miss Carlse who taught you Afrikaans?'

'Yes, but she hated speaking it. She is a Cape Coloured and she called it the language of her oppressors.'

'Ja, I have seen her file, although it is not very thick. She is a supporter of the ANC, is she not?'

'I haven't spoken to Freddie for a couple of years, but I can't imagine she will have switched her allegiance. She holds very strong views about the National Party. She believes it was responsible for the death of her twin brother. She will never forgive you.'

'I was not responsible personally for the death of her brother,' the ambassador said quietly. 'As I am sure you understand, Mister Statton.'

'I understand, Mister Ambassador. But Freddie's brother is still dead.'

Meyer looked at me steadily. 'I am not proud of what was done to people of colour in my country,' he said. 'But times are changing and hopefully we can make amends by building a country in which all our people can live in peace and harmony, whatever their colour, race or creed.'

I had done my own research and knew Meyer was from the liberal wing of the National Party, so I believed his penitence was genuine. However, I knew his was not a view shared by many white people in South Africa. 'I hope you're right, Mister Ambassador,' I said.

'So why did Miss Carlse teach you Afrikaans if she hates it so much?' Meyer asked.

'Freddie preferred to speak English, but she sometimes slipped back into speaking Afrikaans, particularly when she was angry.'

'Your Freddie sounds a feisty young woman,' Meyer said with a smile.

'She was, and in case you wondered, she is back in South Africa,' I explained. 'The British climate didn't agree with her.'

'I know the feeling,' Meyer said. 'I sometimes miss the sunshine myself.' He smiled at me. 'Can I offer you a drink, Mister Statton?'

At first I thought he was offering me tea or coffee, but then I saw he was pointing at a drinks cabinet standing against the far wall.

'That would be nice, but you'd better make it a small one,' I said. 'I'm off to the US Embassy after this meeting and our American cousins can be irritatingly puritanical.'

'So what would you like?'

'Do you have a brandy?'

'Of course,' Meyer said as he opened the drinks cabinet. 'Ten years old KWV. Will that be OK?'

'That will be very much OK, thank you, sir.'

Meyer poured brandy into two balloon glasses and passed one to me. I held my glass up and saw that it was quarter full.

He looked at me anxiously. 'Have I poured you enough,' he asked as he sat down behind his desk and waved me into a seat opposite. 'You did say you only wanted a small one.'

'More than enough,' I assured him. 'I'm pleased you didn't give me a large measure.'

He smiled at me again. 'So what can I do for you, Mister Statton?'

'You told Mrs Thatcher that the influence of the Broederbond stretches into every part of South African society, including the police and armed forces.'

'Yes, and it presents a real problem to the future of my country. This business with the Phoenix Group has highlighted how important it is that my government addresses with some urgency the threat posed by the Broederbond.' He looked at me over the rim of his glass. 'But you still have not told me what you want.'

'I need somebody trustworthy in your security forces with whom I can liaise.'

155

'I was prepared for that,' he said and pulled open a drawer in his desk. 'I have just the person for you.' He took a slip of paper from the drawer and handed it to me. It bore the name and a telephone number of a senior South African police officer.

'Brigadier Alan Pienaar,' I read. 'Is he a member of the Broederbond?'

'No. Although Pienaar has an Afrikaans father, his mother was English. That makes him ineligible. Anyway, Pienaar is a decent lad and I don't think he would join the Broederbond even if he was invited.'

'Does he support what your Government is trying to achieve?'

'Yes.'

'So he can be trusted?'

'He is an honest policeman,' he assured me. 'Now drink up, or I will think you do not like our South African brandy.' He smiled. 'And I would look upon that as an insult, Mister Statton.'

Not wishing to provoke a diplomatic incident I got stuck into his fine 10 years old KWV.

Grosvenor Square, London

When I arrived at the US Embassy in Grosvenor Square, Bob Fletcher met me in its vast foyer. Under his left arm he carried a box file. 'Good to see you again, Mister Statton,' he said.

'Now we're away from the brass I think we can manage first name terms. Don't you, Bob?' I held out a hand.

'That's cool with me, Dave.' He shook my hand. 'Come on, I've booked a meeting room for us just down the corridor.'

'Your ambassador told us that we will have access to CIA support,' I said as Fletcher ushered me into a small meeting room. 'So who'll be my CIA contact, Bob?'

'It will be me, but you probably guessed that.'

'I had a hunch,' I admitted. 'I've never met a military attaché yet who actually served in the armed forces.'

'Not an accusation you can pin on me, pal,' he said with a laugh. 'I was in the Marines before I joined the Firm.'

'In that case, I take it back. It will be a pleasure dealing with you.'

'The same goes for me. I've heard all about you from one of our field agents.'

'Who's that?'

'Hank Graham. He reckons you're one cool dude.'

'You know Hank?'

'Yeah, we go way back. He's one of the good guys.'

'How's he doing?'

'The last time I saw him he was at the Firm's training college lecturing on international affairs.'

'Which one of your suits had that bright idea?'

He shrugged. 'I don't know, but he was seriously pissed off.'

'I'm not surprised. Hank is a fine field agent, but he'd be like a fish out of water in an administrative role.'

'Rumour has it he upset somebody on the top floor at Langley. They have him marked down as a loose cannon.'

'Well that loose cannon saved my life, so pass on my regards when next you bump into him.'

'It will be a pleasure,' Fletcher said with a smile. He took a brown envelope from his box file and slid it across the table to me. 'That's our hotel murder suspect.'

I opened the envelope and took out a grainy black and white photograph. It showed a man dressed in grey trousers, a white shirt, black tie and a dark coloured waistcoat on which was stitched the logo of the hotel. In his hand he was carrying a small bag. Behind the man were the open doors of a lift, from which it looked as if he had just emerged.

'A hotel porter?' I asked.

'That's what he would have us believe. That's the hotel's uniform he's wearing,' Fletcher replied.

'But you have your doubts?'

'Yeah. Big doubts, which is why we think he's our man.'

'Why the doubts?' I asked.

'Because nobody at the hotel recognises him. He's not a member of the hotel staff and he wasn't booked in as a guest.'

I studied the face of the suspect. The man was young, with a round, smooth face and cropped hair. I was disappointed. I had hoped the suspect would be William Butler, but the face in the photograph was not one I recognised. 'How was the victim killed?' I asked.

'He was shot, but no weapon was found.'

'Perhaps the gun was in the bag he's carrying?' I tapped the photograph.

'Yeah. That's what we think.'

'No clues to his identity?'

'Only that he wasn't an American.'

'How do you know?'

'One of the chamber maids remembers going up in the lift with the perp and passed the time of day with him. He got out of the lift a couple of floors before she did. He didn't say much, but she thinks he had a Scotch accent.'

'How would she know that?'

'She once dated somebody from Glasgow.'

'Why didn't the maid raise the alarm?'

'Because she had only been employed at the hotel for a week. She thought the guy was a member of staff she hadn't met.'

I slipped the photograph back in the envelope and tucked it into the inside pocket of my jacket. 'OK, we'll check it out,' I said.

'Something else has cropped up that might be of interest you,' Fletcher said.

'What have you got?'

'A full list of the members of the Phoenix Group.'

'That is definitely of interest.'

He took a sheet of paper from his file and passed it to me.

'Where did you get this from?'

'It was in a briefcase that we acquired.'

'You acquired?'

'Yeah, we were approached by somebody offering to sell it.'

'And of course you didn't ask where it came from?'

'Would you have asked if the briefcase had been sold to you?'

'No,' I replied honestly. 'Who did the negotiations?'

'Me.'

'So you saw the seller?'

'We met in an alley and it was dark, but yeah, I saw him.'

'Did he have long hair and a bushy beard?' I asked.

'As I said it was dark, but yeah, I'm certain he had a beard.'

'I think that was our Irishman. William Butler.'

'Was he the guy that totalled the Ruskie?'

'That's what we think. He must have killed Urinoff so he could steal the briefcase.' I put the list of names in the envelope with the photograph so I could study it at my leisure.

Fletcher passed me a card on which were printed his contact details. 'I have been instructed to give you whatever co-operation you need,' he said. 'You can ring me at any time on one of those numbers.'

'Thanks. Is there anything else?'

'Just one thing. Engels.'

'What about him?'

'Well, should defeating the Phoenix Group necessitate extreme action, we wouldn't lose any sleep if he was part of any collateral damage.'

'You want him dead?'

'Yeah. We're pretty sure he ordered the murder of our agent so we have a score to settle.'

'Why don't you take Engels out?'

'The Firm doesn't do things like that anymore.'

I raised a questioning eyebrow, but Fletcher ignored it. 'Then why not use a third party to do your dirty work? You have no shortage of hitmen in the States.'

'We would prefer if nothing happened to Engels in America.'

'I see,' I said. 'The President wants to keep his hands clean.'

'You're learning the ways of the paleface, Tonto.'

'You mean, like Kimosabe, he speak with forked tongue?'

'You're sharp, Dave.'

'You don't need to be a psychic to read George Bush's mind.'

I stood up to leave and then thought of something. 'Talking of Engels; it would be good to know exactly how much influence he has over the other members of the Phoenix Group.'

'I'll see what we can dig up,' Fletcher agreed as he escorted me out of the meeting room and along the corridor to the exit. 'If we find out anything more about him, I'll let you know.'

DFCO offices.

It was well past four o'clock when I arrived back in my office. After negotiating the delivery of a mug of coffee with Poppy I sat down at my desk and took the photograph of the hotel killer and the list of Phoenix Group members from the envelope. I put them side by side on the desk.

The list of names was of particular interest. It showed how wide the Group's influence stretched. There were representatives from countries across the world, including businessmen from Europe, Australasia, Africa, Asia and North and South America.

This was a list of the world's big hitters. But despite the interesting list of names, my attention kept being drawn back to the photograph of the suspected murderer of the CIA agent. There was something about it that niggled with me. Something I was missing.

Half an hour later Melissa came striding into my office. 'Nothing,' she said without preamble.

'Nothing?' I looked up from the photograph.

'I found nothing about Butler in the Special Branch files.'

'I gathered that's what you meant. So, what you did find.'

'Nothing.'

'Don't keep saying that, Melissa. Explain yourself.'

'OK. I've just spent two days going through six thousand four hundred and twenty one photographs of suspected IRA members and active supporters, looking for a match with William Butler and I found none. The nearest I found were these. What do you think?'

She laid a dozen photographs on my desk next to the one that was already there. All of them depicted men with beards, only one of which I recognised. It was not Butler.

I tapped the photo I recognised. 'That's Gerry Adams,' I said. 'But he's not our man. The guy we're looking for had longer hair and a bushier beard.'

Melissa was staring down at the photograph that Bob Fletcher gave me. She picked it up to get a closer look. 'I've seen him before,' she said.

'Where?'

'In the Special Branch mugshot book.'

'You remember his face out of six thousand photos?'

'I don't remember his face, but I do remember seeing a man whose ear had the lobe missing.'

'A missing ear lobe,' I said, taking the photo from her. I looked closer at the man's face. Melissa was right. His left ear had no lobe. I had missed it. That's when something finally clicked in my mind. 'Do you have the photograph of Butler?' I asked.

'Yes, it's in my handbag.' She rummaged around and eventually pulled out a photo. She passed it to me.

I compared Butler's bearded face with that of the smooth faced suspected hotel murderer. At first glance there was no resemblance, but when you looked closely they both had the same cold eyes, the same thin lips and the same small scar across the bridge of the nose. 'The bastard,' I hissed.

'Boss?'

'It's the same man,' I said.

'How do you know?'

I pointed out the facial similarities. 'In addition, Cole told me that he saw Butler with his hair tied back in a ponytail,' I explained. 'Not only that, but Cole noticed his ear lobe was missing. Butler claimed it was bitten off during a fight in prison. Do you know what I think, Melissa?'

'What?'

'I think the little shit was wearing a wig and false beard when I saw him at the safe-house.'

'What makes you think that?' Melissa asked.

'Because this was taken at the beginning of March.' I tapped the photo of the suspected killer of the CIA agent. 'That photograph,' I tapped the photo of Butler, 'was taken at the end of March. No way could his hair and beard have grown that quickly.'

'I see what you mean,' she said.

I tapped the first photo again. 'There's something else,' I said. 'A maid at the hotel chatted to the porter and said she thought he had a Scottish accent. She was wrong; it was Northern Irish.'

'They're very similar accents,' she said.

'They are indeed.' I smiled at her. 'You've done well again.'

'Thanks,' she said and returned my smile. 'I suppose this means I've got to trawl through the mugshots again to find the guy with half an ear?'

'I'm afraid so, but at least this time you know the person you're looking for is definitely there somewhere.'

'That's what I like about you, boss,' she grinned. 'You have this capacity to make jobs sound easy.'

'If you work very hard, it's a skill you might acquire when you're as old as me, young lady.'

'OK. I'll head back to Scotland Yard. See you in a couple of days.'

'Don't be a pessimist. You might find our Van Gogh impersonator quicker than you think.'

She gave me a sceptical look and left my office shaking her head.

As Melissa disappeared Poppy came in carrying a mug of coffee and a paper plate on which sat a large slice of cake.

'What's that?' I asked.

'Carrot cake,' she said. 'It's Rosie's birthday today.'

'Who is Rosie?'

'She's the girl from the cypher room with the big bum and bad teeth. You must know her.'

'Happily not. I try to avoid the cypher room whenever possible, so I have no idea who Rosie is, or what she looks like. However, she doesn't exactly sound tasty.'

'Perhaps not, but the cake is,' Poppy said as she went out.

She was right. The carrot cake was delicious. I studied the photo of the hotel killer as I ate the cake, sipped my coffee and wondered how Timmy was getting on in Slough.

Chapter 13

The DFCO offices, Friday 6th April

My Friday morning started off with a meeting with Disraeli-Astor. He was at his most irritatingly pedantic. He insisted I repeat almost word for word my discussions with Heinrich Meyer and Bob Fletcher.

'So, what you are saying is that Fletcher is really a CIA agent and not a military attaché?' He asked.

My boss still had a lot to learn about the espionage game. 'Very few military attachés are worthy of the name,' I explained patiently. 'Foreign embassies use that title because the Marshall of the Diplomatic Corps is very unlikely to accept diplomatic papers submitted to the Court of St James by somebody listed as a spy.'

'Are you telling me that military attachés are really spies?'

'Yes.'

'Does the Foreign Office pass our spooks off as attachés?'

'Of course. We Brits introduced the concept of diplomatic deceit to the world.'

'I didn't know that,' he admitted.

'That's because you've spent most of your working life as a soldier and not a diplomat or a spook.'

'And the fellow in this photograph killed a CIA agent?'

'That's what the Yanks think.'

'And you believe he did for poor old Urinoff also?'

'That's exactly what I believe.' I agreed, although I didn't think the KGB general was either particularly poor or old.

'We must find out who this Irishman really is and track him down.'

'Strangely enough, I heard the Prime Minister say almost the same thing on Wednesday.'

'Yes, of course she did. So, what are we doing about it?'

'Well, I don't know about you, but I sent Melissa to Scotland Yard to go through the Special Branch mugshot book of IRA suspects. I sent Timmy down to Slough yesterday afternoon to check out the address we have for Butler.'

'And what did young Fisher find out?'

'His name is Fraser,' I corrected him, 'and I don't know. I told him to ring me if he discovered anything important. He didn't contact me, so I can only assume he found nothing.'

'That's disappointing,' Disraeli-Astor said.

'Not to me. It was always a long shot. I suspect Butler is long gone.'

He stroked his scar thoughtfully. 'That means our only hope is that Melissa comes up with the Irishman's real identity?'

'That about sums it up.'

'How confident are you that she will find him?'

'Very confident,' I replied and explained why.

'What happens when she identifies him? Do we put out an APB?'

'An APB?'

'All-Points Bulletin.'

'You've been watching too many American crime programmes, boss. We don't say that in Britain.'

'But presumably we contact the ports and airports and ask them to look out for our man?'

'What's with this "we" you keep using?'

'OK, do you contact the ports and airports?'

'No, I put out an ATM.'

'What's an ATM?'

'It stands for Ask-the-Met.'

'You're making it up,' he said. 'An ATM is a bank cash dispenser.'

'I can't pull the wool over your eyes can I, boss?'

'Very funny. Now answer my question.'

'I told you. I'll ask the Met. I have a direct line to somebody on the top floor at New Scotland Yard. I'm sure he'll help.'

'Do we really need to involve the police?'

'Yes. They will be able to contact all the other agencies and co-ordinate things far better than Section Two can.'

'That doesn't say much for your team,' he said.

'No, but it does reflect the relative resources of our two organisations,' I replied. 'The Commissioner has over twenty-seven thousand people at his disposal. I have three.'

He looked at me and sighed deeply. 'We've had this conversation before. I know the section is understrength, but...'

'Understrength is an understatement,' I interjected. 'When I came back to the department three years ago there were eight people working for Section Two. Now the team consists of a wet behind the ears university graduate with the common sense of a dead ant. We also have a brilliant researcher who is due to be transferred to the Foreign Office within weeks. Oh yes, don't let's forget a secretary who can only type with two fingers and got her job because of family connections.'

'I don't think that's entirely fair on your team,' he said.

'You keep mentioning my team? I don't recall having had any input into the interview process for any of them. Was there one?'

'I accept that Section Two is short of manpower,' he sought to mollify me and at the same time avoid answering my question. 'But, as I was about to point out, the Cabinet Office has put a block on recruitment. Anyway, I have always made clear that in an emergency you will be allocated spare departmental staff from other sections.'

'So what constitutes an emergency?' I asked. 'And exactly how many spare staff are available? The last time I checked, DFCO had only forty-six people on its books, including management and security guards.'

'Forty-seven actually,' he insisted.

'Sorry, did I forget to include Doris the cleaner.'

'Don't be sarcastic.'

'That's very difficult sometimes,' I said. This provoked a glare, which I ignored. 'Look, the staff shortage in Section Two is impeding our investigations. Surely that constitutes an emergency?'

He nodded slowly. 'Well tackling the Mandela Project is certainly very important, so I suppose the answer is yes.'

'Are there any spare bods in the department I can use?'

'I'll see what I can do,' he promised, before changing the subject. 'Now about this list. Do you recognise any of these people?' He then proceeded to read the names out slowly, as if I hadn't already had a chance to look at them.

'John Derwent Engels, American; Maurice Sevier, French; Jonathan Rhodes, South African; Helmut von Behring, German; Sir Reginald Wren, British …'

'I know him,' I hoped my interruption would stem the flow of names, but he ignored me and pressed on.

'Franz Keller, Swiss; Jacobus van Noort, Dutch; Roberto Giannini, Italian; Richard Baker, Australian; Sunil Patel, Indian;

Grigory Fradkov, Ukrainian; Randolph D Robinson, American; Henri Dumas, French; Brendan O'Leary, Irish…'

It was about then that I switched off and allowed him to chunter on for another few minutes.

'Well?' He asked when he had finally finished reading the long list of names. 'Recognise any of those names?'

'Only Engels and Wren, but I'll get Melissa and Timmy to check the rest of them out on Monday and put together a briefing note for you.'

That made him happy. 'Good! Good!' He rubbed his hands together in anticipation. He loved briefing notes, did the D-G.

'Of course, the list does clear up a couple of things,' I said, pulling a copy of the Mandela Project memo from my file. 'For instance, one of the people who appears to be pivotal to the conspiracy is this MS. I think we can assume those are the initials of the Frenchman, Maurice Sevier.'

'That makes sense,' Disraeli-Astor agreed.

'Then there's Sir Reggie Wren, who no doubt is the SRW mentioned in the memo. Finally, there is BOL, which must refer to Brendan O'Leary. Engels claims that it was BOL who recommended the killer, which makes sense if he is an IRA hitman as we suspect. I'll make sure Timmy checks him out first.'

'One thing puzzles me,' Disraeli-Astor said. 'In his debrief interview Urinoff claimed he had documentary evidence to prove the involvement of a number of influential people in the British Establishment and it was locked away in his briefcase. Where is that evidence?'

'Good question.'

'Surely it would have been with this list that the Yanks gave you? Did Fletcher not mention it?'

'No, but that is not altogether surprising.'

'How so?'

'Because the Yanks will want to keep that information to themselves for future use.'

'For use how?'

'As leverage should they need our co-operation at some time in the future and the Government was reluctant to give it.'

He looked shocked. 'Would the Yanks really do that?'

'Of course.'

'But is it likely to happen?'

'Very likely. Let me give you a for instance. We know there is trouble brewing in the Middle East. Saddam Hussein is making all sorts of threats against Kuwait. What happens if the current tension leads to war? George Bush has made clear that the Americans would step in and support the Kuwaitis. What if they ask for our help?'

'The Foreign Office would not be happy. They are totally opposed to any British military action in the region.'

'Exactly, but they would change their minds like a shot if the Americans threatened to release information that would embarrass leading members of the Establishment, of which members of the Government and mandarins in Whitehall form part.'

'That would be diplomatic blackmail.'

'Yes.'

'Would the Yanks really do that?' He asked again.

'I've just said they would.'

'But they are our oldest allies.'

'No they're not,' I contradicted him. 'That privilege belongs to the Portuguese. The Anglo-Portuguese Alliance dates back to the Fourteenth Century. That is four hundred years before the United States even gained its independence from Britain.'

'Now you're splitting hairs,' he protested. Pot and kettle sprang to mind. 'Oldest or not, they are still our ally.'

'Let me tell you something, boss. The Yanks are only our ally when it suits their national interest. I don't recall them helping us much during the Falklands War. Do you?'

'That is true,' he said before lapsing into silence. 'So what happens now?' He asked eventually.

'Well for a start we pray to God that we catch Butler, or whatever his real name is, before he kills anybody else.'

What I didn't know was that we were already too late.

When I left Disraeli-Astor's office, Colleen Masters looked up from her desk and smiled. It was a nice smile. 'I meant it about looking forward to tomorrow night,' she said.

'Me too,' I replied.

She handed me a buff file. 'Here's today's post for you.'

'I didn't realise I was so popular.'

'It's actually the D-G's post,' she explained.

'I was being facetious.'

'He seemed to think you were keen to deal with it for him.'

'So, when does our boss think I am going to do his bloody paperwork, when I don't have enough time to do my own?'

'You might have more time when you get your extra staff,' she said with a smile.

'What extra staff?'

'He's drafting in three people from other sections, including the deputy head of the Europe desk.'

'Des Hobbins?'

'Yes.'

'Are you sure?'

'Of course. Why do you doubt me?'

'Because Des is experienced and competent. I'm not used to such benevolence from above.'

'You don't give the D-G enough credit.'

'That's hardly surprising.'

'What do you mean?'

'I mean that I've just come from his office. Why didn't he mention the extra staff to me?'

'You were probably being your usual bolshie self,' she said with another smile. 'The D-G doesn't respond well to belligerence and unwanted pressure.'

I stared at her. Obviously, I didn't know our boss as well as I thought I did. I would have to bear that in mind for future occasions.

When I arrived back in the Section Two office the only person there was Poppy. She was painting her finger nails.

'I see you're busy,' I said.

'Very,' she replied with no hint of irony. 'I have to concentrate because it's delicate work getting the top coat perfectly smooth.'

'I'm sure the worry must give you sleepless nights. Perhaps you should give up your day job and spend more time pampering yourself.'

'I'd like to do that, boss,' she said. 'But I need the money.'

I gave up. There was probably a cutting response to this comment, but I was temporarily at a loss to think of one.

I retreated to my office and dumped the file containing Disraeli-Astor's paperwork into my new in-tray. I sat and stared at it for a couple of minutes and then decided it was a job that could wait until Des Hobbins joined my team.

I picked up the file and scribbled on its cover: For the attention of Des Hobbins. Satisfied, I slipped it into my desk drawer.

Chapter 14

The Blue Oyster Club, Soho, London, Saturday 7th April
I took Colleen to La Trattoria for dinner. It was an Italian restaurant in Soho that was handily situated close to the Blue Oyster Club. It was just how I like them: small and intimate. It also had on its menu some of the best seafood dishes in London.

'You certainly know how to pick restaurants,' Colleen said as we left La Trattoria and strolled arm in arm towards the jazz club. 'My prawn Tagliolini Gratinati was to die for.'

The weather was unseasonably warm for early April, which enhanced the feeling of well-being brought on by the good food and the bottle of chilled Soave which accompanied it.

'Good evening, Mister Statton,' the doorman said as he let us through the front door of the Blue Oyster and ushered us into the club. In the basement, the jazz band was already playing. The saxophonist was no Stan Getz, but he was making a reasonable fist of *Here's That Rainy Day*.

'Evening, Herbie.'

The doorman waved to a waitress who sashayed over to us. 'Good to see you again, Mister Statton,' she said with a broad smile.

I recognised her. 'You too, Ruby.'

'There is a table reserved for you,' she said. 'This way.'

As we reached the table, and were taking our seats, Manny appeared, with a lit cigarette in one hand and a bottle of champagne in the other. He put the wine in a chiller filled with ice that was already standing alongside our table. He grabbed Colleen's hand, kissed it gently and then declared: 'It's always good to greet my friend David,' he said, 'but today is special, because he has such a beautiful lady with him.'

'That is very sweet of you, Mister Silver,' Colleen said with a smile.

'You must call me Manny,' the club owner insisted, still clutching her hand. 'David is very lucky.'

'Out of interest, Manny. When was the last time you had your eyes tested?' I asked him.

Colleen pretended to look cross.

'Oy vey!' Manny exclaimed. 'See how you have upset your lady friend. Did your mama not teach you better manners than that, David?'

'Sadly not,' I replied. 'But she did warn me to not let any of my lady friends within a hundred paces of smooth-talking *alte kackers* like you.'

Manny dropped Colleen's hand and covered his heart with his own. 'I am mortified that you would think such a thing of me.'

'Of course you are, Manny.'

He winked at me and I smiled back at him.

'I will leave you to enjoy the music and fizz,' Manny said. He gave a little bow and wandered off to talk to more of his customers.

'It was nice to be chatted up,' Colleen said. 'It doesn't happen often.'

'Don't get too excited,' I warned her as I poured two glasses of champagne. 'Manny bats for the other side.' I handed her a glass,

'You mean he's gay?'

'Yes.'

She sniffed her champagne thoughtfully. 'What's an alte kacker?' She asked eventually.

'It's Yiddish for an old fart.'

'That's not very complimentary. Doesn't Manny mind you being rude about him?'

'Don't worry about him. We understand each other,' I said as I offered her my champagne glass.

She clinked her own glass against mine.

'Cheers,' I said. 'To future friendship.'

'I'll certainly drink to that,' she said.

'Although your boss won't approve of us meeting like this.'

'It's none of the D-G's business,' she said sharply.

'I take it that he's spoken to you?'

'Yes, in his usual gentlemanly fashion.'

'Let me guess; he told you that fraternisation between staff is frowned on?'

'Yes. Did he lecture you too?'

'He did.'

'What did you say?'

'I told him to get stuffed.'

'Really?'

'Not in so many words, but he got the message.'

We sipped our champagne and enjoyed the music that drifted up from the basement. The quartet had been joined by a female singer who was singing *On the Sunny Side of the Street*. I heard Colleen's foot tapping to the beat on the floor under the table.

'I need to pop to the loo,' she said when the song had finished. She looked round the room.

'It's in the far corner.' As I pointed the way, the lights in the club dimmed, making the smoke-filled room even darker.

Colleen weaved her way through the tables to the toilet. Seconds later Manny sidled over to my table.

'David, I need a word with you in private.' He took a long drag on his latest cigarette.

'What is it, Manny?'

He blew a long plume of smoke into the air before replying in a whisper: 'You remember the blonde woman in those dodgy photos I found in the peter you got me to open?'

'Yes. What about her?'

'I've seen her again.'

'Are you sure?'

'Is the Chief Rabbi a Jew? Of course I'm sure.'

'Where did you see her?'

'Here in the club,' he replied, lighting another cigarette from the glowing embers of his last one. He stubbed the fag end out in the metal ashtray that lay on top of my table, and on which was printed the picture of a sailing ship above the name *Senior Service*.

'We live in a free country, and you run a great club.'

'Yeah, yeah, but what would you say if I told you she was with the geezer whose gaff I turned over.'

'Sir Reginald Wren?'

'That's the bloke.'

'When was this?'

'A few days ago.'

'Has Wren been in before?'

'Yeah. He's a regular. He comes at least twice a month. He loves his jazz, does Sir Reginald, but this was the first time I've noticed him with the bird.'

'Any idea when he's likely to visit next?'

'Probably, the week after next,' he replied. 'I have a great trio that plays on the first and third Wednesday of every month. It's his favourite act.'

'Why didn't you tell me you knew Wren when I asked you to burgle his house?'

'Because I didn't know it was his gaff until I saw his photograph in that false passport that was in his peter.'

'You knew it was a forgery?'

'Well, I knew his name weren't Ernest Thomas, so it was pretty obvious.'

'And you didn't think it was worth telling me you knew Wren when you handed the photos over?'

'I know lots of dodgy characters.'

'What makes you think Wren is dodgy?'

'Are you kidding me, David? Anybody who has a forged passport, a pistol and a bag of cocaine in his peter is unlikely to be entirely kosher.'

'Didn't you feel guilty breaking into the house of a regular customer?'

'I told you, I didn't know it was his gaff, and by the time I found out, it was too late. The job was done.'

'That sounds like a cop out to me.'

'Maybe you're right and maybe you're wrong. All I know is that I like to keep a Chinese wall between my business interests.'

'I'm in no position to judge you, Manny, but some people might think you have no conscience.'

'A conscience? Not as far as Sir Reginald is concerned. I'd stab him in the back any day of the week. I lost all my family in Auschwitz and something about that *momzer* reminds me of the Nazis.' Manny was usually pretty easy going, but he spat this out with unaccustomed venom.

'Don't snap at me, Manny,' I said quietly. 'I'm not a Nazi.'

'Sorry, David. But something about Sir-Reginald-Bloody-Wren gives me the heebie-jeebies.'

'You could always ban him from your club,' I pointed out.

'What and lose out on all that dosh he spends on fizz when he comes? I don't think so. He might be a fascist, but his money aint.' He grinned at his own hypocrisy.

'Did you get the impression that the blonde woman was Wren's girlfriend,' I asked.

173

'Well, they weren't exactly shagging on the table, but they looked pretty cosy together.'

'Thanks, Manny,' I said. I now knew that the woman had had some sort of relationship with at least three men: Wren, Douglas Campbell and the effeminate looking man in the Chinese restaurant. However, I was no closer to discovering her identity. Little did I know that puzzle would be solved before the hour was out.

'Here's your lovely lady back again,' Manny said before slipping away into the shadows of the smoke-filled room.

'Was that Manny I saw with you?' Colleen asked.

'Yes.' I refilled our glasses.

'Are you going to tell me what you were talking about?'

I didn't answer her, instead I sipped my champagne.

'It was Manny who broke into Sir Reginald's safe, wasn't it?' She asked.

'You know about that?'

'Of course I do.'

'Do you know what Manny found in the safe?'

'Yes. There was a gun and other stuff.'

'There were also three photographs. Did you see them?'

She shook her head. 'Dizz wouldn't show me.'

'It's Dizz now, is it?'

'Only between you and me. It seems silly to keep referring to him as the D-G, when we both know him so well.'

'Do you remember the blonde girl that we saw in the Chinese restaurant and the Palace Theatre?'

'Yes. I'm convinced I've seen her before somewhere, but I can't put a name to her face.'

'Well she was in a couple of those photos. In one, she was having sex with a man.'

'Who?'

'That is sensitive information. I am sure your mate Dizz will tell you if he thinks you need to know.'

She poked her tongue out at me. 'Sensitive, hey? In that case, it's either a judge, a policeman or a politician. Am I right?'

I ignored her question again. 'In addition, Manny has seen the blonde in here with Wren.'

'Sir Reginald?'

'Who else?'

We lapsed into silence again as we listened to the music. Colleen stared into the darkness of the room as if in a trance. Suddenly she tugged my sleeve.

'What's this tune they are playing?'

'*Misty*,' I replied.

'That's what I thought.' She smiled. '*Play Misty for Me*.'

'What are you talking about?'

'It's a film starring Clint Eastwood.'

I remembered the film then. It was about a radio DJ who was stalked by some loony woman who kept asking him to play *Misty*. 'So what?' I asked.

'So, I remember where I've seen the blond girl before. She was at university with me. I didn't recognise her immediately because I last saw her ten years ago and she's changed a lot. Back then she had pink hair, wore grungy clothes and was overweight.'

She sipped her champagne. 'Her name is Bridget Olafson,' she eventually went on. 'She was the campus bicycle.'

'I don't get you.'

'Oh, don't pretend you're an innocent at large, David. It means she let all the boys ride her.'

'Oh, I see.'

'Actually, she was a couple of years ahead of me and I only knew her for a few months before she was sent down.'

'Sent down?'

'She was expelled?'

'Listen, girl, although I didn't go to a university, I do know what being sent down means. I was questioning why she was expelled? If every over-sexed student was excluded, our universities would be half empty.'

'She wasn't sent down because of the sex thing, it was because she was a complete lunatic.'

'Are you sure the blonde girl is this Bridget?'

'Definitely, but the thing is, everyone called her Misty.'

'Why was that?'

'Because she had the hots for the pianist in the college jazz group. She used to turn up at all their gigs and ask him to play *Misty* for her. The name stuck.'

'But you said she had changed a lot. How can you be so sure?'

'Trust me, I'm sure. There was just something about her. Perhaps it was her eyes.'

'So why was Misty sent down?'

'I told you, she was a lunatic. She turned up unannounced one night in the pianist's room and discovered him with another girl. She flipped and went for them both with a kitchen knife she'd hidden in her handbag.'

'Did she stab them?'

'No. Luckily, a tutor happened to be passing and heard the commotion. Somehow he managed to disarm Misty before she did any real harm. She was ordered off the campus immediately and the whole business was hushed up. I never saw her again until she came into the Chinese restaurant with that man.'

'What happened to her after she left the university?'

'I'm not sure, although the rumour round the campus was that she was working for an escort agency.'

'She was a whore?'

'I was trying to give her the benefit of the doubt, but I suppose the answer is yes.'

'Judging by the photo found in Wren's safe, she's still on the game.'

'At least her time at university was not entirely wasted. I suppose practice makes perfect. I wonder how much she charges.'

'I don't suppose we're talking about ten quid knee-tremblers in an alley. I suspect your friend Misty is a high-class call-girl.'

'She's no friend of mine,' she said sharply and then drained her glass. 'On that note I think it's time to take me home.'

I glanced at my watch. It was well past midnight. 'Let's go.'

The traffic heading west on the A40 was light and we made good time to Bayswater. We were almost at our destination when I spotted the car behind us. It had been following me on and off for a week now and was beginning to piss me off, not least because I hadn't yet had a chance to take a note of its registration number. I was determined to change that.

'There is a BMW tailing us,' I told Colleen.

She looked over her shoulder. 'All I can see are headlights and they are some way back.'

'That's the car I'm talking about. It's a BMW.'

'What are you going to do?'

'Not me, we,' I said.

'OK. What are *we* going to do?'

'I am going to drive past the entrance to your road. Hopefully, that will confuse him.'

'Him?'

'Yes, it's the man who was in the Chinese restaurant with your friend Misty. They followed us home that night too.'

'Is Misty with him now?'

'Not unless she's lying on the floor.'

'So what next?'

'When I get past your road I'm going to take the next right. I will then stop and turn off my lights. Our friend will follow us and will have to slam on his brakes when he sees us parked in the middle of the road. As soon as he stops I want you to take a note of his licence plate number.'

'What if he doesn't stop?'

'Then hold on tight and say a little prayer.'

'Are you serious? You're just going to let him crash into us?'

'Don't worry. That's not going to happen. Trust me, that boy is a real pro.' I tried to sound confident.

'I trust you.' She sounded about as convincing as me.

'That's the spirit, girl.' I glanced in the rear-view mirror for what seemed like the hundredth time in the last couple of minutes. The driver of the BMW was closing the distance between us as he anticipated I would turn into Colleen's road. When I sailed past, I saw the car's tail lights flicker on as the driver touched his brake pedal, only to release it as he realised I was not turning. The gap between our two cars widened momentarily and I used this opportunity to make a sharp right turn at the next junction.

Once I had safely navigated the corner I drew to a halt and turned off all the lights. I looked in the rear-view mirror yet again and saw a car pull into the road, its headlights blazing. I clenched the steering wheel as the lights drew closer and for a moment I thought the BMW was going to hit us.

But just in time, the driver saw us and slammed on his brakes. The car came to a screeching halt and almost immediately started reversing up the road. When it reached the main road the BMW spun on a sixpence and disappeared back the way it had come.

'Did you get his number?' I asked anxiously. The driver had been quicker than I had anticipated.

'Yes,' Colleen replied, waving a slip of paper at me.

'What's that?' I asked.

'My shopping list. It's all I had to hand that I could write on.' She passed it to me.

I took the slip of paper, on one side of which was a list of products. 'Nice ingredients,' I said.

'I'm making red Thai curry for dinner tomorrow. You can join me if you like.'

'It sounds wonderful?'

On the other side of the slip of paper was a car registration number. It started with an F, which indicated it was only two years old. The next three numbers were irrelevant, but the three letters at the end of the plate told me the car had been registered in Kent. Did that mean the driver lived there? A visit to Scotland Yard might answer that question.

The one-way system in Bayswater meant the detour I'd taken resulted in another five minutes driving to get us back to Colleen's road. It was almost one o'clock when I found a parking space near her apartment.

'Are you coming in for a coffee?' She sounded nervous.

'You did suggest that I bring an overnight bag,' I pointed out. 'I assumed it was an invitation.'

'It was an invitation, but I wasn't sure you would accept.'

'How could I refuse?' I said. 'If it still stands.'

'It does,' she said with a shy smile.

'Then I'm happy to accept your invitation, Miss Masters?'

'Mrs Masters.'

'Mrs? I didn't realise.'

'It's only a technicality,' she said. 'Mister Masters left years ago for pastures new.'

'Are there no other men in your life?'

'None.'

'No one? Not even a father?'

'No. He died when I was little.'

'I'm sorry to hear that.'

'You have no reason to be sorry. It wasn't your fault. It's just one of those things.' She stared moodily out into the night. It had started to spit with rain and the street lights shone on the droplets of water on the windscreen making them sparkle like diamonds. 'But sometimes I get lonely not having somebody with whom to share my life,' she added eventually.

'I'm more than happy to be that somebody,' I offered and then suddenly worried again about what I was getting myself into.

She turned and looked at me. Her eyes shone. 'Thank you. That's why I'd like you to stay with me tonight.'

I got out of the car without saying another word. There was nothing more I could say. I opened the passenger door for her and held her hand as she slipped off her seat.

I retrieved my overnight bag from the back seat and then we walked the short distance to the building in which Colleen's apartment was situated. Whilst she took her keys from her handbag and opened the outer door, I looked up and down the road. There was no sign of the BMW.

Her apartment was on the first floor and it didn't take us long to reach her front door. Once we were inside it took even less time for us to reach her bedroom. We bypassed the kitchen and there was no further mention of coffee that night.

Chapter 15

Monday started off well. My mood was light as I drove from my home in Shepherd's Bush to Whitehall. It had been a good weekend; there was a clear blue sky; I could feel the warm spring sunshine on my face; and I had Bob Dylan's Greatest Hits belting out from my car cassette tape player.

The traffic was heavier than usual, which resulted in long queues at the succession of traffic lights I encountered, but even the congestion did nothing to lower my spirits.

Dylan was singing the last verse of *My Back Pages:*

Yes, my guard stood hard when abstract threats too noble to neglect

Deceived me into thinking I had something to protect

Good and bad, I define these terms quite clear, no doubt, somehow...'

And as with the preceding five verses I joined in with the chorus, singing out lustily: 'Ah, but I was so much older then, I'm younger than that now.'

I smiled to myself as the track finished. I really did feel younger today. I thought about why that might be, as the next track started and Dylan began to sing about *Maggie's Farm.*

Perhaps it was the onset of spring; or the adrenalin rush I felt whenever I thought about the Mandela Project operation in which I was becoming increasingly involved. Maybe it was just the after effects of spending the weekend with Colleen Masters.

After an energetic night of love-making we slept in late on Sunday morning, before eventually getting up and going for a light lunch in The Swan, an 18th century coaching inn situated across the road from Hyde Park.

It had been a lovely day and we sat in the sun on the inn's balcony. We ate prawn mayonnaise sandwiches and sipped our way through half a bottle of wonderful Argentinian Malbec. In the afternoon we strolled through the park, chatting about nothing of any consequence, having already agreed to avoid talking about work.

The spring night was drawing in when, several hours later, we returned to Colleen's apartment. She cooked the promised red Thai curry and served it with boiled rice and sweet chilli chutney. We washed the food down with the rest of the bottle of wine, which we had brought with us from our lunchtime trip to the pub.

We then spent the evening making love again. Reluctantly, just before midnight, I left Colleen and headed for home. I was smiling when I clambered into my own bed. I lay awake for some time musing about whether it was possible for the energy of a young lover to re-invigorate an older man. As I fell asleep, with a smile on my face, I decided it could.

There is a small reception room at the start of the corridor that leads to the DFCO offices. It contains a desk, a couple of hard backed chairs and Gwyneth Jones. Middle aged, with tightly permed grey hair and a face on which was etched an almost permanent scowl, she was ostensibly a receptionist.

However, Gwyneth actually served as the department's watchdog, seeing off any unsuspecting members of the Treasury staff who wandered our way by mistake. DFCO didn't welcome visitors, particularly those who turned up in our offices uninvited.

I pushed open the swing doors that separated the DFCO from the rest of the ground floor of the Treasury building. 'Good morning, Gwyneth,' I said as I walked past the reception desk.

'Is it?' She glared at me with cold, unblinking eyes, from behind a pair of heavy framed spectacles.

'Well, it was the last time I looked.' I tried a smile on her, but it had no noticeable effect on her mood.

'It might be for you, but you don't have to put up with my old man,' she said sourly.

'That's true,' I admitted and left it at that. I refused to be drawn into a discussion about the inadequacies of her husband. I had been caught out like that once before. Instead, I walked quickly down the corridor until I reached the door that led downstairs to the basement.

When I reached the main Section Two office there was no sign of Poppy or Timmy, but Melissa was already working at her desk. She stood up and followed me into my office, where she waved a photograph at me as I sat down at my desk. She was beaming.

'I got him!' She declared in triumph.

'Butler?'

181

'Yeah. I eventually found him on Saturday afternoon,' she said as she handed me the photograph. 'This is a copy of the photo from the Special Branch mugshot book.'

I studied the photo and then picked up the original photograph of the guard who had been on duty at the safe-house. I compared the two photos. In one the man had long hair and a beard, in the other he had short hair and was clean shaven. Despite the differences I could see immediately it was the same man.

'His real name is Shaun Brannagan,' Melissa said.

'Unless that's just another alias,' I suggested.

'I'll leave you to decide that,' she said. 'I only provide you with information. It's for you to interpret it. That's why you're the boss.'

'I'm pleased you noticed.' I stared at the two photos and then looked at her. 'Melissa,' I said.

'Yes, boss?'

'Whether Brannagan is Butler's real name or not, finding that photo was damn fine work.'

She did not acknowledge my praise, but the satisfied look on her face spoke volumes.

'Now, I have another job for you.' I slipped the two photos into the pocket of my jacket and passed her the list of Phoenix Group members. 'I would like a briefing note on all the people on that list. Don't worry about Wren, you've already dug up more than enough information on him.'

She cast her eyes down the list. 'This might take some time, because, most of them are foreign nationals. They are unlikely to show up on any of the British data bases I used to track down stuff on Sir Reginald Wren, but I'll do my best.'

'I'm sure you will.' I stood up. 'I'm off out,' I added. 'Get Timmy to help you when he eventually gets in.'

'Will do. Where shall I say you are if anybody asks?'

'Who do you mean by anybody?' I asked. 'There's nobody else in the office. Unless Poppy and Timmy are hiding in one of the filing cabinets.'

Melissa giggled. 'Not in the same drawer I hope,' she said.

'No chance. Poppy would eat Timmy alive.'

'Actually, I was thinking more of somebody like Colonel Disraeli-Astor. What if he calls?' Melissa asked, then added with an inscrutable expression on her face, 'or Colleen?'

'If the D-G wants me, tell him I'm visiting New Scotland Yard to get the Met to put out an APB.'

'An APB?' She queried with a frown.

'Yeah. He'll know what you mean.'

'What if Colleen calls?'

'She'll only be ringing on behalf of the D-G,' I replied cautiously. 'Tell her the same thing.'

New Scotland Yard, Westminster

New Scotland Yard is the headquarters of the Metropolitan Police Service, the force responsible for policing London. The name of the building originated from the location of the Met's original home, which was in Whitehall Place and had a rear entrance in Great Scotland Yard.

Eventually, the Met moved into the Norman Shaw Buildings on the Embankment, and their HQ became known as New Scotland Yard. In 1967 the Met moved again, to a modern building in Broadway, Westminster, and their old building became part of the Parliamentary estate. Now many MPs had their offices in Norman Shaw.

The walk from my office to New Scotland Yard usually took me about ten minutes, but then I'm a fast walker. Today was different. It was a lovely day; the sky was cobalt blue and cloudless, the sun was beating down and the temperature was rising.

I took a leisurely stroll to Parliament Square, where a group of protesters was standing opposite the Houses of Parliament, chanting unintelligible slogans and waving placards declaring their opposition to war. However, the protesters didn't make clear to which war they were referring. Perhaps they didn't know themselves.

I made my way up Tothill Street and when I reached its junction with Broadway the demonstrators were still audible, although I still had no idea what they were chanting.

When I arrived at the Yard I was met by Deputy Assistant Commissioner Kevin Neal, who greeted me with a warm handshake and a friendly smile.

'You were lucky to catch me when you rang,' the policeman said as he walked me to the lift. 'I was just off to Hendon to give a lecture about the Serious Crime Squad.'

'Sorry to spoil your jolly,' I said.

'There's no need to apologise,' he assured me as we reached the top floor and stepped out of the lift. 'In fact, you did me a favour. Talking to a bunch of spotty faced cadets isn't my idea of a fun day. Your call gave me an excuse to pull out and send a detective superintendent in my place.' He led me along a corridor and into his office.

'How's your dad?' I asked as I sat down in the chair opposite him. Billy Neal was an old friend of mine, who I hadn't seen for several years.

'When did I see you last?' Kevin asked as he sat down behind his desk. It stood in front of a large picture window that gave a panoramic view of Westminster. His desk was empty except for a large white blotting pad, a telephone and half a dozen photo frames that were clustered at one end.

'It's probably over a year ago. Why?'

'So you won't have heard.'

'Heard what? Has something happened to him?'

'You could say that.' He smiled wryly. 'He got married again.' He picked up one of the photographs from his desk and looked at it fondly before handing it to me.

A smiling, broken-nosed Billy Neal looked up at me with eyes that twinkled in the light from the camera's flash. He wore an ill-fitting suit, with a white carnation in the button-hole of his jacket.

Next to Billy stood a small woman wearing a lilac dress, the hem of which was several inches above her knees. On her head she wore a feather fascinator. One hand gripped Billy's arm, whilst the other held a bunch of carnations. She was smiling too. There was something familiar about her.

'They look very happy,' I said and then added: 'I recognise her from somewhere.'

'Didn't you visit dad a few times when he had that pub down in Kent?'

'Yes,' I confirmed. In fact, it was in Billy's pub that I first met Alexei Urinoff. 'But the last time was about eight years ago.'

'Well she worked for Dad at the pub.'

'I remember her now. She had an accident whilst juggling some plates.'

Kevin looked at me quizzically.

'She dropped them on the floor when she was clearing up after

184

lunch' I explained. 'Your dad wasn't best pleased.' I tapped the wedding photograph. 'But it looks as if he forgave her.'

'That's dad all over,' Kevin said. 'He doesn't hold grudges. It's one of his most endearing traits. He blows up, has a pop at somebody and then forgives them as soon as he's calmed down.' He smiled proudly as he took the photograph back.

'I'm pleased for him. Your dad was in a bad place after your mum died.'

Kevin's smile faded. 'I know. When the bastard who killed mum got away with just a prison sentence, we thought Dad was going to top himself.' He considered me sadly as memories of his mum flooded back. 'My family will never forget what you did, Dave. We owe you big time.'

I shrugged away his thanks. Billy Neal had thanked me on numerous occasions for having exacted on the man who raped and murdered his wife the death penalty his crime deserved, but which the British justice system refused to deliver. However, it was the first time that Kevin had shown his own appreciation.

'It was the least I could do, Kev,' I said quietly. 'Bobby Hughes was an animal and he deserved to be put down, but it's not something we should be talking about. Don't forget you're a senior police officer now.'

We fell silent, each weighed down by our own thoughts.

'I'm always impressed with the view you have from up here.' I said, pointing out of his office window. Immediately the mood lightened.

Kevin looked over his shoulder. 'That's because you work in a dungeon.' He smiled at me. Like his dad, he could never be miserable for long. 'Ok, Dave, down to business. When you rang and set up this meeting you sounded as if you had something urgent to discuss with me.'

'I assume you are still head of CID?'

'Well, I was this morning.' He smiled. 'But for how long I don't know. There is yet another re-organisation afoot.'

I handed him the slip of paper with the registration number of the car that followed Colleen and me on Saturday night. 'First up, I need to know who owns this car.'

'That's an easy one,' he picked up his phone and dialled a number. 'But you must want more, because you could have rung and

185

asked me to look up the number.'

'Yes, there is something else,' I admitted, but said no more because he raised a hand to indicate that his call was being answered.

He read the number to whoever was at the other end of the phone and then added: 'And I want the information pronto.' He put the phone receiver down and smiled again. 'And the other thing?'

'A bit more difficult,' I admitted as I took a photo from my pocket and handed it to him. 'His name is Shaun Brannagan. The photo was taken from the Special Branch mug shot book.'

'Provisional IRA?' Kevin guessed.

'He was, but I'm not sure now.'

'What about him?'

'We think he's murdered at least two people in recent weeks.'

'Who did he kill?'

I told him. 'But I'd be grateful if you kept that information strictly to yourself. We can't afford any leaks.'

'So what's with all the cloak and dagger stuff?'

'I'm currently involved in a multi-agency operation, which has been sanctioned at a high level.'

'Government level?'

'She who must be obeyed.'

'The Prime Minister?'

'Yes.'

'Holy Moses!' He looked at me intently. 'Is there anything else I should know?'

'Things might get rough.'

'When you say rough, Dave. 'Are you planning actions I probably shouldn't hear about?'

I smiled. 'Let's just say that I might have to do things to which the Metropolitan Police might find it hard turning a blind eye.'

'In that case; don't tell me.'

'Don't worry, I won't but I do need your help. Brannagan is a threat and we have to find him before he kills anybody else.'

'Is that likely to happen?'

'We think so, which is why Mrs T made clear to us that finding Brannagan is our top priority.'

'What do you want me to do?'

I'd like you to circulate Brannagan's details to all your usual contacts.'

'Not a problem. I'll do it straight away.'

'Thanks.' I passed him the second photo. 'Shaun Brannagan also goes under the name of William Butler. This is him wearing a wig and false beard.'

Kevin studied both photos. 'A good disguise. I wouldn't have recognised him.' He looked up at me. 'So what evidence do you have that Brannagan killed those two guys?'

I stared out of the window and pondered that question myself. In the distance I could see the spring sun being reflected off the water of the Thames. A pleasure boat steamed slowly past the Houses of Parliament towards Westminster Bridge. As I watched, the hands on Big Ben reached 11 o'clock, but its chimes were muffled by the double-glazed window.

'We have circumstantial evidence only,' I admitted.

'It's difficult to arrest somebody solely on circumstantial evidence, let alone obtain a conviction.'

'I know that, Kev, but in some ways, this is a bit like the Bobby Hughes business. Brannagan is guilty and he must be punished properly. There's no question of you having to arrest him. If you can track the bastard down, I'll do the rest.'

Kevin's phone rang. He picked the receiver up immediately. 'Neal,' he said before taking a pen from his top pocket and a notepad from the top drawer of his desk. 'Yes, go ahead.' He wrote something on the notepad. 'Thank you,' he added before returning the receiver to its rest. He tore a page from his notepad and handed it to me.

'Justin Bloom,' I read out loud.

'What interest do you have in Bloom?' Kevin asked.

'Have you heard of him?'

'Yes. He runs a private detective agency out of an office in Chelsea. He specialises in high-end clients whose nefarious activities fill the pages of the News of the World and who have more money than sense.'

'Do you know his address?'

'Not off hand, but you'll find it in Yellow Pages.'

'What do you know of Bloom?'

'Not much. He sometimes sails close to the wind and we've had to mark his card on a couple of occasions, but he's never been implicated in any criminal activity. What's your interest in him? Is he involved in the Brannagan business?'

'I'm not sure yet. I might need to have a quiet word with him.' I saw the way the policeman looked at me with his eyebrow raised.

'Is your quiet word going to be one of the things I don't want to hear about?' He asked.

I shook my head. 'Don't worry, it will be words only.'

'Was there anything else, Dave?'

'Just one thing. Have you heard of Sir Reginald Wren?'

'Reg-the-sledge?'

'You know him?'

'Oh, yes. I know him alright. What do you want with that thug?'

'Is he a thug?'

'More than that, he's a psychopath.'

'You don't like him.'

'Does it show?'

'Just a little.'

'Look, Dave. Reg might be a knight of the Realm, dress in fancy clothes and pretend he's part of the gentry, but in my book, once a common little turd, always a common little turd.'

'You called him Reg-the-sledge. What's that all about?'

'When I started out on the beat, back in Nineteen-seventy, I was stationed in the East End. It was a couple of years after the arrest of the Kray Twins, which left a big hole in the East London criminal underworld. That vacuum was filled by the Shoreditch Gang.

'Wren was a member of the gang. He was a young jack-the-lad who aspired to being like the Kray twins. Shortly after being inducted into the gang he took part in an ambush on the leader of a rival gang from Whitechapel that was trying to muscle in on their territory.

'To prove how hard he was, Wren laid into their rival with a sledgehammer and left him within an inch of his life. From that day on, he became known as Reg-the-sledge.'

'Was he prosecuted?'

'No chance. There was no proof of his involvement and his victim refused to press charges. All we had were rumours and circumstantial evidence.'

'Which cannot be used to obtain a conviction.'

'Exactly.'

'So what happened to Wren?'

'Over the next few years he was pretty active in the

neighbourhood and earned a reputation as a ruthless enforcer. He was implicated in loads of physical assaults and at least half a dozen murders. Unfortunately, we were never able to pin anything on him.'

'Why was that?'

'Unlike most of the other tearaways, who had more brawn than brain, Reg had his fair share of both. He was tough enough to attack his rivals when necessary, but smart enough to cover his tracks well, not least by offering bungs to bent coppers. The Force was riddled with them at the time.

Eventually Reg's luck ran out. He was caught by the Whitechapel mob who exacted revenge on him for what he did to their leader. Reg ended up in hospital for a month and when he was discharged he disappeared.'

I guessed there was more and I was right.

'Reg-the-sledge didn't come back onto my radar screen until about eight or nine years ago, by which time he was a millionaire and had been knighted.'

'So what brought him to your attention?'

'It was when I was in the Fraud Squad. We had a tip-off that Wren was heavily involved in insider trading. We suspected his fortune was built on City fraud, so undertook an investigation into his financial affairs. Unfortunately, we could find nothing that proved his guilt. He was very clever and left no evidence that would stand up in court.'

'Frustrating.'

'Very. We were really pissed off, but then we got a break. A City trader was caught passing on sensitive take-over details to an investor for money and during his interrogation he confessed to selling insider information to several other people, including Reg.'

'You had Wren bang to rights?'

'That's what we thought, but we were wrong. Despite our objections the judge released the trader on bail. A couple of days later, his house burnt down with him inside. All that was found of him was his badly burned body. However, at his autopsy a forensic scientist discovered the back of his skull had been crushed.' He paused and stared sightlessly up at the ceiling.

Finally he continued. 'The wound was a deep and long indenture that forensics said could have been caused by a large, heavy blunt instrument. They could not be certain what type of weapon had been used, but I was in no doubt the poor sod was killed with a blow from a sledgehammer.'

'Wren?'

'Yes.'

'But you couldn't prove it?'

'No, I couldn't prove it and once again he got off scot-free.' He gave me a questioning look. 'So what's your interest in Reg-the-sledge?'

'Unfortunately, that's classified and I can't share it with you for now, Kev, but your information has been very useful.'

'Can you at least tell me whether you have him in your sights?'

'Well, let's just say that I might need your help later.'

'That's good enough for me. If there's any way I can help put that bastard away, you only have to ask.'

That was good enough for me as well.

DFCO offices

When I got back to the office Poppy was leaning back in her chair reading Cosmopolitan. On its cover was a pouting actress in a low cut dress and a series of tasters for the main features inside, one of which declared that Christopher (Superman) Reeve was "Sexy, Sensitive and Smart".

I had no idea whether any of those things were true and my secretary probably didn't care either way. 'Where's Melissa and Timmy?' I asked her.

'Melissa has gone to the library,' she replied without looking up from her magazine, 'but Timmy hasn't arrived yet.'

I looked at my watch. It was just after noon. I frowned. 'It's not like him to be late. Has he rung in ill?'

'No. He told me he was driving back from the West Country first thing this morning. Perhaps he's stuck in traffic.'

'Do we have his mum's telephone number?'

'Yes.'

'Okay, give her a ring and find out what time he left Devon. He might have broken down somewhere and need rescuing. That Mini he drives is not very reliable.'

'Will do,' she said, but showed no sign of abandoning whatever article she was reading.

'Straight away, Poppy,' I said sternly.

She closed her magazine with an audible tut and reached for her desk diary.

'And please find me the address for the Justin Bloom Detective Agency. It's somewhere in Fulham.'

'Where will I …?' she started to say.

'Try Yellow Pages!' I pre-empted her question.

With another tut she stood up and stomped over to the shelving unit on which were displayed a range of telephone books. I headed for my office.

Ten minutes later Poppy came bustling into my office. I looked up; it was unusual for her to bustle anywhere. She looked worried.

'What's wrong?' I asked her.

'It's Timmy. He never arrived at his mum's house on Friday and he hasn't been in contact since.' She passed me a square of yellow paper. 'This is the address you asked for.'

I folded the advertisement Poppy had torn out of Yellow Pages and put it in my wallet. I pondered the news about my deputy. I could think of half a dozen good reasons for Timmy's failure to reach his destination, including getting lost on Exmoor, but I had a bad feeling about his no-show. I picked up the phone and rang Disraeli-Astor.

'Good afternoon, this is the Director-General's office. Colleen speaking. Can I help you?'

'Hello, Colleen. How are you today?'

She recognised my voice. 'Still tingling,' she whispered.

'In a nice way I hope?'

'A very nice way. I'd forgotten what it feels like to have a real man, rather than a vibrator, for company in my bed.'

'I take it you're on your own in the office.'

'Of course.'

'So why are you whispering?'

'Was I whispering?' She said in her normal voice and then giggled.

'Yes,' I said, before adding in a whisper. 'But just so you know, I'm still tingling too. For the same reason.'

She giggled again. 'I didn't know you used a vibrator?'

I was about to laugh when I remembered why I had rung. It was no time for levity. 'Is the D-G in?'

She must have recognised something in my voice. 'Is something wrong?'

'Timmy's missing.' I explained what had happened.

'Dizz isn't here.'

'Are you expecting him in today?'

'Yes. In a couple of hours.'

'OK. I'm heading down to Slough, I'd like to see him when I get back. Leave a message with Poppy to let me know what time.'

'Will you be back by five?'

I glanced at my watch. It was almost one o'clock. Time would be tight, and getting back would depend on the traffic, but I decided that four hours should be long enough for what I had to do. 'I think so.'

'In that case I will book you in for a five o'clock meeting.'

'Shouldn't you check that with the boss?'

'Don't worry, he'll agree,' she said confidently.

Chapter 16

Buttercup House was an apartment block close to Slough railway station. It was built in the early Eighties, but looked much older. It was designed in a style that would have fitted in with the post-war council house building boom. Red brick, inexpensive, unassuming and functional.

In front of the block was a car-park in which were parked a couple of vans and half a dozen cars, all of which looked as if they needed extensive work at a body repair garage. There was no sign of Timmy's yellow Mini. That could have been a good sign. Or not.

Number 21 was on the third floor of the block. There was a lift, but the stainless-steel lift door on the ground floor had a cardboard sign attached to it with adhesive tape. It told me that the lift was out of order. The sign was half covered by a single word in large letters that had been sprayed at an angle across it in red paint. It read: **SHIT**. It was a sentiment I shared as I climbed a staircase that smelled of boiled cabbage and urine.

Halfway up the first flight of stairs I almost trod on a used condom. On the landing above I found a discarded hypodermic needle, along with a blackened strip of aluminium foil that had been used to prepare a fix.

On the second-floor landing somebody had vomited in front of the lift, following what looked like a booze and kebab filled night out. In the middle of the puddle of sick was a footprint, which had then spread the mess across the landing in a series of small splodges.

When I reached the third floor landing I found it was surprisingly clean, compared to the floors below. It had been swept recently and on the windowsill somebody had put a row of flower pots filled with pelargoniums.

Set into the wall in the corner of the landing was a large metal chute. Tenants could dispose of their household waste into a communal refuse bin that was housed in an enclosure beneath the block of flats. The lid of the chute was clean and looked as if somebody had recently washed it.

Outside flat number 19 there was a green mat on which was

printed the word **WELCOME**. The front door of the flat was immaculately painted and its brass letter box and knocker shone with a brightness that only hours of dedicated rubbing with metal polish produces. It didn't take a rocket scientist to work out the occupier of this flat was responsible for the cleanliness of the landing.

In contrast, the door to flat number 21 was as scruffy as its neighbour's was neat and tidy. Not only was the door's paintwork battered and chipped, but it was so filthy it was difficult to identify its original colour.

I knocked on the dirty door, but there was no response. I opened the letterbox and looked through. The entrance hall beyond was deserted and the flat was as silent as a grave.

I studied the door carefully. Modern locks are notoriously useless and this one was no exception. In the movies, intelligence agents and cops carry tools in their pocket to pick locks. In real life the only thing needed to break into a flat without a key is a sturdy size nine shoe. Conveniently, that's what I was wearing and I smashed open the door with one kick.

A quick search of the one bedroom apartment revealed it had been cleared of everything except furniture. The bedclothes had been removed from the bed in the single bedroom and the wardrobe and sideboard drawers were empty.

In the bathroom there were none of the usual bits and pieces you would expect to find. There was not even a toilet roll.

The lounge-diner was equally empty and it was only when I went through to the small kitchen that I discovered any evidence that the flat had been occupied recently.

I found a waste bin under the sink containing a dirty floor cloth, a copy of the Daily Mirror dated Friday 6th April and an empty bottle of spirit gum.

My IRA bird had flown.

The newspaper told me that Brannagan had vacated the flat within the last 72 hours; and the gum bottle suggested he left wearing a false beard and wig. The Irishman was once again masquerading as William Butler.

I found something else in the kitchen.

Propped up on the work surface next to the electric stove was a clip board complete with a few sheets of blank A4 lined paper. It was the clipboard that I had suggested Timmy take to Slough with him.

On the top sheet, somebody had used a thick black felt tip pen to print in large letters what looked like a football score: PROVOS 1 – BRITISH SCUM 0

I guessed immediately what the message meant and I felt sick. The spoof football score was the Irishman's way of both mocking and challenging me.

I left the kitchen and noticed a smear of blood on the cheap lino floor covering in the hallway. I got down on my hands and knees to look closer. I noticed specks of blood on the wall.

I opened the apartment's front door and discovered that the metal strip running across the top of the wooden threshold had been damaged. A small part of it was bent up in a jagged hook. The edge of the hook was very sharp and attached to it was a tiny slither of what looked like flesh.

I made my way out onto the landing and found a trail of blood leading to the communal rubbish chute. I swore. I knew what this meant. I made my way back down the stairs to the refuse area in the basement, where I found a row of metal bins overflowing with black rubbish sacks thrown down the chute by tenants.

A couple of the sacks had fallen to the ground and split open and there was rubbish scattered across the floor of the enclosure. Some of the spillage was waste food that had attracted a few of the local rat population. The rodents scattered as I made my way to check the first bin.

I found what I was looking for in the third bin. Buried beneath half a dozen black sacks, I discovered a bundle of blood stained sheets and the blankets that must have been with them on the bed in the apartment upstairs.

Staring up at me through a fold in the blankets were the lifeless eyes of Timothy Fraser.

DFCO offices

'**You** look as if you need a stiff drink,' Disraeli-Astor said as he invited me to sit with a wave of his hand.

I didn't argue with him. My deputy's death had affected me more than I wanted to admit. I could still see his eyes staring up at me. 'Yes, I need a drink. Timmy might have been one of life's innocents and lacking in common sense, but he was a nice lad.'

'Fraser's death wasn't your fault,' he said, reading my mind. He handed me a large cognac. 'Shit happens,' he added as he poured himself a whisky.

'It does, but on this occasion, I helped Timmy step into it. If I hadn't sent him to Slough, he would still be alive.'

'Don't blame yourself.'

'That's easy for you to say, but sending him to confront the Irishman was like throwing a Christian to the lions. He never had a chance.'

'We thought Butler had fled,' he said gently, implicitly accepting some of the responsibility for my deputy's murder.

'I appreciate your support,' I said, grateful that he wanted to share the blame. 'But Timmy's death was down to me. I took the decision alone. Yes, it's true I thought the Irishman had scarpered, but I was wrong.'

'We all make mistakes, Statton.'

'I know, but this particular mistake killed Timmy.'

Disraeli-Astor sipped his whisky. 'So, Butler definitely murdered young Fraser?' He seemed to find it difficult to accept the obvious truth.

I handed him the clipboard I had found in the kitchen.

'What do you think?' I asked.

He looked at the sheet of paper. 'It certainly seems to confirm Fraser was killed by a member of the Provisional IRA.' He looked up at me. 'That message is shockingly callous.'

'Callous is an understatement. Whoever wrote that message, has a very sick mind.'

'And you think it was Butler?'

'Can you think of another possibility?'

'No.'

'Then we are agreed. It was Butler.'

'And you think he wanted you to find the message?'

'That's exactly what he intended. He was taunting me.'

'You have to find him before he kills anybody else,' Disraeli-Astor said earnestly.

'That's exactly what I intend doing, but now I have a different motive for finding the bastard who killed Timmy. Before it was strictly business. Now it's personal.'

'What's happening about Fraser's body?' He asked.

'The clean-up squad is in Slough recovering his body now and will remove any evidence of foul play from the apartment.'

'I assume you didn't notify the local police?'

'Of course not. We'll deal with this in our own way. However, I think Butler used Timmy's car to get away, so I did ring my contact at the Yard and ask him to put a trace out for it.'

'Is there anything you need me to do?'

'Yes. You could break the news to Mrs Fraser.'

'Of course,' he agreed immediately. I suppose he was used to such unpleasant tasks. As a colonel in the British Army he would have had to contact the parents of men and women killed whilst under his command. 'Get Poppy to give Mrs Fraser's details to Colleen and I will contact her.'

'OK, I'll get her to do it in the morning.'

'What else do we have?' He asked.

'For a start, we think Butler's real name is Shaun Brannagan.'

'How do you know that?'

'More good work on Melissa's part. She saw Brannagan's photo in the Special Branch mugshot book and recognised him as Butler.'

'We need to keep hold of that girl.'

'I agree,' I said and then fell silent while I sipped my cognac.

'What?' He asked, sensing that I had something on my mind.

'I have found out some more about Wren's background. He's had a very chequered career.' I repeated my conversation with Kevin Neal.

'Reg-the-sledge?'

'That's what ADC Neal called him.'

'That is shocking. I heard rumours that Sir Reginald had sailed close to the wind occasionally, but I hadn't realised he was a thug. What else?'

'As you know, I tasked Melissa with checking into the backgrounds of the other members of the Phoenix Group and putting together a briefing paper for you. I was going to get Timmy Fraser to help her.'

'Does she need help?'

'Yes. There are a lot of members and it's a long and laborious task. I need a good researcher to help her, preferably somebody with experience.'

He smiled. 'On that subject, I have some good news for you. Following our previous conversation, I took steps to get you additional staff, one of whom has research experience.'

'What's the catch?' I asked suspiciously.

'There is no catch,' he assured me. 'In addition, we are transferring an intelligence specialist to Section Two. Currently she's on maternity leave, but she should be back in time to join you at the beginning of December.'

'Great! She'll be able to help put up the Christmas decorations.'

'Spare me the sarcasm, Statton. This really isn't the time.'

He was right and momentarily I felt contrite, but the feeling didn't last long. 'So, when do we get the researcher?' I asked. 'Next Easter?'

He scowled at me. 'When do you want him?'

'Tomorrow.'

'It will be done.'

'I also need a reliable deputy to replace Timmy.'

'I have already thought of that. I am seconding the deputy head of Europe desk.'

'Des Hobbins?' I asked, not letting on that Colleen had already shared this information with me.'

'Yes. I think that's the chappie's name.'

'He's a good man. How soon can he start?'

'Next week. First thing on Tuesday morning.'

'Why Tuesday?'

'Because Monday is a bank holiday.'

'Of course. I forgot it's Easter weekend.'

'It's good to be one step ahead of you for a change.' He gave me a satisfied smile. 'Hopefully, that is the last I will hear about Section Two being understaffed.'

'I can't guarantee that. However, I certainly appreciate the additional help, however limited.'

Is there anything else I need to know?' He asked.

'Yes, I'm being followed.'

'By whom exactly?'

'By a private detective called Justin Bloom.'

'How did you find that out?'

'Because I made a note of his car licence plate and had my contact at the Yard check it out.'

'Do you think Bloom following you has anything to do with the Mandela Project business?'

'I assume so. I'm not working on anything else.'

'And there's no other reason why this detective chappie might be following you?'

'Well, I'm not knocking off anybody else's wife, if that's what you mean.' I suppose that wasn't strictly true, but I couldn't see why Bloom would be interested in my new relationship with the still technically married Colleen Masters.

'I should hope not,' he said, ever the prude. 'I was wondering more about any past cases in which you might have been involved.'

'I can't think of anything, but I will find out tomorrow.'

'How?'

'Because I intend paying Bloom a visit to confront him.'

'Is that wise?'

'Can you suggest a better way of discovering who he's working for?'

He shook his head and stared at me. 'Well be careful what you do. Don't act the hard man with him.'

'Don't worry. I'll leave the rough stuff to your friend Reg-the-sledge.'

He viewed me sceptically, but he let it pass. 'I will need to brief Jeffery Johnson on what has happened,' he said. 'Should I mention about Bloom?'

I weighed that question up in my mind. I preferred to work on a need to know basis and I wasn't sure my proposed visit to Bloom was something Johnson needed to know. On the other hand, it was possible we might need the politician's support if something did go wrong.

'Okay. I can't see it will do any harm,' I replied, not knowing how wrong I was.

Chapter 17

Poppy and Melissa were already in the office when I arrived on Tuesday morning. I told them about Timmy's death straight away, although I spared them the gory details. Understandably, they were both upset, so I went through to my office and left them to comfort each other.

I gave them five minutes and then returned to the outer office. 'Poppy, please can you let Colleen have the telephone number for Timmy's mum,' I said gently.

'Does Mrs Fraser know about Timmy?' She asked as she dabbed her eyes with a paper tissue.

'Not yet. The D-G is going to ring her. That's why he wants her telephone number'

Poppy picked up her desk diary and without another word she headed upstairs. She could have phoned the information through, but, despite being upset, she probably couldn't resist an opportunity to gossip with Colleen Masters and see if she could find out more about our new relationship.

As my secretary disappeared through the door, the researcher who had been drafted in to my Section Two team turned up. He found Melissa sitting at her desk in tears. I ushered him into my office where he introduced himself as Clive Flack.

I explained the situation to him and then called Melissa and asked her to join us. By then, she had composed herself and greeted her new work mate with a weak smile and a strong hand shake.

'How's the research going?' I asked her.

'Slow,' she admitted.

'Never mind, it should speed up now you have Clive to help you.'

I saw tears well up in Melissa's eyes again and I realised she remembered that it should have been Timmy helping her. She choked back a sob and then the pair of them left my office and returned to the library to continue compiling briefing papers on members of the Phoenix Group.

Poppy had still not returned and I was just about to scribble a note, telling her I was leaving the office to visit the Justin Bloom

Detective Agency, when my telephone rang. It was Kevin Neal.

'Morning, Dave.'

'Kev.'

'We've found the Mini you were looking for,' the policeman said. 'It's parked at Gatwick.'

'In the airport?'

'Yes. The short stay car-park.'

'That was quick work.'

'We got a lucky break. One of the car-park attendants noticed the Mini's road fund licence had expired.'

I was not surprised; it was just like my deputy to forget about renewing his tax disc.

'When the attendant checked it out he discovered the Mini was on the alert list.'

'What about the Irishman?'

'That was the first thing we checked. He was booked on a flight for Belfast in the name of William Butler.'

'When was the flight?'

'Saturday morning.'

'Thanks, Kev. I owe you.'

'Any time, Dave.'

'I might have to take you up on that offer,' I said before hanging up.

Poppy had still not reappeared so, instead of leaving her a note, I decided to track her down. It didn't take me long. As I suspected, she was in the D-G's office still chatting to Colleen.

'Morning, Colleen,' I said. Poppy looked at me and smiled knowingly. I ignored her. 'Is the boss in?'

'Yes, but he's on the phone to Timmy's mother,' Colleen replied.

'Poppy, please can you go back to the office and check the next available flight to Belfast,' I said.

'Will you want a seat booked?' She asked.

'That was the general idea. Why do you ask?'

'Because, the only person in the department authorised to book flights is Colleen.'

'I didn't know that,' I admitted.

'It's a new decree from the Cabinet Office,' Colleen explained. 'They are clamping down on expenses.'

'So do they want us to grow wings?'

'Don't have a go at me,' Colleen said. 'I just do as I'm told. If you don't like the new rules, take it up with the Cabinet Secretary.'

'Since Colleen is the only one who can do the booking, wouldn't it be better if she found out about flights to Belfast for you,' Poppy suggested.

What she said made sense, but I was always amazed at her capacity to avoid work. She got away with it on this occasion as well.

'I'm happy to check for you, David,' Colleen offered. She pulled a form from the drawer of her desk. 'What do you need the flight for?' She asked, with her pen poised.

I sighed and shook my head in exasperation. 'Is this really necessary?'

'Yes,' Collen said. 'It's the rules.'

I was about to say sod the rules, but thought better of it, but I couldn't disguise my irritation. 'In that case let me explain in words that even the prats at the Cabinet Office might understand: William Butler, or Shaun Brannagan, or whatever other name the murderer of Timothy Fraser is using today, has gone back to Ireland and I want to follow him. Will your new rules permit that?'

'Don't whinge.' She started to fill in the form. 'They're not my rules. Even the D-G has to give a reason for his flights now.'

That calmed me down. 'Ye gods! I bet the boss loves that!'

She laughed. 'He's not best pleased.' She looked down at the small telephone switchboard on her desk. 'He's off the phone now if you want to see him.'

I made my way to Disraeli-Astor's office, knocked on his door and went straight in. His was the only office in the Department that had a window and I found him standing, with his hands behind his back, staring moodily out of it. He looked over his shoulder and saw it was me. 'Take a seat.' He moved over to his desk and stood behind his chair.

'How did Timmy's mum take it?' I settled myself down on the chair opposite him.

'What do you think? She was very upset.' He stared at me sadly. 'They always are.' He sat down with a heavy sigh. 'Let me tell you something, Statton.'

'I'm listening, boss.' I was surprised. This was a side of him I hadn't seen before.

'During my time in the Army I often had to contact parents to tell them their loved one had been killed. I always tried to be professional, and divorce myself from the bad news I delivered.' He paused as he fiddled with the large sheet of blotting paper that lay on the desk in front of him.

'But no matter how hard I tried, I never came to terms with the hurt I inflicted on those decent people. It got to me every time. Telling Mrs Fraser her son was dead affected me in the same way.'

'I understand how you feel and I admire you for what you did,' I told him gently. 'It shows you are human.'

'Thank you, Statton.' For once he sounded sincere. He sat quietly for a while. 'But enough of this. You wanted to see me?'

'Yes, the Yard have found Timmy's car at Gatwick. It seems Brannagan took a flight to Belfast on Saturday.'

'What do you think we should do?'

'I want to follow him to Ulster?'

'I thought you would say that. When do you want to go?'

'Straight away. Colleen is checking flights for me now.'

'Do you know where he is?'

'I have an address for him in Londonderry. I'll start there.'

'So, what do you want from me?'

'I intend to eliminate Brannagan from any future enquiries.'

'What sort of elimination?'

'Permanent.'

'You want me to get you an XPD order.'

'Yes. If I'm going to kill Brannagan it would be good to be covered by a piece of paper.'

'I'm not sure how long it will take to get one.'

'It only takes the signature of a Home Office minister. You could get your mate Douglas Campbell to sign it. No point being a member of the Old Boys' Club if you can't make use of your contacts.'

He looked doubtful.

There was a knock at the door and Colleen came into the office. 'There's a British Airways flight to Belfast from Gatwick at two o'clock,' she said to me.

'I understand I need permission to book flights these days,' I said to Disraeli-Astor.

'Book it, Colleen,' he said without hesitation.

'Thanks for your help,' I called after her as she went back to her desk.

'I spoke to Jeffery Johnson this morning,' Disraeli-Astor said. 'He feels we should call a meeting of the AOSC to brief them on what is happening. I agreed and called one for this afternoon, here in my office.'

'In that case, please extend my apologies for absence,' I said.

'I will,' he said. 'However, the point is that Dougie Campbell will be in attendance. I'll ask him to hang around after the meeting and have a word then about an XPD order.'

'Okay. I'll ring you this evening to find out what he says.' I stood up.

'I'll do my best but don't hold your breath. Dougie can be a difficult bugger sometimes.'

'So can I be.'

'Tell me about it,' he said.

I stood up.

'One other thing before you disappear,' he went on. 'What about the private detective? Do you want me to get the Europe desk chappie who is joining Section Two to visit him?'

'No, I want to speak to Bloom myself. He can wait until I get back from Northern Ireland.'

'Well make sure you come back safely,' he said quietly. 'I don't want to make any more telephone calls to any more weeping mothers this week.'

'Don't worry about me. My mum is dead.'

When I left the D-G's office Colleen was at her desk, but Poppy had disappeared.

'Did you book my flight?' I asked.

'Yes, you can collect your ticket from the B.A. desk at Gatwick Airport.'

I thanked her and went to leave, but she touched my arm.

'Please be careful in Belfast, David.'

'Not you as well. The boss has just said the same thing. Why suddenly is everybody so concerned about my welfare?'

'Haven't you seen the news?'

'No, I've been too busy to watch the telly or read a newspaper. What are you talking about?'

'Four members of the Ulster Defence Regiment were killed yesterday morning in Northern Ireland?'

I can't say I was shocked. Like many people in the security services, I had become inured to the violence that had turned Ulster into a war zone over the last couple of decades. 'In Belfast?' I asked.

'No, in Downpatrick. Isn't that close to Belfast?'

'Not really. It's about twenty miles south. What happened to the soldiers?'

'Their Land Rover was blown up by a one-thousand-pound bomb. The Provisional IRA has claimed responsibility.' She looked at me and there was something in her eyes I couldn't fathom. She squeezed my arm. 'I'm worried the same might happen to you.'

'I'm touched, Colleen, but don't worry about me. Brannagan lives in Londonderry, which is about seventy miles in the opposite direction. That's where I'll be heading.'

'But they have bombs in Derry, don't they?'

'Yes, plenty of them,' I had to concede. 'But I'll be okay. I won't be wearing a uniform and I'll keep my head down. I'll be in and out of Londonderry before anybody knows I'm there.'

I should have known better.

Chapter 18

Londonderry, Northern Ireland, Tuesday April 10th.
I stood in a fire gutted two-up-two-down house in a battle-scarred road in the Bogside. The overwhelmingly Catholic district of Londonderry, which lay just outside the old city wall, was home to some of the most fanatical of Northern Ireland's dissident republicans.

The sense of fear and intimidation in the Bogside was tangible. Protestants, and visitors from Britain of whatever faith, were not welcome in the area, particularly those, like me, who were employed by the hated British Government.

It was almost midnight and darkness lay across the street like a soiled blanket. Most of the street lamps had been vandalised beyond repair and the full moon, which had earlier sent its beams to light up the dingy housing estate, was now hiding behind a bank of dark clouds.

In the house opposite, the silhouette of a man moved backwards and forwards across the blinds that covered the bedroom window. I knew the man was Shaun Brannagan and I guessed what he was doing because I had been watching the house since early evening.

When I arrived in Londonderry it was late afternoon. I drove straight to the area of the city where Shaun Brannagan lived and parked my hire car in a road some way from the Irishman's home. I then took a circuitous route on foot to my destination.

I was dressed in denim jeans, a windcheater and trainers. Over my shoulder I carried a small rucksack. I hoped I looked like just another worker on his way home.

By the time I reached 8 Lenahan Street I was confident I had not been followed. The street was deserted, but as a precaution I went straight past Brannagan's house without stopping. I walked quickly, but not so fast that I didn't have time to spot the boarded-up house opposite.

I realised immediately it would make an ideal place from which to stake out my target.

I walked to the end of the road, turned the corner and then took a different route back to where my hire car was parked. I was relieved to discover it hadn't been vandalised and still had four wheels. I drove to a city centre car-park where I knew my car would be safer.

There was a row of public telephone boxes next to the car-park. After trying a couple, and finding the phone receivers had been stolen, I found one that worked. I dialled a special number that took me straight through to the secure internal DCFO telephone system.

'Acme Cab Service.' I recognised the voice of Sam White, the duty switchboard operator.

'Hello, Chalky,' I said.

I knew he recognised my voice too, but sensed him hesitate as he wondered whether to abandon the usual security procedure. He decided to stick to the rules. 'Acme Cab Service,' he repeated.

'OK, Chalky. If we must go through this charade: I'd like a taxi.'

'Where to, sir?'

The current round of passwords was being taken from the standard Monopoly board. I knew this week's destination was one of the stations, but for the life of me I couldn't remember which one. 'King's Cross,' I tried.

'Sorry, sir, but we don't run a service to that station.'

'How about Liverpool Street?'

'We can do that one for you, Mister Statton,' he said with a laugh.

'That's a relief, Chalky, because I can't remember the names of the other two stations. Now, please put me through to the D-G's office.'

There were a couple of clicks on the line and then a phone started ringing. It only rang twice before Colleen answered.

'You're working late,' I said.

'David?'

'To be sure.'

'Where are you?'

'Londonderry and before you ask, I haven't been attacked by the Provos yet, but there's still time.'

'You shouldn't joke about such things.'

'Who said I was joking? Why are you working late?'

'I'm typing up the minutes of today's AOSC meeting. Dizz wants them finished today so he can send them to the PM.'

'The minutes must contain an important item if he wants them that urgently.'

'Something about increasing the operations budget.'

'I might have guessed it would be about money. Is he in?'

'Yes, but he has Douglas Campbell with him.'

'Perfect. Put me through.'

The D-G answered the phone after one ring. 'What's wrong?'

'Why should there be anything wrong?'

'Because you only ever contact me when there's a problem.'

'I told you this morning that I'd ring this evening.'

'Oh, yes,' he said, but I could tell from his voice that he had forgotten our conversation. 'Have you found the Irishman yet?'

'No, but I've found the house where he lives.'

'So what are you going to do?'

'Wait and watch,' I replied and explained about the burned out house in Lenahan Street from which I intended to stake out the Brannagan's home.

'But what happens if he no longer lives at that address?'

'Then he won't turn up.'

'And if he does turn up?'

'Simple. I will kill him. That's why I'm calling. Did you get your mate to sign the XPD order we spoke about?'

'I have Mister Campbell with me now,' Disraeli-Astor said, neatly side stepping my question. He was becoming an expert at such manoeuvres. 'I'll put you on conference call and you can ask him yourself.'

There was a pause and then I heard him whisper. 'It's my man Statton, Dougie. He's asking about the XPD order.'

'So, what's the story? Is the order signed or not?'

'There is a problem,' Disraeli-Astor replied. 'Mister Campbell will explain.'

'Hello, Mister Statton,' the minister said. 'As Colonel Disraeli-Astor hinted, there is a problem.'

'The colonel didn't hint. He was quite explicit. So, what sort of problem are we talking about, Mister Campbell?'

'Let me be honest with you.'

'Why does my heart sink when I hear a politician say that?'

'Hear me out, Mister Statton.'

'Go ahead.'

'Well, the truth is that I'm not willing to sign the XPD order without knowing exactly why you feel it necessary to kill this Shaun

Brannagan character.'

'It's necessary because the little shit is a murderer.'

'Surely that's for the courts to decide.'

'Tell that to Timothy Fraser.'

'Who is Timothy Fraser?' I heard Campbell whisper.

'Statton's deputy,' Disraeli-Astor whispered back. 'He thinks the Irishman murdered him.'

'I don't *think*,' I shouted. I was angry now. 'I *know* Brannagan murdered Timmy and that's why I want that XPD order. I'm going to kill him before he murders anybody else.'

'I'm sorry, Mister Statton, but I'm not comfortable signing the order.'

'Now listen to me, you superannuated twat. Very shortly I will be standing in a burnt-out, dirty, draughty, rat-infested house waiting for Brannagan to return home.

'I could be there for hours and I'll probably while away my time praying that when Brannagan turns up he'll be alone, but I don't hold out much hope my prayers will be answered. It's more than likely he'll be accompanied by some Provo heavies.'

I paused, but there was silence on the other end of the line.

'So, let me be clear about one thing. Whether, or not Brannagan is alone, I will confront him, at which time, no doubt, there will be a gunfight.'

I paused again and let that sink in.

'Mister Campbell, you need to understand something else. If I fire my weapon, I will be shooting to kill, and those IRA bastards will be doing the same. When the bullets start flying, it's going to be my life on the line, not yours. So, I'm not interested in whether you are comfortable or not, I just want you to sign that fucking form and help me do my job.'

'I really am very sorry, Mister Statton,' Campbell said in his smoothest politician's voice. 'Let me assure you that I am not refusing to sign the XPD order as such, I just need more time to weigh up the pros and cons.'

'That, minister, is utter bollocks,' I replied angrily. 'You can take your pros and cons and stick them up your arse.'

'Now, now, Statton,' Disraeli-Astor interjected hurriedly to prevent the row escalating. 'You cannot blame Mister Campbell for being cautious.'

'Being cautious is one thing,' I said. 'But being obstructive is an entirely different matter. Look, I might not have the advantage of an Eton education, but I know when I'm being given the finger.'

'I'm not sure that is entirely fair,' Disraeli-Astor said, defending the now very quiet Douglas Campbell.

I noticed the D-G's use of the word "entirely" and I sensed he agreed with me but, that didn't make me any happier.

'Sod fairness. I want action. Surely there's more than one Home Office minister who can sign the order?' I challenged him.

'There is, but you asked me to approach Mister Campbell on the Q.T,' he made a point of reminding me. 'Of course, I can ask another minister, and I will, but any such request will have to go through the proper channels and it will take time.'

'Don't you understand?' I shouted angrily. 'I am about to go into a combat situation. I don't have time to wait for the sodding Whitehall bureaucratic wheels to turn.' I slammed down the phone and cursed them. However, although describing both men with a string of Anglo-Saxon four letter words made me feel better, it didn't improve my situation. I feared that once again I was being lined up as the sacrificial goat should the operation go tits up.

It was dusk when I left the telephone box and headed back to Lenahan Street, but the night fell quickly and it was dark by the time I arrived at my destination.

The dull yellow light from the few remaining working street lamps, and brighter white light from a full moon, cast shadows that covered the pavements in dark pools and leaked in inky black trickles into the alleyways that ran alongside every other house in the road.

One of those shadows gave me a welcome cloak of anonymity as I slipped unnoticed into the alley next to the boarded up two-up-two-down and made my way to its small overgrown garden. I took a small torch and a jemmy bar from the rucksack and easily broke into the house through a back door that led into a gutted kitchen.

Once inside the house, I made my way carefully through to the front room, the walls of which were blackened by fire damage. There was no furniture in the room, but for some reason there was an upturned tea-chest in the middle of the floor. The air was full of soot, together with the stench of smoke and scorched paint.

Planks of wood had been used to board up the glass-less window and there were gaps between several of them. Through one gap I could see the front of Brannagan's home and by moving my head from side to side I could see also up and down the road. I dragged the tea-chest over to the window and settled down to wait. I tried to forget about the particles of soot that I sucked into my lungs with every breath I took.

Lenahan Street was still deserted, although occasionally I spotted a dark shape appear briefly against the grimy, grey stone semi-detached houses, before slinking away into one of the alleyways. It was a hostile environment and very few residents of the Bogside ventured out after dark. The streets belonged to the gangs and the terrorists.

I had to wait almost four hours before something happened, by which time the moon had disappeared and the only light in the street came from the few lamps that worked.

I was just beginning to think I was too late and Shaun Brannagan had already fled, when a car appeared and sped up the road, with its headlights blazing. It screeched to a halt outside the house I was watching.

The passenger door of the car opened and the interior light came on. I recognised Brannagan immediately. He had discarded his William Butler wig and beard, but his whisker-less face was imprinted on my memory. He got out of the car, strode quickly to the front door with a key already in his hand, opened it and disappeared inside the house, slamming the door behind him.

Seconds later a light was switched on in an upstairs bedroom and a rectangle of light picked out the car like a spotlight. I could see white smoke drifting out from the car's exhaust pipe. The engine was still running. It looked as if the Irishman was planning a quick getaway.

The driver got out of the car and lounged against its side. He was a big man with lank hair hanging down to the broad shoulders of his leather jacket. He looked directly at the house in which I hid.

My heart leapt and I took a step back from the window. Then I realised that it was impossible for the driver to see me through the wooden boards. I relaxed and resumed my earlier position.

The driver was no longer looking my way. He had lit a cigarette and was now casually looking up and down the road. He looked relaxed and unworried, but that might have had something to do with the pistol he held nonchalantly in one hand.

He tapped on the car's window and the passenger door swung open. A man got out. He was as tall as the driver, but thinner with a shaved head. He wore a denim jacket and jeans. He nodded briefly and then headed up the road, quickly melting into the night.

Now, as midnight approached, I watched as Brannagan moved about the bedroom in the house opposite. I guessed he was packing a bag. My bird was about to fly again, but this time I was determined to clip his wings before he flew too high.

I pulled my .44 Magnum from the holster I wore under my left armpit and made sure it was fully loaded. I was ready, but I still had no XPD order so any action I took would be without authority from my masters.

But Brannagan had killed Timmy Fraser, dumped him in a rubbish bin and mocked his death with a football score like message. I was determined he was going to die. Authority or no authority.

Clasping my pistol, and with my rucksack on my back, I headed for the kitchen door. I stepped out into the garden and pressed against the wall. I waited in silence, but all I could hear was the low, steady throb of the exhaust of the car that was parked outside Brannagan's home.

The night was pitch black. The moon was trying to escape from its prison of clouds, but had so far failed miserably. I made my way along the short path that led to the alley and then, keeping close to the side wall of the house, I edged slowly along the alley to its entrance. Now, I was almost opposite Brannagan's house, but its front door was half obscured by the parked car.

The driver moved round to the other side of the car and stood on the pavement. In this new position, his bulk obscured yet another slither of the front door. I swore under my breath and raised my pistol. I aimed it at the small part of Brannagan's front door I could still see. I hoped the Irishman's head would appear in that precise place. It would be an almost impossible shot, but it might be the only shot I got.

The bedroom light went off and I tensed in expectation. 'Come on you bastard,' I whispered to myself. The front door opened, but nobody came out. The driver was now resting his pistol on the roof of the car and it was pointing at me.

I heard a sound behind me and looked over my shoulder. The moon finally decided to leave its cloud shelter and show itself. The garden at the end of the alley was suddenly filled with a bright moonlight.

Silhouetted in the entrance to the alley was the shaven headed man in the denim jacket. He must have walked up the road, crossed over to the other side, doubled back and made his way along a back alley to ambush me from the rear.

That's when I realised I had been set up. Somehow Brannagan knew I was coming for him and had set a trap into which I had obligingly walked. I had no time to worry about how he'd found out I was in Londonderry. There were more pressing matters to worry about. For a start Mr Denim Jacket was pointing a gun at me.

I spun on my heel and dropped down on one knee to reduce the target he had to aim at. He pulled the trigger and I heard a click as the hammer hit an empty chamber.

As I raised my own weapon and fired all in one movement, the thought crossed my mind that, unlike me, my assailant hadn't checked his gun.

My pistol didn't misfire.

The bullet hit the man full in the chest. It lifted him into the air and threw him two feet further away from me. He landed on his back and didn't move. A few very lucky people survive a .44 Magnum bullet in the chest, but Denim Jacket was not one of them.

I jumped to my feet and turned to see the car driver running across the road towards me with his pistol raised. I took aim. Carefully and deliberately I shot him in the right knee. With a scream of pain he collapsed in a heap in the road.

Then Brannagan came running round the side of the car. In one hand he carried a bag and in the other a pistol. He fired a snap shot at me. I threw myself to the ground and rolled to my left as a bullet chipped a chunk out of the wall against which I had been standing.

As I fell, my hand hit a kerb-stone and my pistol was jolted from my grip. I heard it slither across the tarmac road surface. I ended up on my stomach in time to see Brannagan throw his bag into the car and slide onto the driver's seat.

I scrabbled round until I found my Magnum and lifted myself onto my elbows. I aimed at Brannagan through the open driver's door and fired, but I was micro-seconds too late. He had slammed

213

the door closed already and accelerated away with a squeal of tyres. The only damage my bullet did was to drill a hole in the car's back passenger door.

I didn't even think about following Brannagan. Even if my car had been close to hand I would never have caught him. These were his streets and he knew them like the back of his hand.

Instead I walked over to where the wounded driver lay writhing in the middle of the road. I picked up the pistol that lay beside him and slipped it into my pocket. The man looked up at me through pain filled eyes. I pointed my pistol at his head and his eyes widened in alarm.

'I'm going to start counting,' I told him quietly. 'If I can still see you when I reach ten, you can say goodbye to the top of your head.' I started to count slowly.

Despite his agony, the driver clambered to his feet and began hobbling up the street, moaning loudly with each step. By the time I reached eight he had disappeared into the shadows. He would live, which is more than you could say for his friend in the alley. He was never going to sneak up on any other unsuspecting victim.

Using my torch, I spent a few minutes searching the entrance to the alley for the spent cases of the bullets I had fired. I picked them up and put them in my rucksack with the pistol I had taken from the injured man. I then searched for the gun with which Denim Jacket had tried to shoot me. I found it in a bed of marigolds.

I went over to the dead man and using his pistol I shot him through his temple at close range. The gun didn't misfire on this occasion. I wiped any finger prints off the pistol, put it in the dead man's hand and wrapped his fingers round the butt.

Any half competent pathologist would know the man's head wound was inflicted after death. However, the now bizarre crime scene posed enough unanswerable questions to discourage the Royal Ulster Constabulary from launching a protracted investigation into the shooting. Instead they could log it as just one more example of the para-military violence that had blighted the province for so long.

Half hour later I arrived back at the city centre car-park and got into my car, by which time Shaun Brannagan was already across the border, safe in the Republic of Ireland.

Chapter 19

'**Are** you sure the Irish chappie was dead,' Disraeli-Astor asked.

'He was dead,' I assured him.

'Did you have to kill him?'

'Yes. It was either him or me.'

'I've heard that before.'

'Are you referring to Dermot O'Neill?'

'It did cross my mind.'

'That was a long time ago. However, it was true then and it's true now.'

'Well, true or not, it's a damn nuisance.'

'I apologise for being a nuisance, but when I was looking down the barrel of that thug's pistol, the last thing on my mind was wondering if defending myself might inconvenience you. I was about to have my head blown off. What did you expect me to do? Stand to attention and whistle the National Anthem?'

'Look, I'm not criticising you, Statton,' he said hurriedly, 'but, if the proverbial hits the fan, it's me who will be hauled up before the parliamentary security select committee to explain your actions.'

'Sadly, that is the lot of a Director-General,' I pointed out. 'But when I lie awake at night worrying about the cross you have to bear, I cheer myself up by reminding myself how much money you earn. Perhaps you should try doing the same.'

'Spare me your juvenile wit,' Astor said tetchily. 'The point I am making, is that I might have to answer some tricky questions. To do that I need to know the truth, the whole truth and nothing but the truth.'

'So help me God,' I added. 'Look, the truth is exactly as I told you. I shot him in self-defence.'

'And what about the second man?'

'I only hit him in the knee.'

'Only? With your Smith & Wesson?'

'Yes.'

'He didn't have much of a knee left then?'

'That's true. But, as far as I know he's not dead. Unless he's allergic to lead.'

'So, remind me. Why did you shoot him?'

'Because he came running towards me waving a gun.'

'Did he actually fire at you?'

'Nope. I didn't give him a chance.'

'So there is no evidence he was going to shoot you.'

I looked at him scornfully.

'He could have been innocent.'

'Look, when somebody points a gun at me, I shoot first and ask questions afterwards. That bastard was going to kill me.'

'That is only an assumption,' he insisted.

'Whose side are you on? You're beginning to sound like a member of the bloody select committee.'

'I'm sorry to grill you, Statton, but you don't know what those MPs are like. If I have to appear before the committee, the members will throw all sorts of questions at me, so I want to be prepared with some reasonable responses. For instance, what do I say if they insist the chappie you killed in the alley might have been innocent?'

'You tell them that it serves the chappie right. You say the chappie shouldn't have been carrying a gun and hanging out with such dangerous friends.'

He shook his head. 'I wish it was that easy. The committee members will be out to get me. They will only be interested in pinning another unjustified Catholic death on the security services so they can win a few brownie points from the civil liberties lobby and get a headline in the Guardian newspaper.'

'I'm sure you'll see them off. You've faced greater danger. Just remember Goose Green.'

He smiled at that. 'What about Brannagan?'

'I told you, he escaped.'

'I understand that, but I need to know whether, given the chance, you would have killed him too?'

'You never got me an XPD order for him.'

'That's not an answer.'

I stared at him in silence for a moment. 'Surely, all that matters is that Brannagan is still alive,' I said.

'That is still not an answer,' he said letting a hint of irritation creep into his voice again. 'You didn't have an XPD order for the other men you shot, but one of them is dead and the other is likely to be crippled for the rest of his life.'

'That's different. I didn't plan to harm them. They were collateral damage. They attacked me first remember. It was either them or me.'

'So you did plan to kill Brannagan?'

'That's a silly question, boss. You know I did. That's why I wanted the XPD order.'

'I meant, did you plan to kill Brannagan despite not having the necessary authority?'

'It's best you don't know,' I said softly. 'You wouldn't want to lie to the select committee would you?'

'Probably not,' he said and fell silent. He considered me thoughtfully. 'But at the end of the day what they think is irrelevant,' he went on finally. 'We have our own priorities.'

I was impressed. This was yet another side of him that I hadn't seen before. 'Which are?' I asked.

'Our number one priority is to track down Brannagan,' he said. 'And by the time you find him, I promise you will have a signed XPD order. That will give you all the authority you want and the Department will be covered.'

'That's great, but I've heard promises like that before. I'll believe it when I have an order in my hand.'

He was about to protest when I cut him off.

'OK, boss, let me be frank with you. As far as I am concerned, the only authority I need to shoot that murdering Irish bastard is the knowledge that Timmy Fraser is currently lying in a mortuary with his throat cut. The bloody security select committee can either like it, or lump it.'

'As Francis Urquhart might say: "You can say that, but I couldn't possible comment."'

I was surprised my boss had read House of Cards, but I nodded my understanding. I was pleased he supported me, albeit only by implication.

Disraeli-Astor continued to study me for what seemed an age, then changed the subject: 'Look, I know young Fraser's death hit you hard and I'm sorry to burden you at this time, but I need your help.' He passed me a thick buff folder. 'The bumf keeps piling in. Can you sort some of it out for me?'

I opened the file and the first document was the annual budget requisition memo from the Cabinet Office, with its thick form still attached. The form hadn't been started, let alone completed in triplicate. 'I've already seen this once,' I protested. 'I sent it to Roly. The department's budgets are his responsibility.'

'I appreciate that. However, as Lafarge pointed out, quite reasonably, he will be retiring soon. Next year's budget won't affect him. He thought it would be better to leave the form to somebody on whom it would have an impact.'

'In that case, shouldn't that somebody be you?'

'In principle.'

'In principle? What does that mean?'

'It means that ultimately I am responsible for the budget, but in practice, as Director-General, I delegate some of my tasks to my deputy, the budget being one of them.'

'But I'm not your deputy,' I pointed out. 'Unless you're offering me Roly's job if I fill this bloody form in for you?'

He didn't respond to this and his face gave nothing away. He changed the subject again. He was a dab hand at doing that. 'There is something else you ought to know. Fraser's funeral is taking place next Wednesday afternoon at Kensal Green Cemetery.'

'Not in Devon?'

'No, his mother only moved to the West Country a couple of years ago, until then she lived all her life in London. She wants her son buried next to his father.'

'I'll attend,' I said.

'I thought you might.'

'And I dare say Poppy and Melissa will want to come with me to pay their respects.'

'Of course,' he said with a nod. 'Des what's-his-name is joining your team next Tuesday. He, and that other bod I transferred, can man the office while the rest of you are at the cemetery.'

'It's Des Hobbins,' I pointed out. 'And the other bod's name is Clive Flack.'

'Of course it is.'

'Are you coming to Timmy's funeral,' I asked.

'I'll try to make it, but I can't promise.'

I took that as a no.

'What about the detective chappie?' he asked.

'Justin Bloom.'

'Was that his name?'

'Yes. I'm off to see him now.'

'I'll be interested to hear what he has to say for himself.'

'You can come with me if you like.'

'I think not. I am up to my eyes in work.'

I tapped the file. 'Most of your work appears to be destined for my desk.'

He smiled patronisingly at me. 'You simply do not understand, Statton. My job is not all about paperwork. There is a wide range of responsibilities involved with being Director-General. You have no idea how many management problems I face on a daily basis. For instance...'

'Managing your very large pay packet?' I interrupted him.

'That's the second time you have mentioned my salary, Statton. You sound resentful. I'm beginning to wonder if you are a closet communist.'

'I'm no commie, boss, far from it, I'm border line Tory. I don't mind money, in fact I love it. No, I'm just a working-class boy who wishes he was paid as much as you. I'm not resentful, I'm just jealous.'

'As I was saying before you so rudely interrupted me,' he went on, ignoring my comment. 'For instance, later this afternoon I have a meeting at the US embassy. They want to discuss how we can work together on this Mandela Project business and I have to find a way to diplomatically tell them we don't want any interference from the State Department. Then, when I get back, I have to prepare today's report for Jeffery Johnson.'

'That's not going to take up much paper. What's to report?'

'Not a lot,' he conceded. 'That's why I want to know what Bloom has to say for himself. I can include that in my report. I will be staying in the office late today, so brief me when you get back.'

'OK.' I stood up.

'Oh, and Statton,' he paused and put on his spectacles. He had only just taken to wearing them for reading. I wasn't convinced they were necessary, because sometimes he forgot to put them on. They had bi-focal lenses and purple frames.

He thought they made him look cool. Personally I thought they made him look like a nerd. Now he peered over the top of them and gave me the sort of warning look to which I had become accustomed. 'Whatever you do, please do not come back and tell me that you have killed the detective.'

'Very droll,' I said over my shoulder as I left his office carrying the file of paperwork. Somehow I resisted the temptation to slam the door behind me, but I admit it pushed my self-control to its limit.

Fulham, London

The Justin Bloom Detective Agency was located in a large Victorian house in the King's Road that had been converted into offices. Bloom's agency was tucked away at the top of a flight of stairs.

I wondered how many of his high-end clients had ever actually visited his less than salubrious office. Probably not many. I guessed that Bloom was the type who would find any excuse to meet his clients in some fancy club, or bistro, and bill them for the privilege.

The office door was painted white and there was a black sign screwed to it bearing the agency's name. I knocked but there was no answer. I tried the lever handle and heard a click. The door was not locked. I pushed gently and it swung open silently. I stepped into a deserted reception area.

The advertisement for the detective agency, that Poppy had found for me in Yellow Pages, boasted it operated out of offices that were "inviting, luxurious, spacious, inviting and yet discreet". Looking round I could only assume the advert predated the 1987 Trades Description Act.

The reception area was tiny and contained a small desk, behind which was positioned a rickety dining-room chair. However, there was no sign of the other things needed by a receptionist, such as a telephone, typewriter or appointments book. There was not even a chair in which a client could wait, but I suppose that hardly mattered since there was no room to sit anyway.

I walked through to the main office, which was as devoid of life as the reception area from which I had just come. The first thing that struck me was all the lights were on, which was odd because it was mid-afternoon.

The desk in this room was larger than the one in the reception area, but not by much. However, it did at least have a telephone, a large diary and a cheap plastic container in which I could see a collection of pens, pencils and paper clips. The only other things on the desk were an almost empty bottle of white wine and two glasses.

Behind the desk was a large, plush executive style chair - the only nod that I could see to the promised luxury suggested by the advert - and in front of it stood an identical chair to the one in reception. Alongside the desk was a waste bin half full of the usual paper litter found in any office. Laying on top of the rubbish was a foil condom wrapper.

Set into one wall was a small, old-fashioned casement window, which overlooked an overgrown, postage-stamp sized garden. Against the opposite wall stood two grey metal filing cabinets, above which was fixed a shelf containing a neat row of ledgers, kept in place by two mahogany cubes.

There was a door in the far corner of the office, which I guessed was a toilet. I tried the handle but the door was bolted on the inside. I pressed my ear against the door, but there was no sound from behind it.

There were three round holes in the door's front panel.

I didn't have to expend much effort to kick open the door, because it was secured by only a single small bolt. The electric light was on in the toilet, despite there being a small frosted glass window set into the back wall, through which the sun was shining.

I tried to push open the door, but it was jammed against the leg of a man who was slumped on the floor. His upper body was lying across the toilet pedestal and his head was propped against a low-level cistern.

The man was wearing dark slacks and a shirt that had once been brilliant white. Now, much of the shirt was a dark scarlet colour, stained by the blood that had seeped from three holes in the man's back.

If the man stood up, the holes in his back would match those in the door panel, but he would never stand up again. He was dead.

I put all my weight against the door and pushed hard. The body moved slowly, inch-by-inch and then, suddenly, slid over onto its back. I looked round the door at the dead man's face. It was Justin Bloom.

I squeezed into the toilet and saw that his trousers were undone and urine had splashed all over the toilet seat and floor.

It didn't take a first class honours degree in criminology to work out that the detective had been relieving himself when he was shot in the back through the toilet door.

In the toilet pan a used condom floated on the surface of the yellow stained water. He had obviously enjoyed his last moments of life, but with whom had he had sex?

Poking out of Bloom's shirt pocket was a folded piece of paper. I pulled it out delicately with thumb and forefinger. It was a Bank of Ireland cheque for £250, issued against the account of Five Continents Travel Ltd. I had never heard of it.

I made my way back to the office. The ledgers on the shelf above the filing cabinets all had white labels on their spines. In neat hand-writing on each label was the name of the ledger. I pulled down the one that was marked: **Accounts Day Book**.

I opened the ledger and turned to the income section. The accounts were written up in the same hand-writing as that on the labels. The page for April 1990 showed only a handful of entries, all of which were early in the month. One entry, dated 3rd April, showed a cheque receipt for £250. The client was shown as Five Continents Travel Ltd.

I flicked back a page to March and found three similar entries, all for the same amount. They were dated 13th, 20th and 27th. I guessed this weekly payment was a retainer for his services. No doubt, if Justin Bloom hadn't been killed, there would now be an entry dated 10th April.

The dead man was an organised person. Each of the filing cabinet drawers was labelled with its contents. One of the cabinets contained case files in alphabetical order. I pulled out the top drawer, which was marked *A-H*. It was full of buff cardboard files, each with a coloured label tab. I soon found the file for which I was looking.

I took out the file for Five Continents Travel Ltd. It was empty. As I returned the file to the drawer, I saw the corner of a sheet of paper poking out from an adjacent file. I pulled it out and removed the paper.

It was a letter on Five Continents Travel headed notepaper giving authority for the Afro Mining Corporation to act on its behalf in all dealings with the Justin Bloom Detective Agency. The letter was dated 10th March 1990 and was signed by the company's Chairman, Brendan O'Leary.

I flicked through the rest of the papers in the file, but found nothing else relating to Five Continents Travel or the Afro Mining Corporation. I folded the letter and slipped it into my jacket pocket. I closed the filing cabinet drawer and walked over to the desk. I opened the appointments diary at the page for 10th April 1990. There were just three entries.

The first was a 12.30 luncheon date at Mario's Restaurant with somebody called Celia Browne. I assumed this was either a client, or a prospective client. The second was a four pm appointment at Companies House, but there was no indication about the purpose of the visit. The final entry was for a meeting at 8 pm and just said BO. I wondered if this stood for Brendan O'Leary.

I checked back on the dates when the other Five Continents Travel cheques were issued and found a similar meeting scheduled for the same time on each of the days. In addition, there were a number of other entries for meetings with BO at different times on other days during April and March, but none before Five Continents Travel sent the letter to Bloom. That triggered a couple of questions in my mind.

The first was, if Brendan O'Leary was BO, did that mean that he killed Bloom? Secondly, why had he visited the private detective so many times, particularly since he had appointed Wren's company as his agent in London?

It made no sense, but what was new? Nothing in my life made sense at the moment, including my feelings for Colleen Masters. Suddenly, the thought of her made me want to see her, touch her and hold her.

DFCO offices.

Colleen was getting ready to go home when I arrived in her office on the way to see Disraeli-Astor.

'How did you get on with Justin Bloom?' She asked.

'The D-G told you?'

'No, Poppy did. I rang your office but you weren't there. She told me you had gone to see a Justin Bloom, but she didn't say why.'

'That's because I didn't tell her why.'

'So who *is* Bloom?'

'Was.'

'Why the past tense?'

'Because he's dead.'

'But who was he?'

'Remember the bloke who was with your friend Misty at the Chinese restaurant and theatre?'

She nodded.

'That was Bloom. He was a private detective.'

'Was he following you?'

'Perhaps. Or you.'

'Why would he be following me?'

'I don't know. That's why I visited him. I wanted to find out what he was up to.'

'Did you find out?'

'No, but I have my own idea.'

She suddenly looked at me sharply. 'You didn't kill Bloom, did you?'

'Don't you start; your boss seems to think I spend my life keeping undertakers in business.'

'Then who did kill him?'

'I don't know that either, but again, I have my own idea. Now, why did you ring me?'

She glanced towards the D-G's office door and lowered her voice. 'It's Easter this weekend and I wondered if you had anything planned,' she said before lowering her voice even more. 'If not, would you like to replace my vibrator again?'

I smiled at her. I couldn't think of anything better to do with my time. 'On one condition. That you let me take you away somewhere.'

'That's not a condition. It's an invitation I'd be foolish to turn down.'

'So you'll come?'

'Lots of times hopefully,' she giggled.

'You know what I mean.'

'Yes, I'd love to come with you. Where do you have in mind?'

'Kent.'

'A lovely county, but large. Which part?'

'Have you ever been to Wye?'

'No. I've never heard of it.'

'It's about ten miles from Canterbury.'

'I've heard of Canterbury.'

'I should hope so. Well, Wye is a little village with a fantastic restaurant called The Wife of Bath.'

'As in *The Canterbury Tales*?'

'Yes, that's the connection with Canterbury.'

'The restaurant also has a few guest rooms and I thought we

could stay in one of those. Wye doesn't have much of a nightlife so it will be a quiet, unexciting weekend, but relaxing.'

'It might be quiet and relaxing. However, I'm sure we can generate a little excitement.' She grinned impishly.

'I'll pick you up at six o'clock on Friday evening,' I said.

'Eighteen hundred hours it is, sir,' she confirmed with a mock salute. 'I've been learning!'

I clapped my hands silently and then made my way to Disraeli-Astor's office. I knocked on his door.

'Come in,' he said, but I was already halfway through the door. He didn't seem to mind. He was writing and didn't look up as I sat down opposite him.

I didn't say anything either. Instead I sat there and thought about how best I could break the news of Bloom's death to him. Although I didn't kill the detective, I knew my boss would find some way of blaming me.

I stared out of the window. It was almost seven o'clock and the sun was already on its way to bed. It was sinking slowly down behind the roof of the building opposite. The sun's rays flooded through the window and highlighted the few strands of grey in Disraeli-Astor's cropped dark hair.

'Well,' he said when he eventually looked up and took off his spectacles. 'How did you get on with Bloom? What did he have to say?'

'Not a lot.'

'Enough of the Paul Daniels impressions, Statton. Did Bloom say anything worthwhile?'

'Nothing.'

'So did you actually talk to Bloom?'

'That would have been difficult.'

'Why?'

'Because when I found him he was lying face down in his own piss.'

'What are you telling me?'

'I'm telling you that Mr Justin Bloom is currently in the Home Office pathology lab being cut up into little pieces.'

'He's dead?'

'Completely.'

'I think you had better explain,' he said with a heavy sigh.

So I told him how I had discovered Bloom in the locked toilet and what else I had found in the office.

'Who killed Bloom?' He gave me a suspicious look.

'I'm not sure. Not least, because I wasn't present when he was killed.'

'Take a guess.'

'OK. This is what I think happened. Somebody with the initials BO visited Bloom to deliver his weekly retainer cheque from the Five Continents Travel Ltd. I think BO had a glass of wine with him.' I told him about the entries in the appointments book.

'At some time during the evening they had sex, after which Bloom went into the toilet for a pee. When his visitor heard the click of the toilet door bolt, he fired three shots through the door into Bloom's back.'

I took from my pocket the letter I had found in the filing cabinet and passed it to him. 'Read that.'

'You think that BO stands for Brendan O'Leary?' He asked after he had read the letter.

'It's a possibility.'

'So O'Leary killed Bloom.'

I hesitated before saying: 'That's what it looks like.'

'You don't seem overly confident.'

'I'm not. It doesn't smell right. Why would O'Leary deliver the cheque himself? Powerful men like him have flunkies to do menial jobs like that. Anyway, O'Leary had hired Wren's company as his London agent.'

'But you said Bloom had written in his appointments book that he was meeting O'Leary.'

'That's not true. What I said was that he was meeting BO.'

'Who you think is O'Leary.'

'Who *might* be O'Leary,' I emphasised. 'But the identity of BO is just one of several unanswered questions.'

'Like?'

'Well, for a start why was Justin Bloom following me and why would O'Leary want to kill him?'

Astor looked at the letter again. 'Could it be connected to the Mandela Project operation?' He tapped the letter. 'After all this letter confirms that O'Leary is working with Wren?'

'We knew that already. If you remember, they were both on the list of Phoenix Group members given to us by the Yanks. Talking of whom, how did your meeting at the embassy go?'

'Not good.'

'They want something,' I guessed.

'Yes. They want more input into the operation.'

'What sort of input?'

'You won't be happy.'

'Try me.'

'It might be better if I let them explain. They have suggested a meeting between Bob Fletcher and you to thrash out the details.'

'Thrash out what details?'

He looked uncomfortable. 'They requested direct field involvement.'

'What the hell does that mean?'

'They want one of their agents to work with you when you're operating in the field.'

'Over my dead body.'

'Don't mention dead bodies. You seem to attract them the way meat attracts flies.'

I found it difficult to argue with him on that point. Instead, I asked: 'So when is this meeting with Fletcher?'

'I told the Ambassador you would arrange a meeting.'

'That was nice of you. What else?'

'I said you would contact Fletcher and meet up before you undertook any further field work.'

'Great!'

'I did try to put them off, but the ambassador reminded me that the Prime Minister had specifically requested their help.'

'I don't mind CIA help. I just don't want them trying to take over the operation.'

'On that, Statton, we are in complete agreement.'

'OK. I'll ring Bob Fletcher first thing in the morning and set up a meeting for some time next week.'

'Thank you. I have every faith you will find a way to prevent interference from our American cousins.' He smiled at me.

I didn't smile back at him. I hoped his faith was not misplaced. My past dealings with the CIA had not been auspicious.

Chapter 20

Colleen and I made love twice before eventually she fell into a deep sleep in the early hours of Sunday morning, but despite the hour, and my heavy eyes, slumber eluded me. Thoughts swirled round in my mind and I could not get rid of them.

It had been a great weekend so far. When we left London on Good Friday, the bank holiday evening traffic was a nightmare. We were stuck in a succession of jams. But we didn't care. We spent the time listening to Bob Dylan and Dave Brubeck cassette tapes, chatting a little and laughing a lot.

By the time we reached The Wife of Bath it was late and we were too tired to eat a proper meal, but the chef put together a plate of delicious sandwiches, which we ate in our comfortable bedroom. The chilled bottle of Moet and Chandon, with which we washed down our late meal, pushed us over the edge from tiredness to sleepiness.

It was gone midnight when we washed, brushed our teeth and fell into bed completely exhausted. There was no love making. We were both asleep as soon as our heads hit the pillow.

At some time during the night my sleep was disturbed. Colleen was restless. I could feel her tossing and turning and mumbling incoherently. I lay listening, not quite sleeping and not quite awake.

My befuddled mind could make no sense of what she was saying and I soon drifted back to sleep. By the time I awoke in the morning I had forgotten most of what she said. Most but not everything.

Saturday started well with a full English breakfast, which set us up nicely for a seven-mile countryside hike along the North Downs Way and Stour Valley Way to the village of Chilham.

After wandering round the garden of Chilham Castle, and exploring the pretty village, with its many timber-framed buildings, we had a pub lunch in the White Horse before taking a leisurely stroll back to Wye.

In the evening we had dinner in The Wife of Bath. It was expensive, but top quality. I had a T-bone beef steak that had been hung and matured for a month. Colleen had Lobster Thermidor, which, when I smelt it, I half wished I had chosen. That is often the way with food.

For pudding, we both chose the crème brûlée, followed by local Kentish cheeses accompanied by water biscuits and a 10-year old port.

We drank our coffees sitting in the restaurant's small lounge in front of a roaring fire. The heat was welcome because the warm spring day had given way to a chilly evening.

By the time we made our way upstairs to our bedroom we were relaxed, happy, and wanted each other badly. We both got what we wanted.

We made love.

Although it would take something approaching the Spanish Inquisitors to make me admit it publicly, but that last word summed up my growing feelings for Colleen Masters.

And now I lay awake thinking about our time in Wye. It had been a good visit and we had enjoyed ourselves. There were lots of positives to take from our weekend, and I would, but it was a more negative thing that kept me awake. It was something that Colleen mumbled during her disturbed Friday night's sleep.

Most of what she had said was incomprehensible, but one thing stuck in my mind. It might have been a figment of my imagination, but still I could not forget the words that I thought she mumbled: 'I'm sorry, David, I didn't mean to hurt you.'

I had no idea what this meant. I wasn't aware she had hurt me in any way. Maybe she said something entirely different and I had imbued her words with more meaning than was intended.

As I mulled over this riddle, sleep finally crept up on me. That's all I remember until I woke up at eight o'clock on Easter Sunday to the feel of Colleen's hand massaging my groin.

I didn't stop her. The chocolate Easter egg that was hidden in my overnight-bag as a surprise for her could wait.

Chapter 21

Wembley, London, Monday, April 16th

Colleen and I stayed in Kent until after lunch on Easter Monday before travelling back to town. We reached Bayswater by mid-afternoon, where I dropped her off at home and headed straight for north-west London.

Wembley Way was packed with people heading towards the pop concert being held in honour of Nelson Mandela. There was a hint of rain in the air, but judging by the rapidly dropping temperature, snow was a distinct possibility.

The concert was sold out with 74,000 people expected to attend. The weather forecast was not good and those who had tickets to stand on the soccer pitch in front of the stage, were going to be cold and wet by the end of the evening.

When I arrived at Wembley Stadium, I made my way to the police control room. I found the head of Special Branch briefing his senior officers. They were standing in front of a large plan of the stadium, pinned to a cork-board.

I introduced myself and explained why I was there. The reception I received mirrored the frosty climate outside.

'I'm pleased to meet you, Mister Statton,' Assistant Deputy Commissioner Gerald Hughes said, although he didn't look particularly pleased, nor did he offer me his hand.

'You too, sir,' I responded with an equal lack of enthusiasm. Kevin Neal had already tipped me off about ADC Hughes. In Kevin's opinion, his colleague was a pompous, ambitious arsehole who looked down on those of inferior rank, but sucked up unashamedly to the Commissioner and his political masters.

'However, I am not entirely clear why you are here,' Hughes added.

'I'm here so you can give me an update on the security measures you have put in place for the concert.'

'I'm always happy to co-operate with our colleagues in the Secret Service, but, unfortunately, I don't have time to brief you right now.' He turned away from me.

'That's very disappointing, Mister Hughes,' I said staring at his back. 'Is there any other message you would like me to give the Prime Minister?'

Hughes turned to face me again. He frowned. 'I don't understand.'

'It was a simple question, sir. Would you like me to repeat it?'

'I understood the question,' he said sharply. 'I just didn't understand your reference to the PM?'

'Because my orders came direct from her.' I paused and let that information sink in. 'And she specifically asked that I double check the security arrangements for today's concert and report back to her.' I stared at him. 'So, other than that you don't have time to brief me, do you have any other messages for Mrs Thatcher?'

ADC Hughes stared right back at me and weighed up his options. He soon realised I had put him in an impossible position and that he had none. His face flushed red with restrained anger. 'So what do you want to know?' He asked crossly.

I stepped closer to the cork-board and pointed at the plan. Some of Hughes's senior staff were looking at their boss uncomfortably, but that was his problem, not mine. 'Thank you, Mister Hughes,' I said, ignoring his hostility. 'Let's begin with what measures you have put in place so far.'

'I would rather begin by assuring you that everything is in hand,' he said pompously

'I'm sure the PM will be pleased to receive your assurance. However, I think she will probably expect me to provide her with a few more details.'

At last the policeman got the message and he started to brief me properly. He began by telling me that the whole arena had been thoroughly searched by sniffer dogs, which would continue to tour the stadium throughout the concert. He then explained the security arrangements for the evening.

The plan was that Nelson Mandela, and his wife, Winnie, would appear briefly in the upper tier of the stand, along with Oliver Tembo's wife, Adelaide, who was representing her husband because he was in hospital. They would be joined by Archbishop Trevor Huddleston and the ANC representative in London, Mendi Msimang.

Mandela would be introduced and wave to concert goers to show he was actually in the stadium. Immediately after this brief appearance, the ANC leader's group would be whisked away to a

231

private room, located in the administration area of the building, to which there was no public access. The group would stay there until it was time for Mandela to make his speech.

The only other people allowed into the private room would be Special Branch police officers and a few specially invited politicians.

'When Mandela eventually makes his way to the stage I will accompany him with some of my officers,' Hughes explained. 'In addition, there will be armed policemen positioned around the stadium monitoring the audience and watching for any suspicious activity.'

'Thank you, Mister Hughes,' I said when the briefing was finished. 'Just one other thing, what time will Mister Mandela be making his speech?'

Hughes hesitated, and then he said. 'For security reasons that decision will be taken at the last moment.' He paused and looked at me when I didn't respond. 'We were thinking eight o'clock,' he added reluctantly. 'Just as it's starting to get dark.'

'That makes sense,' I agreed. 'Dusk is a difficult light for any sniper.'

'That's what we thought,' he said and for the first time I saw a flash of respect in his eyes, but it didn't last long, it was soon submerged under his resentment. 'But the actual time is fluid and will depend on circumstances. The speech will only take place when I am satisfied all potential firing positions for a sniper have been identified and secured.'

This made sense as well. 'OK. I'll let you get on,' I said. 'However, if it's alright with you I'll wander round the stadium and check out what's happening. A fresh pair of eyes and all that.'

'We welcome your help, Mister Statton,' Hughes said without wasting too much energy putting sincerity behind his words. His attitude didn't worry me. I am far too old to take umbrage at being treated like dirt by somebody whose sense of self-importance and ambition was greater than his ability.

I spent the next couple of hours visiting different parts of the stadium, until I ended up standing in front of the stage, facing the audience. Either side of me was a phalanx of security guards and policemen.

On stage behind us, a bespectacled Lou Reed was laying down a half decent guitar solo. A few flakes of snow fluttered down from the sky, but it didn't appear to worry either the rock singer or his enthusiastic audience.

As I listened to the music, I used a pair of field glasses to work out the various fields of fire in different parts of the stadium. I was pleasantly surprised to see that each of the potential sniper firing positions I spotted were already occupied by a police marksman. I just hoped none of the cops was Brannagan in disguise.

It was ten to eight when I finally left the front of the stage and headed for the administration section of the stadium. By then Ben Elton was firing off, at machine-gun speed, rude comments about Margaret Thatcher.

When I reached the door at the bottom of the staircase leading up to the room in which Mandela and his entourage were closeted, I found it was locked. There was an armed policeman standing outside the door. I showed my Met Police warrant card. 'Can you unlock the door?' I asked.

'No, sir,' the policeman replied. 'The only person with a key is ADC Hughes and he is already upstairs.'

I didn't complain. Locking the door to the private section, and keeping personal control of the key, was a good move by Hughes. I headed for the public staircase that was further round the stadium.

It took me some time to make my way to the administration offices from the public area. There was no direct access to the corridor that led to the staircase leading down to the back of the stage, but eventually I discovered an office that appeared to be close to where I was heading.

The door to the office was locked, but when I knocked a woman opened it a fraction. She viewed me suspiciously. I wasn't surprised. On a desk behind her were piles of money she had been counting.

I showed her my warrant card. Although her expression softened slightly, she didn't fling her arms round me and greet me as a bosom buddy. However, she did open the door fully and allow me into the office, before immediately locking the door again.

On the other side of the office, was another locked door and through its glass panel I could see a corridor beyond. This was what I was looking for. The woman let me out and I left her to return to counting the concert's takings. It looked as if it would be a long job.

Once in the corridor I turned right and headed for the private room in which Mandela was being entertained. I glanced at my watch and saw it was almost eight o'clock. I was probably too late to help escort the African leader down to the stage, but at least I would know he was still safe.

I turned a corner and almost bumped into a man who seemed to be loitering in the corridor. He looked shocked to see me. 'Who the hell are you?' He asked.

'Don't worry, Mister Hollingsworth,' a deep voice said. 'I know this man. Good evening, Mister Statton. It is good to see you again.'

Nelson Mandela emerged from a toilet. I looked along the deserted corridor. 'Where is your security detail, sir?' I asked.

The African pointed towards the end of the corridor. 'They are on their way downstairs,' he said. 'I needed to use the toilet.'

'Did you let ADC Hughes know?' I asked.

'No, it was a last minute decision. Not to worry though, we will soon catch up with him.'

'Then let's go, sir,' I said shepherding him towards the end of the corridor and down the steep staircase. I was closely followed by Tony Hollingsworth, who by now had introduced himself as the funder and organiser of the concert.

At the bottom of the staircase we found the exit door was locked. I banged on it, but there was no response from the other side. I knew from my earlier experience that the noise in the stadium was deafening. It would be difficult for anybody standing outside the door to hear me.

'What do we do now?' Hollingsworth asked. 'If Mister Mandela doesn't turn up on the stage there will be a riot. I'll be ruined.'

'Follow me,' I said, more worried about Mandela's safety than Hollingsworth's money. 'I know another way out.' I headed back up the stairs.

I resisted the temptation to take the stairs two at a time. I was conscious of the age and physical condition of Mandela, who I knew was still suffering the effects of his lengthy stay in prison.

When we reached the top, I led the pair back down the corridor past the toilet to the accounts office door. I looked through the window and saw the woman was still counting money. I knocked on the door.

She looked up, but at first didn't see me, instead she saw Nelson Mandela's black face. She didn't appear to recognise the ANC leader, because a wary expression spread across her face. Then she saw me and relaxed. She stood up and walked over and unlocked the door to let us in.

I led the two men through the office and headed for the door that led to the public corridor. When we reached the football pitch, snowflakes fluttered in the air again. We pushed ourselves through the crowds of concert goers, who were so intent on watching what was happening in front of them that they took no notice of us as we elbowed our way to the stage.

When we arrived behind the stage I ran up the steps and immediately found ADC Hughes.

'Are you missing somebody?' I asked.

He gave me a quizzical look. 'Who?' He asked and then scanned the short line of people who waited patiently in the wings. Blood drained from his face. 'Where's Mandela?' He stammered.

'So much for your security,' I said angrily. 'I found him upstairs. He was all alone except for Mister Hollingsworth, who doesn't strike me as somebody who would be much good in an emergency.'

'I don't understand. I assumed Mister Mandela was with us. What happened to him?'

'He needed a leak. Did you think to ask whether he, or any of his group, wanted to use the toilet?'

'Hollingsworth asked them, but they all said no.'

'Mister Mandela changed his mind.' Hollingsworth explained as the two men joined us in the wings and overheard the conversation.

'Unfortunately, these things happen as you get older,' Mandela added with a smile.

'Never mind. No harm was done,' I said, which was true, although such a lapse in security was unforgiveable. However, I didn't have time to make a fuss because Nelson Mandela was already being ushered onto the stage.

As he was picked up by a spotlight, a huge roar went up from the audience. He raised a hand and almost immediately the cheers subsided into silence. That was the power of the man. He began to speak.

'Master of Ceremonies, Distinguished artists, Members of the International Reception Committee, dear friends here and elsewhere in the world.

'Our first simple and happy task is to say thank you. Thank you very much to you all. Thank you that you chose to care, because you

235

could have decided otherwise. Thank you that you elected not to forget, because our fate could have been a passing concern.'

I eased my way to the front of the stage, but ensured I stayed out of sight in the shadows. I looked out at the crowd, on my guard for potential trouble. I could see that the audience was mesmerised as it listened to Mandela. The stadium was silent except for his deep voice.

As I stared into the gathering gloom, I could see nothing more suspicious than the occasional flashbulb as somebody took a photograph of their hero, but I kept my hand close to the butt of my Magnum anyway.

'Let us continue to march forward together for the realisation of that glorious vision,' Mandela said as he came towards the end of his speech. 'It will be a proud day for all humanity when we are all able to say that the apartheid crime against humanity is no more.

'Then shall we all converge on the cities, towns and villages of South Africa to celebrate that moment when by ending the system of white minority domination, humanity will have ensured that never again shall the scourge of racial tyranny raise its ugly head.

'You will all be welcome to attend those historic victory celebrations.'

When Mandela finally finished his speech a tremendous roar went up from the crowded stadium. As I watched him raise a clenched fist and soak up the adulation, I remembered the question Freddie had posed eight years before: Would Nelson Mandela ever take control of South Africa?

I hadn't known the answer then and I still didn't have one. However, I was determined to do all I could to keep the man alive long enough to at least give him a chance to deliver if he could.

Seeing a Mandela led government in her country was what Freddie always dreamed of. We might have drifted apart, and were now separated by two continents, but my deep rooted respect and affection for her made me determined to make that dream come true.

Chapter 22

Des Hobbins made a good start. He was in the office by 09.00 hours on Tuesday. That was ten minutes after me, but a half hour before the rest of my staff.

Like many of the longer serving employees of the department, Des was an ex-military man. In his case, he left the Army, after 22 years' service, as a staff sergeant in the Military Police. From what I knew of Des, he was a tough, but fair-minded red-cap.

I wasn't surprised Des was on time. That was his style. I was pleased to have him on my team.

'Morning,' he said as he came into my office to report for duty. 'Sorry to hear about your deputy. He was a decent lad.'

'In the words of the D-G, shit happens.'

'I know, but why does the shit usually end up on the heads of nice people like young Fraser?'

'That, my friend, is something on which I do not feel qualified to comment. Only whichever God you happen to believe in knows the answer to that particular question.'

Des nodded and looked at me with sad eyes. 'Do you remember Rosa Müller?' He asked.

'Wasn't she married to the pastor who ran the Wittenberg Ring?'

'Yes. Franz Müller.'

'A brave man,' I said.

'They were all brave.'

My mind went back three years to what was my first assignment when I re-joined the Department. 'As I recall, we were sent over to the East to help track down a member of Müller's group who disappeared.'

'The language teacher.'

'That's right, the language teacher.' I stared at him silently for a few moments. 'There is something that's always puzzled me,' I said eventually. 'You were the group's field contact, so were an obvious choice go, but why did the D-G send me with you?'

'Because I asked for you,' Des said.

'He never told me that.'

'The D-G keeps his cards very close to his chest.'

'Don't I know it. So, why did you ask for me?'

Des didn't respond immediately, instead, he pulled on his bottom lip and looked thoughtfully at his wedding ring.

'The Wittenberg Ring was very important to me,' he said suddenly. 'Those people were feeding us with invaluable information about the deterioration in the country's economy. They understood the way in which Erich Honecker was rapidly losing control over the civilian population, as Perestroika in the Soviet Union impacted on the East German Communist Party apparatus.'

I knew all this but let him carry on. I guessed he needed to get something off his chest.

'The language teacher was key to the information flow, because he was used as a translator during Stasi interrogations of those local people picked up for anti-state activities. When he went missing, the Müllers found out he had been arrested and asked for help to rescue him.'

'Which we did.'

'Yes we did,' he agreed. 'But I could never have rescued him if it hadn't been for you. I had heard you were resourceful, which is why I wanted you with me, but you never told me how you discovered where the teacher was being held.'

'I knew somebody in the KGB who owed me a favour. I couldn't say at the time, but it doesn't matter now.'

'Would I be right in thinking that was our friend Alexei Urinoff?'

'How did you guess?'

'Because it had to be somebody whose identity needed protecting in nineteen-eighty-seven, but doesn't need protecting now. I just put two and two together.'

'Urinoff was based in East Germany back then and had a couple of contacts in the Stasi. He found out the teacher was being held in Dessau, but was being transferred to Berlin in an unmarked car. He gave me details of the route, the vehicle being used, the date and the time. You know the rest, because you were there.'

I remembered again the way we had ambushed the car in which the teacher was being transported. The Stasi had decided to use back roads to reach Berlin, rather than the autobahn. We chose a heavily wooded area in which there was no option other than for them to stop when they came across the large tree that blocked the isolated road.

There were only two Stasi officers in the car with the teacher; one driving and the other on the back-seat guarding their prisoner. When they arrived at the tree the car stopped and the driver got out. He soon realised the tree was too heavy for him to move on his own. His companion forced the teacher out of the car with his pistol and ordered him to help the driver move the tree.

I hit the guard across the back of his head with the cosh that I carried in my right hand. He fell with a grunt and there was a clatter as his pistol bounced on the road. The driver looked over his shoulder and saw me immediately. He didn't move to confront me, no doubt deterred by the pistol I carried in my left hand, which was pointing at his head.

The driver didn't have long to worry about the awkward situation he faced, because Des Hobbins poleaxed him with a baseball bat.

It was all over in seconds and soon we had the teacher in our car, which was parked on the other side of the tree, and were heading for Berlin.

'And I suppose it was Urinoff who hired the undertaker in East Berlin who smuggled the teacher across to the West in that coffin?'

'Yes.'

'Wasn't that a risk?'

'Everything in life is a risk, Des. However, it was less risky than it seems. The teacher was sharing the coffin with a dead British Army officer who had a heart attack whilst attending a conference in East Berlin and was being transported back to the West.'

'So why did Urinoff help?'

'It was his insurance policy. Even back then he could see the writing on the wall and wanted to earn brownie points in case he decided to defect to the West.'

'I never knew.'

'You didn't need to know. Now what about Rosa Müller?'

Des looked sad again. 'She was a lovely woman in every sense of the word. She was beautiful and had the serenest air about her that I have ever known in a woman.'

'It was pretty obvious you had a soft spot for her.'

He nodded. 'But you need to understand that our relationship never went beyond mild flirting.'

'Why?' I asked.

He looked again at his wedding ring. 'It would never have

worked. We were both married.'

'You used the past tense when talking about Rosa,' I pointed out gently.

Des looked upset. 'Did you know that Franz and Rosa had a son?' He asked.

I shook my head.

'He was seventeen and was the apple of their eye.'

'What happened?'

'He was shot whilst trying to get to West Berlin.'

'When?'

'About a year ago. It destroyed Franz. He made a fuss about what he called state murder and was picked up by the Stasi. The next time Rosa saw him he was lying on a slab in the mortuary. The authorities claimed he fell out of a window whilst trying to escape. However, they never successfully explained to Rosa how Franz managed to squeeze through the metal bars on his cell window.

'About a month after Franz's death, I heard that Rosa had committed suicide.' He stared into a distance that was not visible in my small office.'

'I'm sorry, Des. I didn't realise.'

'As you said, Dave. Shit happens.'

'I know, but I just wish it didn't always happen to people like Timmy and the Müllers.'

He shrugged. 'That's life.'

'Life is what happens when you're busy making other plans.'

'Very philosophical, Dave.'

'Blame it on the late John Lennon.'

'Eh?'

'It's from a song Lennon wrote.'

'Oh, I see.' He tried to smile, but I could see it was difficult for him.

'It's good to have you with us, Des.' I changed the subject.

He got the message and snapped out of his dark mood. That was a credit to his professionalism.

'We have been given the task of putting together the Department's annual budget requisition,' I told him.

'Is that the Royal we?'

'You could say that,' I replied with a smile.

'I thought it was Roly's job to do the budget.'

'So did I, but the D-G has tasked me with it.'

'And I suppose you're handing the task over to me?'

He looked at the buff file suspiciously. 'I've never put a budget together.'

'Join the club.'

'So what am I supposed to do?'

'I thought of that and I've come up with a solution that will make your job easier.'

'I'm all ears.'

'The file contains all the necessary budget forms. It also includes a copy of the department's current budget. I had Poppy dig it out from central administration. What I suggest is that you take this year's figures and add twenty percent to them all.'

'Will the Cabinet Office accept such a large increase?'

'Of course not, but I take the view that the bean counters in Downing Street will object to any requisition we make. They will just allocate us what they want anyway.'

'So submitting a budget is a big waste of time?'

'Not entirely, because it does give the Deputy D-G something to do.'

'Not this year it didn't.' Des laughed as he got to his feet.

'By the way,' I said as he headed for the door. 'There are a few other bits and bobs of paperwork in the folder. I'm sure you'll be able to deal with it on my behalf.'

'Thanks for the vote of confidence,' he said glumly. 'I can't wait.'

'Great minds think alike. That's exactly what I told the D-G.'

Des stopped and looked back. 'Is knowing I'm as bolshie as you supposed to make me feel better?'

'Nope,' I said with a smile. 'But it's good to have somebody else in the club. I was getting lonely.'

Des returned my smile and left my office. As he disappeared, my phone rang. It was Colleen Masters.

'Dizz would like to see you. Can you pop up?'

'How can I refuse?'

'You can't. So get yourself up here now.'

'You can't talk to me like that. I'm a member of the management team.'

'That didn't seem to worry you on Saturday night and Sunday morning,' she whispered.

'Sadly I must plead guilty to the charge of hypocrisy.'

'You're forgiven. I look forward to seeing you very soon.'

'Is the coffee brewed?' I asked.

'Of course, the D-G cannot function without his morning infusion of caffeine.'

'In that case, tell him I'm on my way.'

Disraeli-Astor was reading when I sat down in a chair opposite him. 'Is Colleen bringing the coffee?' He asked without looking up.

'I think so, unless she's going to feed the houseplants with that brown stuff that's bubbling away in the corner of her office.'

'It's too early in the morning for your smart arse comments, Statton,' he said with a sigh.

'I apologise for trying to add some light relief to an otherwise gloomy day,' I said.

'I take it you had a good Easter weekend?' This time he looked up and removed his spectacles.

'You mean apart from having to give up most of my bank holiday to visit a freezing cold football stadium and listen to a succession of over-the-hill singers and so-called comedians.'

'I thought you were supposed to be checking up on security.'

'I did that too. I can multi-task.'

'And since Mister Mandela appears to be safe and sound, I take it security arrangements were satisfactory?'

'What do you think? It was organised by the Special Branch.'

'There was a problem?'

'No, but that was more through luck than judgement.'

'Explain.'

'There was a cock-up, but no harm was done.' I explained what had happened when Mandela decided at the last moment that he wanted to use the loo.

'So it was just as well you were there to rescue him then?'

'I think that would be stretching the truth somewhat. I'm sure even the Special Branch would have noticed eventually that Mandela wasn't on the stage and, to be honest, he was safe enough locked up in the administration offices.'

Disraeli-Astor looked at me silently and then said: 'I still don't approve of you fraternising with the staff. Bad form.'

'Who says I have been fraternising with anybody?'

'I know everything that goes on in this building.'

'In that case I'll make sure that any future fraternisation takes place in other buildings.'

'Do you ever take anything I say seriously?'

I frowned and scratched my head. 'Um. Let me think about that for a moment.'

He shook his head and gave me an exasperated look. He tapped the document he had been reading. 'I have received two pathology reports.'

'For Bloom and Timmy, I take it?'

'Yes. There's not much to report on Bloom except that he was shot three times in the back with nine millimetre Parabellum bullets.'

'A Glock semi-automatic fires nine mill bullets,' I pointed out.

'Nine mill bullets are standard NATO ammunition. They're used in a number of small arms. What made you mention a Glock?'

'That was the pistol in Wren's safe.'

'Is that significant?'

'Probably not, but I never close my mind to any possibility.' As it happens I believe in going with my gut instinct, but I didn't tell him that. 'With that in mind, I think it is about time I talked to Sir Reginald Wren.'

He looked at me sharply. 'What exactly do you have in mind?'

'I found out he'll be visiting Manny Silver's jazz club tomorrow evening. I think it will be a good opportunity for a quiet word with him to see what sort of reaction I get.'

'Okay. I don't suppose it will harm letting Sir Reggie see we're watching him,' he agreed. 'However, I don't want any rough stuff. Is that clear?'

'Very clear.' I smiled at him. 'Was there anything else in Bloom's autopsy report?'

'Only that it confirms Bloom had sex shortly before he died.' He was interrupted by a knock on the door. It opened and Colleen came in carrying a coffee tray. She put it down on a side table.

'Do you think the sex angle is significant?' He asked me as we watched Colleen pour coffee into two cups.

She looked up sharply. 'I beg your pardon, sir?'

Disraeli-Astor blushed. 'I'm sorry, Colleen. I was talking to Statton,' he said hurriedly.

She smiled at him. 'Don't worry, sir. I understand. Boys will be boys.'

His blush deepened, bringing his scar once again into sharp relief. 'I didn't mean what you think I meant. I was talking about that private detective chappie, Bloom. It seems he had sex just before he was killed.'

'That's what I thought you were talking about. I don't know what else you imagined I was thinking,' she teased.

'It doesn't matter.' Disraeli-Astor fought desperately to regain his composure. 'Thanks for the coffee.'

Colleen left the office. She caught my eye as she passed me and arched an eyebrow. I kept my face impassive.

'To answer your question,' I said when she had gone. 'The sex thing might be significant, but, on the other hand, it might not. It depends on a number of factors. For instance, did Bloom have sex with his killer? I think so, but we don't know that for sure. Then there is his sexuality. I think he was a homosexual, but does that mean the killer was gay too? If so, was Brendan O'Leary his gay killer? If not, who was the killer?'

'I see what you mean. It's a tricky one. So what now?'

'I'll have Melissa do some digging into Bloom's background. You never know, that might throw up something. Now, what about Timmy?'

Disraeli-Astor took a document from his desk and passed it to me. 'Read this. I would be interested to know what you think.'

The document was the Home Office pathologist's report following the autopsy on Timmy's body. It showed the back of my deputy's head showing signs of a serious injury consistent with having been struck with a heavy blunt object. Based on the shape of the wound, the pathologist suggested that the possible weapon was a hammer.

The report listed a number of minor bruises and abrasions on Timmy's chest, back, buttocks, legs and heels. This was consistent with him falling after having been hit on the back of his head. There was also a deep scratch on the palm of his left hand, which could have been caused by a shard of glass or metal.

Despite the horrific damage to Timmy's head, the pathologist was certain this was not the cause of his death. The report made clear the wound would have rendered my deputy senseless before his throat was cut, which was the wound that actually killed him.

I studied the report carefully and then sat silently for a moment pondering its meaning.

Disraeli-Astor broke the silence. 'More coffee?'

'Yes, please.'

'So what do you think?' He re-filled my cup.

I didn't respond immediately, because I wanted to choose my words carefully. I sipped my coffee, which was up to his usual excellent quality.

'OK. Let me tell you what I think.' I said eventually. 'Timmy turned up at Brannagan's flat and knocked on the door. There was no answer so he tried again. Still no answer. Thinking Brannagan had scarpered, he turned away and took two or three steps towards the stairs. Brannagan opened the door silently, stepped out onto the landing and hit him on the back of the head with a hammer.

'Timmy collapsed, falling hard on the ground. Brannagan turned him over and dragged him back into the hallway of his flat, where he slit his throat. He stripped the sheets and blankets from his bed and wrapped Timmy's body in the blankets and then threw him down the rubbish chute. He used the sheets to clean up the blood in the flat and then threw them down the chute as well.'

'How do you know all that?' Disraeli-Astor asked.

'A little logic and lot of guesswork,' I replied. 'For instance, I'm guessing that Timmy rang the bell more than once, because that's what any conscientious field agent would do, and he was.

'That he walked a couple of steps away from the door is a guess, but makes sense because Brannagan would not have wanted to drag Timmy too far, to reduce the risk of being seen. He must have hit the ground hard, because there were bruises on his chest.'

'How do you know Brannagan didn't open the door when Fraser knocked?'

'Because if he'd done that Timmy would have been facing him, and he wouldn't have been able to hit him on the back of his head.'

Disraeli-Astor nodded his understanding. 'And what about Brannagan dragging Fraser back into the hall? How do you know that happened?'

'A number of reasons. Firstly, Timmy's back, buttocks and heels were bruised. Secondly, I found a slither of skin on the threshold of the door. I suspect that came from the palm of his left hand. And finally, there was blood in the hall, it could only have come from his body.'

We sat drinking our coffee in silence for a few minutes and then Disraeli-Astor said: 'I sense there is something else. You look worried.'

'I am.'

'What's wrong?'

'I think we might have a problem. 'If the scenario I have just set out is right, it would mean Brannagan knew in advance Timmy was going to see him.'

'I don't know what you mean.' He looked puzzled.

'Ask yourself this. Why didn't Brannagan open the door when Timmy rang?'

'Perhaps he did. Perhaps Fraser told Brannagan who he was.'

'Why would he do that? All he was doing was checking that Brannagan was still there. If the Irishman had opened the door, I'm sure Timmy would have pretended to be from the local council.'

'Why would Fraser do that?'

'Because it's what I told him to do if Brannagan was in. Incidentally, that's why Timmy was carrying a clip-board.'

'So the clip-board on which Brannagan wrote his message belonged to Fraser?'

'Yes.'

Disraeli-Astor thought about that for a while. 'OK, so it looks as if Brannagan did not open the door when Fraser knocked.'

'Exactly. So why not?'

'Perhaps he was just being careful.'

'If that was the case, why did Brannagan kill Timmy? Why didn't he just let him walk away?'

'Perhaps Brannagan peeked through the window and recognised Timmy.'

'How would he recognise him? As far as I know, they never met.'

'I thought you said that Timmy went to the safe-house with you? Could Brannagan have seen him then?'

'I'm pretty sure not,' I replied and explained what happened when Timmy forgot the tape recorder. 'So I repeat. Why did Brannagan kill Timmy?'

'I don't know,' Disraeli-Astor admitted.

'Exactly. It makes no sense. Timmy could have been the rent collector for all Brannagan knew, and despite the unpopularity of rent collectors there would have been no reason to bash him over the head with a hammer and cut his throat.'

He nodded and I could see he was beginning to understand.

'But the clincher is the message that Brannagan left on the clipboard.'

'Provos 1 – British Scum 0?'

'Yes. It proves Brannagan knew who Timmy worked for and had already made up his mind to kill him.'

'But how did he know Fraser was going to visit him?'

'I can think of only one way.'

The D-G thought about that. 'A tip-off?'

'There is no other explanation.'

'But who tipped him off?'

'That I don't know, but I'm going to find out.'

He considered me silently for several seconds before he spoke again. 'That's damn good detective work, Statton.'

'I can't help being brilliant.'

'Whatever happened to modesty?'

'It got beaten to the winning post by honesty.'

'Sometimes you are insufferable.'

'I know. But you love me really. Why else would you put up with my smart arse comments?'

'Get out!'

'Yes, boss.'

Chapter 23

Kensal Green Cemetery was over one hundred and fifty years old and it showed. Much of the once beautifully kept grounds were now unkempt and on many of the graves the crosses and headstones had become lopsided with age.

Momentarily I felt sad for the past, and those who were buried in the cemetery, mostly long forgotten by their descendants. At one time many of the gentry from West London had been interned in what was an attractive rural setting. Now the cemetery was surrounded by housing estates.

I had never met Timmy's mother and she was a surprise to me. I had imagined she would look like her son, who was short and slightly built, with mouse coloured hair and a shy, diffident look about him.

Mrs Fraser was none of those things. Instead, she was a tall, statuesque woman, with flowing blonde locks and an air of calmness and confidence, which was not diminished by her obvious distress at being at the funeral of her only son.

She stood next to the open grave with a comforting arm round her daughter, who bore a remarkable resemblance to Timmy. I could only assume their father had been short in stature and that brother and sister took after him.

Lieutenant Commander Fraser was a pilot in the Fleet Air Arm. He was seriously wounded during the Falklands War, and died of his wounds a year after his return to Britain. I knew Timmy was very proud of his father, so it was fitting that he was being buried alongside him in the same grave.

There was a surprisingly large number of mourners. They stood three deep round the grave, listening to the priest as he intoned the burial rites. Those who could not get close to the internment were forced to stand in the spaces between neighbouring graves. It was a tribute to my deputy's popularity that so many had turned up to mourn his passing.

I noticed several other women wore veils like the Frasers. One of them caught my eye. She wore a tight, bottle-green coat that accentuated her shapely curves. However, she too wore a veil, so I had no idea if her face matched that heavenly looking body.

The priest brought the ceremony to an end by tossing a handful of dirt into the grave. As it rattled onto the coffin lid, Timmy's sister began to sob. A number of other women joined her, including Poppy and Melissa. Even some of the men dabbed their eyes with handkerchiefs.

Mrs Fraser had retained her composure throughout the ceremony and still showed no sign of distress.

With the burial service finished, the mourners moved off to make way for the grave diggers to complete their task. Now they stood in little groups on the wide tarmac path that ran through the cemetery. On the grass verge, a row of wreaths had been laid out by the undertakers. They would be placed on Timmy's grave once it had been filled and re-turfed.

Poppy and Melissa had already headed back to the office, but I stayed behind to look at the wreaths. Having read the tributes to Timmy, I stared off into the distance, mulling over one message in particular that preyed on my mind.

'I'm pleased you came, Mr Statton,' a voice broke into my thoughts.

I turned to find Mrs Fraser standing behind me. She was alone. 'It was the least I could do. Your son was a fine lad and an important member of my team.'

'Timothy worshiped you,' she said. She had a quiet cultured voice and spoke in a measured tone that reminded me of her son. She had removed her veil to reveal a face that was closer to being attractive than beautiful, but it was still appealing, particularly the sharp blue eyes that looked at me steadily. Up close, I could see that although her clothes were clean and well ironed, they showed noticeable signs of wear and tear.

'He was a fine lad,' I repeated, slightly embarrassed by her words. 'But, I'm not exactly the best role model for him to worship.'

'That's not what Timothy told me. He said you were always fair and honest with him.' She smiled sadly. 'My son knew he wasn't perfect, Mister Statton, and he had a lot to learn, but you taught him a great deal.'

I shrugged and thought about the cruel things I had said about Timmy at times. This made me feel guilty. I looked over her shoulder and saw a group of people a few yards up the path. Behind them I could see the shapely woman in the bottle-green coat. She stood apart from the others, as if she was ill at ease in their company.

'You called Timothy a lad,' Mrs Fraser said. 'But he wasn't a lad. The truth is that you took my boy under your wing and turned him into a man.'

Her words touched me and my sense of guilt deepened. 'Mrs Fraser there is something I must tell you.'

She shook her head and the strengthening wind caught her hair and blew it across her face in a fine blonde curtain. She pulled it away with both hands and tucked it behind her ears. 'I think I know what you're going to say and it's not necessary.'

'Hear me out,' I insisted.

'If you must,' she said softly.

'Yes I must. The thing is, Mrs Fraser. I sent your son to his death.'

She looked at me steadily. 'No you didn't, Mr Statton. Timothy was a field agent and you sent him to do the job he was paid for.'

'He was an inexperienced field agent and I sent him to confront a killer.'

'Did you really?'

'What do you mean?'

'This killer you sent Timothy to Slough to confront, did you actually think my son would find him?'

She was sharp.

'No, I thought he would be long gone,' I paused and momentarily wondered whether I should tell her the whole truth. I decided she needed to know and would understand. 'You said I taught Timmy a great deal. Well, I tried to teach him the ropes. In fact, his visit to Slough was part of the learning process. He should have checked out that address before and I only sent him to Slough to teach him a lesson.'

'I am sure Timothy would have understood your reasons.'

'That's as maybe, but it doesn't make me feel any less responsible for his death.'

The woman took my hand. 'Let me tell you something, Mr Statton. My husband flew a Wessex helicopter during the Falklands War…'

'I know. Timmy told me,' I interjected.

'Did he tell you that Angus was badly injured when his helicopter crashed in bad weather on Fortune Glacier a couple of months before the end of the war?'

I nodded but didn't interrupt her again. Timmy told me everything about his dad, but I sensed that this was something that she needed to talk about. In some way it was cathartic for her, and perhaps me as well.

'Angus was rescued and was eventually flown back home, but he never fully recovered. Despite the best treatment available, my husband passed away seven years ago, almost to the day.'

'I'm sorry, Mrs Fraser.' There was nothing else I could say.

'But I never blamed Margaret Thatcher, or the Defence Chiefs for sending my husband to war. He knew what he was doing and so did I. We both celebrated when the Falklands were liberated and we were proud of the fact Angus had been part of that liberation. Timothy was proud of his father too.'

'He was,' I agreed.

'Timothy wanted to follow in his father's footsteps and do something to help our country. He could have followed Angus into the Armed Forces, but chose instead to join the Intelligence Service. He felt it was the best way of using his intellect.' She looked at me again and now I could see moistness in her eyes. 'Timothy was very intelligent, Mr Statton.'

'I know he was, Mrs Fraser.'

She fell silent, but continued to look at me with her tear filled blue eyes. 'What I want to know,' she said eventually, 'and I don't expect you to divulge any state secrets, but was Timothy working on something that was important to our country.'

I was on safer ground now, because I could tell the unfettered truth. I realised I was still holding her hand. I squeezed it. 'Mrs Fraser, we are at war again, but it is not a military war. We are fighting against people who are threatening our country's economic well-being and that of our allies. Your son was helping to defeat our enemies. He was a brave and honourable man who was killed in the course of that war. You can be very proud of him.'

That's when the tears finally came. I put my arms about her and hugged her to me. She sobbed against my chest for a couple of minutes and then pulled away. With a noticeable effort she straightened her back and smiled at me wanly.

'I'm pleased there was such a good turn-out for Timmy,' I said.

251

'He had a lot of friends.'

'Yes, most of the young people who were here today were at university with him. They all loved Timothy.' She sobbed again, but soon controlled herself.

'Will you be coming to the wake?' She asked. 'It's being held at the Kensal Arms. My daughter is there already ensuring everything is ready. You will be most welcome.'

'Thank you, but unfortunately I have an important meeting at the American Embassy this afternoon. I can't miss it because it relates to the business that Timmy was working on.'

She smiled. 'I understand,' she said, then paused before adding: 'There is one thing I would like to ask of you.

'What is it?'

'I want you to track down the bastard who murdered Timothy and make sure he never kills anybody else's son.' With that she turned on her heel and walked away, leaving me alone with my thoughts.

All the mourners had disappeared by now, presumably to make their way to the Kensal Arms. I wondered if the woman in the bottle-green coat had joined them. I still had no idea who she was, or what her relationship was to Timmy. However, I knew instinctively that it was her who had brought the wreath with the inscription that read: *I didn't want it to end this way.*

Grosvenor Square, London

My appointment at the US Embassy in Grosvenor Square was to see Bob Fletcher. However, this time he didn't meet me in reception. Instead I was greeted by a smart young lady wearing high-heels; a tight pencil skirt; starched white blouse; and long, red-painted nails that looked as false as her welcoming smile.

'Please step this way, Mr Statton,' she said in an accent straight out of *Gone with the Wind*.

She led me towards the same small meeting room in which I had met Fletcher on my previous visit. The CIA man was sitting waiting for me.

'Thank you, Jolene,' Fletcher said, as he stood to shake my hand. 'It's good to see you again, Dave.'

I thought he sounded about as sincere as Jolene's smile, but that might just have been my cynicism, so I gave him the benefit of the doubt. 'And you too, Bob. Sorry I'm a bit late, but I was delayed at a funeral.'

'It's not a problem, pal,' he said, but glanced at his watch to remind me what a busy man he was. 'Anybody I know?'

'I don't think so. He was my deputy. His name was Timothy Fraser.'

'Been with you long?'

'No, he wasn't long out of university.'

'How'd the kid die? An accident?'

'We think he was murdered by the same guy who killed your agent and our Russian defector.'

'The Irishman?'

'Yeah.'

'What evidence do you have?'

'Only circumstantial,' I replied and then went on to tell him what I believe happened to Timmy. 'So what would you conclude from all that?'

'Circumstantial or not, the evidence is good enough for me. That bastard has now killed three people.'

'At *least* three people,' I corrected him.

'At least,' he agreed. 'But that's not why you wanted to see me is it?'

'No. I understand that Colonel Disraeli-Astor agreed with your ambassador that you and I should work out how we can best co-operate on the Mandela Project operation.'

He raised an eyebrow at me. 'He said that?'

'Well, words to that effect.' I smiled. My boss had said nothing of the sort, but nothing ventured, nothing gained.

'So let's do it. Shoot.'

'OK. We'd like to accept the CIA's offer of help when I'm in the field. However, we have one condition.'

'Which is?'

'That you are the agent assigned to work with me.'

He shook his head. 'No can do, Dave.'

'Look, Bob. You know the score. When I'm out in the field, it's my neck on the block. If I must have a CIA agent tagging along, then I want that person to be somebody I can trust to watch my back properly. I've done some research on you and I was impressed with what I found. I would trust you.'

'I'm flattered, Dave, and I would love to back you up, but I'm no longer a field agent. I'm far too long in the tooth and my heart wouldn't stand up to the excitement. That's why the Firm put me out to grass and I ended up as the military attaché here in London.'

'That's a shame. It makes it difficult to accept your help.'

'There are plenty of other good agents coming through who are a lot younger and fitter than me,' Fletcher insisted.

I grimaced. 'I'm afraid my experience of CIA agents has not been good.'

'So I understand. Hank Graham told me what happened between Joe Welensky and you.' It was his turn to smile. 'He said there was bad blood between you.'

My mind went back to my encounter with Welensky on a riverbank in Kent. It ended in the CIA agent punching the metal girder of a bridge, instead of my face, and ending up in the A & E department of Maidstone Hospital with shattered bones in his fist and a badly bruised pride.

'Most of the blood was on Welensky,' I said.

Fletcher grinned. 'That's what Hank told me. What about his boss, Gavin Rogers? I know he had something to do with that South African business. What happened between him and you?'

'Rogers shot me in the arm and would have killed me if Hank hadn't stopped him.'

'How did Hank stop him?'

'Didn't he tell you?'

'No he clammed up when I mentioned Rogers.'

'In that case my mouth will remain shut tight also, except to say that the last I saw of Rogers he was heading towards a Russian submarine.' This was a lie, but what the hell?

'Rogers has never been seen since,' Fletcher probed.

'Is that so?'

'Yeah. We wondered whether he was dead.'

'Who can say? He could be sunning himself somewhere on the Black Sea for all I know.'

'Does Hank know what happened to Rogers?'

'That's something only he can tell you,' I said. 'But talking of Hank, what about him working with me? I trust him.'

'Hank Graham?' He pretended to sound surprised at my suggestion, but I got the impression he agreed with my opinion of his colleague.

'Yes. He's a damned good field agent. Can you swing it for me, Bob?'

'It might be difficult, Dave, but I'll try.'

'Thanks, I can't ask for more than that. Now what have you found out about John Engels?'

He took a file from a briefcase that was standing on the floor beside his chair. He pulled a paper from it and handed it to me. 'The CIA managed to get another agent into Engels's company. She came up with some interesting information.'

'Such as?'

'Well, for a start, it's quite clear Engels is the head honcho of the Phoenix Group. He pretty well runs the whole caboose with the help of four other senior members.'

'I would lay odds that one of them is our Sir Reginald Wren?'

'Bull's eye!'

'Who else?'

'Maurice Sevier, Jonathan Rhodes and Brendan O'Leary.'

I recognised the names immediately. 'Your agent did well. She must have managed to get herself into a position of real trust.'

'Yeah,' Fletcher said, but didn't enlarge.

'Is there more?'

'Yeah. She hit pay dirt. A real nugget. She found out the next meeting of the Phoenix Group will take place in South Africa.'

That grabbed my attention. 'That's a gold plated nugget,' I said.

'More like solid, twenty-four carat gold. Our girl found out a lot more than that. For instance, we now know that the meeting will include delegates from the Broederbond and the P.A.C.'

'That's very interesting. If somehow the meeting can be infiltrated, it would be a great opportunity to discover if they still plan to assassinate Mandela.'

'My thoughts exactly,' he said. 'And if that *is* the case; when and where such an attempt will take place.'

'Did your agent find out when the meeting is taking place?'

He smiled. 'She sure did. Saturday, May Fifth.'

'That's only two weeks away. It doesn't leave much time to arrange things.'

'For sure, but no doubt you'll think of something.'

'Do you know in which part of South Africa the meeting's being held?' I asked.

'Yeah. It's in a place called Nordhook. Does that name mean anything to you?'

'Yes, except it's Noordhoek.' I pronounced it the Afrikaans way. 'It's near Cape Town. Are you sure that's the location?'

'That's what our agent heard. You sound surprised.'

'I am. I used to know that area pretty well and I can't think of a suitable venue for such a meeting in the area. However, I haven't visited that neck of the woods for at least eight years. Things could have changed. I'll make some enquiries and see what I can find out.'

'Thanks. It would be good to have our information confirmed. When can you let me know?'

'I'm not sure. I'll speak to the South African Ambassador first, but if he can't help me, I'll track down an old friend of mine. However, that could take some time.'

'We don't have a lot of time.'

'Don't worry. I'll try to get details of any potential venue to you by the time you obtain permission for Hank Graham to be assigned to work with me.'

'Are you trying to stiff me, Dave?'

'Let's just call it an exchange of favours.'

'You mean a quid pro quo?'

'Well, where I grew up we used to say; you scratch my back and I'll scratch yours.'

He laughed. 'OK, pal. Ring me when you've checked out this Nordhook place.'

'No, I have a better idea, Bob. You ring me when you've convinced Langley to assign Hank to help me.'

He held his hands up in surrender. 'I'll do my best.'

The Blue Oyster Club, Soho

Being a Wednesday night the jazz club was half empty and there were plenty of seats. I found one against the wall facing the entrance, from where I could see who came and went.

Despite being half empty, the Blue Oyster was far from quiet. It was eight thirty and the trio was already into its set and blasting out a version of *Blueberry Hill* that made the floor vibrate. There was a general hubbub as customers talked louder so they could be heard over the music. I said nothing. I had nobody to talk to. Wren hadn't arrived yet.

I sat drinking a Bishop's Finger and waited. By nine o'clock, and well into my second beer, I was beginning to think he was not going to come, but then I saw him.

He sauntered through the door, with the blonde-haired Misty Olafson on his arm and a huge unlit cigar in his hand. They headed for a table in the far corner of the room. As they sat down, Manny Silver hurried over to the table from the bar with two flute glasses in his hand. He was followed closely by Ruby carrying an ice bucket, out of which jutted the neck of a champagne bottle.

Manny put one glass in front of Misty with an exaggerated sweep of his arm and a little bow of his head. He placed the second glass in front of Wren, before supervising the waitress as she positioned the ice bucket alongside the table.

Manny pulled the champagne from the bucket and ostentatiously held it in front of Sir Reggie so that he could see the label. Wren indicated his approval with a perfunctory nod of his head. Satisfied, the club owner handed the bottle to the waitress.

Ruby opened the champagne with a well-practiced expertise that popped the cork, but ensured not a drop of the precious liquid was wasted. Meanwhile, her boss took a box of matches from his pocket and carefully lit Wren's cigar, which soon added to the already smoke filled atmosphere.

The waitress poured wine into both glasses and words were spoken, but it was far too noisy in the club to hear what they were. Manny, bowed deeply again and then headed towards the bar, with Ruby in tow.

Their table was positioned in a shadowy part of the room, however, I was able to see them clearly. Wren touched glasses with Misty, who was sitting opposite him. They both took a sip of their champagne. She put her glass down on the table and with a smile gently stroked his hand. In turn, he took her hand and kissed its back.

This display of intimacy set me wondering about them. Were Misty Olafson and Wren an item and if so, were they already in a relationship when the girl had sex with Douglas Campbell? Or did they get together afterwards? Or was she simply being paid to escort Wren about town?

I pondered on this for a few minutes while I listened to the trio playing *Sweet Lorraine*. As they finished, and moved effortlessly into *Fly Me to the Moon*, I shrugged my thoughts aside and got to

257

my feet. I picked up my beer and made my way across to Wren's table. He looked up as I approached.

'May I join you?' I asked as I pulled a chair from a neighbouring empty table and placed it between them.

Wren sucked hard on his cigar and then blew smoke in my face. 'Do I know you?' He asked coldly.

I waved away the smoke. 'Not personally, but it's highly likely one of your friends mentioned me.'

'Who would that be?'

'It doesn't matter one way or the other. The important thing is what I know about you, Sir Reginald.' I sat down and put my beer on the table. 'Or, should that be Reg-the-sledge?'

Wren stiffened. Now there was real menace in the look he gave me. 'What do you want?' He got straight to the point.

'Just a friendly little chat.'

'Are you the filth?'

'No. However, someday you might wish I was.'

'Why?'

'Because the police just arrest people. They then refer them to the Crown Prosecution Service, who eventually hand them over to a court to be tried. If found guilty by a jury, those people are punished by a judge.' I picked up my glass and drank another half inch of Bishop's Finger.

'But I'm different. I'm from the Department for Covert Operations.' I said this without taking my eyes off Wren. I put my glass back down on the table. 'Section Two, to be precise.'

'You're Statton,' he said. It was not a question.

'So, I was right. One of your friends did tell you about me. I assume it was Douglas Campbell.'

Wren shrugged nonchalantly. 'Who's Douglas Campbell?'

'He's the Home Office minister who's been feeding you information about me. Did he tell you what Section Two does?'

Wren said nothing.

'No? In that case, let me explain. Section Two cuts out the middle men. So, when it comes to punishing people who are a threat to our country, I'm the police, CPS, jury, judge and executioner, all rolled into one.'

'What threat? I don't know what you're talking about. I've done nothing wrong.' Wren balanced his part smoked cigar in an ashtray and started playing with the ring he wore on the pinkie of his left hand. I thought this was a sign of nervousness on his part, but maybe it was just his way of showing me the huge diamond that adorned the gold band.

'Don't take me for a fool, Reg. It makes me very angry when people do that and you wouldn't want to see me angry.'

Wren shrugged.

'So let's be clear on a couple of things. One, I know the Right Honourable Douglas Campbell MP is a friend of yours. And two, I know he's been providing you with sensitive information that could harm Britain.'

Wren picked up his cigar again and looked at its tip to check it was still alight. It was. He sucked on it, making its tip glow.

'I also happen to know that Mister Campbell is well acquainted with your lady friend here,' I went on, nodding towards Misty, who looked at me through narrow, hostile eyes. She reminded me of a lioness eyeing up its intended prey. Perhaps she was. 'Very well acquainted, if you get my drift.'

Wren blew more smoke at me and returned his cigar to the ashtray.

'But for the time being I'm not interested in Mister Campbell. Instead, I'd like to talk about another friend of yours. Shaun Brannagan.'

This got Wren's attention. He began to say something but I held up a hand to silence him. 'Before you deny knowing him let me remind you who he is. Brannagan is an ex-IRA thug who has been hired by the Phoenix Group as its resident assassin.' I stared at him, but his own gaze didn't waver. However, somewhere deep in the darkness that lay behind his eyes, I detected the flicker of madness.

Those eyes reminded me they belonged to a man capable of using a six-pound sledgehammer to smash somebody's skull. I would have to be careful to make sure his next victim wasn't me.

'That's right, Reg. We know all about the Phoenix Group. We know Campbell is helping the Group and we know that Brannagan has killed people for it, including a member of my staff.'

'I know nothing about that.' Perhaps, on this point, he was telling the truth.

'That doesn't absolve you of responsibility.'

Wren casually took a sip of champagne. 'You still haven't told me what you really want, Statton.'

'That's easy. I want you to do something for me.'

'Are you fucking mad?'

'Yes and I'm getting madder by the minute.'

For the first time Wren didn't seem as sure of himself. He studied me with hooded eyes and tried to second guess my motive for confronting him. He picked up his cigar and looked at the tip again. This time he discovered his cigar had gone out. He pulled a lighter from his pocket and relit it. I got the impression he was playing for time. 'What do you want me to do?' He asked eventually.

'I want you to pass on a message to Brannagan.'

'Brannagan?' He echoed. 'What message?'

'Tell him that I'm coming for him. Tell him there is nowhere for him to hide. Tell him this is now between him and me and there will be only one winner. Me.'

'What if I refuse?'

I slowly pulled my Smith & Wesson from its holster. I rested my hand on the table with the pistol pointing at Wren's head. For the first time since our conversation started, his eyes moved from my face, now they looked down the barrel of my Magnum. He didn't move a muscle.

'It would not be wise to refuse, Reggie. With or without your help I am going to track down the Irish bastard who murdered my deputy in cold blood. That boy was like a son to me.' This last was a lie, but Wren didn't know that.

Out of the corner of my eye I saw Misty reach towards her handbag. 'Don't do it, darling,' I told her without taking my eyes off Wren. 'Not unless you want your boyfriend's brains to join the beer stains on the wall behind him. Now, put both your hands on the table in front of you.' She did as she was told. 'Good girl.'

'Do you understand, what I'm saying?' I said to Wren. 'Originally, I was just doing my job, but now it's personal. Now I'm going to find Brannagan and kill him.'

'You *are* mad,' Wren sneered. 'Brannagan is one dangerous bastard. He will eat you alive.'

'Just pass on that message to him.' I stood up, still pointing my pistol at his head. I kept the weapon low so that nobody else in the room could see it, but my aim didn't waver. 'And you'd better hope you're right, Reg. Because once I've killed Brannagan, I'm coming after you and the other scumbag members of the Phoenix Group.'

I backed away from the table, watching him carefully, but he didn't move. He just continued to stare at me with his mad eyes. He didn't look scared, he just looked very angry.

I smiled to myself. It was just the reaction I wanted. I was satisfied.

Chapter 24

'It was good of you to find time for me at such short notice, Mister Ambassador,' I said as we shook hands. 'I'm sure you must be busy.'

'It is not a problem, Mister Statton,' Hendrick Meyer assured me with a smile. 'As it happens, your request for a meeting was propitious, because I have some highly confidential information I want to share with you. Please take a seat and tell me what I can do for you.'

'It's about the Phoenix Group,' I explained as I sat down in a chair opposite him. 'I have received information it intends holding its next meeting in your country.'

'Is that so? I wonder what they are up to.'

'Well, there might be a clue in the fact that representatives from the Broederbond and the PAC are attending the meeting.'

'Are they, by God?'

'That's what we've been told.'

'When is the meeting?'

'Next month. It's being held in Noordhoek, on the Cape Peninsula.'

'I know Noordhoek well. My family home is located not far away in in Constantia.'

'Very nice,' I said. Constantia is one of the most affluent and exclusive of Cape Town's suburbs.

'I know what you're thinking, Mister Statton,' the Ambassador said with a slightly self-conscious smile. 'Yes, I'm lucky enough to live in a big house in a good neighbourhood. But it hasn't always been like that. I was born and raised in District Six, which, when I was growing up, was inhabited only by Cape Malays, coloureds and poor-white families like my own.'

Meyer stared out of his window, towards where Nelson's Column dominated Trafalgar Square. 'But although we were poor, we were happy.' He smiled nostalgically. 'And do you know what, Mister Statton? We got on well together, whatever our race, colour or creed.'

'How times change.'

'They certainly do. In the Seventies, the friends with whom I grew up, were forcibly removed from District Six. Most of them ended up on Mitchell's Plain.' His expression changed to one of sadness. 'I still feel partly responsible for what happened.'

'Why?'

'Because I supported, and now represent, the National Party Government that evicted them from their homes.' He stood up. 'I think I need a drink.' He walked over to his drinks cabinet. 'You?'

'If you're offering me some of your delicious KWV brandy, the answer is yes.'

'I've something better than that. I've just received a couple of cases of Klipdrift Gold from home. If you liked the KWV, you will definitely like this.' He held up a bottle to show me. 'This, my friend, is the nectar of the gods.' He poured a generous measure into two glasses, before handing one to me as he returned to his seat.

'So you feel responsible for the forced removals policy?' I asked before taking a sip of the Klipdrift. He was right, the brandy was delicious.

'Responsible and guilty. Which is why I am determined to do everything I can to help bring change to my country and make amends for the past mistakes that were made.'

'I'll drink to that, Mister Ambassador.'

'Please, Mister Statton. Call me Hendrick. I get fed up with all the pomposity that goes with being an ambassador.'

I nodded. 'Then you must call me David.'

'Very well, David it is. So, getting back to the Phoenix Group meeting in Noordhoek. How can I help you?'

'I couldn't think of anywhere in Noordhoek suitable as a venue for such a meeting. Have you any idea where it could be held?'

Meyer took a sip of his brandy and looked thoughtfully out of his window before he replied. 'I can think of only one place. When were you last in the area?'

'Eight years ago.'

'Then you probably don't know the Mountainside Reserve Hotel.' I shook my head.

'It's a hotel set in a nature reserve at the foot of Chapman's Peak. It hasn't been open long. Its accommodation consists of a range of individual wooden lodges that are situated on the side of the mountain in the middle of a Milkwood forest. It's very rustic and ecologically-friendly.

'The resort has good access, but is very secluded and is surrounded by barbed wire fences. There is a fine restaurant and a conference centre. It would be perfect for a discreet meeting, because May is out of the holiday season and the area will be very quiet.'

'It certainly sounds an ideal spot.'

'Assuming the hotel is the venue, what do you propose?'

'Wherever the meeting is held, it's important we find out what the Phoenix Group is planning. Originally I thought about infiltrating the meeting, but I've had second thoughts. Getting somebody into the meeting could be tricky, so I think it would be better to bug it.' I paused and then asked: 'Hendrik, is this something your police or security services can handle, or would you like our help?'

Meyer thought about that for a while. 'Under normal circumstances we could deal with it, but because of the involvement of the Broederbond, the risk of a leak would be too great. If the Phoenix Group got wind of what we were doing, they might be scared off. It would be easy for them to find an alternative venue in another part of the country. So, yes, David, I think this is something you Brits will have to handle.'

'That won't be a problem,' I assured him. I had already decided that my first job was to visit Cape Town to check out for myself the Mountainside Reserve Hotel. It was not an unpleasant prospect. 'You said there was something you wanted to tell me, Hendrick.'

'Yes. It is about Nelson Mandela. Firstly, I would like to thank you for looking after him so well when he attended the Wembley pop concert. He was full of praise for the way you protected him following the lapse in security by your Special Branch.'

'You know about that?'

'Of course. Mister Mandela could have been in danger of his life if it hadn't been for you.'

'I was just doing my job.'

'And a good job it was.'

'Thank you. So what about Mandela?'

Meyer again looked thoughtful. 'When exactly in May will the Phoenix Group meeting take place, David?'

'Saturday the fifth.'

'I wonder if that is just a coincidence,' he murmured to himself.

'What?'

'On Friday the fourth there are to be secret talks between the

South African Government and the African National Congress. President De Klerk will lead for the Government and Nelson Mandela will head up the ANC delegation.'

'Where are the talks being held?'

'At the President's Groote Schuur home.'

'And what are they about? Can you tell me?'

'Yes. That is the confidential information I mentioned earlier. I have been asked by my Government to let you know about the talks. They are the first stage in negotiations we hope will result in an agreement that will bring to an end the violence and intimidation that is making life a misery for so many of our people.'

I mulled over the significance of this information and whether the talks would have an impact on my own operation.

'My Government hopes also that the talks will break down barriers that are preventing the start of full negotiations. They'll include immunity from prosecution for returning ANC exiles and the release of political prisoners.' He paused and looked at me earnestly.

'As you can imagine, David, there will be many who are opposed to the talks, so they are immensely sensitive, which is why I am telling you about them in the strictest confidence.'

'I understand,' I assured him. We sat in silence for a while as we both sipped our brandy. 'It's certainly odd the Phoenix Group plans to meet at the same time as the secret talks are being held at Groote Schuur. However, perhaps it's just a coincidence.'

'I hope you're right, David, because if it's not, then those talks are not so secret after all.'

We looked at each other. 'Do you think the Phoenix Group plans to attack the ANC leaders while the talks are taking place at Groote Schuur?' I asked.

'You must have been reading my mind,' Meyer said with a smile. 'I was asking myself that exact question, and the answer is no, I don't think so. Even if there has been a leak and the Phoenix Group found out about the talks, they will also know that security is very tight at the presidential residence.' He lapsed into silence and took another sip of his brandy.

'But it would be foolish to be complacent,' he said eventually. 'I am sure my Government would welcome any help and advice you can offer that will make Groote Schuur even more secure.'

'I am happy to pass on that request to Colonel Disraeli-Astor. Is there anything else I should know?' I asked.

'Not really, except to confirm that two weeks after the Groote Schuur meeting, Mister Mandela will be visiting London. He has been invited to address both Houses of Parliament on Thursday seventeenth of May, but I expect you know that already.'

'Of course,' I lied.

The DFCO offices

What on earth were you thinking?' Disraeli-Astor asked when I finished telling him about my visit to the Blue Oyster Club and what had happened when I confronted Wren.

'Since you ask, I was thinking that putting the fear of God up Wren would be a terrific way to flush out Brannagan.'

'Well you could have told me what you planned to do,' he protested.

'I did tell you what I planned.'

'No, you just said that you… and I think I am quoting verbatim: "I thought it would be a good opportunity for a quiet word with him to see what sort of reaction I get." He said this with an odd cockney accent that I assume he thought sounded like me.

'And as I recall, you said, and I *am* quoting verbatim: "I don't suppose it will harm letting Sir Reggie see we're watching him."'

'That's as maybe, but you said nothing about threatening him with a gun,' he added, reverting to his usual cultured voice.

I shrugged. 'I didn't threaten him, I just showed him how big my Smith & Wesson .44 Magnum was. Now, since we are talking about sharing information with each other, why didn't you tell me that Nelson Mandela was coming to London next month?'

'What on earth are you talking about?'

'You didn't know?'

He shook his head. 'Know what?'

'Mandela has been invited to address both Houses of Parliament.'

'Who told you that?'

'The South African Ambassador. He assumed I knew. Silly sod.'

'But we should have known, Statton!' He hammered his fist angrily on the top of his desk. 'The Ambassador must have thought you were incompetent not knowing anything about Mandela's visit.'

'Don't worry. I didn't let on that I had no idea what he was talking about.'

'That's not the point. It could have made us look like idiots.'

'Speak for yourself.'

'I'm serious, Statton!'

'I'm sure you are.'

'It's quite outrageous that we were kept in the dark!'

'Well it's not my fault, so don't shout at me.'

'I was not shouting!'

'You were and you're still doing it.'

He took a deep breath and then said more calmly: 'I'm sorry, I didn't mean to take my frustration out on you. However, such a breakdown in communication is simply not good enough. After all, we are responsible for Mandela's safety when he visits Britain.'

'Are we? I thought that was the job of Special Branch.'

'Technically they are, but under our supervision. They might be the muscles, but we are the brains.' He tapped his temple. 'I will contact the Cabinet Office and the Home Office immediately to find out how this happened.'

'Good plan, and while you're about it, you might like to ask them about the XPD notice we requested for Brannagan. I might need that if and when he comes after me.'

'Authorisation has never bothered you in the past. As the Irishman you shot in Londonderry would be able to testify, if he wasn't dead.'

'It's true that sometimes circumstances require me to take immediate and drastic action. However, it makes me feel better having a piece of paper in my pocket when I pull the trigger.'

'Do you really believe your visit to see Sir Reggie will provoke Brannagan into showing his hand?'

'Nothing is certain in life, but when Wren passes on my message, then I think there is a good chance Brannagan will try to kill me and he will want to strike first. Certainly, that's what I would do if the roles were reversed.'

'Is Sir Reggie likely to pass on your message?'

'Now Wren knows I'm onto him, he and his mates in the Phoenix Group will want me out of the way. So, yeah, he'll make sure Brannagan comes after me alright.'

'And the blonde girl in the photographs you showed me with Dougie... What did you say her name was?'

'Misty Olafson.'

'Of course. Are you sure it was Misty Olafson who was with Sir Reggie at the club?'

'Quite sure.' I remembered the look on the woman's face as she reached for her handbag when I pulled my gun on Wren. 'And unless I am very much mistaken, she is as dangerous as a black widow spider.'

Disraeli-Astor opened a folder on his desk. 'Now about this budget requisition form you sent up to me,' he changed the subject abruptly. It was a habit he had that was becoming irritating.

'What about it?'

'Didn't you say Dobbins completed it for you?'

'His name is Des Hobbins and yes he did complete it. Why?'

'Has he ever done a budget before?'

'No, but I gave him a couple of pointers.'

'I thought so. The form has your fingerprints all over it.'

'If you didn't want my input, perhaps you should have filled the form in yourself.'

'You miss my point, Statton. The Cabinet Office is looking for a ten percent reduction in our budget and yet by my reckoning Hobbins is actually asking for a ten percent increase over last year.'

'Good man! I'm pleased he followed my advice. I took the view that the bean counters will cut whatever figures we put in anyway, so the more we ask for, the more we are likely to get.'

'I'm afraid it doesn't work like that, Statton. I have to justify every penny for which we ask. As an example, take the travel and subsistence budget. That's one area they always query because they think we are extravagant. In the current economic climate, how can I justify any increase, let alone this extortionate amount Hobbins has asked for?' He tapped the budget papers.

'None of it is for Des,' I pointed out.

'I know that. It was a figure of speech. I still need to justify the increase.'

'You can justify it by explaining about my trip to South Africa. I will be there for at least two weeks and that will take a sizeable bite out of the amount for which we've asked.'

'So, while we're on that subject, why do you need to spend so long in Cape Town?'

'Don't you trust me?'

'Of course I trust you, but I'm the one who has to explain it to the bean counters at the Treasury, so humour me.'

'Well you could start by explaining to them that the trip has been sanctioned by the Prime Minister in response to a request from the South African Government. That should shut them up.'

'Sadly, you have a lot to learn about the Treasury, Statton. They think it's their Permanent Secretary who runs the country, not Mrs Thatcher. Rest assured they will still query our figures.'

'OK. Let me spell it out. Firstly, I need to check out this Mountainside Reserve Hotel.'

'But the Phoenix Group meeting is not scheduled to take place until May fifth. Why do you need to go there so early?'

'I think you'll find those fellers don't leave anything to chance. The meeting might not be taking place until the fifth, but they'll have people visiting in advance to check everything is properly organised for them.'

'How can you be so sure?'

'Because, I've already made enquiries at the hotel. They are fully booked for the last few days in April and the first week of May. That's very unusual, because it's out of season this time of year. My guess is the Phoenix Group has block booked all the accommodation for that period.'

'Why would they do that?'

'Because it will ensure maximum privacy while preparations are made for the meeting and at the same time allow the members to start arriving early. If I was to rock up at the hotel during that period, and start nosing around, alarm bells would ring from New Hampshire to New Delhi.'

'I see.'

'Which means I will need to stay at the Mountainside Reserve for a few days this coming week in order to have enough time to work out how best to bug the conference centre. Booking in as a paying guest well before the meeting is due to take place will enable me to poke around without raising any suspicions.'

'I suppose that makes sense,' he acknowledged grudgingly.

'There is another consideration. As you know, although the South Africans are not anticipating an attack during the meeting between the government and the ANC, as a precaution they have requested our help to check out security at Groote Schuur.'

He nodded his understanding.

'The ANC meeting takes place on May fourth, so I need to visit the presidential residence in advance to check their security arrangements. I am anticipating returning to the UK immediately after the Phoenix meeting, unless something dramatic happens.'

'Like what?'

'Like if the Phoenix Group try to take out the ANC leaders whilst I'm in South Africa, or they reveal plans at their meeting that necessitate me staying in the country. Don't worry though, if I need to stay longer I will clear it with you first.'

'That's very good of you.'

'Do I detect a hint of insincerity in your voice?

'Yes. I don't see why you should have a monopoly on sarcasm.' He looked pleased with himself. 'Is there anything else I should know?'

'Yes, I want to hire a security company to help me check out the Mountainside Reserve and install listening devices in its conference centre.'

'Do you have a company in mind?'

'Yes. It's run by an old friend of mine. His name is Paul Helsdon.'

'Is he trustworthy?'

'I'd trust him with my life. In fact, I owe him my life.'

'How so?'

I told him how Paul had been with me in Laos fighting with anti-communist insurgents who were being backed by the Vietnamese. Our patrol was ambushed and all my men were killed except for Paul who managed to escape.

I was captured and taken back to the insurgents' base. They were preparing to torture me, but I was saved from being sodomised by a red hot bayonet when Paul ran into the camp firing his automatic weapon. He wiped out all the insurgents and we both escaped unscathed.

'I see what you mean,' he said when I finished my story. 'However, no doubt your friend will charge for his services?'

'Of course. You get nowt for nowt.'

'How much?'

'I haven't a clue. Until I have checked out the Mountainside Reserve Hotel conference centre, I have no idea what will be needed. I then have to discuss the situation with Paul.'

'OK. Get Colleen to book you a flight to South Africa.'

'That's a relief, because I've already booked into the hotel. They're expecting me on Saturday evening.'

'Why am I not surprised?' He said in a resigned voice.

'Because you know me too well, boss.'

'If you can only stay at Mountainside Reserve Hotel for a few days, what will you do for the rest of your time?'

'I don't know. I'll make a plan when I'm there. It depends how I get on. There are plenty of hotels in the area. I'll let you know once I decide.'

'OK. Now, what about the Irishman? Will he be a threat?'

'I hope so. That's why I wound up Wren. I want Brannagan to follow me, but don't worry, I'll be watching out for him.'

'And...?'

'And what?'

'What if you see him?'

'I'm not sure you want to know.'

'I want to know,' he insisted.

Okay. It's simple. If I see the bastard, I'll take him out.' I stared defiantly at him. 'With or without an XPD order.'

'Very well. Whatever happens, Statton, you have my full support. That Irish bastard murdered Fraser in cold blood. He cannot be allowed to get away with killing one of our own.'

'Thank you, boss.' I was surprised at this uncharacteristic disregard of the rules. 'However, there is something else.'

'What's that?'

'The thing about bugging the conference centre.'

'What about it?'

'I think we should keep it strictly to ourselves.'

'You don't want me to mention it to the AOSC members?'

'Definitely not the AOSC.'

'I take it you're worried about Dougie finding out?'

'What do you think? We know your mate is almost certainly passing information to Wren. The last thing I want is that bastard tipping off the Phoenix Group about my plans to eavesdrop their meeting. Security at the hotel is going to be as tight as a duck's arse as it is. I don't want to encourage them to step it up still further by giving advance warning of my intentions.'

'What about within the department?'

'No. I believe it should be treated on a strictly need to know only and right now I can't think of anybody in the department who needs to know.'

'Not even Dobbins?'

'It's Hobbins, and the answer is no. Tell no one.'

'Understood.' Disraeli-Astor pointed to a box on his desk. 'Before you go, perhaps you'd like to make a donation.'

'What's it for?'

'We're having a whip round for Fraser's mother.'

'A whip round? What's that all about?'

'It's Poppy's idea. She got chatting with his sister at the funeral. Apparently, Mrs Fraser is struggling financially. It seems she has barely enough in the bank to pay for the boy's funeral. Her daughter said that her mother is dreading the undertakers' bill. Poppy thought it would be a nice gesture to help her pay it.'

I pulled my wallet out and removed two £20 pound notes. 'Happy to contribute, but I'm not sure Mrs Fraser will take the money. She struck me as a very proud woman who is unlikely to accept charity.'

It was late afternoon by the time I finished my meeting with Disraeli-Astor and returned to the Section Two offices. They were deserted except for Des Hobbins.

Melissa and Clive were still at the library researching members of the Phoenix Group. Poppy had taken a couple of days off to spend a long weekend with her married lover, Roger. I asked Des to join me in my office.

'I'm off to South Africa...' I started to say

'You told me,' Des interjected as he settled himself into a chair opposite me.

'Let me finish.'

He raised his hands in an apology.

'I'm going tomorrow. While I'm away I want you to see if you can track down Brannagan.'

'Will do.'

'If you suspect he is following me to Cape Town, I want to know straight away.'

'Of course.'

'And remember he might travel as William Butler.'

Des nodded his understanding.

'Pull Melissa off the Phoenix Group research job to help you.

Young Clive will be alright to carry on with the research on his own,'
I said this with a confidence I didn't really feel. In my heart of heart I
knew the new researcher was in the Timmy mould and would be lost
without Melissa's intuitive guidance.

'That might be difficult,' Des said.

'Why?'

'Because Melissa is on holiday starting on Monday.'

'For how long?'

'Two weeks.'

'Bugger. I didn't know that. Who the hell authorised that?'

'Don't you remember?' He asked with an amused smile.

'Me?' I guessed the answer.

'Well, it's your signature on her holiday request form.'

That's when it came back to me. 'But that was weeks ago,' I
protested feebly, angry at myself for not remembering.

'There's no time limit on authorisation, boss.'

'Thanks for stating the bleeding obvious.'

Des laughed.

'You might well laugh, but that doesn't change the fact that
Melissa is on leave.'

'I'm sure I'll get by on my own. I'm a big boy now.'

'I wasn't casting doubt on your ability,' I assured him. 'But
Melissa has a talent for tracking people down. She has a sixth sense.'

'I could ask her to postpone her holiday.'

I shook my head. 'I don't think so. It wouldn't be fair on her. I
think you'll find she's off to Thailand.'

'Don't worry, boss. I'll be fine working on my own.'

'I'm sure you're right. However, should you need help from
Scotland Yard, liaise with ADC Neal.' I passed him the contact
details for Kevin. 'He's one of the good guys.'

'Thanks, access to the Yard's computers might be useful.'

'It might. However, although I trust Neal, I don't have the same
faith in some of his colleagues, so be careful who you talk to.'

'OK, I'll be discreet and if I need more help from within the
department, I'll let you know.'

'I think you'd be better off speaking to the D-G. I'm not sure
exactly where I'll be and you might not be able to reach me. I'll be in
touch with the office every so often to check on progress, but I can't
guarantee when. Anyway, I won't be able to sort out manpower from

South Africa. Let the boss earn his corn.'

Des got to his feet. 'When do you leave?'

'First thing in the morning. Hopefully Colleen is booking my flight as we speak.'

'Okay. I'm off home. Have a safe journey.'

'Thanks, but I'll be quite safe. The only risk to life and limb on the plane will come from the cruddy food. Statistically, you are more likely to get run over by a bus whilst crossing the road than you are being involved in an airplane crash.'

'Bollocks to statistics,' he snorted.

'I forgot you don't like flying.'

'I *hate* flying! If God had wanted me to fly he'd have given me wings instead of arms and stuck a jet engine up my jacksie.'

I laughed. I had heard Des use the same joke before, usually when he was holding forth in a pub, but the image was still funny.

'Anyway, I was thinking more about when you actually arrive in Cape Town. My recollection is that the motorists in South Africa are maniacs and the roads are death traps.'

'That's true, but I'm used to driving in the Cape. I'm more likely to get grief from a woman driver in a car-park.'

It was his turn to laugh.

I didn't join in because the phrase many a true word is spoken in jest suddenly popped into my head and I had no idea why.

Chapter 25

The only seat Colleen could find for me was on a British Airways flight from Heathrow to Johannesburg. We took off at 9 pm on Friday night and landed at 10 am the following morning. This gave me ample time to transfer to the Cape Town bound South African Airways plane that took off at midday.

By mid-afternoon I had picked up an Avis hire car, which was waiting for me at D.F. Malan Airport, and was heading towards Somerset West.

As I drove down the N2, my mind went back to the last time I had arrived in the Cape, eight years before. On that occasion, when I left the airport terminal building, it was to step into driving rain. By the time I reached my car, I was cold, wet and miserable.

Today was different. The sun was shining and there was such a balmy feel to the autumn afternoon I was able to drive with my window wound down and savour the sweet African air.

In the distance, I could see the Constantiaberg Mountain range, of which Chapman's Peak was part. In its foothills lay my destination. Noordhoek.

I was in no rush and drove at a leisurely pace, but it still took me only twenty minutes to reach the turn off onto Baden Powell Drive. Soon I was driving along the shore of False Bay towards Muizenberg.

Three and a half miles out into the bay was a small, rocky outcrop. The low-lying black islet rose from the dark azure coloured waters of the bay like a humped-back whale. Its name was Seal Island.

The only time I had visited the islet was when my team and I were making our preparations to visit another island, ironically, named after seals also, although it was better known by its Dutch name: Robben Island.

Our visit to Seal Island took place in thick fog, when I was testing a ski-boat with my friend Paul Helsdon. It was memorable for being the first and only time I had been close to a great-white shark. I smiled to myself as I remembered the look on Paul's face when a shark surged from the water with a struggling seal in its jaws. He was terrified of sharks.

When I reached Muizenberg, I picked up Main Road, which took me along the coast through the communities of St James, Kalk Bay and Clovelly. As I drove through this latter hamlet, my mood darkened.

Clovelly was where I had stayed during my previous visit to the Cape Peninsula and painful memories from the past forced themselves into my mind. They were about as welcome as gate-crashers at a party.

However, I managed to exorcise the unwelcome ghosts, and my spirits had risen again by the time I reached the neighbouring town of Fish Hoek. From there I took the Kommetjie Road, which links False Bay, with its relatively warm Indian Ocean waters, to the colder Atlantic Ocean waters on the west side of the peninsula.

After a couple of miles I turned onto the Ou Kaapse Weg and, shortly after that, onto Noordhoek Main Road. Ten minutes later I pulled into the car-park of the Mountainside Reserve Hotel.

The air was still balmy, but the sun was lower in the sky and the trees that surrounded the car-park cast dark shadows across the dusty surface. I checked in at reception and then followed a porter up the narrow path to the wooden lodge that would be my home for the next few days. I slipped him a fifty-rand tip and in return he gave me a wide smile and his name.

Piet explained that in addition to being a porter, he was also the hotel's handyman and general dogsbody. He urged me to contact him if I needed any more help. That was exactly what I planned.

The tip I had given my new best friend was well over the odds for carrying a single suitcase up a slight slope and ten steps. However, I looked upon it as a part payment in lieu of future services rendered.

I had no idea for what information I might need to pump him, but I was confident that knowing I was a generous tipper would help lubricate his mouth.

My cabin was marketed as an Executive Suite, but the hotel management didn't make clear what level of executive they were hoping to attract. It was adequate, but hardly luxurious. I'm sure many company high-flyers would turn their noses up at the décor and facilities on offer in the cabin. I wasn't so demanding.

Apart from a bedroom, there was a small lounge area, which

comprised of a slightly shabby double sofa; an upright wooden chair; a coffee table with a scratched top and a sideboard. A portable television and a telephone stood on the sideboard, whilst a wicker basket of chopped wood stood on the floor alongside it. This was for use with the open fire that was set into the side wall.

In addition, there was a bathroom, with the usual fittings, and a curtained window, in front of which stood a bath that looked out onto the dense foliage of the milkwood forest.

Beyond the trees, Noordhoek beach curved in a long and beautifully clean crescent of sand that led all the way to the lighthouse in Kommetjie, which was already flashing out its warning as dusk grew closer.

There was no mini-bar in the cabin, but this didn't matter because I had picked up a couple of bottles of Pinotage and a bottle of brandy at the airport.

I found a corkscrew in a drawer in the sideboard, which suggested that previous guests had done the same as me and brought in their own supply of booze. I opened a bottle of wine and poured some into a glass tumbler I found in the bathroom.

Outside the bedroom window was a private balcony that overlooked the building in which was located the reception and restaurant. I went outside with my glass of wine, sat down on one of the wooden chairs that had been provided and waited for the sunset.

By the time the sun sank spectacularly into the Atlantic Ocean I was into my second glass of Pinotage and was starting to feel relaxed after my long journey.

Once the sun had disappeared, the temperature dropped rapidly and dramatically and by the time I retreated to the comfort of my bedroom it was bitterly cold. I used wood from the wicker basket to lay a fire and lit it with firelighters and matches that I found in the same drawer as the corkscrew.

I kicked off my shoes and sat in front of the roaring fire. I sipped yet another glass of the deep red wine and let the warmth flow over me whilst I thought about my next move.

When I had last visited South Africa, Paul Helsdon was living in Johannesburg, but I knew he had now moved to Cape Town, which I took to be a good omen. I contacted him before I left England and arranged to meet him for lunch. He insisted on treating me to a meal at the Mount Nelson Hotel. I tried to object at this show of generosity, but he refused to listen. I didn't complain.

I was looking forward to seeing Paul again. I hoped to persuade him to visit the Mountainside Reserve Hotel with me to check out the lie of the land. I was sure he would agree.

I didn't get any further ahead with my plans before tiredness, three glasses of wine and the heat from the fire overcame me and I fell into a deep sleep.

When I awoke in the early hours of the morning, the fire was out, I was cold, stiff and had a full bladder. I visited the toilet and then clambered, still clothed into bed. I was soon asleep again.

Sunday, April 22nd

I awoke at eight o'clock Sunday morning and tugged open the curtains of my bedroom to be confronted by low dark clouds. Rain blew in from the Atlantic and hammered against my window with the steady staccato rhythm of a snare drum.

I had a quick shower and then made my way down to the restaurant. By the time I finished a light breakfast the rain had abated and only a fine drizzle remained in the air. On the way back up the pathway to my cabin I saw Piet coming out the front door of the conference centre.

He gave me a warm smile, before locking the door using a key from the large bunch he was holding. I guessed these were the master keys to all the cabins in the hotel.

I smiled back at him. 'Is there a way to get down to the beach from here, Piet?' I asked.

'Ja. If you walk along this path, and keep going, you'll reach the end of the hotel's property. There's a gate, but it's not locked at this time of day. Go through the gate and keep on down the hill and eventually you'll reach the beach.'

'How far is the beach?'

'A couple of kilometres, but be careful, meneer, because the path is full of sharp rocks and pot holes.'

I thanked him and headed towards the path

'Hey, meneer,' he called after me.

I turned to face him.

'Don't forget to contact me if there is anything I can do for you.'

'I don't have anything right now, but I'll bear it in mind.'

'I could wash your car,' he suggested with a smile.

'My car is clean, but I'm sure I'll find another job for you before I leave.'

Piet's smile widened.

Piet was right about the state of the path. Where it ran through the hotel grounds it was not too bad, but once I went through the gate and out onto the hillside the surface deteriorated rapidly.

The path became increasingly steep as it meandered through the thick milkwood forest. As I got further down the hill the composition of the path's surface changed from compacted dirt - which in places had been turned into mud by rain - to a softer sandy mix. Just as Piet had warned, there were numerous rocks and potholes in my way and a couple of times I stumbled and almost fell over.

Eventually I found myself at the bottom of the path in a small clearing, surrounded by boulders, on a narrow sandy shelf about ten feet above the beach. There were a number of treacherous, rock strewn, tracks leading down through the boulders to the beach.

I chose one track and, with some difficulty, managed to make my way down until I ended up on the beach, looking back up at what now appeared to be an almost impenetrable forest.

I could see a number of the hotel's cabins poking above tree tops and raindrops sparkled like diamonds on their roofs as the morning sun broke through clouds that previously had wrapped it in a dark shroud.

I stared thoughtfully up at the narrow dark slit in the trees at the back of the sandy shelf. This was the start of the path that led back up to the hotel. I wondered how many people actually ventured into the forest from the beach.

I considered the inhospitable view of the dense forest from the beach; the precarious state of the tracks leading up to the shelf; and the difficulty in spotting the entrance to the path. I guessed only people who knew the path would use it. They would be few and far apart, particularly at this time of the year. That suited me just fine.

Rather than walk back up the path, I made my way along the beach. It stretches six miles south all the way to Kommetjie, but I only walked for about three miles before heading east towards Noordhoek village.

I made my way through a scattering of large houses until I reached the main road that led back to the Mountainside Reserve

Hotel. When I eventually arrived back at my cabin, I had time to shave and dress before heading for the city to meet Paul for lunch.

Gardens, Cape Town
The Mount Nelson was the best five-star hotel in South Africa, and arguably anywhere on the African continent. Its reputation for grandeur stretched back almost a hundred years, to the original opening in 1899. More recently its pre-eminence was further burnished when in 1988 it was taken over by Orient-Express Hotels, which added its own cachet to Mount Nelson's already stellar status.

I turned off Orange Street and drove through the columned main gate. It was built at a time when South Africa was still one of the jewels in the British Empire, reminding me of the turbulent times the hotel had witnessed since it first opened.

I followed Parliament Avenue as it swept in a gentle arc past the imposing colonial style pink building, on the front of which flew the flags of half a dozen different countries. I parked my hire car alongside a collection of Rolls-Royces, Bentleys, Mercedes-Benz and the odd Porsche. My modest Volkswagen Passat didn't seem overawed at the company it was keeping. Neither was I.

Paul Helsdon was waiting for me in the hotel lobby with a wide grin on his handsome face. I held out a hand for him to shake, but the big man ignored it and instead grabbed me in a bear hug that almost squeezed the air from my lungs. I hugged him back briefly, then we pulled apart.

'Ag man, I've missed you.'

'It's been a long time,' I replied.

'Too bloody long, man,' he said as he led me into the restaurant. 'It's six years since I visited Freddie and you in Scotland.'

'Good afternoon, Mister Helsdon,' the maître d' said, giving Paul a slight bow and the sort of beaming smile that no doubt was reserved for regular customers who were generous tippers.

'Hi, Franco,' Paul shook the man's hand. 'This pale looking rooinek is David Statton,' he introduced me in his customary irreverent fashion. 'He's an old friend of mine.'

The smile the maître d' offered me was half-hearted, but I suppose he had worked out that I was unlikely to be frequenting the Mount Nelson often. He waved over a waiter and asked him to show us to our table.

'I have allocated your usual table, Mister Helsdon,' the maître d' said, whilst making disappear the large denomination note that my friend slipped discreetly into his hand.

'Have you seen Freddie recently?' I asked as we sat down at a table that looked out onto a sprawling tropical garden.

'Ja. I bumped into her a couple of weeks back. She's working for one of my new clients.'

'How is she?'

'She's lekker.' Suddenly the big South African looked sad. 'Sies man, it broke me up when you guys split. I thought you'd stay together forever.'

'Me too, but perhaps I was expecting too much taking Freddie to live in the wilds of Scotland.'

'Ja. I sensed she was unhappy when I visited you.'

'She was and your visit probably didn't help.'

'Is that so? Ag man, I'm so sorry.'

'Don't worry, Paul. I wasn't trying to pin a guilt trip on you. I think she would have left anyway. She had been pining for Cape Town for ages. She tried to hide how she felt, but I saw in her face how much she missed her friends and family. I think you reminded her of home.'

The waiter was hovering; waiting to take our order. We paused for a moment to look through the menu. I chose calamari peri-peri to start and lobster thermidor to follow. Paul chose pan fried perlemoen as a starter, followed by a fillet steak stuffed with Stilton cheese.

'We'll have a bottle of chardonnay with the starters and pinotage with the main meal,' Paul added.

'Very good, sir,' the waiter said, before slipping silently away.

'Do you miss Freddie?' Paul asked.

'Yes.'

'Then why don't you contact her while you're here?'

'I'm not sure that's a good idea. She might be in another relationship.'

'So what?' Paul said, then paused again as a wine waiter appeared carrying an ice bucket containing a bottle of chardonnay. He poured a splash of wine into a glass and Paul sniffed it appreciatively. 'Fine,' he said and watched as the waiter poured a generous measure into both our glasses.

Paul waited until the man left. 'In my experience, women aren't put off agreeing to a date even if they're in a relationship,' he said with a knowing smile. 'In the right circumstances.'

'What are the right circumstances?'

'That she fancies you.'

'Is that it?'

'And there's no risk she'll be found out,' he added with an impish grin. 'Of course, you won't know whether Freddie has found somebody else unless you ask her.'

'We haven't spoken for a couple of years. I wouldn't even know how to get in touch with her.'

'But I do,' Paul said with another grin. 'I told you earlier, she works for one of my clients. I have their telephone number in my diary.' He lapsed into silence again as our waiter arrived carrying two plates and put them down on the table in front of us.

'OK, give me the number before we leave and I'll ring her.'

I cut off a piece of calamari, dipped it into the peri-peri sauce, which was served on my plate in a small glass bowl, then popped it into my mouth. Paul tucked into his perlemoen and we ate in companionable silence.

'So, howzit with you, man?' Paul asked eventually. 'What's it like back working for the British Secret Service?'

'It's a secret.'

'And what about this job you've lined up for me? Is that a secret also?' He laughed.

'No, I can talk about that.'

'So, what do you want me to do?'

'A couple of things, but first tell me about yourself.' I used my fork to point around the dining room. 'You seem to know your way round here pretty well. You must come here regularly. Mount Nelson doesn't come cheap. I take it your security company is doing well?'

Paul nodded. 'Not bad. By the end of this year I could be a millionaire.'

'Rands?'

'No, US dollars.'

I whistled quietly. 'I'm impressed. The private security game must be very lucrative.'

'It is now, but sies, man, it hasn't been easy. As you know, I used all the money I earned from that job back in eighty-two to start up my own company. For the first few years I struggled to make ends meet, but now, it's starting to pay dividends.'

'What changed?'

'The release of Mandela has alarmed a lot of people and private security is booming. Everybody but everybody wants the latest burglar alarms fitted to their homes and armed security guards regularly checking up on their properties.'

'Has crime got that bad?'

'Not yet, but punters know that change is coming. Within a couple of years there will be an election that the ANC is expected to win. People have now woken up to the fact that South Africa is going to have a black government. Whites, Coloureds, Asians and even the black middle classes, are worried that policing will be one of the first public services hit. They believe that will lead to an increase in lawlessness, as it did in Zimbabwe.'

We finished our starters and, as if by magic, a waiter came from nowhere to whip away our plates and top up our glasses with what remained of the white wine.

I sipped my chardonnay before saying: 'But as far as you're concerned, Paul, every cloud has a silver lining. Yes?'

He looked at me and shook his head. 'No, Dave, in my case the lining is golden.' He drained his wine with one swallow and then grinned. 'Now tell me what you want me to do.'

'Have you heard of the Mountainside Reserve Hotel?'

Paul looked surprised. 'The Mountainside Reserve? Sure I've heard of it. It's in Noordhoek A few weeks back I submitted a tender for a security job for them. Apparently they were acting on behalf of a client.'

'You quoted for work? Are you able to tell me what it was for?'

'I didn't get the job so I don't see why not. The tender was for undertaking a security sweep of the buildings and grounds.'

'When was the sweep to take place?'

'At the end of this month.'

That would make sense if the hotel's mystery client was the Phoenix Group.

'In addition, I was asked for a quote to supply security guards to patrol the grounds during the weekend of the fifth and sixth of May.'

'But you didn't get the job?'

'No it was won by Titan Security.'

I shook my head. 'Not a company I've heard of.'

'Probably not. They operate only in SA, but they are on a par with your Securicor.'

'That big?'

'Ja, which is why I wasn't surprised they won the contract.'

'Why not?'

'Because I can't compete with their prices. Titan can afford to cut their margins to win additional business like the Mountainside Reserve job. To companies like them it's no more than icing on an already very large cake.' He smiled at me. 'But give me a couple of years and I'll give Jonathan Rhodes a run for his money.'

'Jonathan Rhodes?' I muttered.

'Do you know him?' Paul asked.

I shook my head. 'No, but the name sounds familiar.'

'It ought to be. He's one of the wealthiest men in Southern Africa. His grandfather was a cousin of the Rhodes.'

'You mean Cecil?'

'Yes. As you probably know, Rhodes had no children himself, but he ensured his relatives were looked after when he died. Not only does Jonathan own Titan Security, but he has significant mining and brewing interests.'

We lapsed into silence as we finished off the bottle of chardonnay.

'Tell me, Paul,' I said eventually. 'As part of the bid process did you have to survey the Mountainside Reserve?'

'Of course. I wanted to know how many guards would be needed.' He paused as our waiter wheeled a lidded trolley alongside our table. He was accompanied by the wine waiter who carried a bottle of red wine, which he proceeded to uncork whilst the first waiter opened the roll lid of the trolley to reveal our main courses.

Immediately an aroma of lobster thermidor mixed with steak and cheese wafted our way. Smoothly the waiter transferred our plates onto the table and then returned to the kitchen pushing the trolley.

The wine waiter asked Paul to taste the pinotage, of which the big South African approved with a satisfied nod of his head, then the waiter poured each of us a glass before following the first waiter towards the kitchen.

My mouth watered as I looked down at the steaming lobster shell full of succulent meat mixed with mustard and herbs. I put a forkful of lobster into my mouth. Like the starter it was delicious.

Paul was already eating his steak, but it didn't stop him talking.

'So what about the Mountainside Reserve?'

Between mouthfuls I told him about everything that had happened to me since arranging for the defection of Alexei Urinoff and his murder by William Butler. I explained about Butler's involvement with the Phoenix Group, their agenda to destabilise South Africa, their upcoming meeting in Noordhoek and how important it was that we found out what their intentions were. It was only when I had finished briefing Paul that I remembered where I had seen the name Jonathan Rhodes before.

'Rhodes is a member of the Phoenix Group,' I told him.

Paul looked at me in silence for a while. He put his knife and fork down on his empty plate. 'So it might not have been only price that won the contract for Titan?'

I didn't answer him, because it sounded like a rhetorical question. Instead I said: 'I want you to come to Noordhoek with me and see if we can work out a way of bugging the conference centre without being detected.'

He frowned. 'I think the receptionists might recognise me. I joshed those girlies a bit.'

'Don't worry. I don't plan to go anywhere near the reception. I know a more discreet way into the resort.' I explained about the path up from Noordhoek beach. 'Once it's dark, I think we can get in by the back door.'

'When I checked out that path down to the beach it was late evening and the gate was locked,' he said.

'Leave that to me. I have a plan.'

'OK. I trust you. When do you want to do it?'

'How are you fixed this coming Wednesday evening?'

Paul pulled a slim black diary from the inside pocket of his jacket and flicked through it. 'That will be lekker. I have a couple of appointments during the day, but I'm free in the evening. Where shall we meet?'

'You know how to get to the Mountainside Reserve, don't you?'

'Ja. It's off Beach Road.'

'Well, at the very end of Beach Road you'll find a car-park.'

'I know it,' Paul confirmed.

'Good. I'll meet you there at nineteen hundred hours.'

The waiter came back to clear our plates away and bring us the dessert menus. We both decided on a plate of cheese, accompanied by a vintage port.

'Where are you staying, Dave?'

'At the Mountainside Reserve, but that's only until the end of this week.'

'Then what?'

'I'll find somewhere else.'

'I have a spare room in my apartment in Newlands. Why don't you stay with me?'

'Are you sure?'

'Of course, I'm sure. I'd welcome your company. In fact, why don't you check out of your hotel and move in straight away?'

'It's a tempting offer, but I need to stay where I am until at least after we give it the once over on Wednesday. Let's take a rain check and I'll decide on Thursday.'

'That's cool with me.' He downed the last of his wine and then studied me. 'You mentioned you had a couple of things for me. What else?'

I explained about the meeting between the Government and ANC leaders. 'But the meeting is top secret,' I told him when I had finished. 'So, keep it to yourself.' I had been given the information in confidence, but I knew I could trust Paul to keep his mouth shut. As if reading my mind, he pulled an invisible zip across his lips.

'I have been asked to visit Groote Schuur in advance of the meeting and check out their security arrangements for them,' I explained. 'I'd welcome your input. How are you fixed for time the week after next?'

'This coming Friday I have to travel to Durban for a few days.

'When do you come back?'

'Wednesday week. The first of May,' Paul said.

'Are you free on Thursday of that week?

Paul looked at his organiser again. 'Ja. Free as a bird.'

'Excellent, that fits in well. We can check out Groote Schuur during the day and make any last minute arrangements at the Mountainside Reserve when it's dark.'

Our cheese and port turned up and we spent the rest of the afternoon leisurely finishing off our meal and reminiscing about old times. It was good to be working together again.

Before we parted, Paul flicked through his diary and found Freddie's work telephone number. He wrote it down on the back of a business card. I looked at it, but said nothing. I no longer had an excuse not to ring her. I was committed.

Noordhoek, Cape Peninsula, Monday, April 23rd
I spent Monday morning reconnoitring the grounds of the Mountainside Reserve Hotel. Starting each time at the conference centre I made my way through the forest in a dozen different directions. I noted the location of each cabin and worked out the sight lines to and from the path that led down to the beach.

By early afternoon I had worked up an appetite so I headed back to my cabin to change for lunch. I saw Paul's business card on the coffee table and picked up the phone to ring Freddie. I started to dial her number when I had a sudden attack of nerves. I returned the receiver to its rest. I decided to contact her after I had eaten.

But after eating a hearty lunch in the restaurant, I put off ringing Freddie yet again, deciding instead to track down Piet the porter. I found him cleaning out the swimming pool with a long handled pool brush connected to a suction hose. His face lit up when he saw me. I told him there was a problem with the toilet cistern in my cabin. He promised to fix it as soon as he had finished what he was doing.

Piet turned up at my cabin half an hour later. There was nothing wrong with my toilet, but it was a good excuse to get him on his own. We spent fifteen minutes in good natured negotiation, before we reached an agreement. I would give him five hundred rand in exchange for his silence and two of the spare keys that he told me were kept in the reception office.

Piet left the cabin with a smile on his face and ten minutes later he came back with a large water melon, from which a slice had been cut. He had small pieces of melon down the front of his overalls, so I guessed he had eaten the slice for his lunch.

He smiled at me again and stuck two fingers into the red flesh of the melon and pulled out first one key and then another. He handed them to me and I paid him. This time his smile was even wider when he left my cabin to find somewhere to eat the rest of his water melon.

I washed the keys under a tap in the bathroom sink, drying them on a towel. Satisfied, I mixed them with my home keys, which were on a key-ring in the pocket of my holdall. The best hiding place is always the obvious one.

Now I had what I wanted, I spent the next couple of hours

drawing up a plan, which I would flow past Paul on Wednesday. When I was finished I put through a long distance call to London.

Colleen answered the phone. 'The Director-General's office, Colleen speaking, how can I help you?'

'Very efficient.'

'David? Is that you?'

'You guessed.'

'Where on earth are you?'

'You should know. You booked my flight.'

'Don't be difficult. I know you're in Cape Town, but where exactly? It's a big city.'

'I'm in a little place called Noordhoek. I thought you knew.'

'You had Poppy book your hotel, which, I might add, is strictly against the new rules,' she said in a voice that reflected her disapproval at the way I had bucked the system. 'And she hasn't been able to brief me about your whereabouts, because she is still on her long weekend, which, no doubt, she spent screwing Roger.'

'You sound jealous.'

'Don't change the subject.'

'I wasn't changing the subject. It was you who mentioned Poppy. Was that because you wish we were doing, what she and Roger are doing?'

I could hear her struggling to hold back a giggle. 'See what I mean? You're trying to start a discussion about Poppy's love life in the hope that I will forget you ignored departmental procedures and didn't channel your hotel booking through me.'

'You found me out.'

'You're incorrigible.'

'How do you spell that?'

Finally she laughed.

'I like it when you giggle,' I said.

'Stop it, David. I'm cross with you.'

'Of course you are. Because I'm a very naughty boy.'

'It's no joking matter. Rules are rules.'

'Some rules were made to be broken. Anyway, your boss knew where I was staying. Why didn't you ask him?'

'I did, but he couldn't remember.'

'Great! I could have been murdered in my hotel bed and nobody would have known about it.'

'It would have been your own fault, for not telling me. You know what the boss's memory is like.'

'Is he there?' I asked.

'Yes, I'll put you through, but first I want to tell you something.'

'What's that?'

'I wish we could have another dirty weekend like Poppy and Roger,' she said quietly, then there was a click on the line and she was gone.

I heard the D-G's phone ring twice, then the receiver was picked up.

'Disraeli-Astor.'

'Is it really? There was me thinking I was ringing the Chinese takeaway.'

'Is that you, Statton?'

'I's me.'

'Where are you?'

'Don't you start, I've just been asked the same question by your PA. Don't you talk to each other? Look, I told you where I was staying and we had a conversation about how long I would be staying here.'

'I don't recall exactly what was said. Never mind, it's time to move on.'

'I think you're mixing too much with politicians. That's the stock response they give when they know they're in the wrong.'

He ignored me and carried on. 'So, just tell me what's happening down there in Cape Town.'

So I gave him a quick briefing about the Mountainside Reserve Hotel; my meeting with Paul Helsdon at the Mount Nelson; and the involvement of Jonathan Rhodes' company in the security arrangements for the meeting.

'Rhodes is a member of the Phoenix Group,' he said.

'You remember?' I couldn't conceal my astonishment.

'Don't sound so surprised. I studied the history of Cecil Rhodes at Eton and the name stuck in my mind when I saw the list of Phoenix members. Is there a family connection?'

'Yes. His grandfather was Rhodes' cousin.'

'It is widely thought that Cecil had a preference for male company. If you get my drift.'

I did. 'You mean he was homosexual.'

'Nobody is sure and it has never been proven. The only certainty is that Rhodes never married and he had no children.'

'I know. When Cecil died, he left a sizeable part of his fortune to Jonathan Rhodes' grandfather,' I pointed out.

'And no doubt part of that fortune was eventually inherited by his father.'

'Quite likely. Jonathan's family certainly wasn't short of a few bob. I understand he was educated privately in the UK. Was he by any chance at Eton with you?'

There was a silence on the other end of the telephone and then he said in a good-humoured voice: 'Look, Statton, I know what you're trying to do and I refuse to let you provoke me.'

'It was worth a try. I don't want to get out of practice.'

He had the good grace to laugh at that, before saying: 'So, you have to leave your hotel by the end of this week?'

'Yes. I'll probably move out on Thursday.'

'Where will you stay?'

'Well, the food at the Mount Nelson is excellent. I was thinking of booking in there for a few days.'

'The Mount Nelson?'

'Yes. The bedrooms are very comfortable.'

'Are you serious?'

'Very serious. They're almost palatial.'

'You know what I mean, Statton. The Mount Nelson is very expensive. I'm not sure such extravagance is appropriate.'

'I see. So we field agents are second class citizens are we?'

'I didn't say that,' he said defensively. 'The point is that your trip is already costing the Department a small fortune, we can't afford for you to stay in a luxury hotel as well.'

'As I recall we included expenditure for this operation in the budget.' I pointed out.

'And as I recall, I told you that all our expenditure has to be justified to the Treasury. So, however large our agreed budget, we still cannot have you spending money as if it's going out of fashion.'

'Money isn't everything, boss,' I quoted back to him his own words. 'It's more important to have a feeling of self-worth. And staying at the Mount Nelson would give me a wonderful feeling of self-worth.'

There was another silence at the other end of the phone, then he said: 'Don't try my patience, Statton.'

'Don't worry,' I said. 'I have no intention of staying at the Mount Nelson. That really was a wind-up. It's good to see I haven't lost my touch.'

He sighed heavily. 'Sometimes I worry about your so called sense of humour.'

'I read somewhere, that worry is just a state of mind. Perhaps you should see a doctor.'

He chose to ignore me. 'So, where *are* you going to stay?'

'Paul Helsdon has offered to put me up in his apartment. It should save the department a few bawbees.'

'That will certainly please the Treasury.'

'It's always a pleasure to make the bean counters happy.'

'Do you have the address?'

'No. I'll let you have it as soon as I've moved in. Now, is there anything else at your end that I need to know?'

'A couple of things. First up, I had that military attaché chappie from the American embassy onto me.'

'Bob Fletcher?'

'That's him. He told me Langley has agreed that somebody called...' he paused and I imagined him looking through the note pad he kept on his desk, '...Hank Graham will shadow you in the field. Does the name mean anything to you?'

'Yeah, Hank's OK. Did you tell Fletcher I was in South Africa?'

'I had no choice.'

'How did he take it?'

'He was not amused.'

'I bet he wasn't. What did he say?'

'He said Graham could not be released from his current duties for at least two weeks, so wouldn't be able to join you in Cape Town until the second week of May.'

'I assume you told him you were disappointed about that?'

'Of course. I also explained that you might well be back in London by the beginning of May.'

'No lies there then. I bet that made Fletcher even unhappier.'

'Well, he did mumble something about submitting an official complaint to the Foreign Secretary.'

'What does he think that will achieve?'

'What do you mean?'

'I mean the mandarins at the Foreign Office are useless. They will make all the right noises to the Yanks; apologise profusely; deny all knowledge of our activities; and then send you a patronising letter about how important it is to work closely with our allies. It will be like being whipped with a wet lettuce.'

'I don't think that is altogether fair. I'm sure it must be jolly difficult keeping everybody happy. The Foreign Office does an important job. After all we don't want to start another war, do we?'

'Well the F.O. certainly doesn't. They're still fighting World War Two and they can't handle more than one conflict at a time. Their problem is they have learnt nothing since Nineteen Thirty-Nine. They still prevaricate, appease and ignore real threats.'

Disraeli-Astor grunted, but I couldn't tell whether he was agreeing with me or not. I suppose that was another sign of his bureaucratic skill.

'The F.O. hasn't yet grasped that the world has moved on and we are already fighting another war,' I went on. 'Only it's a different kind of war, against a different kind of enemy. When the F.O. is confronted by the reality of something like IRA terrorism; Islamic fundamentalism; plain old fashioned espionage; or, in this case, the threat from a secret organisation; it confuses them. So, they simply close their eyes and hope the problem goes away.'

'I'm not surprised the F.O. mandarins get confused,' he said. 'I often feel the same way when I see some of the things that are going on in the world.'

'Yeah, but at least you have some understanding about what those things mean, boss.'

'Is that a compliment?'

'It wasn't a criticism,' I said.

'I'll take that as a yes then.' He sounded happy. 'Talking of the Foreign Office, they are insisting you liaise with the British Consulate in Cape Town.'

'Bollocks!'

'That's what I thought you would say.'

'So what did you tell them?'

'In order not to create any inter-departmental conflict I negotiated a compromise.'

'What sort of compromise?' I asked suspiciously.

'We have agreed that the military attaché at the British Consulate in Cape Town will organise regular telephone conferences involving the Ambassador and him; the department here in London; and you. The first one will take place on Wednesday morning at eleven hundred hours.'

'Terrific. I can't wait.'

'Don't be grumpy. It's the best I could do.'

'Do we really want the F.O. to know all our secrets?'

'Certainly not!'

'So what are we going to do?'

'I suggest we go through the motions of using the conference calls to deliver progress reports.'

'And?'

'And we do not discuss anything we would prefer to keep within the Department. We will restrict such business to separate private conversations between ourselves. Is that understood?'

'Yes.' It was a good move, but then inter-departmental politics was Disraeli-Astor's speciality. 'Now what was the other thing you wanted to tell me?'

'It's about your holiday request form.'

'What about it?'

'I've signed it off.'

'But the application was for next week.'

'I know. I thought you might like to spend your holiday in Cape Town. It will save you the cost of an airline ticket.'

'Tell me you're joking, boss.'

'Have you ever known me to joke?'

'No,' I admitted.

He laughed. 'There's always a first time, Statton.'

'That's not funny, boss,' I protested.

'Perhaps now you will understand how you make other people feel,' he said and put the phone down.

I sat and stared at the phone, steeling myself to ring Freddie. I had no idea why I felt so nervous. I told myself it was irrational. Okay, so she had walked out on me, but I understood the reason for that and we parted much closer to being friends than enemies.

We had spoken on the telephone a few times in the early days, but these calls had petered out because we were separated by six thousand miles. Eventually, we lost contact completely when I lost the notebook containing her phone number. I kept meaning to track her down, but never got round to it.

Now, the lack of a contact number was no longer an excuse. I picked up the phone and dialled her work number.

'Goeie middag. Hoe kan ek jou hel?' The receptionist asked and then repeated in English: 'Good afternoon. How can I help you?'

'Freddie Carlse please,' I said.

'Please hold, sir, I'll check whether he is in.'

He? I was puzzled, but before I could query it the receptionist put me on hold.

There was a click in my ear and she was back. 'I'm afraid Mister Carlse is not in today, sir.'

'I was actually looking for a Miss Carlse,' I explained.

'The only Miss Carlse we have in the company is Bridgette, who works in the property section.'

'That would be her. Please could you put me through?'

'Not a problem, sir. Hold the line.'

As I waited to be connected, I remembered it was Freddie's father who started calling her by that name. She told me this was her dad's way of compensating for the loss of her twin brother, whose name was Frederik. I mulled over how some people, like Freddie, were known by their nicknames, rather than their given name.

This rang an alarm bell in my mind and I had a feeling I was missing something important in the chain of events in which I had been involved over the past few days. I didn't have time to pursue this line of thought because a voice said: 'Bridgette Carlse, can I help you?'

'Hello Freddie.'

'Who is this?'

'Do you really need to ask?'

'Is that you, Dave?'

'The very same.'

'Where are you ringing from?' She asked.

'A hotel in Noordhoek.'

'You're here in South Africa?'

'Well, the last time I looked that's where Noordhoek was.'

She sighed audibly. 'I see you haven't lost your penchant for sarcasm.'

'It's difficult to kick a habit of a lifetime.'

'What are you doing here?'

'That's not something I would feel comfortable talking about over an open telephone line.'

'I heard you were employed by the British Government.'

'In a manner of speaking,' I replied cautiously.

'I see. In a manner of speaking are you here on business?'

'Yes. Now what do I call you? Freddie or Bridgette?'

'I'm happy with either,' she said stiffly, as if I had brought back a bad memory for her. 'At work they call me Bridgette.'

'I don't work with you and I'm a creature of habit, so if it's OK with you I'll stick with Freddie.'

'If that's what you want.' She paused for a moment and then asked: 'How did you get my number, David?'

'Paul gave it to me.'

'You've been in touch with him?'

'Yeah, we had lunch together yesterday. Can we meet?'

There was a lengthy silence and at first I thought she had put the phone down on me, then she eventually said. 'If we meet will you tell me why you're in SA?'

'Yes,' I replied immediately. I knew I could trust her.

'Then the answer is yes. When and where?'

'How are you fixed tomorrow tonight?'

'I'm free,' she replied without hesitation.

'Do you want to meet me somewhere, or would you like me to pick you up?' I asked and then added: 'Do you have transport?'

'Yes, but I'm happy for you chauffeur me.'

'Where are you staying?'

'I have an apartment in Claremont.' She gave me the address before asking: 'Where shall we eat?'

'I thought about that little place in Fish Hoek we used the first time we had dinner together. Do you remember?'

'How could I forget? It was The Galleon Grill.'

'That's it.'

'Unfortunately, we can't go there.'

'Why not?'

'Because it closed down. It's now a supermarket.'

'What a shame. Can you suggest somewhere else?'

'Yeah. There's a nice place in Constantia. It serves great food and is smart without being pretentious.'

'That sounds perfect. A bit like me.'

'You wish!' She retorted with a laugh.

'How does seven o'clock suit you?'

'That will be lekker.'

'OK. I'll pick you up then.'

'See you,' she said and was gone.

Suddenly, I realised how much I had missed Freddie and the prospect of seeing her again excited me.

Chapter 26

Cape Town, Tuesday, April 24th
Central Police Station in Cape Town is located in Plein Street, close to the Parliament Buildings. Parking in the city centre was usually a nightmare, but not for me. Not that day anyway.

Having an appointment with the head of police, and bearing the official seal of the British Government, ensured that I was allocated a reserved space in the small car-park that adjoined the police headquarters.

How times change. My previous visit to Cape Town was to buy equipment for our raid on Robben Island. That day my friends and I went out of our way to avoid contact with the police. Today I was in the city at their invitation. Such irony.

It was early afternoon and the weather was fine. There was a clear blue sky and a south-easterly breeze had picked up white clouds and spread them in a fluffy cloth across the top of Table Mountain. The clouds spilled over the edge of the mountain top like frothy milk rolling down the sides of an over-filled cup of latte coffee.

When I arrived at the police station there was a uniformed cop waiting for me in the car-park. He was young, with the build of a rugby player and a cauliflower ear that suggested his position might be somewhere in the front row of the scrum.

The policeman checked my identity and then escorted me through the front foyer without stopping at the desk to sign me into the visitor's book.

We took the lift up to the seventh floor, where the young cop led me down a corridor to the end office. On its door was a sign reading: Brigadier Alan Pienaar.

My escort knocked once, opened the door, let me in and then disappeared. During the few minutes we were together that boy never once uttered an intelligible word. However, he was an expert at grunting and making hand signals.

Pienaar was sitting behind his desk. He stood up and waved me into a seat. He didn't offer to shake my hand and there was no warmth in the token smile he threw my way.

He was a big man with broad shoulders and a cannonball head

stuck on top of a thick neck. Like the young cop earlier, he had a rugby player's cauliflower ears and a weather-beaten face that could never in a million years be described as handsome.

This somewhat battered look was accentuated by a large nose that had plainly been broken on more than one occasion; more evidence of the policeman's time playing for Northern Transvaal.

'Welcome back to South Africa, Mister Statton.' There was little enthusiasm in the policeman's greeting.

'It's always a pleasure to visit your beautiful country, Brigadier,' I responded neutrally.

'It's best if we get one thing clear from the start,' Pienaar said. 'I have been tasked by my Government with helping you whilst you are in South Africa. I have been fully briefed on the threat posed to both of our countries by the Phoenix Group and its friends in the Broederbond and Pan Africanist Congress.'

'Well that's a good start,' I said.

'I understand the implications of allowing our enemies to succeed and for that reason I will do everything in my power to assist you, but I do so with a sense of deep distaste.'

'That's not so good.'

'What do you expect? I know what you did when last you were in my country. You were responsible for the deaths of four of my police colleagues and almost fifty sailors.'

I looked at him silently and my mind went back to the terrible events I had tried so hard to forget. I was still haunted by what happened when my friends and I were forced to use blend-brand-hand-grenades, otherwise known as *brandies*, when we were confronted by a South African naval vessel on our way back from Robben Island.

When a *brandy* explodes, it generates white-hot smoke that reaches temperatures of twelve hundred degrees Celsius. At that heat, any combustible material with which it comes in contact is ignited, including human flesh and bone.

In our case, it took only a handful of the grenades to destroy the naval vessel and all who sailed in her. That same night I also used a *brandy* to stop a police car that was chasing me. I still had nightmares about the devastation the grenade wrought.

'Whatever you might believe, Brigadier, we didn't set out deliberately to harm anybody. We only used our weapons as a last resort. When we were forced to retaliate, we only fired warning shots at first. However, the sailors on the navy boat were shooting to kill, so eventually, we had no option but to follow suit.' I stared at him, hoping he would understand. 'I know it's no consolation to you, but I lost three friends that night.'

'You're right. It is no consolation. One of the sailors who died on that ship was my nephew.'

'I'm sorry to hear that.' What else could I say?

'So you see, Mister Statton, I have no reason to like you. However, my personal feelings must take a back seat behind loyalty to my country.'

'I'm truly sorry about your nephew, but the sailors opened fire on us first. Sometimes we are forced to do things which we must live with for the rest of our life. I'm afraid that was one such time.'

The policeman nodded but said nothing.

'Look, Brigadier, I'm not proud of what happened and I can understand how you feel.'

He nodded again.

'I know we will probably never be friends,' I went on, 'but I hope that at least we can work together.'

Pienaar looked at me steadily for a few moments and for the first time I could see a glimmer of respect in his eyes. 'Ja,' he said finally. 'You have it about right, Mister Statton. I too have done many things of which I am not proud.

'So it seems we are alike in some ways, Brigadier.'

'Ja. We do what needs to be done at any given time but you were right to point out we have to live a long time with the consequences of our actions.'

He leaned forward and held out a hand. 'As you say we might never be friends, but let us work together now to defeat this threat to our countries.'

We shook hands on that.

'So how can I help you?' Pienaar asked.

'I assume you know about the meeting that is taking place at the Mountainside Reserve Hotel next month?'

'Ja, I have been briefed by our National Intelligence Service about the attendance at the meeting of the Afrikaner Broederbond and the Pan Africanist Congress. However, they were unable to provide much information about the foreign businessmen who appear to be bankrolling them.'

So, I told him what I knew about the Phoenix Group, its plan to murder the ANC leaders, and install the Broederbond and its Pan Africanist Council allies as the new South African government. 'But the members of the group are not all foreigners,' I explained. 'Have you heard of Jonathan Rhodes?'

'Ja. He is one of the wealthiest men in South Africa. Why do you ask?'

'Because he's a leading member.'

'Is he, by Jove!'

'Yes. Do you have a police file on him?'

He shook his head. 'He has never been in trouble with us.'

'Would it be possible for you to get somebody to put together a background paper on him for me?'

'Of course. I can let you have something within a couple of days. I will contact you when it's ready.'

'I'm not sure of my exact movements this week. So it will be better if I contact you. Can you have the briefing paper prepared by Thursday?'

'Ja. That should not be a problem. Why don't you drop in and collect it. You can tell me all about your plans at the same time.'

'Happy to do that. Briefly, your Government has asked my Prime Minister for help and I have been tasked with finding out what the Phoenix Group is planning.'

'I am aware of that request and the reasons for it,' he paused and gave me another of his intense looks. 'I am not happy with the situation.'

'Why's that, Brigadier?'

'Because I am embarrassed.'

'About what?'

'That we had to come cap in hand to you Brits for help because fear of the Broederbond prevents us South Africans from handling this business ourselves.'

'There is no reason for you to feel embarrassed,' I assured him. 'All countries have troublemakers that pose a threat to state security. Just think of the IRA in my own country.'

'I appreciate your understanding.'

I smiled at him. 'So, what can you tell me about the Broederbond? Does it really have as much influence as you suggest?'

'If you equate influence with the number of its members, then the answer would be no. However, if you gauge the influence of an organisation on its ability to get members into positions of power, then the answer is yes.'

'So, does that mean the answer is yes?'

'Since nineteen-forty-eight every South African Prime Minister, and more recently, State President, has been a member of the Broederbond. Does that answer your question?'

'I had no idea.'

'Well, it is true. More to the point, the patronage that goes with those positions has ensured that throughout the apparatus of government, members of the Broederbond have been in control of the levers of power since South Africa was first created.'

'It's the same in Britain. Except in my country it is Old Etonian's who run the country.'

'It's not the same thing at all. Going to a public school divides people by wealth and such privilege happens in all countries. Even the Soviet Union. Here it is different. Setting aside the racial divide, there are many other things that divide us.' He paused and gave me another of his intense looks. 'Let me tell you what happened here in South Africa,' he continued eventually.

'I'm listening.'

'Civil servants, policemen, members of the armed forces and other state employees who happened to be English speakers, were effectively side-lined and replaced with Afrikaans speaking Broederbond members who could be relied on to support the National Party Government.'

'You've reached the rank of brigadier,' I pointed out. 'Does that mean you're a member of the Broederbond?'

'No. I was just lucky. My first language is Afrikaans so I was trusted and allowed to progress in the police force. However, because my mother was British, I was never invited to join.'

'That must have been a disappointment.'

He shook his cannonball head. 'Not at all. I would not have joined them even if I had received an invitation. It is not my way.'

'You mentioned earlier that all the leaders of your country since nineteen forty-eight have been members of the Broederbond. Does that include F.W. De Klerk?'

'Ja.'

'But I thought he was instrumental in releasing Mandela and opening up dialogue with the ANC?'

'One thing you need to understand, Mister Statton, is that the current generation of Afrikaner politicians, like De Klerk, are more pragmatic than some of their predecessors. They might be members of the Broederbond, but they are not stupid. They understand the current status quo is unsustainable and change is inevitable. They want some control over that change when it comes.'

'So, why is the Broederbond trying to undermine De Klerk?'

'Because it is dominated by Afrikaner hard-liners for whom even suggesting the possibility of a black government is an anathema.'

'But the Broederbond is proposing a coalition with the Pan Africanist Council. They are black.'

'True, but the PAC is weak and would end up as very junior partners in any administration. They are being manipulated by the Broederbond leaders, who will stop at nothing to get their way.'

'Including selling their souls to the Phoenix Group?'

'Ja.'

'Do you know who the ring-leaders are?'

'We know them all,' he confirmed.

'So why can't you take them out?'

'We have no evidence of illegal activity.'

'That has not always stopped the SAP in the past.'

'I know, but that does not make it right. In fact, the systematic abuse of power used in the past, is one of the things of which I am not proud.'

'You weren't answerable for the actions of your colleagues,' I pointed out.

He smiled wryly. 'That is true, but turning a blind eye to what they were doing made me an accomplice. My predecessor in this job, Kobus Coetzee, was one of the guilty men.'

I had heard of Brigadier Coetzee. He was a cop with a soft voice and a hard fist. He had tortured Freddie's father in an effort to find out more about our plan to rescue Mandela from Robben Island.

'As it happens, this is different,' Alan Pienaar was saying. 'The people in question are well protected. If we made a move against the troublemakers, the wider Broederbond membership would rally round them.'

'But you implied earlier that membership was relatively low. Would it matter?'

'Ja. It would matter because those members in positions of power would not support such a move without the necessary evidence. Even moderates, like De Klerk, would feel obliged to protect the ring-leaders. It is tribal. To turn their backs on them would be tantamount to treason against the Volk itself. It would be political suicide and South Africa would return to the dark days of the nineteen sixties.'

'And I assume hard-liners still hold sway in the police force?'

'Ja, and the armed forces.'

'Which is why De Klerk is relying on the British Government, and its allies, to defeat the Phoenix Group and protect the ANC leaders?'

'That is about the truth of it, Mister Statton, but as I said earlier, I don't like the situation.'

'So, right here and now, it's down to me?'

'Not entirely. There are moderates throughout the machinery of Government who are determined to defeat those who would do us ill. You will be able to call on their support, but we are in a difficult position and must handle the situation delicately. Which is why we need your help.'

'We?' I queried.

'Ja. I back what De Klerk and his colleagues are trying to achieve. They know I am loyal, which is probably why I was asked to liaise with you. I will give you as much assistance as possible.'

'Thank you. It will be helpful knowing I can call on you in an emergency. Meanwhile, I'd be grateful if the reason for my presence in your country could be kept strictly between ourselves.'

'That would be my intention anyway. It is the only way to ensure there are no leaks.'

'If anybody asks, tell them I'm visiting South Africa to advise your Government on security matters, which is close enough to the truth.'

'Very well.' He fell silent and considered me thoughtfully. 'Do members of the Phoenix Group really have the capability to assassinate Nelson Mandela?' He asked eventually.

'Yes. They've hired an Irish hitman to do their dirty work.' I told him what I knew about Shaun Brannagan.

'And is this Brannagan any good?'

'Judge for yourself. I believe he's killed three people since being hired by the Phoenix Group. The first was a CIA agent, the second was a Soviet KGB colonel who defected to Britain and the third was my deputy.'

'Your deputy?'

'Yes.'

'So catching Brannagan is personal?'

'Very personal.' I explained what had happened to Timmy Fraser. His murder still weighed heavily on my mind. I was conscious that by sending him to Slough I had effectively signed his death warrant. 'He was a good lad and didn't deserve to die.'

'That's the problem. It is always the good who die young,' Pienaar said. I could see he was thinking about his nephew. 'But we cannot bring them back. We must just get on with life.'

'You're right. So, back to the here and now. What can you tell me about the Pan Africanist Council?'

'The PAC? Well, unlike the Broederbond, they are not much of a threat. For a start, their organisation leaks like a sieve, which makes them very useful to us. Much of our current intelligence information comes from the ANC, who have several moles in the PAC, including, at one time, a man at the very top of their organisation. Have you ever heard of Anthony Sibeko?'

I shook my head. 'No, but I've heard of David Sibeko. Wasn't he assassinated in Tanzania?'

'Ja. He was shot dead in nineteen-seventy-nine by members of the Azanian People's Liberation Army following an argument with them at his home in Dar es Salaam.'

'So is Anthony Sibeko any relation to David?'

'Ja, his cousin. Anthony was one of the leaders of the PAC. He was also an ANC spy.'

'Was he one of the moles you were talking about?'

'Ja. He provided the ANC with some good stuff. It was Sibeko who gave us what limited information we have about the Phoenix Group.'

I looked at Pienaar thoughtfully and wondered whether Anthony Sibeko was taking part in the meeting with the Phoenix Group. If so, he would be able to provide us with information about what was being planned for Nelson Mandela and his ANC colleagues. It would be a good back-up to the bugging devices we planned to install in the conference centre.

'Can you find out if Anthony Sibeko is taking part in next week's meeting with the Phoenix Group?' I asked.

'I don't have to,' Pienaar replied without hesitation. 'Sibeko will not be at the meeting.'

'How do you know?'

'Because his body was found dumped in a ditch outside Nyanga. We suspect he was tortured to find out the names of other informants in the PAC.'

'Did he identify any of his colleagues?'

'We'll never know for sure. However, the flow of information to the ANC appears to have dried up.'

'That could just be a coincidence,' I suggested.

'That's what we're hoping. Perhaps Sibeko's murder has frightened off the other ANC moles.' Pienaar said. He looked at me thoughtfully. 'You looked disappointed at his death.'

'I am. I hoped he might be able to tell us more about the Phoenix Group's plans.'

'Well, he won't be able to tell us anything now. Not unless he sends us a message from the grave,' Pienaar said sardonically. 'Was there anything else?'

'Yes,' I said. 'Are you aware of the meeting on Friday week between your Government and ANC leaders?'

'Ja, I have been fully briefed on that as well.'

'Are you in charge of the security arrangements?'

'Not directly. They will be handled by an elite unit of Special Forces, working directly for President de Klerk. However, I will be providing back-up manpower at Groote Schuur.' He looked at me and gave me a tight smile. 'I understand you have been asked to... how do you English put it? Give the place the once over?'

'Well, that's how some of the more hackneyed crime writers describe undertaking a risk assessment,' I said and returned his smile. 'Is my involvement likely to be a problem?'

'I wouldn't think so. I like to think our Special Forces are very efficient, but none of us is perfect and even the best men sometimes miss the obvious.'

'Don't I know it,' I replied and quickly told him what happened at the Nelson Mandela concert in London.

'That explains why Mister Mandela holds you in such high

esteem,' Alan Pienaar said.

'I need to visit Groote Schuur. Can you arrange it?'

'Of course, I am visiting it myself on Thursday week, you are more than welcome to join me. It will fit in perfectly with your cover as a security advisor and another pair of eyes will be useful.'

'With your permission, there will be two pairs of eyes,' I explained about Paul Helsdon's involvement in my operation.

If the policeman associated Paul's name with the destruction of the navy boat, he didn't mention it and he raised no objection to him joining me on my visit to Groote Schuur.

When I left Central Police Station I joined the traffic driving down Plein Street, but when I turned into Spin Street there was a commotion behind me when a car driver hit his horn in a long, loud blast. I looked in my rear view mirror and saw a racing green Porsche 911 Carrera come from the direction of Corporation Street and push its way into the line of cars that had followed me round the corner.

What is it with Porsche drivers that makes them think they own the road? They might spend a fortune on their fancy cars, but that gives them no more rights than anybody else.

Once free of the city centre I made my way towards Sea Point, where I picked up the coast road heading south. It was now mid-afternoon and there was a steady flow of traffic as shoppers, and a few out-of-season tourists, left the city early to escape the rush-hour.

However, by the time I reached the northern outskirts of Llandudno only a handful of cars was following me down the road, including the Porsche 911.

Llandudno is home to scores of expensive homes that line a dozen roads cut into the western slopes of the Table Mountain National Park.

The main coast road from Cape Town to Hout Bay, bypasses Llandudno, almost cutting the seaside community off from the rest of the Peninsula. There is one spur off the coast road, which winds its way through the houses and eventually ends up at the sea front.

When I reached the entrance to this beach road, I took a sharp right turn, without indicating, but with a squeal of tyres and a hoot of protest from the car that was travelling immediately behind me. I apologised under my breath to the driver.

I drove down to the beach and parked in the car-park. I sat and stared out to sea where fishing boats plied their trade on the horizon. I was not joined by any other cars and after half an hour I convinced myself that I was mistaken about being followed out of Cape Town by the Porsche.

By the time I made my way back to the highway, the traffic had increased as early commuters from Cape Town made their way home. I had to wait for a few minutes before there was a long enough gap in the stream of vehicles for me to join the south-bound flow. At least this gave me the opportunity to double check that nobody was following me.

It took me only ten minutes to reach the centre of Hout Bay, but I didn't stop. Instead, I carried on along the coast road and eventually found myself on Chapman's Peak Drive. It zig-zagged up the western slopes of Constantiaberg, until 8 miles, and over 100 tight bends later, it reached Noordhoek, which lay in the southern foothills of the hump-back mountain.

At the top of Chapman's Peak I pulled off the road into an observation lay-by and got out of the car. It was a lovely late afternoon and I could see clearly cars coming up the winding road from Hout Bay. None of the drivers showed any interest as they passed me and there was no sign of the Porsche.

The lay-by overlooked the inlet in which Hout Bay nestled and I could see the sweep of the bay in all its glory. A number of trawlers were steaming out of the harbour into the Atlantic Ocean. The mountain is almost 2000 feet high, and from that height the trawlers looked like toy boats on a pond.

The water in the bay was clear and I could see a small pod of whales lying submerged just beneath the surface, perhaps resting before leaving for their feeding grounds.

I returned to my car and drove along the road until eventually I came to another lay-by. This one overlooked Noordhoek. I got out of my car and again looked up and down the road. A steady stream of vehicles drove past where I was parked, but none of them was a racing green Porsche 911.

The lay-by was directly above the Mountainside Reserve Hotel and my position gave me an excellent panoramic view of its layout, including the restaurant, the conference centre, and the cabin in which I was staying.

The forest in which the buildings were located looked even denser from this angle, making the task Paul and I faced much easier. We would be well hidden from prying eyes, particularly at night.

That was my hope anyway.

Constantia, Cape Town

Freddie was waiting for me when I arrived at her flat in Claremont. The apartment block was situated on Main Road, officially designated as the M4, which runs all the way from Cape Town's southern suburbs to Simon's Town.

Main Road passes through a number of communities, including the neighbouring suburb of Wynberg, which is where Freddie lived when I first met her.

It was from her apartment in Wynberg that I had collected her on the day we used a ski-boat to reconnoitre landing places on Robben Island, following which we shared a picnic in the middle of Cape Bay. Tonight we would be having a somewhat more substantial meal and it was unlikely our evening would end as it had on that occasion.

Following our picnic, on that sunny afternoon in the Atlantic Ocean, we drove back to her apartment, showered together and then made love. There was little chance of that happening tonight. For good or ill, the world had moved on since the day, six years before, when I took Freddie to catch her flight back to South Africa.

I rang the bell and she opened her door before I could ring a second time. She had changed very little since the last time I saw her. Her black hair was cut shorter, in a style that framed her pretty face, but there was little other difference.

Intelligent, dark-brown eyes still peered through heavy framed glasses. She still had the same pretty, fresh-faced appearance that made her look no older than a teenager and the same petite, yet shapely, figure. She looked absolutely sensational.

There was so much I could have said. I could have told her how I felt about her. I could have said I missed her. I could have said I was sorry I let her go. I could have said I wished things had turned out differently. I could have said a hundred nice things. Instead I said: 'You were waiting for me.'

She smiled. 'You still seem surprised I can get ready on time.'

'Well, you are still a woman.'

'And you are still sexist.'

'You remember?' I asked. We held a similar verbal joust on the day of our picnic.

'Of course.'

'How are you?'

'I can't complain. What about you?'

'My boss tells me that I complain too much.'

She laughed. 'So you haven't changed.'

'Nor have you. You're looking good.'

'For a thirty year old?' She raised an eyebrow.

'Are you really that young?'

She poked her tongue out. 'I don't know what I ever saw in you.'

'As I recall you told me you liked older men.'

'I was just a silly young girl.'

'You were twenty-two when we met.' I looked down at her. 'And you don't look a day older now.'

She put a finger in her mouth and pretended to be sick. 'Compliments and you don't go together, Dave.'

'It wasn't a compliment. It was the truth. You do look young.'

'There are a few extra lines on my face and the odd grey hair on my head.'

I studied her carefully. 'You hide them well.'

'Yeah. Good make-up and hair dye.'

'An ugly woman can use the most expensive lipstick and rouge going, but she will still be ugly. You're not ugly and you don't need make-up.'

She looked at me silently for a few moments. 'I'm waiting for the punchline,' she said eventually.

'There isn't one.'

Her brown eyes narrowed. 'No punchline? No sarcasm? Are you really Dave Statton, or are you an imposter?'

'Don't worry. I'm the real thing. So, no more Mister Nice Guy this evening. I don't want you overdosing on kindness.'

She laughed again and took my arm. 'That's much better. Now get me to the food or I'm going to faint from starvation.'

Constantia, Cape Town

The Tuesday evening traffic was light and it took us only ten minutes to travel from Claremont to Constantia. The Garden Restaurant was exactly how Freddie had described it: smart but unpretentious. It was small enough to offer a warm and friendly atmosphere, but there was sufficient space between the tables to be able to talk without being overheard.

The restaurant boasted an interesting menu and an extensive wine list. An added bonus was it had its own large car-park, something that few eating houses in the city are able to offer.

A waiter in tight, pink trousers turned up to take our order, which he wrote down with flamboyant exclamations of approval at our choices.

'And we'll have a chilled bottle of gewürztraminer,' I said.

'So what's with using the name Bridgette?' I asked when the waiter had disappeared with a flick of his hair and a wiggle of his backside.

'It's the result of typical bullshit bureaucracy. When I joined my company there was already a Freddie Carlse working for them. The personnel department said they could not have more than one person of the same name on the books and insisted that I be listed in the directory as Bridgette. It stuck.'

'There's nothing wrong with that. After all, it is your real name,' I pointed out.

'I know, but I was always Freddie to my family and being called Bridgette every day seemed odd, but I'm used to it now.'

'I like the name Bridgette.'

'I know. You said it suited my femininity.' She sounded pleased at the memory.

'It does.'

'I thought you were just saying that to be nice.'

'There is nothing wrong with looking feminine.'

'I understand that now, but when we first met I was in my feminist phase. I considered such compliments patronising.'

'And now?'

She grinned. 'I say bring it on.'

'So what name would you prefer?'

'I don't care,' she said quietly. 'Just hearing your voice is enough.'

Before I could respond, Pink Pants turned up with our starters, he was followed by a second waiter carrying our bottle of wine in an ice bucket. Pink Pants insisted on explaining what was on our plates and how the food had been cooked.

By the time he finished I had forgotten both why I'd ordered moules marinière in the first place and what I wanted to tell Freddie. 'Enjoy,' I said to her instead.

She had ordered calamari and she got stuck into it with relish. She said she was hungry and it showed. We munched away in silence. Both lost in our own thoughts.

When she finished her starter, she looked up and was about to say something when Pink Pants turned up to clear our plates and deliver our main meal. We had both selected Lobster Thermidor, which was what we had ordered for our first meal together.

'When we ate at the Galleon Grill we drank special Appletisers.' I said.

'I remember,' she said with a smile. Restaurants in Fish Hoek are not allowed to sell alcohol, so The Galleon Grill got round the local bye-law by replacing apple juice with white wine for any trusted customer who ordered a special Appletiser. I was trusted.

'It's nice to be able to enjoy this gewürztraminer openly.' I lifted my glass towards her.

'I agree.' She touched my glass with her own, before starting to tuck into her lobster. However, after a couple of mouthfuls she stopped eating and looked at me intently. She was no longer smiling. 'There is something I need to tell you, David.'

The use of my full name grabbed my attention. 'I'm listening.'

She loaded a fork with lobster flesh and mustard sauce but didn't eat it, instead she looked at me with sad eyes. 'There's something I want you to know.'

'Go on.'

'Since we split up I've dated a number of men.'

'That's hardly earth-shattering news, Freddie. You're single and there's nothing wrong with dating men. It might make the SABC news if you were caught dating women, but even that's debatable these days.'

'That's not everything.'

'So what *is* everything?'

She forked the lobster into her mouth and was silent while she ate it. Finished she put her fork down on her plate and said: 'I went to bed with a couple of them.'

I shrugged. 'You're a big girl now.' I spoke nonchalantly, but I was surprised at the kick in the stomach her words gave me. 'And

311

you're not a nun.'

'You're jealous.'

'Of course I'm not,' I lied. 'You're an independent young woman and I have no monopoly on your affections.'

'You *are* jealous,' she repeated. 'I can tell by your voice.'

'For Christ sake, Freddie, or Bridgette, or whatever you decide to call yourself.' I wanted to shout, but instead I kept my voice low. 'Of course I'm bloody jealous.' My words came out as a hiss, which I immediately regretted. I paused, wondering if I should tell her how I felt. I decided I would. 'And I'm jealous because I still love you.' There it was out.

She smiled at me and for the first time that night she looked genuinely happy. 'I'm pleased about that, because I love you too.'

'But what about all those other men?'

'All? I only went to bed with two of them.'

'Two is *all* to me.'

'Don't worry, Dave. Neither of them was a patch on you.' She smiled again and carried on eating her meal. 'What about you? Has there been anybody else?'

I didn't respond immediately, finishing off my Lobster Thermidor first. It gave me time to find the words I wanted. I felt the need to rationalise my actions. 'Yes, there was somebody else. The truth is I was celibate from the day you left me, right up until a couple of weeks ago. I always hoped you would change your mind and come back to me, but you didn't and eventually my loneliness got the better of me.'

'Who was she?'

'Just somebody from the office. A secretary. It started when I took her to see a West End show and then one thing led to another.' I looked into her eyes. 'Are you jealous?'

'I hate the thought of you making love to somebody else.'

'I'm not sure the word *love* would describe the reason behind what I did.' I refused to admit, even to myself, the feelings I was beginning to have for Colleen Masters before I left England. 'It was more a case of loneliness and lust.' I changed the subject. 'And what about those two guys you went to bed with? Who were they?'

'Just somebody from the office.' She threw my words back at me. It didn't make me feel any better. She took my hand. 'Look, Dave. Who, when, or where is irrelevant. It doesn't matter. I screwed two men and you screwed your little secretary. There's no point beating ourselves up over what happened. We can't turn back the clock. What counts is how we both feel right now.'

'And how do you feel right now?' I asked her.

'I feel we should pass on the deserts. Instead, I want you to take me home and make love to me.'

She didn't have to ask me twice.

Claremont, Cape Town
When we arrived at Freddie's apartment block, I drove down the slope leading to the underground car-park and at the bottom I was confronted by a metal security shutter.

I stopped and Freddie jumped out of the car and punched a code into a key pad that was fixed to the wall. The shutter rolled up and I drove through the gate and into a well-lit car-park. Once we were safely inside, the shutter automatically closed behind us.

Freddie directed me towards an empty space next to her red Mini-Cooper, which was parked adjacent to a set of lift doors. The lift took us up to the top floor, where Freddie's apartment was located. It was only a few paces from the lift to her front door. It was just as well, because she was already unbuttoning my shirt with one hand, as she unlocked the door using a key held in her other.

She pulled me inside and kicked the door closed with the heel of a foot from which she kicked her shoe in the same movement. Her other shoe followed quickly as she pulled me down a short passage to her bedroom.

We didn't waste any time on small talk.

Within seconds of reaching the bedroom we were both naked. I removed her spectacles and put them on a dressing table. Without her shoes Freddie was at least four inches shorter and her head only came up to my lower chest. She was still as light as I remembered and I easily lifted her from her feet and held her so that our mouths were level. I kissed her softly and then flicked my tongue delicately across her lips.

Freddie had always liked that. She groaned and pressed herself against me, wrapping her legs around my body. I could tell that she was already aroused, but I made her wait for what she wanted. Gently I laid her on the bed with her legs dangling over the edge with her feet just about resting on the floor.

I pushed her legs apart and knelt between them. I lowered my head and licked the inside of one thigh and then the other. Freddie groaned again. She knew what was coming. This was something I had done to her so many times before and I knew that it drove her wild. I licked the inside of each leg again, but this time I directed my tongue at the groin area. I repeated the action, but as I moved from one groin to the other I flicked my tongue against her clitoris.

Freddie gasped and grabbed the back of my head with both hands. I allowed her to take control and direct my tongue towards the spot on which she wanted me to concentrate. I obliged.

After a few seconds I heard her breath quicken. She shuddered slightly and I knew that she was about to reach a climax. It was now time to give her what she wanted most.

I lifted Freddie into the centre of the bed and laid beside her. I spread her legs again and then rolled over on top of her. She cried out as I entered her and pushed her hips upwards to take me in as deeply as she could.

Still inside her, I twisted with her until she was laying on top of me. She sat upright and taking my hands she put them on her breasts, pressing down on my hands to encourage me to knead them. I squeezed her breasts and she closed her eyes in ecstasy.

'Oh, yes, my darling,' she murmured as she started to move up and down on me.

I took her nipples between my fingers, one in either hand, and squeezed them gently until she groaned.

'Oh, yes, my darling,' she repeated, increasing the speed of her upward and downward rhythm. 'More, more, more…' She mumbled, repeating the words continually as her movement grew faster, until finally she screamed: 'I'm coming! I'm coming! Oh, God! I'm coming.'

She fell forward against me, her body slippery from the perspiration. I rolled her on her back. I was still hard and I pushed myself gently in and out of her, letting her enjoy my own rhythm until she started moving with me, as she reached for another climax. It didn't take her long and this time I gave myself up to my own needs and we peaked together.

Afterwards we lay for some time in companionable silence, neither of us wanting to break the magical spell we had created.

'I've missed that,' Freddie said eventually.

'Me too,' I agreed. 'Nobody can compare with you.'

'Nor you. Those two guys I went with could learn a lot from you. They were both only interested in satisfying themselves as quickly as possible. It was strictly wham, bam, and thank you mam. They had no consideration for my needs.'

'That, Freddie, is the difference between love and lust.'

'Well I know which one I prefer.'

I tightened my hold on her. 'I've missed you, Freddie,' I said quietly.

She didn't respond for a while, but then said: 'I missed you too, Dave, and there have been times when I wished I'd stuck it out in the UK. I often thought about asking you to take me back.'

'So why didn't you?'

She lapsed into silence again, before saying in a quiet voice: 'A couple of reasons.'

'Like what?' I asked.

'Pride,' she whispered, so quietly that I could barely hear her.

'I didn't catch that.'

'Pride,' she said louder. 'Pride and fear.'

'Pride I understand, that's you all over, but fear? That doesn't sound like the Freddie I used to know.'

'On this occasion, it's true. I was frightened you wouldn't want me back.'

'I would have had you back in a shot. After all, it was my fault you left in the first place.'

'How do you work that out?'

'Because it was selfish of me expecting you to live in the wilds of Scotland. That sort of quiet, sedate life style is OK for old geezers like me.'

'You're not old,' she insisted.

'I am forty-seven. Compared to you, that's old.'

'But I like older men.'

'That's beside the point. I could see you weren't happy in Scotland. You're young and needed the sort of lifestyle that the Highlands can't offer. We should have moved down to London.'

'Where you live now.'

'You know?'

'Yeah. I kept track of you through Paul.'

'Would you have stayed with me if we had lived in London?'

'Maybe. Perhaps I could have got a job and we could have gone to the theatre and the cinema and I could have visited the shopping centres. So, yeah, maybe I would have stayed.'

'You could still move back in with me and do all those things. What do you think?'

'Let's just say it's slightly more than maybe.' She hugged me. 'As I said before, I do sometimes think about moving back to the UK and being with you. Indeed, in my madder moments I even hanker for the quiet life in your Scottish cottage.'

'I can live with slightly more than maybe,' I said.

She hugged me again and dropped her hand between my legs. She started to stroke me gently. I reacted immediately.

'That's my boy!' She giggled. 'Now show me again how old geezers can perform in bed.'

So that's exactly what I did.

Wednesday, April 25th

When I woke up the following morning it was to the thought that although the world had moved on, perhaps Freddie and I hadn't moved with it after all. I felt content. Freddie and I hadn't seen each other since she decided to leave Britain and return to South Africa, but we had made up for lost time, talking and making love into the early hours of the morning.

Now as I opened my eyes the smell of cooking bacon wafted into the bedroom, mingling with the aroma of the freshly ground coffee I could faintly hear percolating from the same general direction. I might be an old geezer but there is nothing wrong with my hearing or my sense of smell.

I heard the clatter of a pan hitting the tiled floor, followed by Freddie's voice speaking Afrikaans: 'Kak! Kak! Kak!'

I got out of bed, pulled on my underpants and padded barefoot along the passage to the kitchen. I found her on hands and knees picking up rashers of bacon from the floor and putting them back into the frying pan she had dropped.

'I thought you hated speaking the language of the oppressor,' I reminded her.

'I do, but swearing in Afrikaans is so much more satisfying.' She looked up me.

'Shit is shit in any language,' I said.

'I suppose.' She handed me the frying pan. 'The bacon will be fine,' she assured me. 'The floor was clean.'

'The floor aint clean no more, madam,' I pointed at the splats of fat on the black tiles.

'I'll soon clear that up. Pass me the paper towels.' She waved a hand to where the roll stood on top of the fridge. 'Thanks for a lovely time last night,' she said as she wiped the tiles clean. 'I had forgotten what making love could be like. I'm still tingling. You were fantastic.'

'You weren't so bad yourself.'

'Thanks. You obviously taught me well. Would you like eggs with your bacon?'

'I'll pass. I'm happy with just a bacon sarnie and some of that wonderful smelling coffee.'

'Personally, I would prefer more of your wonderful sausage.' She giggled sexily. 'But sadly I have to be in work by ten o'clock for our monthly strategy meeting.'

'Thank God for that. I have a meeting at the British Consulate this morning and you're insatiable. I'd never get there on time.'

'Is it to do with that business you told me about last night?'

'Yes, the military attaché has arranged a telephone conference call with my boss in London. It's to discuss progress, so it's likely to be a quick call.'

'Will I see you tonight?' She asked as she buttered some bread and made our bacon sandwiches.'

I shook my head. 'I'm afraid not. I'm meeting Paul.'

'The same business?'

'Yes. We're working on it together. We need to find a way of bugging the conference centre at the Mountainside Reserve Hotel without the devices being spotted, and, more importantly, think of a way to monitor the bugs without us being seen.'

'Paul and you working together.' She smiled. 'Just like old times.'

'Let's hope this operation turns out better than the last one.'

'Me too. You're running out of friends.'

'Cruel, but true.'

'I worry about you, Dave.'

'Don't worry. Paul and I will be OK.' I had my fingers tightly crossed as I said this. 'We could meet up for a meal on Thursday evening,' I offered.

'I'd really like that. Particularly if my dessert is as delicious as it was last night.'

'You're terrible,' I scolded her.

'Dead right,' she said with an impish grin.

Cape Town

The last person I expected to host the conference call was the Ambassador himself. It was the first time I had met him and I was pleasantly surprised.

Sir Robin Renwick, was nothing like the other British diplomats I had met. He was a genuinely nice person and not at all pompous. How he had succeeded in the stuffy Diplomatic Service was one of life's mysteries.

'Come in, my dear chap.' Sir Robin greeted me with a wide smile as I was ushered into his spacious office by the military attaché, who had already introduced himself as Jamie Callaghan.

'Please take a seat over there.' Sir Robin pointed to where a wide wooden coffee table stood surrounded by matching easy chairs. 'I see you have already met Jamie. He will be joining us.'

I sat down on one of the easy chairs and Callaghan took one next to me. The Ambassador sat opposite us. 'This is really Jamie's show,' Sir Robin said modestly, 'so I apologise for intruding. However, my office is the only one in the embassy that is equipped with conference call facilities.' He pointed to a large telephone that stood in the middle of the coffee table.

At exactly 11 o'clock the telephone rang.

Sir Robin picked up the receiver. 'Good Morning. This is Robin Renwick speaking.' He paused as he listened, before saying: 'I'm very well, thank you, Rupert. How are you?' He waited for Disraeli-Astor to answer. 'That's good. Now I have my military attaché, Jamie Callaghan, with me in the office and your man, David Statton. I am now switching to conference call so they can hear you as well.'

The Ambassador pressed the conferencing button and we all heard the tinny voice of Disraeli-Astor say: 'I have Statton's deputy with me at this end, can you hear him?'

'Hi there, this is Des Hobbins talking.'

'Morning, Des. We're receiving you loud and clear.'

'Morning, Dave,' he responded.

'Morning, guys,' Jamie Callaghan chipped in. 'I'm the military attaché and will be co-ordinating any actions arising from this conference call.'

'Understood,' the D-G said. 'So how are things going at your end, Statton?'

'There's not much to report I'm afraid, Colonel. I've made contact with the policeman who the South African Ambassador directed us to. His name is Brigadier Alan Pienaar and I think he's somebody we can do business with. We have agreed my cover will be that of a security consultant. Pienaar has promised to assist as much as he can, but his hands are tied somewhat.'

'OK, let me know if you need me to put pressure on anybody from this end,' Disraeli-Astor said. 'What else?'

'Not much. I've met with Paul Helsdon and he has agreed to help me to check out Groote Schuur in advance of the meeting being held there Friday week.'

'Good. I will pass that information on to the South African Ambassador,' he said.

'Yes, sir,' I acknowledged, although, I was pretty sure Hendrik Meyer would have been briefed by Alan Pienaar already.

'OK, let me know how you get on at Groote Schuur. Now, I think Hobbins has something for you.'

'Do you want the good news or the bad, Dave?' Des asked.

'I'll let you choose,' I replied, 'I like surprises.'

Des laughed. 'Well the good news is that one of ADC Neal's men came across Brannagan. It was a chance find. The lad was checking through the passenger lists for flights out of London looking for a drug smuggler they have been following. He didn't find the guy they wanted, but he did notice the name William Butler and remembered he was on the alert list.'

'That lad must have some memory,' I said.

'That's what I said to him, but he insisted it was sheer luck.'

'Most detective work is luck, Des, but a good memory helps improve the odds. Which flight was Brannagan on?'

'London to Cape Town.'

I wasn't surprised. 'So it looks as if he has followed me to South Africa?'

'That's what we thought.'

'When was his flight?'

'Sunday night.'

319

'So he arrived Monday morning.'

'Yes and no.'

'What do you mean, yes and no?'

'Well that's the bad news.'

'You're losing me, Des.'

'Well a William Butler arrived in Cape Town alright,' Des said. 'But it wasn't our man.'

'How do you know?'

'Because as a precaution I sent a photo of Butler to security at Cape Town airport and asked them to check it against their CCTV footage. They phoned me about an hour ago and told me that nobody of Butler's description was recorded going through immigration control at any time on Monday.'

'I suppose we shouldn't be surprised,' I said. 'There must be hundreds of people in the world named William Butler. I expect if you check the telephone books for Northern Ireland you will find a couple of dozen listed there alone.' I tried to hide my disappointment. I thought I had flushed the Irishman out and he had followed me to Cape Town. It seemed I was wrong. 'Never mind, Des. It was worth a shot and Neal's lad still did well.'

'Do you have anything else?' Disraeli-Astor asked.

'Nothing that I can think of, boss.'

'In that case I'm going to terminate this conference call. It's costing the department a fortune.'

'Perhaps next time you ought to reverse charges,' I said just before the connection was broken.

'You really should not put ideas like that into his head, Mister Statton,' Sir Robin said with a smile. 'I've known Colonel Disraeli-Astor for a long time and he'll try anything to save money.'

'Tell me about it, sir,' I said with feeling.

Noordhoek, Cape Peninsula

Paul turned up for our rendezvous in the beach front car-park in a Leyland Sherpa van. The windows had been blackened and a small radar dish had been fitted to the roof. He parked next to my car and got out of the van carrying a small bag.

I locked my car and joined him. 'It looks like a BBC television detector van.' I patted the side of his vehicle.

'That's what it is. I had it shipped over from the UK.'

I tried to peer through the window, but could see nothing. 'What's the equipment like inside? It's supposed to catch people who watch TV without a licence, but I was told it doesn't actually detect anything. Apparently, the Beeb uses the vans as a deterrent.'

'That's what I heard too, but I don't know whether that was an urban myth.' Paul locked the van. 'It could be a double bluff.'

'I wouldn't put it past the BBC to pull a stroke like that. Whatever the truth, let's just hope the equipment works.'

'It doesn't matter whether it works or not, because we won't be doing much TV detecting. As it happens, much of the original equipment wasn't suitable for my type of surveillance, so I stripped it out and installed my own gear.'

'Are you sure your equipment will work for us today?'

'Ag ja, man, this baby will pick up a signal from a listening device three kilometres away. By my reckoning the conference centre is less than a couple of Ks away from us, as the crow flies, so we should be well within its limit.'

'I hope the crows fly in a straight line around here.'

'That's what we're here to find out, my friend.'

'OK. Let's get on with it.'

We headed towards the beach.

The night was cloudless and the Milky Way twinkled its way across the black canvass of the sky. A lopsided Southern Cross was stitched against the tapestry of the distant galaxy, with its two companion stars pointing the way to the South Pole.

A full moon rose slowly in the sky and this gave more than enough light to make our way across the sand without having to use the flashlights we carried.

However, it was different when we reached the rocky outcrop at the edge of the beach. Once we clambered up onto the ledge I found the previous day, we were walking though deep shadows cast by the moon. I didn't want us to slip and injure ourselves, so we used our flashlights to navigate the treacherous surface. This increased the chance that we would be seen, but I decided it was a risk worth taking.

We had to use our flashlights also to make our way along the path leading to the hotel, because the moonbeams didn't penetrate the thick canopy of trees through which the dirt track meandered. Every so often we stopped and strained our ears to see if we could hear any sign of movement up ahead, but all was quiet.

We made our way slowly, but safely, to the boundary of the Mountainside Reserve. When we reached the gate through to the hotel, we found it was locked. I used the key Piet had purloined for me and the padlock sprang open silently.

'Where did you get the key, Dave?' Paul asked as we made our way through the gate.

'From a friendly handyman.'

'How much did you bung him?'

'A monkey.'

'Five hundred rand? Sies, man, no wonder the oke was friendly. That's probably double what he earns in a month.'

'His price did include a key to the conference centre.'

'You have that as well?'

'Yes.'

'That's lekker,' he said. 'I was worried we might have to break open the door. Titan Security don't employ the brightest people, but if a forced entrance was discovered, even those domkops would wonder who broke in and why.'

'But presumably they will check the conference centre out as part of their security check?'

'Of course, but there is checking and checking. I suspect Titan will only give it a cursory once over.'

'Are they really that lax?'

'Yeah, if my experience is anything to go by.'

'In that case, let's hope they haven't improved since.

'Amen to that.'

Now we were on the hotel side of the gate, the path improved and we made good progress. We soon reached the first cabin in the complex, which was next to the one in which I was staying.

The grounds were deserted and no lights could be seen anywhere. There were fewer trees in this part of the grounds and the bright moon lit our way, so once again we turned off our flashlights.

There was a set of steps close to my cabin. They led down to the conference centre and swimming pool. We made our way down the steps and when we reached our destination it too was in darkness. We could hear the low throb of music coming from the direction of the restaurant, but there was no other sign of life.

I unlocked the door to the conference centre and pulled it opened without a sound. I said a silent thank you to Piet, who had lubricated the hinges.

We switched on our flashlights again and swept them round the room. Barely more than a large meeting room it was stretching poetic licence somewhat to market it as a conference centre.

However, I guessed it would hold all those attending the Phoenix Group meeting. John Engels and his colleagues were far too professional not to have had somebody check out the hotel's suitability before booking it as a venue.

At one end of the room was a table, behind which were positioned four chairs. More chairs filled the floor space in front of the table. I counted three rows, each containing ten chairs.

To the right of the table was a lectern, connected to the front of which was a microphone. There was also a number of microphones on the top table.

'The mikes?' I suggested.

'Too obvious,' Paul said as he opened his bag and took out a tiny electrical device. 'If Titan check anything, it will be them.'

'So where?'

'The lights.' Paul pointed at the concealed fluorescent strip lights in the ceiling.

'I thought strip lights affected listening devices.'

'That used to be true, but these are the very latest technology from the States.' He held up the small device. 'They can transmit anywhere without interference. Even from fluorescent lights. Unless I'm very wrong, it's the last place Titan will think to look.'

I held my flashlight and shone it at the wood beamed ceiling while Paul jumped up on top of the table. He removed the diffuser from the strip light, unscrewed the starter control box, and connected the listening device to the power input leads.

Next he taped the bug to the control box and screwed it back into position so that the device could not be seen from below. Finally he replaced the diffuser.

He connected devices to three other lights in a similar fashion.

'What happens if they don't turn on the lights?' I asked.

'It won't matter,' Paul said as he jumped down from the table. 'I've wired them so that the bugs are on permanently. Unless we are very unlucky at least one of those babies will work, but we'll test them to make sure.'

323

'How will we do that?'

Paul took another gadget from his bag.

'It's a pager,' I said.

'Well spotted!' He pressed a button on the side of the pager and handed it to me. 'It's now activated. I want you to wait here while I return to the van. Give me about twenty minutes…'

'No, I'll give you half an hour,' I interrupted him. 'That path is treacherous. It's better you take a bit longer and get there safely.'

'Fear not, boss. I'll take care.' He picked up his bag. 'As soon as I have the equipment in the van set up, I'll page you the message *Go!* I want you to stand at the lectern and count to ten in a normal voice. If everything is cool I will page you the message *Come Home!* At which time you return to the car-park.'

'OK,' I confirmed.

'If there's a problem, for instance if I haven't picked up a signal within half a minute of my first message, I will repeat the *Go* message and you to count to ten again. Is that clear?'

'Quite clear.'

'Once we're sure everything is OK, I'll wait half an hour and if you haven't returned to the van I'll come find you.'

'Don't worry. You sort out the electronics and I'll get back to the car-park as quickly as possible. Now, get out of here and leave me to practice counting up to ten.'

Paul left and I locked the door behind him. I settled down on the floor behind the lectern with my back against the wall.

Apart from the faint sound of music coming from the direction of the restaurant, the only noise to be heard was a slight rustling. The branches of surrounding trees were being swept back and forth across the roof by a strengthening breeze.

The conference centre was in total darkness, with no sign of external light shining through any of its windows. As I looked out of one window, I could see a star twinkling through a gap in the thick forest, but of the moon there was no sign.

I closed my eyes and let the silence wash over me as I thought about my conversation with Des Hobbins.

I was disappointed my plan to flush out Brannagan hadn't succeeded. I had been convinced my confrontation with Wren would provoke him into passing my message on to the Irishman, if only to ensure he came after me. Thinking of the Irish hitman gave me an uneasy feeling that I was missing something important and I hoped Brannagan was not even cleverer than I had calculated.

I was jolted from my daydream when the pager vibrated in my hand. The little screen had lit up and read *GO!* I glanced at my watch. Twenty-three minutes had elapsed since Paul left me. He'd made good time getting back to the van.

I sprang to my feet and stood behind the lectern. I began to count out aloud, but before I reached eight the pager vibrated again. *Come home!*

Slipping the pager in my pocket I let myself out of the conference centre door and locked it behind me. Using my flashlight, I made my way quickly down the path to the gate that marked the boundary of the hotel's grounds.

Paul and I had left the padlock open in case we were forced to make a speedy exit from the hotel grounds, but once I was safely through the gate I locked it behind me.

I took my time navigating the lower part of the path, because I didn't want to risk any accidents, but it didn't take me long to get back to the car-park. My car and the van were still the only vehicles to be seen.

Paul must have been watching for me because he opened the side door of the van and a shaft of light lit up the car-park. I stepped inside the van and he pulled the door closed behind me.

The van was fitted out with a table running along one side on which was arrayed a range of electrical equipment, including a couple of computers with keyboards and monitors. The largest piece of equipment looked like an old-fashioned radio receiver, but I guessed it was as sophisticated as all the other kit in the van.

Attached to the receiver by jack-plugs were two pairs of headphones, one of which Paul was already wearing. He was sitting in one of two chairs positioned in front of the table and he waved me to take the other seat. 'Put them on.' He pointed to the spare headphones.

I sat down and did as I was told. At first I could hear only the hiss of static, then I heard the sound of music.' I turned to him and raised an eyebrow. 'Is that music coming from the restaurant?'

'Cool, huh?' He asked with a grin.

'So you heard me when I counted?'

'Loud and clear, in fact, so loud I had to turn you down a bit.' He pointed to a knob on the receiver. 'That's the first device. It's the same with all four.' He twisted a second knob and the music disappeared briefly and then resumed. 'I've now tuned in to the second bug.' He twisted the knob twice more and the same thing happened.

I took off my headphones and laid them on the table. I turned to him. 'I didn't know you were an electronics expert, Paul.'

'I wasn't, but new technology is becoming increasingly important in the security business, so I had to learn quickly, or risk falling behind my competitors.'

'I'm impressed.'

'Ag, man. Coming from you, that's a real compliment. Just keep your fingers crossed that Titan Security maintain their usual level of incompetence and don't find the bugs.'

'Perhaps we can return to the hotel after we've visited Groote Schuur, and make sure the listening devices are still working,' I suggested.

'OK with me. If we come back to the car-park we can see whether the equipment is still picking up the bugs. Hopefully, we won't need to visit the hotel.'

'But what if we can't hear anything? The music might not be playing in the restaurant that night.' I said.

'In that case, we'll just have to check out the conference centre again.'

'Let's hope it doesn't come to that, because Sod's Law is that we'll bump into somebody at the hotel who recognises me.'

'You could always wear a disguise,' he suggested.

I stared at him. 'Like a false beard,' I mused as I remembered the little piece of information I had missed whilst sitting on the conference centre floor.

'What is it?' Paul asked.

I told him about the passenger by the name of William Butler who boarded the plane in London. 'But nobody with a beard matching his description disembarked in Cape Town,' I explained.

'So?'

'So what if Butler got rid of his false beard somewhere? What if he is now masquerading as Shaun Brannagan again?'

Paul nodded thoughtfully. 'Maybe you're right, or maybe you're just trying to make two and two add up to five.'

Maybe.

Chapter 27

Newlands, Cape Town, Thursday April 26th

Shaun Brannagan was still on my mind two days later when I paid my bill and checked out of the Mountainside Reserve Hotel. I had decided to take up Paul's offer and had arranged to drop my bag off at his apartment in Newlands on my way into Cape Town to see Alan Pienaar.

One reason for my decision was because I thought there was little that my presence at the hotel would achieve now the listening devices were in place. As Paul pointed out, in an emergency I had keys to the gate and the conference centre.

Another consideration was that I had convinced myself that Brannagan was in South Africa. Staying in one place too long would make it easier for him to ambush me.

If I had succeeded in provoking the Irishman into following me to Cape Town, a confrontation was inevitable. However, I wanted to control when that happened. To do that I needed to find him before he found me.

My sports loving friend had chosen the right location for his home. His top floor luxury flat was within walking distance of both Newlands Cricket Ground and Newlands Rugby Stadium. I could take or leave the sports, but a bonus for me was that his apartment had a fantastic view of Table Mountain.

Paul showed me to his guest bedroom and made me feel welcome by giving me a spare front door key so that I could come and go as I pleased.

'I'm seeing Freddie again tonight,' I explained to him.

'What do you mean again?' He looked surprised.

'Didn't I tell you?'

'Tell me what?'

'I took your advice and rang her. We met up for a meal on Tuesday evening.'

'Sies, man! You didn't tell me.' He punched me gently on the arm. 'That's real lekker. I'm delighted you guys are getting it together.'

'It's early days yet,' I insisted.

'Of course, but at least you're seeing each other again. Hey?'

'Yes, we're having dinner again tonight. If I'm late back, I'll try to be quiet.'

'Ag, don't worry about that. Just give Freddie my love.'

'I will,' I promised. 'And if you're gone before I get up in the morning, have a safe journey to Durban.'

'What other plans do you have for today?' He asked.

'First up, I'm going to Central Police Station and then later I need to make a phone call to London, will it be alright to use your phone?'

'Help yourself,' he said without hesitation. 'What are you doing at the police station?'

'I'm going to collect a file on Jonathan Rhodes that Brigadier Pienaar promised me. At the same time I'll let him know Brannagan is in town. I want him to check something out for me.'

'Do you really think that mad oke is here in Cape Town?'

'Yes.'

'What makes you so sure?'

'Intuition.'

'Sies, man. If you're right, be careful whilst I'm in Durbs. Remember, you won't have me to watch your back.'

'I can look after myself.'

'Izit?' He offered me a grim smile. 'You didn't look after yourself so well in Laos, did you? As I recall you almost let that commie bastard stick a red hot bayonet up your butt. Hey?'

There was no answer to that.

Central Police Station, Cape Town

Unlike my previous visit, when I arrived in the car-park of the Central Police Station there was nobody waiting to escort me to the Brigadier's office. I hadn't told Pienaar at what time I was going to arrive, so this was neither unexpected nor a problem. I made my way to reception where a very nice young lady greeted me with a smile.

'Goeimore, meneer,' the receptionist said in Afrikaans.

'Goeimore, mevrou,' I replied and then asked for Pienaar.

She telephoned through for me. 'Please take a seat over there, sir.' This time she spoke English, which was perhaps a commentary on the proficiency of my Afrikaans. She pointed to a row of seats against the far wall. 'The Brigadier is tied up currently, but somebody will be down to collect you shortly.'

I took a seat and settled down to wait. I opened a copy of the Cape Times I had bought from one of the young newspaper sellers who ply their trade at traffic lights in the city.

I started reading a report about Dirk Coetzee's appearance before the Harms Commission. He was the former commander of the Vlakplaas counter-insurgency unit and the Commission had been set up to inquire into alleged murders and unlawful action taken by the security forces during the Apartheid era.

However, I had only been reading the newspaper for a few minutes when Alan Pienaar slammed his way through the double-doors. He stood looking round the reception area, his cannonball of a head swivelled from side to side like an angry bull looking for the matador de toros. I stood up and he spotted me. He beckoned for me to follow him. Who was I to argue? I'm no matador.

'I was expecting one of your flunkies to fetch me,' I said as we rode up to his office in a lift he seemed to fill with his bulk.

'I'm afraid flunkies are in short supply today,' he said with the merest hint of a smile. 'We have a major problem in Nyanga. A gang from Guguleto tried to muscle in on the shebeen business operated by the local mob and a full-scale turf war has broken out.'

The lift doors slid open and Pienaar stepped back to let me out first.

'There have already been several killings, and the local station commander cannot cope,' he continued, 'I have had to send reinforcements to help him sort out the problem and I was already short of manpower, because of sick leave and holidays. In addition a number of my officers have been called to Jo'burg to appear before the Harms Commission, so I'm down to the bare bones.'

'I was reading about the proceedings while I was waiting,' I said as he showed me into his office. 'Frankly, it all seems a bit of a whitewash.'

'Ja,' Pienaar said sadly. 'I'm afraid the decision by Mister Justice Harms to limit the inquiry to actions committed in South Africa has undermined the integrity of the whole process.'

'Inquiries are the same the world over. They're too often an expensive farce.'

'Do I detect an element of bitterness in your voice, Mister Statton.'

'I've been the victim of an inquiry,' I admitted. I explained about the departmental inquiry into the death of Dermot O'Neill.

'And this O'Neill. He was a terrorist?'

'A terrorist, a murderer and a thug.'

'In that case, you did the right thing to shoot him.' Pienaar looked at me with renewed respect. 'Listen, Mister Statton. We didn't get off to a good start at our first meeting and that was my fault.' He held his hand out. 'Shall we start again?'

I shook his hand. 'Suits me,' I said with a smile. 'But if we're going to start again, please call me David.'

'I'm Alan,' he said. This time there was some warmth in the smile he gave me, but I was never going to get sunburnt by it. 'So, David, here is the file you wanted on Jonathan Rhodes,' he slid a folder across his desk. It had a buff cover. The colour of official files the world over.

'Thank you,' I said, but didn't open the folder. 'Do you remember I told you about the hitman hired by the Phoenix Group?'

He stroked his misshapen nose thoughtfully. 'The Irishman? Shaun Brannagan?' He asked suddenly.

'You have a good memory, Alan.'

He shrugged. 'What about him?'

'Do you remember also I told you he sometimes goes under the name of William Butler?'

'Ja.'

'Well, the Metropolitan Police Special Branch discovered that somebody by the name of William Butler boarded a plane to Cape Town from London Heathrow.'

'When was that?'

'The flight arrived at DF Malan on Monday morning…'

'I sense a "but",' he interrupted me.

I smiled and continued my sentence: '…*but* our suspect wasn't on it.'

'How do you know?'

'One of my colleagues in London faxed over a photograph of William Butler to the security officers at the airport. He asked them to check the CCTV record of passengers who arrived on that flight. There was nobody of his description on the tape.'

'So, it was a different William Butler who arrived in Cape Town?'

'Apparently.'

'It sounds as if you have some doubts?'

'I do.' I told him why.

'Do you have a photograph of this Shaun Brannagan?'

'Not in South Africa. I can get London to send one over, but that will take time. However, I have another suggestion.'

'What do you have in mind?'

'I know what Brannagan looks like. If he was on that flight I'll recognise him immediately. Can you arrange for me to see a copy of that airport CCTV tape?'

'Of course, when would you like to see it?'

'As soon as possible.'

'I have somebody stationed at the airport who I trust. Let me make a quick phone call and we can go there straight away.'

'We?'

'Ja, I'll come with you. Unless you object to my company?'

'Of course not. In fact, I'd welcome it. I'm sure I'll get greater co-operation from the security staff if I have a senior police officer with me. On my own, I'm just another bloody civilian rooinek.'

He grinned. 'That, my friend, is one of the reasons I offered to come with you.'

'Are you sure you have time?'

'Ja, I have time, but I'd like to make a quick detour to Nyanga on the way back.'

'I'm cool with that,' I assured him.

Whilst Pienaar made his phone call I opened the folder he had given me and read through the three A4 sheets of paper of briefing notes it contained. Attached to the notes were two photographs, the first of which was a head and shoulders shot of a good-looking man, who stared up at me with arrogant eyes.

Jonathan Rhodes wore an open neck white silk shirt, on which the top three buttons had been undone to reveal a hairy chest and a heavy gold chain. He had dark brown eyes, with long lashes and well-defined, almost black eyebrows. His hair was the same colour, but with smudges of grey at his temples. He wore a pencil moustache between his long nose and thin, slightly cruel looking lips. All in all he had the looks that set the pulse racing of a certain type of woman.

The second photograph showed an immaculately dressed Rhodes standing in front of a row of shiny, expensive cars. There was everything from a Rolls Royce Silver Spirit to a Maserati Spyder. He stood with his arms outstretched in a gesture of ownership. He had a wide smile on his face. I started mentally to add up the rough value of the vehicles in front of which he stood and quickly passed the £1 million point. No wonder he looked so pleased with himself.

'Time to make a move,' Alan Pienaar said, breaking into my thoughts of Jonathan Rhodes and his wealth, which the file in front of me told me stood at over two billion Rand. In the currency recognised by my bank manager, that equated to £400 million. 'It's all set up. The tape you want to see will be ready for you to review within the next half an hour. If we leave now we can be at the airport by noon.'

I stood up with the Rhodes file in my hand. 'Let's do it.'

DF Malan International Airport, Cape Town
We were welcomed at the airport like royalty. There was a great deal of saluting and kow-towing as Brigadier Alan Pienaar strode into the suite of offices in which the airport security was based.

I followed him, but few of the staff took much notice of me. This wasn't something over which I would lose sleep. The greatest compliment you can pay a field agent is that he is not noticed.

Pienaar escorted me to a small office where he introduced me to a young policewoman who was waiting for us. Her name was Megan. The girl was no midget, but the brigadier, who stood at her side, towered over her like a genial giant. She was pretty, with intelligent eyes that studied me with undisguised interest as she grasped my hand.

'I am pleased to meet you, Mister Statton,' Megan shook my hand with a firm, confident grip. She spoke with a South African accent, but her voice had the hint of a lilt. However, I couldn't put my finger on what it was.

'I have the equipment set up for you over here,' the girl added as she showed me to a chair behind a desk on which was positioned a monitor screen and a video tape player.

'Thank you for organising this so quickly, Megan,' Pienaar said as he positioned a chair next to, but slightly behind mine. He sat down and the policewoman inserted a video cassette into the machine and pressed a button. After a few seconds clear black and white images appeared on the screen. There was no sound.

I watched as a member of the airport staff silently opened the doors into the arrivals area that led through to immigration. A flow of passengers came through the doors in single file, carrying an assortment of hand luggage.

'Can you slow the tape down?' I asked Megan.

'Of course, sir,' she said and slowly turned a knob on the side of the video screen. 'Say when.'

'That's perfect now,' I said as the progress of the passengers slowed to a crawl. The tape stuttered slightly as the speed at which it was fed through the head was reduced. This made the passengers move like robots, but it gave me longer to examine each face.

I studied the travellers intently. There was a weariness about most of them; probably the result of a twelve-hour flight without much sleep. They shuffled across my vision like people on their way to an unwanted appointment. In some cases they probably were.

There were young faces and old. Male and female. Black, white and every shade in between. There were ugly faces and beautiful faces. My eye was drawn to the owner of one such face. It belonged to a young woman, wearing a low cut top that showed off a generous cleavage.

My mind went back to an earlier visit to South Africa when I had positioned myself in the queue behind an equally shapely woman to distract the immigration officials. It's an old trick and on that occasion it had worked for me.

Now it crossed my mind that Brannagan might try something similar. Suddenly I was alert and watchful, but as the young woman drifted from the screen she was replaced by an elderly Indian woman wearing a sari. This was not my target. The Irishman might be a dab hand at disguise, but he was not that good.

I relaxed as the Indian woman was followed by a young white man with his hair tied back in a ponytail. He had both ears intact. Like all the men who had gone before, this was not Brannagan.

And so the procession went on for another five minutes. I was just beginning to think my hunch was wrong when I finally saw the man I was looking for.

'Stop!' I shouted.

Megan froze the tape.

I pointed at the screen. 'That's him,' I said to Pienaar.

'Are you sure?'

'Quite certain.'

'So you were right.'

'It looks that way.'

'So, how did Butler metamorphose into Brannagan?'

'That's easy. He boarded the plane at Heathrow using his William Butler passport, showing him with a beard and long hair. That's the photograph London sent to your people and was what your guys were looking for at this end.'

Pienaar leaned forward and tapped the monitor screen. 'But Brannagan has short hair and is clean shaven.'

'Exactly. Butler was wearing a wig and false beard,' I explained. 'As I recall, there's a toilet in the corridor between the entrance door from the concourse and the arrivals hall.'

'There is,' Megan chipped in. 'Some passengers find they need to relieve themselves as soon as they get off the plane. I suppose it's something to do with the stress of landing.'

'Well, I think you will find that Butler nipped in and used one of the cubicles to remove his wig and beard, stuffed it into his flight bag and then came out as Brannagan. He probably hung around in the cubicle for a few minutes, so that anybody who saw him go in with a beard, would have disappeared before he came back out clean shaven. That's why he was near the back of the queue.'

'What about his passport,' Alan Pienaar asked.

'He used his Shaun Brannagan passport. No doubt the immigration officer simply checked his face against the passport, stamped it and didn't notice that the name Brannagan didn't appear on the flight passenger list.'

'So your man *is* in South Africa?'

'Yes.'

'Can you get me a still photograph of him, Megan?' Pienaar asked, pointing at the screen.

'Certainly, sir. Straight away.' She removed the video tape cassette from the player and disappeared out of the door.

'I'll distribute a copy of the photograph to all the police stations in the Cape and ask them to keep their eyes open for Brannagan,' Pienaar said. 'But whether we can trace him is another matter. He seems as slippery as an eel that one.'

'I'm afraid he's deadlier than even a conger eel, Alan. He's more like a Cape cobra.'

'Then you must be on your guard.'

'I will be,' I assured him.

Megan came back with an envelope, which she handed to Pienaar. 'I printed off a dozen copies for you, sir.'

'Thank you, my dear,' he said and then led me out of the terminal building to the car-park where his car was parked.

'That Megan seems a smart cookie,' I said as Pienaar opened the passenger door of his car for me and waited for me to climb in.

'Ja. She gets that from her father.'

'Out of interest, Alan, do you call all your police officers by their first names, or only the pretty ones like Megan?'

'Just her,' Pienaar said as he settled into the driver's seat.

I raised an eyebrow at him.

He gave a shrug of his wide shoulders. 'She's my daughter.'

'I don't wish to appear rude, but I'm puzzled. Megan might have inherited your intellect, but she obviously doesn't get her looks from you.'

He gave me a lopsided grin. 'She got those from my wife.' He pulled out his wallet and took a photograph from it. He passed it to me. It showed an older, but equally pretty, version of Megan. 'That's my wife,' he said proudly. 'She's Welsh.'

I thought about the slight lilt in the girl's voice and realised it must be an accent inherited from her mother.

'She's from the Valleys. Just like my ma,' Pienaar went on. 'We named Megan after her grandma.'

I handed back the photograph. 'How did an ugly sod like you attract somebody so beautiful?'

He looked at me gravely, but his eyes were twinkling with good humour. 'Ag, you wouldn't understand, rooinek. It's called charisma.'

Nyanga Township, Cape Town

It took us only ten minutes to reach the outskirts of Nyanga.

The township resembled a war zone. A pall of black smoke hung in the air above the lines of ramshackle corrugated-iron homes that made up the shanty town.

Nyanga was born following an influx of people from the Western Cape's rural hinterland, who had migrated to the outer limits of urban Cape Town in search of a better life. Sadly, they were destined to be disappointed. Their new home had turned into one of the most dangerous places in South Africa.

As we drove through the township we saw police vehicles parked on every corner and squads of heavily armed riot police forming cordons across all the main roads.

Pienaar manoeuvred through the rubble strewn streets until we found the police control centre, set up to manage the increasingly violent situation that had arisen in the last twenty-four hours. We came to a stop at yet another road block.

We were met by a young police captain wearing a blue flak jacket. He recognised Pienaar's car and was already saluting as he approached us.

'How goes it, Bekker?' Pienaar asked in English as we got out of the squad car.

'The local commander is useless,' the young captain answered disparagingly, 'but I think we now have the situation under control.' Although he addressed his remarks to his superior officer, he managed at the same time to study me curiously.

'This is Mister Statton,' Pienaar explained. 'He is from Britain and is in our country to learn how we deal with terrorists.'

'From Britain is it?' Bekker asked and looked at me more intently. 'Do you know Margaret Thatcher?'

'I've met her several times,' I said.

'You've met the Iron Lady?'

'Yes, most recently a couple of weeks ago.'

'That's incredible,' Bekker said. 'You are so lucky to have Mrs Thatcher as your leader. She is my idol. She has been a great friend to our country. She...'

Pienaar cut the young officer off in mid-sentence: 'Sorry to bring your expressions of devotion to an end, Captain Bekker, but I would be grateful for an update about the current situation here in Nayanga. What's happening?'

A deep blush flushed the policeman's face red. '*Verskoon my, Brigadier. Kom saam met my, here.*' Then, remembering me, he repeated in English: 'Come with me, gentlemen.'

Bekker led the way to a wooden shack that stood about twenty yards from the junction at which the roadblock had been set up. He pushed open the door and walked in. Pienaar and I followed.

We were confronted by a shocking sight. Lines of blood stained bodies were laid along both walls. Fat black flies buzzed above each. Several of the dead men against the right wall wore red bandanas around their heads. Bekker pointed to them.

'Those okes are gang members from Guguleto. They are all Zulu.' he explained. 'And on this side, are local gangsters, mainly Xhosa.' He nodded towards the left wall.

'Why are the two gangs separated?' I asked.

'It would make the situation much worse if word got out that we mixed up the bodies,' Pienaar explained. 'It would be seen as disrespectful to both Zulu and Xhosa.'

I found it sad that even in death the two sides were divided by tribal loyalties and historic hatred.

'How many dead so far?' Pienaar asked.

'We're now up to thirty-seven, sir,' Bekker replied. 'But the good news is that we haven't had a fatality for over an hour.'

'What's the response from the locals?'

'They are fed up to the back-teeth with the violence and say we should be doing more to protect them from the skellems. The civic leaders are complaining that we didn't act quickly enough.'

Pienaar shook his head in despair and turned to me. 'That's the dilemma we often face, David. If we move in quickly we are accused by the locals of over-reaction and discrimination against the residents. However, if we hold back we are accused of negligence and not protecting the residents. We can't win.'

I didn't argue. Dealing with unfair criticism is the lot of police officers the world over. Such hypocrisy is used also to discredit members of the security services, or the armed forces, when they are forced to use to violence to protect themselves or the public.

'Well done, Bekker. You seem to be on top of things,' Pienaar said.

The young captain's face lit up at the compliment. 'Dankie, Brigadier.'

'Come on, Mister Statton,' Pienaar said. 'There is nothing more we can do here. Let's get out of Captain Bekker's hair.' With that we headed for his car.

As Pienaar drove me back to Central Police Station I opened the file he had given me about Jonathan Rhodes and stared again at the photo of the South African magnate in front of the line of expensive cars.

'Alan, how many racing green Porsche Carrera's do you reckon there are in Cape Town?' I asked.

'Is this some kind of quiz?' He asked with a laugh.

'No, it's a serious question.'

'Well, the serious answer is that I have no idea, but my guess would be very few. Those cars cost a small fortune and only the very wealthiest people can afford to buy one.'

'Men like Rhodes?' I tapped the photograph. 'There is a green Porsche in this photo.'

'Is that significant?'

'It could be. There was an identical car behind me when I left Cape Town after visiting you a couple of days back.'

'You think it was following you?'

'It did cross my mind.'

'You think it was Rhodes'?'

'I wouldn't bet against it,' I said as we drew up outside Central Police Station.

'It could have been a coincidence.'

'Perhaps. But coincidences are often Fate's way of kicking you in the balls when you least expect it.'

He laughed. 'Very profound.'

I didn't argue with him, but I didn't laugh either.'

Newlands, Cape Town

By mid-afternoon I was back in Paul's apartment making a telephone call to London. Colleen answered the phone.

'Good afternoon, Colleen.'

'Good afternoon, David,' she said in a flat voice.

'What's wrong?'

'It's Mister Lafarge.'

'Roly? What about him?'

'He was rushed to hospital this morning,' she explained. 'He had a heart attack during the monthly management meeting.'

'That's the second one this year. How is he?'

'The latest report from the hospital is that he is comfortable.' She didn't sound convinced.

'Being 'comfortable' sounds promising.' I tried to sound reassuring. I knew she had a soft spot for the Deputy D-G, for whom she worked before being poached by Disraeli-Astor.

'I hope you're right. I suppose you want the D-G?'

'If he's there.'

'He's here. I'll put you through,' she said and was gone.

There had been none of the usual flirtatious banter between us and I was relieved. My private life was becoming complicated. Because of my rekindled feelings for Freddie, my relationship with Colleen weighed heavily on my conscience. I couldn't get out of my head that not that long ago we had shared a bed.

'Disraeli-Astor.'

'Not good news about Roland Lafarge,' I said.

'No, he's very poorly. I'm not sure we'll see him back.'

'That bad? I got the impression he was over the worst of it. Colleen told me the hospital said he was comfortable.'

'Well he's not at death door, if that's what you mean. However, this is the second attack he's had this year. Climbing back into the saddle might finish him off and he is due to retire later this year anyway. I am trying to convince him to go early. I told him I would ensure he does not lose any of his pension. Meanwhile, until a new Deputy D-G is appointed, I'll be a man down so I'm transferring Les Hobble back into my team.'

'I assume you mean Des Hobbins?'

'That's the chappie. Good with budgets, so I hear.'

'What about my team? Des was my acting two I.C.'

'I was thinking of promoting Melissa.'

'Melissa will be off to the Foreign Office soon,' I pointed out.

'Don't worry, I'll find somebody to replace her.'

I snorted, but either he didn't hear, or chose to ignore me.

'Anyway, perhaps a promotion will persuade Melissa to stay with the Department.'

'If it does, I'll get her to look after our herd of flying pigs.'

'You are far too cynical, Statton.'

'I have every right to be cynical,' I retorted. 'I might not be Albert Einstein, but by my calculation, even if by some miracle Melissa does decide to stay with the department, it will still leave my team a man down.'

'I think in today's world of increasing sexual equality you have to start thinking in terms of being a person down, Statton. Now as it happens I met an excellent young lady at the weekend. Jasmine has just come down from Oxford.'

'Jasmine?' I was immediately suspicious.

'Yes. I think she would make a damned good researcher. She got a first in PPE,' he paused and then added: 'That is a degree in philosophy, politics and economics.'

'Well I didn't think she was at Oxford studying to be a personal physical education teacher.'

He ignored me. 'She comes from an excellent family. She would fit well in your team.'

'An excellent family? Well that's alright then. I suppose you went to school with her father.'

'As it happens, no, I didn't.'

'That's a first. You usually only recruit people with a family connection. Are you going all egalitarian on us?'

'Certainly not. In my experience egalitarianism is somewhat overrated. Which is why I favour elitism. I much prefer to use people whose families I know and trust. On this occasion I happen to know Jasmine's grandfather. He was the colonel in charge of my regiment when I joined from Sandhurst. But we can discuss all this when you get back from South Africa, now what is it you want to tell me?'

I told him how Paul and I had installed listening devices in the conference centre and of our intention to return on the Thursday before the Phoenix Group meeting to test them again.

'Don't forget we need to keep this strictly to ourselves,' I added. 'That's why I'm telling you personally, as we agreed.'

'Of course I haven't forgotten,' he said frostily. 'You make me sound as if I'm going senile. My memory isn't that bad.'

I didn't bother to question this statement. I knew he would prove himself wrong soon enough. I didn't have long to wait.

'Is there anything else?'

'Yes. Shaun Brannagan is in South Africa.'

'Who is Brannagan?' He queried.

'You know him better as William Butler,' I reminded him.

'Of course. We thought he was on a plane to Cape Town, but, I thought Hobble said he never arrived.'

'That's what Brannagan wanted us to think,' I said and went on to tell him my theory about how the Irishman had abandoned his Butler disguise and entered South Africa on his own passport.

'Should I report this development to Jeffery Johnson?'

'No.'

'What about the AOSC?'

'Are you joking?'

341

'What do you mean?'

'Think about it, boss.'

'I was thinking about it,' he snapped. 'That's why I asked the question.'

'So why do you think Brannagan is in Cape Town?'

'I can think of at least two reasons,' he responded. 'One: he is there to attend the meeting next month.'

'Most unlikely,' I pointed out. 'If that *was* the case, why did he arrive on Monday, rather than next week when members of the Phoenix Group start arriving?'

'Good point, which only leaves the second option. He followed you so that he can kill you.'

'That's what I think.'

'But that's a good thing, isn't it? You deliberately provoked him into coming after you.'

'I did, but his presence in the Cape begs another question.'

'What's that?'

'When I had my conversation with Wren I never mentioned my visit to South Africa. So how did Brannagan know to follow me here?'

'What are you getting at?'

'Did you tell the ASOC members about my trip to South Africa?'

'Yes. It wasn't a secret.'

'Well, it's certainly not a secret now.'

'So what are you saying?'

'Somebody tipped off the Phoenix Group that I was coming to Cape Town,' I explained patiently.

'You still think Dougie is passing information to Wren?'

'Can you come up with a better suggestion?' I asked.

He did not respond.

'Of course it was Campbell,' I said, 'and when I get back to the UK I will deal with it. I think a quiet word is called for.'

'I would be grateful if you would clear any action with me first,' he insisted.

'Of course,' I assured him.

'I still can't believe Dougie would do such a thing. Perhaps it's another member of the AOSC.'

'That's most unlikely,' I said. 'Just consider the make-up of the committee. Apart from your mate Campbell, there is you, me and two other members. That narrows the possible sources of the leak considerably.'

'But it still doesn't prove Dougie is guilty.'

'Except that Wren as good as admitted that Campbell was feeding him information,' I said. 'Anyway, whether or not your mate is the culprit, we know that somebody is passing information to the Phoenix Group, which is why we have to keep my plans strictly to ourselves. If they find out about the listening devices, my trip will have been a waste of time.'

'And money.' Disraeli-Astor could never resist any excuse to have another dig about my expenses. 'But don't worry, Statton,' he added. 'Mum's the word.'

As I put down the phone I prayed silently that I could trust my boss's mother to keep a secret, because it was more than I could her son.

Claremont, Cape Town

I arrived early at Freddie's apartment. She had just come home from work and was about to have a shower so I sat down in her lounge to read the rest of my *Cape Times*.

'Instead of reading the newspaper wouldn't you sooner come and wash my back?'

I looked up. Freddie was standing in the doorway to the bedroom. She was stark naked and held a sponge in her hand. She smiled at me, turned on her heel and disappeared in the direction of the bathroom with a seductive wiggle of her backside. A few seconds later I heard the hiss of water as she turned on the shower. 'Are you coming?' She shouted.

I decided the editorial in the *Cape Times* could wait. A minute later I joined Freddie in the shower. She already had a soap ladened sponge waiting for me, which I used to lather her body all over, then I threw it to the floor and used my hands to wash away the suds.

When we were finished I turned off the water, wrapped her in a towel, lifted her from the shower and carried her through to the bedroom, where I laid her gently on the bed. She lifted her arms, grabbed me and pulled me on top of her. We were both ready for what followed.

Later we ate a meal in a Chinese restaurant in Wynberg. It was one that Freddie used a lot when she lived in the area. The food was okay, without being exceptional, but then I was comparing it with the Golden Dragon in London.

Thoughts of Jian Ming's restaurant reminded me that my last visit had been with Colleen Masters and this made me feel guilty. My feelings towards her and Freddie were complex. I knew I wanted Freddie, but wasn't sure how I could extricate myself from my relationship with Colleen without hurting her.

'Do you remember the first shower we had together?' Freddie asked, breaking into my thoughts.

I remembered it well. It was after we had been out for the day looking for a way to land on Robben Island. 'Yes,' I replied, shrugging aside my misgivings.

'Do you realise that was eight years ago?'

'It was actually the Eighth of May,' I said.

'How on earth do you know that?' She asked.

'Because the timetable for Operation Seal Island is indelibly printed on my brain.'

She was silent for a while as she let her mind drift back through the years. 'I enjoyed that day,' she said eventually. 'We used your brand new ski-boat to get to Rock Cove and you let me launch it with a bottle of bubbly. I felt just like your Queen Elizabeth.' She gave a nostalgic smile. 'Do you remember what I named that boat?'

'*The Spirit of Freedom.* How could I forget? You wrote the name on her hull in bright pink lipstick.'

She giggled. 'It was all I had available at the time.'

I thought again about the mission to get the Russian nuclear scientist out of the prison on Robben Island. I lost three of my friends in the process. One was buried on the narrow beach we had used to get onto the island. I had a sudden idea. 'Have you visited Rock Cove since you returned to South Africa?'

'Yeah. I went diving for crayfish a couple of months ago.'

'At night?'

'No, during the day. The authorities are a bit more lenient about people approaching the island these days. They don't encourage visits, but they no longer shoot anybody who gets too close.' She looked sad. 'But I haven't been back since.'

'Why not?' I thought I knew the answer. I was right.

'Because my visit reminded me of Mister Mac's death.'

344

'I was thinking about Mister Mac too. I'd very much like to visit his grave. Would you like to join me?'

'Yeah,' she said.

'How would we get there?'

'I borrowed my cousin's boat. I'll ask him if I can use it again.'

'Andre must be a very generous cousin.' I said.

'He is,' she assured me. 'He pretends to be hard but he's a pussy-cat really.'

'When can we go?'

'Well, Andre uses the boat himself most weekends, so it would be better if our trip was on a week day. How does next Monday suit you?'

'That's fine with me, but what about work?'

She smiled. 'I'll take the day off. I'm owed some holiday time.'

I settled the bill. 'I'd like to visit Bloubergstrand and pay my last respects to Charlie and John as well,' I said as we left the restaurant.

'I have no idea where their remains were buried,' she said when we reached the car. 'If they ever were.'

'I'd just like to see where they were killed.' I opened the passenger door for her

'I know where they died,' she said quietly. 'I'll come with you if you like.'

'I'd like that.' I settled into the driver's seat.

Freddie looked at me with an expression that I could not quite fathom, but she nodded her agreement. I started up the car and drove out of the car-park.

'I'm working on Saturday, but we could visit Bloubergstrand on Sunday,' she suggested.

I eased the car into a gap in the steady flow of traffic that was heading towards the main road linking the city centre to the Cape Peninsula. 'Sounds good to me,' I said.

'Will I see you tomorrow?' She asked when we eventually drew up outside her apartment.

'Paul is going to Durban for a few days, which means I'll be on my own tomorrow night. So I have the option of sitting in his apartment staring at the walls, or seeing you. What do you think?'

'I think you will be joining me for dinner.'

'Right answer.'

'Cool. I'll get in some steaks and you can bring a nice bottle of pinotage with you when you come.'

'It's a done deal.' We got out of the car and I walked her to the entrance of her apartment block.

'I'd like to ask you to stay the night,' she said, 'but you would probably keep me up half the night.'

'I wish that was true,' I said. 'At my age the spirit promises the earth, but the body delivers sod all.'

She punched me lightly on the chest. 'Listen, buster, I've seen you perform and you can still turn me on. Once that happens I can't get enough of you.'

I hugged her. 'You know how to make a chap feel good,' I whispered. 'And we have a lot of wasted time to catch up on.'

'We do,' she agreed. 'But not tonight. I have an early meeting in the morning with an important client and I need to be at my best.'

I kissed her on the end of her nose. 'Don't fret. As it happens I want to get back to Paul's place tonight. He's leaving first thing in the morning and I need to have a chat with him before he goes.'

She gave me a hug. 'Thank you.'

'What for?' I asked.

'For being you and for being here with me.'

'Beggars can't be choosers,' I said.

She punched me on the chest again. This time harder. 'Jy vark!'

'Only joking,' I laughed and kissed her full on the mouth to prevent any further protest. She didn't complain. 'I'll see you tomorrow night,' I said eventually. 'What time?'

'Make it seven-thirty and don't forget to bring the wine and a toothbrush.' With that she pushed open the outer entrance door.

I waited until she was safely through the internal security door and into the lift before heading back to my car. As I opened the driver's door, I sensed I was being watched.

I looked up at Freddie's apartment, expecting to see her looking down at me, but although there was a light at her window, the curtains were tightly drawn.

I looked up and down the street, but there was no sign of life. There were a few cars parked further up the road, but none that I recognised. I shrugged and climbed into my car.

As I drove back to Newlands the racing-green Porsche weighed heavily on my mind. I still had a nagging suspicion it was following me when I left the police station, but a sense of well-being and half a bottle of wine almost helped convince me I was being paranoid. That's when a quote by American author Edward Abbey popped into my mind.

He wrote: "Anyone not paranoid in this world must be crazy. Speaking of paranoia, it's true that I do not know exactly who my enemies are, but that, of course, is exactly why I'm paranoid."

I couldn't have put it better myself.

There was something else on my mind. Something that made me feel guilty again. Freddie had called me a vark. That is the Afrikaans word for pig. The last person to call me that in mock anger had been Colleen Masters.

Chapter 28

Bloubergstrand, Cape Town, Sunday April 29th

Since my arrival in Cape Town the weather had been mainly grey, cool and miserable, with only the occasional glimpse of sunshine to lift the spirits. Typical autumnal days in the Cape.

But today the sun had pulled out all the stops. It shone down from a clear blue sky with a warmth that had encouraged Freddie to dress in a pair of skimpy shorts and a vest top that showed off her shapely figure.

But Freddie was as sensible as she was beautiful, and as she threw her bulky bag onto the back seat of my car I could see a heavy jumper poking from its top.

'You've come prepared.' I pointed at the bag.

'Of course. There's a pair of jeans in there too.'

I smiled. 'Let's hope you don't need them.'

'Don't worry. I should be alright until this evening. The weather forecast for today and tomorrow is fine with bergwind conditions.'

I hoped she was right. A warm north-easterly wind blowing down from the Karoo would make our sea trip to Robben Island the following day much more pleasurable.

Our drive to Bloubergstrand from Claremont took just over half an hour, which included a stop at a service station near Milnerton to fill up with petrol. In addition to filling my fuel tank the forecourt attendant insisted on cleaning my windscreen. On hearing my accent, he grilled me on whether any other team would beat Arsenal to the English First Division title that season.

My response that only Liverpool would come close to the Gunners was greeted with good-humoured derision by the attendant, who proudly declared himself to be a Manchester United supporter. He then insisted on cementing our short period of male bonding by shaking my hand in the multi-grip African fashion.

'What was that all about?' Freddie asked when I returned to the car.

'Man talk.'

'I bet it was all about bloody football!' She snorted.

'It might well be bloody football, to you girlies, but it's great at breaking down racial and social barriers.'

'Girlie, is it? So that's why you left me on my own for almost half an hour with nothing better to do than sit and look at the cars come and go.'

'Don't exaggerate,' I said with a laugh. I started the car and drove out of the service station, steering with one hand. 'We were chatting for no longer than five minutes.' I handed her the red rose the pump attendant gave me in exchange for the generous tip I slipped him. 'For you.'

Freddie sniffed the rose and smiled. 'You're forgiven. I'd sit here all day looking at cars being filled up with fuel if it meant you were going to be romantic more often.'

'Don't hold your breath. You've had your annual quota of romance from me in one hit.'

She thumped me on the thigh, but I could tell she didn't believe me.

We left Milnerton and drove north in companionable silence, but as we drew closer to our destination our mood became more sombre. This was a place with so many bad memories for us both.

When last I had visited Bloubergstrand, it was a small seaside hamlet. Now, as we reached its outskirts, I was struck by the change to the local skyline. The area had changed dramatically with new developments all over the place.

In front of me I recognised the tall apartment block, from which Paul Helsdon and I laid our plans to use a small beach to land on Robben Island's east coast.

But the last time I saw the block it had been surrounded by only a scattering of bungalows and holiday homes. Now, as we headed towards it, we were driving through a network of residential roads lined with an assortment of new houses.

I drew up outside the apartment block, next to which stood an empty plot covered in weeds and dirt. At the far end of the strip of wasteland was a row of garages.

'I see they're still there.' I pointed at the ramshackle structures, where we had stored the ski-boat we used to get to Robben Island. 'Do you remember the trouble we had getting the boat trailer hooked up to the truck? There was torrential rain that night and the mud outside the garage was thick and slimy.'

'Yeah, I remember. But the mud wasn't as thick and slimy as the guy who rented you the garage.'

More memories flooded back. Freddie was with me on the day I negotiated to rent the garage. She was wearing a revealing top, similar to the one she had on now.

The garage owner was dressed in a colourful Hawaiian shirt. He had the look of an Italian gigolo about him and spent more time ogling Freddie's chest than he did letting the garage to me.

She had called him a slime-ball. It was an apt description.

I drove on, heading up the coast road that led to Melkbosstrand and, much further north, the Koeberg Nuclear Power Station, but we didn't go that far. Instead, just outside Bloubergstrand, I turned off the main road onto a track that led through sand dunes to an isolated beach. It was empty, except for the ghosts of the tragic events that took place on the beach eight years before. We covered the final few hundred yards in silence, both of us nagged by our dark memories.

I parked in the lee of a high sand dune and turned off the engine. The last time I had been on the beach was at the wheel of a truck. A Russian scientist, Alexei Zamyatin, was in the back after we freed him from the high security prison on Robben Island.

Before driving off to my rendezvous with Gavin Rogers - the CIA agent who had contracted me to deliver Zamyatin - I watched as Freddie reversed a Toyota pick-up truck down the track, along which we had just travelled. In the back was Paul Helsdon, John Brandon and Charlie Le Roux. They carried Kalashnikov AK47s and enough ammunition to start a small war.

I never saw John and Charlie again.

Freddie and I got out of the hire car. I took a rucksack from the backseat and slung it across my shoulder. We headed through the sand dunes and trudged down the track in silence.

After we had walked a hundred yards, Freddie stopped and touched my arm. I looked down at her. Tears welled in her eyes.

'This is where I stopped the bakkie when Charlie was shot,' she said softly. 'It's the first time I've been here since it happened. It makes me feel so sad.'

'Me too.'

'But it's not the same for you, David,' she said in a strangled voice. 'You weren't there when the actual shooting started. You weren't there when Charlie was killed. You weren't there when John was shot in the back.'

Her words made me feel guilty, because she was right. She had been forced to watch as our friends were killed. I knew it had taken her many months to get over the trauma caused by the carnage she had witnessed that day. 'I'm sorry. I should never have brought you back here.'

The tears were now flowing down her cheeks. She clutched my arm. 'No, I'm sorry, David. I shouldn't have spoken to you like that. It wasn't your fault then and it isn't your fault now. You didn't want to leave me behind. You offered to take me with you when you went to the rendezvous with Rogers, but I was stubborn and insisted on staying with the rest of the team.'

'You were very brave.'

'No, I was very stupid,' she insisted. 'I wanted to prove I was as good as a man, but when the chips were down, I reacted like a silly little girl.'

She pointed up at the top of the sand dune.

'That's where Paul and I stood and watched as John drove towards the police road block with Charlie's body in the back of the bakkie. John told us he was going to light a fuse in a petrol can and then jump out before the bakkie hit the police car.'

'John was a film stunt man,' I reminded her. 'He was used to danger.'

'But he didn't jump,' she sobbed.

'It was probably an unfortunate accident.'

She shook her head. 'No. he blew himself up on purpose,' she said quietly. 'And if I'm completely honest, Paul and I knew what he intended to do.'

I took her in my arms. 'It wasn't your fault, Freddie,' I told her gently.

'We should have tried to stop him,' she sobbed into my chest.

'Paul told me John was too badly injured from the wound in his back to survive,' I explained. 'John knew he was going to die and decided to take the police with him. I expect he reasoned it would give Paul and you time to escape.'

'John was the brave one, not me,' she said eventually.

'And that's why we're here. To pay him and Charlie our last respects. Now, are you OK to show me exactly where John died?'

Freddie pulled away from me and wiped the tears from her cheeks with the back of her hand. 'Yeah, I'll be fine now.' She smiled up at me wanly and started walking down the track towards the road.

When we reached the end of the track, she stopped. 'This is where the police road block was set up,' she explained. 'A squad car was parked across the track and behind it were two personnel carriers. The bakkie blew up when John drove it into the police car, causing its petrol tank to explode, which in turn set light to the personnel carriers. It was horrible. So many men died.'

We stood in silence for a while and then she asked: 'Do you remember I told you about the cop who tortured my papa?'

'Yeah. Brigadier Coetzee.'

'I found out later that he was in the police squad car. He was killed in the explosion too.'

'Poetic justice, if ever there was one.'

'I suppose, but knowing that doesn't make me feel any better. His death never brought my papa back.'

I looked around me, but could see little evidence of what I knew was a huge explosion, but I suppose after eight years, a lack of debris was understandable. Off to my right something metallic glinted in the sun.

I walked over and found part of a round object poking out from the sand. I bent down and pulled the disc free. It was a blackened and distorted wheel hub-cap, on the surface of which I could just make out the Toyota emblem. Probably it had been blown from the pick-up during the explosion.

'This is as good a spot as any.' I put my rucksack down on the ground and unzipped it. I took out two of the wooden crosses I had picked up from an undertakers the day before.

I took a wooden mallet from the rucksack and hammered both crosses into the ground, side by side. The first cross had a simple message inscribed on it: *R.I.P. John Brandon. Died May 15th 1982.*

The second cross was identical, except for the name, which read *Charlie Le Roux.*

Freddie laid a small posy of freesias at the base of each cross and then read the first verse of a poem by A E Housman:

These, in the day when heaven was falling,
The hour when earth's foundations fled,
Followed their mercenary calling,
And took their wages, and are dead.

Our little service of remembrance seemed to be cathartic for Freddie, because she was more cheerful as we made our way back down the track to the beach.

When we reached the car, I threw my rucksack on the back-seat and took a picnic basket and cool-box from the boot. I helped Freddie spread out a blanket on the sand in front of the car.

Although the north-easterly wind was warm, and little more than a stiff breeze, it was strong enough to whip fine sand from the beach's surface. However, the car acted as an effective windbreak and we managed to keep sand from the food Freddie had prepared for the wake we were holding for our dead friends.

I opened the cool-box, removed from it a bottle of champagne and popped its cork. Freddie sat down on the blanket and took two glasses from the hamper. I joined her and filled the glasses that she held towards me. I put the wine back in the cold box and took a glass from her.

'To absent friends,' I said as we both held a glass aloft.

'To absent friends,' she repeated.

'If Charlie is looking down on us I know he will be pleased we're drinking champagne to celebrate his life,' I said.

Freddie agreed. 'He was a proud Frenchman.'

'And champagne connoisseur,' I added.

'That doesn't surprise me,' she said, 'But I don't know about John and Mister Mac. Neither of them struck me as being champagne types.'

'They weren't. I'm sure John would have opted for a nice ice-cold Coors Light and Mister Mac's preference was a wee dram of whisky.'

'Talking of Mister Mac, will we do the same little ceremony for him tomorrow?' Freddie asked.

'Yes, I have another cross in my rucksack.'

It was a lovely autumn day and we spent the afternoon sitting in the sun, eating our picnic and chatting about our time together. As we talked, I realised how much Freddie had meant to me in the past; how much I missed her in my life; and how much I wanted her to figure in my future. I sensed she felt the same way, but neither of us was yet ready to suggest the next logical step, which was that we should get back together.

By now, it was after four o'clock and the sun was starting to slide

353

down the western sky as it made its way slowly towards its six pm cold bath in the Atlantic Ocean. The temperature on the beach was dropping so I cleared up as Freddie changed into jeans and jumper.

As I loaded the picnic basket and cool-box into the boot, I saw a flash of light out of the corner of my eye from the direction of the sand dunes. I stared that way and tried to work out what it was.

Something had reflected the sun's rays and I could think of a number of possibilities. For instance, I knew there was another track leading through the dunes further to the north, because I had driven along it eight years before. It was possible there was a vehicle parked there now and the sun had reflected off its windscreen.

Alternatively, it could just be another hub-cap protruding from the sand, or a discarded bottle, or an aluminium can, or even the metal barrel of a weapon. Any one of these suggestions was possible, but the one thing that I could not get out of my mind, was that the sun could have been reflecting on the lens of a pair of binoculars.

I decided it was time to leave the beach. We got into the car and I drove back down the track to the road. I headed for Bloubergstrand and from there onwards to Cape Town.

During the journey I checked my rear mirror regularly, but there was no sign we were being followed.

This should have reassured me.

It didn't.

Chapter 29

Table Bay, Cape Town, Monday April 30th

Sunday's unseasonably hot weather rolled over into Monday and the Victoria and Albert Basins were bathed in sunshine when I arrived at the Foreshore car-park on my way to meet Freddie.

I had dropped her off earlier, before heading to the British Embassy to brief the Ambassador. There was little new information to share with Sir Robin, so the meeting didn't take long, but traffic in the centre of Cape Town was horrendous and I didn't get back to the basins until late morning.

I parked my car, slung my rucksack over my shoulder and headed for the marina where Freddie had told me her cousin's boat was moored. However, she had forgotten to tell me which boat to look for, and, stupidly, I hadn't thought to ask, so I had no idea where she was. I walked up and down the pontoons, with their extensive moorings, hoping to spot her.

Eventually she saw me first and waved frantically to attract my attention. She had already collected the key to her cousin's boat and was on board waiting for me.

I'm not sure what I had expected, but I was not prepared for the huge motor cruiser on which she stood. It was magnificent, with pure white paintwork, sparkling windows and gleaming chrome rails

'Does your cousin really own this beauty?' I asked as I clambered up the ladder that led to the fly-bridge helm station where Freddie stood. I dropped my rucksack onto the deck.

'Yeah,' she replied as she hugged me.

'And he lets you use her?'

'Andre trusts me. He knows I'm a good sailor.'

Having seen Freddie's seafaring skills for myself, I knew she wasn't being immodest. 'But isn't the boat a bit large to get through that narrow channel through the rocks?'

'Far too large,' she acknowledged. 'That's why we'll use the dinghy to land,' she pointed to a small boat that was lashed to a pair of stern-mounted davits. 'Come on, let me show you round her.' She led me down to the galley and saloon.

'Very impressive,' I said when we had finished our short tour.

'Your cousin has done well for himself.'

'Yeah, we're all very proud of Andre,' she said as we climbed up to the wheel-house. 'He started off with just one taxi touting for business in Mitchells Plain. Now he has a fleet of taxis, employs fifty drivers and covers the whole of Cape Town.'

'What about the taxi-wars?' I watched as she sat in the chair behind the wheel and started the boat's twin engines. 'Have they affected him?'

'Not really. The trouble was mainly in Jo'burg. There hasn't been much sign of it down here.'

'So, it's all been peace and light in Cape Town?'

'Oh, I wouldn't say that. Some of Andre's drivers were threatened by a rival firm that tried to muscle in on his trade.'

'I don't suppose he was happy about that.'

'He wasn't but the situation was soon resolved.'

'How?'

'The office of the rival firm burnt down with the owner inside and the threats suddenly stopped.'

I raised an eyebrow. 'Did your cousin do that?'

'Andre has always denied any involvement, but...'

'But?'

'We'll never know the truth. However, what I do know is that Andre can look after himself and would never be pushed around by anybody. Now are you going to just stand there gossiping, or go and cast off?'

'Aye, aye, captain!' I headed for the stern. I jumped down onto the jetty; untied the rope from the mooring post; and then clambered back on board the motor cruiser.

By the time I re-joined Freddie in the wheel house, we were already steaming towards the marina's entrance, leaving a wake of foaming water behind us. We were both relaxed and in no hurry. We took our time and our journey across Table Bay was made at a gentle cruising speed.

Freddie dropped anchor just outside the crescent of rocks from which Rock Cove derived its name. It formed a barrier several hundred yards off the short stretch of sandy beach, as if guarding one of the very few landing places on Robben Island.

We lowered the dinghy into the water, using the cruiser's electric hoist. I picked up my rucksack and climbed down before helping

Freddie down.

My previous visit to the island was on a stormy, pitch-black night, with gale force winds and a heaving sea. Despite the conditions, Freddie had showed her sailing skill by navigating *The Spirit of Freedom* through the narrow channel that was the only way through the rocks into the cove.

John and Mr Mac were in the boat with Freddie, with Charlie, Paul and me following in the second ski-boat. Attached to the stern of *The Spirit of Freedom* were two lights, which I used as a guide to steer our way safely through the choppy waters.

Today was different. Much different. There was a clear blue sky above and the sea was calm, with just a gentle ripple of the surface to set the dinghy bobbing. Freddie started the outboard motor and pointed our bow towards the channel through the rocks.

She increased speed and we made our way quickly and effortlessly into Rock Cove. She eased back on the accelerator as we neared the shoreline and manoeuvred the dinghy so that it ran parallel with the beach, then she cut the motor.

I jumped into the water with a rope and waded the short distance to dry land. I pulled the dinghy, bow first, far enough up the beach to allow Freddie to jump onto the sand. Once safely ashore, she helped push the boat away from the water's edge.

I looked around the strip of sand and was surprised to see in the far corner the remains of the two wrecked ski-boats. We had abandoned them on the beach eight years before.

They were hit by a boulder, torn loose from an overhanging rock formation by a bolt of lightning and we had commandeered a police launch to escape from the island.

The boulder had crashed down, destroying the two craft, and injuring Freddie in the process. It still lay where it had landed, straddling both ski-boats across their shattered sterns.

'What's that over there?' Freddie pointed at the steep, treacherous slope in front of us.

'Let's find out,' I said, although I guessed what it was. I lifted my rucksack from the dinghy and we walked over to get a better look at what she had noticed. It was a rope, the frayed end of which hung about three feet above the sand. The other end of the rope was tied to one of the manatoka trees in the woods above our heads. I knew this, because my friends and I had used it to help us down the slope during our escape from the island.

At the other end of the beach there was a larger cluster of rocks, which, over perhaps a thousand years or more, had fallen onto the sand. It was on one of these jagged rocks that Mr Mac had struck his head and been killed. I headed along the foot of the slope, with Freddie close behind me.

When we reached the rocks, I looked for the rudimentary grave in which Charlie and I had buried Mr Mac. We had scraped a shallow trench for our friend, covered him with sand and piled a few small, rocks on top. It was not much, but it had been the best we could do in the circumstances.

But the grave was no longer there.

The smaller rocks had been scattered, with only one larger rock still in place, at what had been the head of the grave. The covering of sand had been washed away by the sea and there was no sign of Mr Mac's remains. They had either been swept out to sea, or had been dragged away by jackals or other scavengers.

I took the last cross from my rucksack and used my mallet to knock it into the ground behind the large rock. I had used Mr Mac's dirk to chisel into its surface a similar message to that contained on the cross: R.I.P. Mr Mac.

Freddie read the same poem she had in Bloubergstrand the day before. Then, with our job done, we left the beach in silence and returned to the cabin cruiser.

She had made up some sandwiches and stored them in the fridge in the cruiser's galley, along with some beers. We spent a couple of hours sitting in the sun in the aft cockpit, eating sandwiches, drinking Castle lager and chatting about what we had both been getting up to since she left our little cottage in Scotland.

I told her how I had been recruited back into the Department for Covert Operations mentioning a bit more of the work in which I had been involved. Freddie was most interested in my most recent assignment to help protect Nelson Mandela.

In turn, she told me how on her return to South Africa she finally discovered what happened to her father. We always assumed Johan Carlse was killed when, as a member of an ANC assault group, he was ambushed when attacking the Koeberg Nuclear Power Station.

It transpired that he actually survived the attack, but was captured by the police and later committed suicide in his cell by hanging himself with his belt. At least that was the official version given by the police when her father's body was eventually handed over to Freddie's uncle.

The family never believed the police story, not least because it was the stock explanation for prisoners who died in custody. Their suspicion was reinforced when the undertaker discovered on Johan's body a mass of burns, bruises and abrasions consistent with torture.

Subsequently, evidence was discovered suggesting Carlse had been tortured during interrogation by Kobus Coetzee. Freddie was convinced the allegation was true.

'This coming Friday would have been papa's birthday,' she said sadly. 'He's buried next to mama in Ocean View Cemetery. I usually visit his grave on his birthday. Will you come with me?'

'Of course,' I said without hesitation. I remembered my last conversation with Johan Carlse, during which he made me promise to look after his daughter. I owed it to him.

Freddie stood up and came over to my chair and hugged me. 'Thank you, Dave,' she whispered. 'Under that cold, cynical exterior you are a warm-hearted, wonderful person and that's why I love you so much.'

I hugged her back. 'I love you too. I looked at my watch. 'But shouldn't we be getting back? Didn't you say your cousin was coming to meet us at the marina at four o'clock to collect the keys to the boat?'

She glanced down at her watch-less wrist. 'What time is it?' She asked.

'Half past three.'

'Not a problem.' She headed towards the ladder that led up to the fly-bridge. 'We'll be back before four. Hold on to your hat sailor!'

She was right. The return journey was nothing like the leisurely trip we had taken to get to Robben Island. She pushed the throttle up to full power and the twin Volvo Penta diesel engines drove us through the water at an eye-watering speed.

We made it back to the marina with five minutes to spare.

Freddie locked up the boat and we made our way to the car-park, where we found a young man leaning against a Jaguar XJ-S convertible, with gleaming red paintwork and its hood down.

The man straightened when he saw us. 'Hi, Coz,' he called out with a broad smile. 'Howzit, babe?'

'Don't you babe me, Andre,' Freddie scolded as we approached the man. She tossed the boat keys to him.

He caught the keys and, in one smooth move, slipped them into his pocket. 'Chill, Coz. Don't hit me with your women's lib vibes. I was only jibing you.'

He turned to me. 'Howzit, man? So, you're the cool dude, Freddie's hot on.'

'Drop the black-ghetto shit, Andre,' Freddie warned him. 'Just talk normally.'

'Sorry, Coz,' Andre said with a grin. 'Just joshing you in front of your fellah.'

'Andre! I said stop it.'

The man held out a hand to me. 'I'm pleased to meet you Mister Statton,' he said with a wide smile. 'I've heard a lot about you from my feisty cousin here.'

I shook his hand. He was a handsome young man with sparkling, good-natured eyes and a natural smile that must have melted the heart of more than one Cape Town girl.

Freddie had once shown me a wedding photograph of her mother and father. As I studied Andre, I was struck by how much he looked like Johan Carlse, before sorrow and drink drained the vitality from him after the death of his wife.

'Call me Dave. It's good to meet you too, Andre. And thanks for letting us use your boat today.'

'Ag, it's not a problem. I owe Freddie big time. She loaned me the money to buy my first taxi. Without her help I'd probably be a skollie walking round the waterfront hustling tourists.'

'Instead of which,' Freddie interjected, 'he's a skollie driving a flash car round the waterfront hustling tourists.'

Andre laughed. 'Harsh, babe!' He cried as he climbed into his Jag and started it up. 'But now you come to mention it, I think it's time to get back to the office and make sure my drivers are out there working hard to pull in the punters.' With those words, and a cheery wave of his hand, he was gone with a roar of the Jaguar's 228 horse power, 6-cylinder engine, and a squeal of its tyres.

'You loaned him the money for his first taxi?'

'Yeah. Do you remember you gave me a briefcase to look after containing the twenty-five thousand rand that papa earned for his part in your operation?'

I remembered and didn't have the heart to point out that her father did nothing to earn the money, because he disappeared before the operation began. 'Yes.'

'Well I hid it at the bottom of my wardrobe. However, the police discovered it when they raided my apartment. When they handed my father's body over to Uncle Rolf, they gave him also the briefcase. Miraculously, the money was still in it.

'Uncle Rolf opened a bank account in my name and deposited the money in it. When I arrived back in South Africa I found that, with interest, there was almost thirty thousand rand waiting for me. It was a pleasant surprise.'

'You earned that money,' I told her. 'After all, you took your father's place and guided us to Robben Island. We would never have made it without you.'

'Thank you,' she said with a smile. 'That means a lot to me. I always felt slightly guilty taking papa's money. Anyway, that's where the money came from to help Andre, but he paid me back years ago.'

'He certainly made good use of your loan. Not only has he a fantastic boat, but that's a great looking Jag he's driving.'

'Yeah, it's his pride and joy. But I'm not keen on it. I don't like them big and long.'

'That's a relief. I'd hate to feel inadequate.'

'Don't be so rude,' she scolded me, but then dissolved into a fit of giggles. 'I was talking about his car,' she went on when she was able to talk again. 'I prefer small cars. Like that little sports job that followed us into the petrol station yesterday.'

Alarm bells rang in my mind. 'I didn't see a sports car.'

'That's because you were too busy bonding with the forecourt attendant,' she said with a laugh.

'What make of car was it?'

'Sies, man, I didn't notice the make. I just remember it was a lovely green colour.'

'I think you'll find it's called racing-green.'

Chapter 30

Rondebosch, Cape Town, Thursday May 3rd

The house that dominates the Groote Schuur estate has been in existence since the Seventeenth Century, but the original farmhouse was converted into its current magnificent structure by Cecil Rhodes over two hundred years later. The resulting Cape Dutch building, designed by Sir Herbert Baker, sits in the shadow of Table Mountain on the slopes of Devil's Peak.

After the death of Rhodes, Groote Schuur eventually became the official residence of the South African Prime Minister, and in 1984, home of the President.

The gardens surrounding the house were designed to provide an almost year round display of colour, with a host of flowers, including bougainvillea, fuchsias and a world-famous collection of roses. Although it was the beginning of autumn, there were still a lot of vibrant blooms visible as Paul and I drove through the estate to the house.

We had already navigated our way past two heavily guarded barriers and now, as we approached the house itself, we were confronted with a third checkpoint.

'Those crunchies are really taking security seriously,' Paul murmured.

'It's certainly an impressive start,' I agreed softly.

For the third time in less than ten minutes I handed over our passports for inspection. It was a different police sergeant who took the documents from me, but the eyes that studied them did so with the same level of suspicion.

As at the previous two checkpoints, the policeman was flanked by several uniformed cops carrying lethal looking assault rifles. Those boys had been well-trained. Their weapons were pointing at us. They meant business.

Satisfied the sergeant handed back the passes. 'Dankie, meneer,' he said in Afrikaans, before switching to English. 'Brigadier Pienaar is expecting you. He has requested you use the special police parking area to the left of the house. There is a space reserved for you.' He pointed with his hand towards where a handful of police squad cars were parked.

'No problem,' I said as I let out the clutch and headed along the gravel road to the car-park. The sergeant was true to his word. There was an empty space with a yellow and white painted traffic cone stood in front. Attached to the top of the cone hung a sign reading: *Reserved for Major Statton.*

'Major?' Paul queried.

'I have no idea. Perhaps I've been promoted and Disraeli-Astor forgot to tell me.'

'Did you see the car-park on the other side of the house?' Paul asked once we had parked in the allocated space.

'Yeah. There were a lot of cars parked there.'

'Exactly. I thought the meeting was taking place tomorrow.'

'Me too,' I agreed as we got out of the car. 'Perhaps Pienaar will be able to explain. There he is.'

We headed to where the brigadier was standing on the front steps of the house chatting to a group of senior police officers with enough stars on the shoulders of their dress uniforms to start a new galaxy.

'What do you think so far, David?' He asked and then glanced at Paul.

I introduced my friend and then said. 'I'm impressed so far, Alan, but one question. Who do all the cars belong to? I thought the peace talks were tomorrow.'

Pienaar shook his head and grimaced in disgust. 'A break down in communications I am afraid. Until Tuesday that's what I thought, but I was then told that informal talks between Government and the ANC officials were taking place yesterday and today. The final talks will take place tomorrow, when an agreement will be signed committing both parties to work together to bring an end to the current violence and intimidation.'

'Mandela and the other ANC leaders haven't arrived yet?'

'No. They won't be here until tomorrow when the agreement is actually signed.'

'Excuse me for being thick,' Paul said, 'but if both sides already know what is contained in the document, why can't it be signed today?'

Pienaar smiled. 'Don't ask me. I am just a humble policeman. I have never understood the minds of politicians and bureaucrats. I'm sure they know what they are doing,' he added hurriedly.

'Are there any other ways of accessing Groote Schuur, brigadier?' Paul asked.

'There are security fences all around the estate so it should be pretty secure,' Pienaar replied.

'With all due respects, that's not what I asked,' Paul insisted.

Pienaar shrugged. 'I'm not being evasive, Mister Helsdon, and I'm not complacent. However, you must understand that the Groote Schuur grounds are extensive. Inevitably, a determined person could break in if he wanted to.'

'That's what I thought,' Paul said. 'So what steps are you taking to counter that threat?'

'We have set up a cordon of security guards, supplemented by my own men, one hundred metres apart, round the outer perimeter of the grounds. In addition there is another cordon, closer to the house, made up of men from the Special Forces Brigade.'

Paul looked around. 'I saw the guards patrolling the outer fence. However, I didn't notice an inner cordon.'

Pienaar smiled. 'I would be annoyed if they were visible. The Specials are supposed to see, but not be seen.'

'Can we have a look around inside the house?' I asked.

'Of course,' Pienaar said. 'Follow me.' He led us up the steps to the front door, where a soldier wearing the maroon beret of the South African Special Forces Brigade and carrying a Heckler & Koch MP5 sub-machine gun stood. At first the soldier barred our way, but he stepped aside when he recognised the brigadier.

We entered the front door and found ourselves in a spacious entrance hall. Pienaar led us down a corridor towards an ornate set of double-doors. Standing outside the room was another soldier carrying an identical gun to his colleague at the front door.

He too recognised the brigadier and moved to one side as we approached. Pienaar opened the doors without knocking. 'This is the dining room where the meeting is being held.' He led us into a long wood panelled room, down the centre of which ran an ornate dining table surrounded by chairs.

Scattered across the table-top was an assortment of note pads, pencils, glasses and jugs of water. 'They are currently having lunch in the breakfast room,' Pienaar explained.

Paul wandered across to the windows and looked out at the expanse of lawn that lay there. He nodded with satisfaction when he saw there was nowhere in the immediate vicinity where a sniper could hide and fire into the dining room.

In the distance there was a line of trees at the edge of the lawn, but two figures dressed in black uniforms were standing guard at either end. In addition, yet another soldier was positioned directly outside the dining room window, looking across the lawn.

Paul walked over to the large fireplace, with its Zimbabwe soapstone surround. He knelt down and looked up the chimney.

'You won't see anything, Mister Helsdon,' Pienaar said. 'The chimney has been blocked up at the top. We don't want some skollie dropping a grenade down it.'

'I'm impressed,' Paul said,

'I think we have covered all the bases.' Pienaar smiled.

'Is the breakfast room protected like this?' Paul asked?

'Ja,' Pienaar confirmed.

'Are any of the other rooms in the house being used by attendees of the meeting?' I asked.

'Ja, the study, which is being used when one side or the other wants to discuss something in private. However, it has no windows and the chimney has been blocked up also, so the room is not susceptible to an outside attack.'

'Where will Mandela and De Klerk sign the agreement?'

'In here,' Pienaar explained. 'The signing will be in private and then there will be a photo-shoot with all the other delegates on the steps outside the house.'

'And how will the ANC leaders arrive?' Paul asked.

'In a convoy of cars, accompanied by police motorcycle outriders,' Pienaar answered. 'By the way, I have something for you.' He took two cards from his pocket and handed one to each of us. 'Passes. You will need these tomorrow.'

I glanced down at my pass and saw it was made out to Major Statton. 'What's with the Major Statton? Is there something you're not telling me?'

Pienaar smiled. 'Don't worry. There's nothing untoward going on. I did it to help you. My men are simple souls. If they believe you are a major they will treat you with far more respect than if you were a civilian.'

'Then Major Statton, it shall be.' I slipped the pass in my pocket.

'Any other questions?' Pienaar asked.

'Yeah. Why don't I have a rank?' Paul waved his pass in the air. 'Don't I deserve a little respect?' He tried to sound affronted, but didn't put much effort into his protest.

'It's not necessary, Mister Helsdon, because you'll be accompanying Major Statton. One ranking officer will be more than enough to ensure respect for both of you. Anything else?'

'Nope,' Paul said.

Pienaar looked at me.

'One more thing,' I said. 'Have there been any sightings of Shaun Brannagan yet?'

'I'm afraid not,' the policeman said. 'But I'm confident he will be spotted if he's still in our area.'

'He's in the area alright. I can sense it.'

'In that case, we will catch him. Don't worry. There is a general alert across the region and all my men have been issued with his description, including his William Butler disguise.'

'That's as maybe, but I won't stop worrying until that tricky bastard is safely locked up in Pollsmoor Prison.'

Noordhoek, Cape Town

It was dusk when we arrived at Noordhoek and the beach car-park was empty when we parked the detector van in the same place as on our previous visit. Now Paul and I sat in the back of the detector van with headphones on.

Every so often one or other of us looked out of the window to ensure that we were not being observed, but we had nothing to worry about. The Noordhoek beach car-park remained deserted and we would have noticed the arrival of any other vehicle because it was now in complete darkness.

There were no other vehicles to be seen and what would eventually turn out to be a full moon was still only a sliver of silver rising from the depths of the Atlantic Ocean.

'Anything?' Paul asked.

'Nothing but static.'

'Bollocks! Me neither.' He twisted a few knobs on the control box in front of him, but this made no difference to the sound coming through my headphones. The static was still static.

'It looks as if we might have to check out the bugs,' I said.

'I hope not. It won't be as easy as last time.'

'That, my friend, is what's called stating the bleeding obvious. There will be guards crawling all over the place, which means we won't be able to use torches. I don't relish trying to navigate our way through the woods without a light.'

'We might not have a choice.'

'Let's give it another half an hour,' I suggested. 'If we do have to go in, it won't be any more dangerous then, than it is now.'

We sat and waited, listening to the hiss of static in our headphones and glancing occasionally at our watches.

'By the way,' I said eventually. 'Freddie has asked me to move in with her.'

'Are you joshing me?'

'No. It means moving out of your place. Do you mind?'

'Hell, man, of course not. Does this mean you guys are getting back together?'

'I'm not sure we've reached that stage yet. But, we saw a lot of each other while you were in Durban, so it seems sensible to stay at her apartment rather than keep travelling to and from Claremont.'

He grinned at me. 'You're getting back together, only you won't admit it.'

I was about to deny his allegation when there was a clicking noise in my headphones. I touched Paul's arm.

'I hear it,' he whispered.

'Somebody is unlocking the door,' I whispered back.

'Yeah.'

There was a creaking sound as the door to the conference centre opened and another click as somebody switched on the lights. This was followed by footsteps walking across the wooden floor and what sounded like the rattle of glasses.

Paul raised both thumbs in the air. 'Sounds like somebody has put a tray of glasses on the table,' he said in a low voice.

'That's what I think,' I agreed.

'Not that it matters what they're doing,' he whispered. 'The important thing is that the bugs are working perfectly.'

'Good work, Paul.'

'Thank you, boss.'

'All ready for our listening session on Saturday,' I said softly.

'I hope so, but I think I'll come back tomorrow evening just to double check.'

'Do you want me to come?' I asked.

'No, but I'll contact you if there is a problem,' he said, still whispering. 'You just get that gal of yours to sort us out some sandwiches for our Saturday session and I'll get some beers from the bottle shop.'

'Sounds a good deal to me,' I agreed. 'Now let's get out of this place.'

'I'll Roger that,' he murmured.

'Paul?'

'Yes?'

'Why are we whispering?'

'Sies, man. Buggered if I know!' He laughed loudly as he closed down the listening equipment. 'Nobody can hear us.'

Chapter 31

We finished the week the way we started it; honouring dead friends. In this case it was Johan Carlse.

It was still early when we arrived in Ocean View and the sun was just rising above the Kommetjie skyline. Our early start was because Freddie had an important meeting later that morning.

The time suited me. Later that morning I was visiting Groote Schuur with Paul to witness the signing of an agreement between F.W. De Klerk and Nelson Mandela that was destined to change the future of South Africa.

I had only visited the coloured township of Ocean View once before. That was on the night I met Freddie's father for the first time. Johan was already half-drunk by the time I arrived at his house and as the evening wore on he finished the job.

I met Freddie for the first time that night as well. Her father introduced her as his intermediary, who would liaise with me. He then proceeded to fall asleep and she had to help him to his bed.

Johan had promised to take Freddie home that night, but, because he was already in a drunken sleep, it eventually fell on me to drive her to her apartment in Wynberg. That was the start of our relationship.

Now, that evening, eight years before, came back to me as Freddie drove me in her Mini Cooper through the coloured township of Ocean View, which is located a couple of miles south of Noordhoek.

The roads in the township had been laid out in a grid style and the houses that lined them were small, identical buildings with little room for individuality.

'Isn't that where your father lived?' I pointed to a house whose front garden was cemented over to create a parking space.'

'You have a good memory.' She slowed down to allow me to get a better look. 'The last time you visited was at night and it was pitch black.'

'I see they have installed street lights,' I said.

'Only a few, in some roads. They did that a couple of years back.

Long after papa died,' she explained as she drove on.

The cemetery was at the far end of the township, nestling in the foothills of the northern end of the Swartkopberg mountain range. It was surrounded by graffiti covered, cement-panelled walls.

Running along the top of the walls were inwards sloping three-strand barbed wire fences. Set into the wall were a pair of metal gates, which were also topped with barbed wire.

There was no car-park in the cemetery so Freddie parked her car in the road outside. When we got out of the car, she took two bunches of flowers from the back seat. She locked the car and we made our way through the gate on foot.

We walked along the tarmac drive for a couple of hundred yards and then veered off across the grass, weaving our way between the graves until we reached the far end of the cemetery.

Her father's grave stood in the shade of a giant milkwood tree. It was one of the better maintained in the line of graves that made up that part of the cemetery. The grass had been neatly cut and large shiny pebbles had been used to mark out the outline of Johan Carlse last resting place.

Most of the graves had a simple cross as a memorial and some had marble headstones. Carlse's grave had neither, instead a black painted anchor had been positioned at its head, with its crown sunk into a cement block. A plaque had been attached to the anchor where its stock joined its shank. It was inscribed with the names of Freddie's parents and the dates of their respective births and deaths.

Freddie laid her flowers on the ground alongside the grave. 'Although Papa was baptised a Christian, he was never very religious, but after the death of my brother and mother, he refused to believe in the existence of any God.' This explained the absence of a cross or any other religious symbol on his memorial.

Attached by wire to the bottom of the anchor were two large metal vases, one on either fluke. Each vase contained a bunch of flowers. Although the blooms were wilted and losing their petals, they didn't appear to have been there long.

Freddie read my mind. 'One of Andre's drivers lives in Ocean View. I pay his wife to replace the flowers once a month.' She removed the dead flowers from the vases and handed them to me. 'Can you take those to the bin over there?' She pointed to a white building at the end of the tarmac drive. 'Next to the bin is a tap and a watering-can. Bring some water back with you.'

'I'm on my way,' I replied as she bent down and picked up the fresh bunches of flowers. By the time I returned with a full watering-can she had arranged the new blooms in the vases.

'Thanks.' She took the watering-can from me and poured water into both vases. Finished, she stood with her head bowed. She was crying.

I took the watering-can from her and placed it on the ground. I gently put my arm round her shoulders. She turned, threw both arms around me and buried her head in my chest. She sobbed silently.

'Oh, David, I've missed you so much,' she said between sobs. 'There have been so many times when I needed a hug and you weren't there to comfort me.'

'I'm here now,' I said softly.

She looked up at me and smiled. 'That makes everything so much better.' She hugged me tighter and then looked at her watch. 'But I need to get to work and you wanted me to drop you off at Paul's first.'

We made our way back to the car and she didn't glance back once at her father's grave. I decided that was progress of sorts.

Rondebosch, Cape Town
Security at Groote Schuur was tighter than when we had visited the previous day and it was more noticeable. The invisible inner security cordon had been reinforced with three large police personnel carriers fitted with heavy machine guns and manned by a couple of dozen armed policemen wearing body armour.

We used the security passes Pienaar gave us to make our way through the three security cordons. However, when we reached the front door of the house our way was blocked by the same SADF Special Forces soldier who had guarded it on our last visit.

The guard nodded to welcome us and acknowledge that he recognised us as we flashed our passes at him, but he didn't step aside. 'Sorry, Major Statton,' he said to me. 'Those passes are only valid in the grounds. You are not allowed in the house unaccompanied.'

'Well done! Excellent work, soldier,' I tried to sound like a British Army major. 'Can you contact Brigadier Pienaar?'

'Of course, sir.' He pulled a two-way radio from inside his flack-jacket, turned away and spoke rapidly in Afrikaans into the mouthpiece of the handset. A tinny voice answered in response. It didn't sound like Pienaar, but then it didn't sound like any human being. However, the guard seemed to understand because he nodded and then turned back to us. 'The Brigadier will be with you shortly, sir.'

Two minutes later Alan Pienaar joined us. He was dressed in a suit, the jacket of which was stretched a little too tightly across his barrel chest. 'Good morning, gentlemen,' he greeted us with a somewhat harassed smile. 'Your timing could not be better. You have arrived just as the agreement is about to be signed. If you follow me, you will be able to witness this very historic event.'

When we arrived in the meeting room, it was full of people. Unlike the day before, every seat at the table was taken and there were people standing two deep against the wall.

As we eased our way silently into the room, the State President, F.W. De Klerk, was speaking. 'Thank you, gentlemen,' he said in his soft voice. 'I am delighted that we have finally reached an agreement that will start the process of dismantling the current Apartheid system and allow all of our people to unite as equal citizens of our nation.'

'Amen to that, Mister President,' Nelson Mandela said with a smile.

De Klerk returned his smile and then said: 'And so, all it remains for us to do, Mister Mandela, is to sign the minute that sets out what we have agreed over the past few days.'

An official standing behind the President placed a leather folder in front of him, which he opened to reveal a single sheet of paper.

'To avoid any doubt or misunderstanding I will read out the minute,' De Klerk said as he picked up the sheet of paper. He looked around the unnaturally still room. The air of expectation was tangible.

I too looked around the room and made eye contact with a tall man standing in front of the window, but he looked away quickly.

'The Government and the African National Congress agree...' De Klerk began to read, '...on a common commitment towards the resolution of the existing climate of violence and intimidation from whatever quarter as well as a commitment to stability and to a peaceful process of negotiations ...'

I studied the man by the window. He was young, with broad shoulders and the distinctive open face of somebody from Afrikaner farming stock. There was something familiar about him, but I couldn't put my finger on what it was.

'Flowing from this commitment, the following was agreed upon,' De Klerk read. He glanced up at Mandela, who was sitting opposite him.

The black African nodded his encouragement. His face was immobile and I wondered what was going on in his mind. He was witnessing an event he must have hoped would take place, but probably never believed would happen.

'One. The establishment of a working group to make recommendations on a definition of political offences in the South African situation; to discuss, in this regard, time scales...'

I listened as De Klerk resumed his reading of the minute, but continued to watch the man by the window out of the corner of my eye. I saw him glance at me surreptitiously, but when I turned my head, he quickly looked away again and patted his pocket as if checking something was still there.

I stiffened. Paul had loaned me one of his pistols and I wore it in a holster under my arm. I discreetly slipped my hand inside my jacket and made sure the weapon was easily accessible. It was.

De Klerk was still reading. He had reached the last of the five objectives set out in the agreement.

'...Efficient channels of communication between the government and the ANC will be established in order to curb violence and intimidation from whatever quarter effectively.

'Finally, the government and the ANC agree that the objectives contained in this minute should be achieved as early as possible,' De Klerk finished with a flourish and then, without further ado, he signed what was to become known as the Groote Schuur Minute.

He passed the leather folder to the official who took it round to the other side of the table and laid it in front of Mandela. The ANC leader added his signature to the document before it was whisked away for safe keeping in the library of the South African Parliament.

'Gentlemen. That document represents the future of our nation,' F.W. De Klerk said in a sombre voice.

'A rainbow nation,' Mandela added.

'Ja. A rainbow nation,' De Klerk agreed, raising his voice to he heard above the loud and enthusiastic applause that greeted Mandela's words.

I didn't applaud. I was too busy watching the young guy by the window and I didn't start to relax until Alan Pienaar ushered De Klerk and Mandela out of the room. They were followed by a line of other attendees. Paul and I stood back to let the queue pass.

'What's wrong with you?' Paul whispered.

'What do you mean?' I asked.

'Sies, man, you're like the proverbial cat on a hot tin roof.'

'How so?'

'You keep checking your gun.'

Bang goes my efforts to be discreet, I thought. I should have guessed my friend would notice. 'I checked it only once,' I insisted.

'Why?' Paul asked.

'Goeie more, meneer,' a voice said. It was the young man from the window.

'Good morning,' I replied.

The youngster smiled at me shyly. 'You probably don't recognise me. I met you in the car-park when you visited Central Police Station and I took you up to the Brigadier's office.'

So, the young policeman with the grunt did have a voice after all. I smiled at him. 'I remember. You had a uniform on that day,' I pointed out.

He smiled back. 'Ja. I'm on plain-clothes duty today.' He seemed proud of this. 'The Brigadier didn't want any uniformed officers in the room while the signing was taking place, but it feels odd wearing a suit.' He patted his jacket pocket again. 'I miss a gun on my hip,' he said with a shrug. 'Well, I'd better go find my boss.' With that, he bid his farewell and followed the last of the attendees out of the room.

'So, why *did* you check your pistol?' Paul asked again as we headed for the door.

'It doesn't matter,' I replied.

Claremont

Paul dropped me off at Freddie's apartment in Claremont. She was still at work, but I knew she would not mind me using her telephone to ring London to speak to Disraeli-Astor.

It was over a week since I had last spoken to Colleen. On that occasion she had sounded subdued and distracted, which I put down to her being upset that Roland Lafarge had been rushed to hospital, but today she was back to her usual cheerful self.

'David? Is that really you?' She asked.

'Well it was definitely my face looking back at me in the shaving mirror this morning,' I said. 'And my voice sounds the same to me. How does it sound to you?'

'Actually, it sounds rather good,' Colleen said softly. 'I've missed your voice and I've missed you.'

Her words made me feel guilty again. 'How's Roly?' I turned the conversation away from a subject I didn't want to pursue.

'He's much better, but Dizz has placed him on gardening leave.'

'Gardening leave? That's a good move,' I said.

'It's not like you to be complimentary.'

'It wasn't a compliment, Colleen. It's called satire.'

'I don't get it,' she said in a puzzled voice.

'Then you have more in common with your boss than I thought.'

'I still don't get it.'

'Roly doesn't even have a window box in his apartment.'

'I see. So, it was sarcasm rather than satire,' she pointed out correctly, then added: 'I see your stay in South Africa hasn't changed you.'

'No, thank God. In fact my trip has been a bonus. Good food, good wine, sunshine and a healthy dose of cynicism. What more could I ask for?'

'I can think of at least one thing,' she replied suggestively.

I tried to laugh it off. 'I don't know what you mean. Now, perhaps you would like to put me through to the Director-General.'

'Spoil sport,' she whispered, before putting me on hold.

'Where the hell have you been?' Disraeli-Astor asked without preamble when he came on the line. 'You were supposed to be keeping me informed of progress.'

'That's what I'm doing now,' I said.

'Well, it's not good enough. This is your first call for over a week.'

'That's because I had nothing to report for over a week.'

'Well you've been too quiet for my liking. I suppose you've been sunning yourself on the beach.'

'Don't equate my silence with a lack of work. As for sunning myself, have you any idea what autumn weather in the Cape is like?'

'So what have you got to report now?' He side-stepped my question, which was answer enough.

'A few things. The first is that the police have had no luck finding Brannagan, however, I think I'm being followed.'

'By him?'

'I don't know.'

'Who else could it be?'

'I'd put my money on Jonathan Rhodes.'

'Ah, yes. The South African.'

'That's right.'

'What makes you think it's him?'

I explained about the racing-green Porsche I thought had been tailing me, although I didn't mention that Freddie had seen it too. In fact, I didn't mention her at all.

'Well watch your back, Statton. I don't want you being killed. The department can't afford another funeral.'

I hoped he was joking, but I didn't hear him laugh.

'So what else do you have?' He asked.

'Well, yesterday Paul Helsdon and I checked out the listening devices we planted in the conference centre at the Mountainside Reserve Hotel. They were working perfectly.'

'What if they're discovered today?' He asked. It was a good question, which reminded me that my boss was not totally stupid.

'Paul is going to check the bugs again tonight. If there's a problem we'll still have time to activate Plan B.'

'Which is?'

'I don't know, we haven't worked one out yet, but we'll think of something.'

Disraeli-Astor didn't respond to this news, instead he fell silent and I could picture him sitting behind his big desk fiddling with the expensive executive toy his wife bought him for his birthday. It was one of those perpetual motion things and it looked like a miniature solar system. He said it helped him to think.

I'm not sure why, because he hadn't yet worked out how to make the top circular section spin properly. He'd been trying for weeks to keep it going for longer than a few seconds without success and he stubbornly refused to let anybody interfere.

He was so determined to sort the damn thing out himself, I didn't have the heart to tell him that all the toy needed was a battery in its base to power the magnet that made it work.

Anyway, it was keeping him quiet now, so I took the opportunity to tell him about the ceremony I had just witnessed at Groote Schuur. His reaction was one of disinterest. He seemed not to understand the historic significance of the document that had just been signed by President De Klerk and Nelson Mandela.

'So, Mandela is safe then?' Was all he could think to ask.

'Yes,' I confirmed with a resigned sigh. 'The South Africans know how to do security. Short of parking tanks in the grounds of Groote Schuur, there was little more Pienaar could have done to protect Mandela and his ANC colleagues.'

'What's your next step?' He asked.

'On the assumption that the bugs are still working, we will be spending tomorrow cramped in a van, monitoring the Phoenix Group, their partners in the Broederbond and the PAC.'

'My heart bleeds for you. At least you will be under cover. When I was in the Falklands I spent a whole day,' he paused for effect, *'twenty-four hours,'* he emphasised, as if I didn't know how long a day was, 'with my company, lying in mud in the pouring rain. We were waiting for a signal from brigade to launch an attack on an Argie battalion. You ought to try it some time.'

My boss's attitude didn't surprise me. He would never change. He was an ex-soldier who believed that everybody should at some time have to experience the deprivations he experienced during his service years.

I couldn't be bothered to point out that during my time working for the department, I had suffered similar hardship on a number of occasions. Instead I said: 'If you don't mind, I'd rather not. I think I'll stick with the van. At least I won't freeze to death and put you to the inconvenience of having to attend my funeral.'

'Who says I would attend?' Disraeli-Astor said lightly.

He was probably joking, but I was not amused. The thought he hadn't bothered to attend Timmy's funeral still rankled with me.

'That's true. You usually get somebody else to represent you,' I replied, then before he could respond I added: 'I'll contact you again on Monday, sir.'

With that I put the phone down on him and left him to play with his executive toy.

Claremont

When Freddie came home from work I could see she was still upset. I gave her a hug and stopped her from taking off her coat.

'Leave it on. No cooking for you tonight, my girl, I'm taking you out for a meal.'

She hugged me back. 'Are you ordering me about?'

'Yeah.' I grinned.

'Well, you know how I feel about that,' she said sternly, but she smiled and her face lit up. 'However, on this occasion I'll let you get away with it.'

So we went to The Garden Restaurant in Constantia. I had managed to book the same table we used before. It was tucked away in one corner of the restaurant and was cosy and intimate. It was just what we needed.

I had already pre-ordered a bottle of gewürztraminer and it was waiting for us in the ice bucket that was standing beside our table when we took our seats.

We were escorted to our table by the same waiter in the pink pants who had served us on our first visit. 'Shall I pour wine for sir and madam?' He asked as he went to hand me a menu.

'Yes please, but I won't need a menu. I already know what I want to order.'

'Very good, sir,' the waiter said as he lifted the gewürztraminer from the bucket and expertly removed the cork almost in the same movement.

'I'm going to have the same as last time,' I told Freddie. 'What about you?'

'Me too,' she said.

'So that will be calamari and lobster Thermidor for madam, and moules marinière and tartare of Wagyu beef for sir?' Pink pants said as he poured some wine for me to taste. It was excellent and I told him so.

Freddie clapped her hands softly in delight. 'What a memory you have,' she told the waiter as he filled her glass.

Pink pants preened himself at her words and offered her an extravagant bow. He poured my wine with a wide smile on his face and disappeared towards the kitchen, writing our order on his pad as he went.

'Thank you for bringing me here, Dave. It's just what I needed.'

'I thought you might like to talk about your father. Perhaps remember the good times.'

'Yes, I'd like that.'

So we sat, drank wine, ate and chatted away the evening. By the time we drove home she was much happier and when we went to bed she pulled me to her.

'Will you take me home with you?' She asked in a small voice.

'Back to the UK?'

'Yeah.'

'Are you sure that's what you want?'

'I'm sure.'

'But won't you miss your family?'

'Yeah. I love them dearly, but not as much as I love you.'

I hugged her tightly. 'But what about the cold weather?'

'Are you trying to put me off? Don't you want me to come with you?'

'Of course I want you with me. I was just pointing out the obvious. It was you who couldn't handle the British weather. I don't want you leaving me when the winter chill sets in.'

'I won't ever leave you again, Dave,' she assured me.

'And the snow and ice?'

'I'll buy myself some new warm winter clothes. It will be a good excuse to go shopping. Will you come with me?'

'Happy to, but I won't be able to make it tomorrow. Paul and I have to spend some time in Noordhoek.'

'Tomorrow's out for me too. I have to work. How are you fixed on Sunday?'

'Are the shops open on a Sunday?'

'Yeah. In the city anyway.'

'Then Sunday it is.'

'Can we take your car? It has a larger boot than my Mini.'

'What's it worth?' I asked.

'This.' She wormed her way down in the bed, so that her head was level with my groin, she started to kiss me.

I ran my fingers through her hair. 'Do your worst, wench. I'm easily bought.'

Chapter 32

Noordhoek, Cape Peninsula, Saturday May 5th

When Paul picked me up from Freddie's apartment to take me to Noordhoek, the big South African reported that the listening devices were working when he checked them the previous evening.

The Phoenix Group meeting was scheduled to start at 11 am, but Paul and I were in position an hour earlier. As soon as we arrived at the car-park, we switched on our wireless equipment. The bugs were obviously working still, because the sound of last minute preparations in the conference centre could be heard clearly.

I gave Paul a thumb up and took off my headphones.

He followed suit. 'So far, so good,' he said.

We were concerned somebody might notice the aerial on the van's roof, so Paul concealed it by fitting a roof rack, holding wide colourful surfboards on either side. This camouflage had led to another concern, which was whether the dish would pick up the signal properly, but we need not have worried, because reception was excellent.

There were half a dozen other vehicles in the car-park, several also with surfboards strapped to their roofs. We were safe from any prying eyes, because our van had smoked glass windows, which allowed us to see out, without anybody being able to look in. In addition, there was a partition between the driver's cab and the main section where the equipment was installed. To all intents and purposes, we were invisible.

From where we were parked, I looked out across Noordhoek beach and watched the breakers turn the surface of the sea into foam, which was coloured grey by the van's windows. Several people walked past our van, but nobody gave it a second glance.

A line of horse riders came slowly across my vision as they made their way down the track leading from the nearby stables and out onto the beach. One by one, they spurred their mounts into a canter and headed off across the sand.

'I'm thinking of leaving the department,' I said.

He looked at me as if thunderstruck. 'Sies, man. Why?'

'It's Freddie.'

'What's wrong with her?'

'Nothing, except she wants to return to the UK with me.'

'Hey, man, but that's great!'

'I'm not so sure.'

'Why the doubts?'

'Because I don't think she'll be happy in London.'

'Why not? At least you'll be together.'

'I know, but she'll miss South Africa.'

'How do you know? Have you asked her?'

'There's no point. I know Freddie too well. She'll insist she doesn't mind leaving Cape Town.'

'Ag, man, what's the problem?'

'The problem is she'll only be trying to please me.' I looked at him. 'I don't want that, Paul.'

'So, what are you going to do?'

'I'll let her join me in London, see out this Mandela Project assignment, however long it takes, and then resign.'

'What will you do then?'

'We'll come back to South Africa and settle down here.'

Paul stared at me. 'Sies, man. Are you serious?'

'Deadly serious. However, I haven't discussed it with Freddie yet, so keep it to yourself for now.'

'No problem, you can trust me to keep my mouth shut.'

I said nothing. He was right. I could trust him.

'Tell you what, Dave. I've a proposal for you.'

'What's that?'

'If you guys do come back to SA, why don't you become my partner? I need somebody like you to help me grow the company.'

'Thanks, Paul. If that's a genuine offer, I'd be delighted to accept.'

'Ag, man, it's a genuine offer alright.' He held out a hand. 'Let's shake on it.'

I took his hand and shook it warmly.

Paul glanced at his watch. 'It's almost time.' He reached down to a cool-box that stood on the floor next to his seat and pulled out a couple of Castle lagers. 'But we have time for a quick beer. Let's drink to our future partnership.'

I took the proffered beer and we clinked the necks of our bottles together.

'Here's to the future!' He raised his bottle.

'Let's see how things pan out first,' I said cautiously. 'This Mandela business might drag on for years.'

'Sies, man! I bloody well hope not!'

The sun was shining down from a cloudless blue sky and the temperature was beginning to rise inside the cramped van. We both took a long drink of our cold beer. A few moments later we put our headphones back on and Paul turned up the volume on the receiver.

We were only just in time. Seconds later the meeting started.

The first voice had a distinctive Texan drawl. 'It's good to see so many of my Phoenix Group friends here today. I would like to welcome y'all to South Africa.'

There was a slight pause.

'Can I also welcome our colleagues from the Broederbond and the Pan Africanist Congress who are joining us for today's meeting.'

Another pause.

'Now, for the benefit of our South African guests, I suggest we begin by introducing ourselves. Let me start the ball rolling: My name is John D Engels and I am Chairman of the Phoenix Group.'

The attendees then introduced themselves one by one. When it was the turn of the representatives from the Broederbond and the Pan Africanist Congress the only person of whom I had heard was Edward Bhengu, one of the founding members of the PAC. Once the introductions were over, the meeting started in earnest.

Engels began by reporting several apologies for absence from members of the Phoenix Group, including Sir Reginald Wren. There were no apologies from the other two organisations.

The American had a quiet, measured manner, however, when he moved onto the next item a hint of concern tinged his voice. 'Gentlemen, it falls on me to report some breaking news.'

There was another pause, this time longer than the first. I imagined Engels looking around the room to ensure he had the attention of all the delegates.

'Y'all should know that President De Klerk has just announced the South African government and the ANC yesterday signed a document they are calling the Groote Schuur Minute.'

I plainly heard an intake of breath.

'For those who do not know, Groote Schuur is the official

residence of the South African President. De Klerk made clear during his announcement that the agreement is the first step towards an election at which all races in the country will be able to vote. There is little doubt those elections will be won by the ANC.'

There was a sudden burst of hubbub in the background as delegates digested and reacted to Engels' statement.

'Gentlemen! Gentlemen!' the American raised his voice and the hubbub slowly subsided. 'I share your concern, but it was in anticipation of an ANC government that we formed the Phoenix Group in the first place, so we all knew this was likely to happen sometime. This announcement should come as no surprise.'

There were a few murmurs of agreement.

'However, it was surprising we were given no warning of the Groote Schuur meeting. A key to our plans to prevent the ANC from taking control of South Africa is to take out its leaders. If we had been told a ceremony was taking place yesterday, we could have worked out a way of achieving that important task then.'

Engels paused and when he spoke again there was a hard edge to his voice. 'When we invited our South African friends to work with us, we were assured by them they had excellent intelligence sources. Perhaps they would like to explain why those sources failed to warn us about yesterday's ceremony. What about it guys?'

There was another silence, when all I could hear through my headphones was the hiss of static. I glanced over at Paul and frowned. I was about to ask what was wrong with the equipment when the leader of the Broederbond delegation, Schalk Van de Merwe, spoke up.

'Meneer Engels, I am deeply embarrassed to admit this, but the truth is we knew nothing about the meeting at Groot Schuur.' Van de Merwe spoke in heavily accented English.

'But why didn't y'all know what was going on?' Engels asked. 'I thought your outfit had the cops sewn up?'

There was another silence before Van de Merwe spoke again. I imagined the Broederbond leader's look of discomfiture as he prepared to answer the question.

'That used to be the case, Mister Engels,' he eventually said. 'But things have changed.'

'In what way?'

'Unfortunately, we have fewer friends in the police,' Van de

Merwe explained. 'Although the Broederbond has considerable support amongst junior ranks, important intelligence came from senior police officers. Sadly the flow of information from that source has all but dried up.'

'Why is that?' Engels asked.

'Because they had the riot act read to them by the Minister of Law and Order, Adriaan Vlok.'

'I've heard of him,' Engels said. 'He's supposed to be one tough cookie.'

'Ja. Vlok frightened most of our best sources into silence and the few officers who refused to be cowed by him were summarily dismissed and replaced by supporters of De Klerk.'

There was yet another silence before Van de Merwe spoke again: 'But it would not have helped even if we had known in advance about the meeting. Security at Groote Schuur is tight, so there is no way we would have been able to eliminate the ANC leaders during the signing ceremony.'

'I'm sorry, but I do not accept "no way". In my experience there is always a way. It is all about will, means and knowledge.' Engels said. 'The Phoenix Group has the will and the means, but we were relying on you to provide us with the knowledge.'

This admonishment led to another silence, eventually broken by Van de Merwe. 'I can only apologise for our failure,' he said. 'However, if it is any consolation, we do have a little good news to report. However, I will leave my PAC colleague, Edward Bhengu, to tell you about that.'

'Mister Bhengu? What do you have for us?' Engels asked.

'As you will recall, Mister Chairman, for many months the PAC operations were being hampered by police activity,' Edward Bhengu intoned in a deep African voice. 'The authorities always seemed to be one step ahead of us and knew in advance what we were planning. We now know why. We had a spy in our ranks.'

'A spy? Have you been able to identify the bounder?' Asked a new voice. Because of its pronounced accent, I guessed it belonged to the Indian member of the Phoenix Group, Sunil Patel.

'Yes, his name was Anthony Sibeko and he was feeding information to the ANC jackals, who in turn were passing the information onto their Government puppet masters.'

'Who is this Sibeko fellow?' Patel asked.

'He was the relative of another traitor to our cause. His cousin was David Sibeko, who was executed eleven years ago.'

'You twice referred to the spy in the past tense,' Patel said. 'Why was that?'

'Because three days ago we dealt with comrade Sibeko. He will never betray us again.'

'Is it possible there are more spies in your organisation?' Engels asked sharply.

Bhengu didn't answer immediately and when he did it was in an apologetic voice: 'We think Sibeko was working alone. However, we have no way of knowing for sure.'

'Your lack of knowledge is hardly reassuring,' Engels said.

'I can understand your concern, Mister Chairman,' Bhengu said. 'However, I hope you will be reassured to learn we are restricting decision-making to trusted comrades in our top leadership team.'

'The Chairman might be reassured, Mister Bhengu, but I'm not.' This comment was delivered by a voice with a distinct South African accent. I guessed the speaker was Jonathan Rhodes. 'The loyalty record at the top of the PAC is not an auspicious one. Presumably you thought David Sibeko was trustworthy and look what happened to him.'

'As I said earlier, Mister Rhodes, Comrade Sibeko was a traitor. None of our current leaders is like him,' Bhengu insisted defensively.

'But surely Anthony Sibeko was also in your leadership team. Rhodes pointed out. 'And he was a traitor like his cousin.'

'There is little point wasting precious time on a problem our friends in the PAC have already resolved, Jonathan,' Engels interjected, bringing the spat to an end. 'Such things can happen to anybody. As you know, not that long ago, my own company was infiltrated by a spy who chose to meddle in our business.'

'A spy wouldn't last long in any of my companies,' Rhodes insisted.

'Nor did he last long in mine,' Engels pointed out. 'I had the CIA agent eliminated as soon as his presence was discovered.'

There was another pause, but Rhodes did not respond.

It was Engels who broke the silence. 'However, let's set aside the issue of spies and address the substantive issue,' he said.

Now Rhodes spoke up again. 'And what issue is that, JD?'

'A simple one. We in the Phoenix Group must now accept that

385

our South African colleagues have major internal problems and probably will not be able to provide us with any useful information. That makes even more important the intelligence gathered by our other sources.'

'Are we still receiving information?' Rhodes asked.

'We are indeed,' Engels said. 'In fact, one of our contacts has come up trumps yet again. As y'all know, Sir Reginald Wren usually gives a report about what is happening in London, but business commitments prevented him joining us today.

'However, Sir Reginald briefed our good friend Brendan O'Leary, who will give an update in his absence. Now, in handing the floor to Brendan, can I say how wonderful it is to see him back with us after his recent illness.'

'It takes more than a heart attack to keep a good Irishman down, JD,' O'Leary said.

'I'm delighted to hear it, Brendan,' Engels said. 'Now, perhaps you would update us on the news from London.'

'No problem,' the Irishman said. 'Gentlemen, I can report one of our contacts found out that Nelson Mandela is to make a speech in the British Parliament later this month.'

'That's very interesting,' a new voice joined the discussion, 'but what does it mean?'

'Sir Reginald and I believe it could provide us with an ideal opportunity to assassinate him, Maurice,' O'Leary said, identifying the speaker as Maurice Sevier, one of two Frenchmen present.

'Is that feasible?' Sevier asked. 'Surely security will be so tight that nobody will be able to get close to Mandela?'

'As I told Schalk earlier, Maurice, there is always a way,' Engels replied. 'But perhaps it would be better to let Brendan explain the situation.'

'JD is right, Maurice,' O'Leary said. 'It's definitely feasible. Security at the Palace of Westminster is surprisingly lax.'

'I can vouch for that,' Engels chipped in. 'The Brits have this quaint notion that the public should have easy access to Parliament so they can lobby their representatives. It's complete madness, but it does mean that people are coming and going all the time.'

'It would never happen in France,' Sevier said. 'We have much more respect for the privacy of our politicians.'

'The lack of security at Westminster suits us,' Engels said. 'It means that targeting Mandela during his visit to Parliament will be even easier than trying to take him out here in South Africa, where he is better protected. Isn't that so, Brendan?'

'To be sure, JD, to be sure,' O'Leary agreed. 'Sir Reggie and I think a single assassin, working alone, will be able to breech easily what limited security there is on the Parliamentary estate. Obviously that person would have to be an expert but as you know, we have such a man available to us.'

'Shaun Brannagan?' Sevier asked.

'Yes.' It was Engels who confirmed this. 'Brannagan would be perfect. He is fearless. We just need to point him in the right direction and let him loose.'

There were a few murmurs of assent.

'But first, we have another little problem that needs to be addressed,' Engels went on. 'Something must be done about the British Secret Service agent.'

Paul pointed at me and raised an eyebrow. I shrugged.

'We have received information that David Statton is in South Africa and becoming a nuisance,' Engels was saying. 'He poses a big threat to our plans and must be neutralised.'

'How will such a satisfactory solution be achieved?' Sunil Patel asked.

'Don't worry, my friend. That is in hand,' Engels replied. 'Shaun Brannagan is in Cape Town already and is working closely with Mister Rhodes. Is that not so, Jonathan?'

'Yes. We're on Statton's case and he will not be a nuisance for very much longer,' Rhodes said. 'We know where he's holed up and we're going to deal with him.'

'But what if your plan to kill this fine fellow Statton fails?' Patel asked.

'We will not fail,' Rhodes said emphatically.

'That is reassuring, Jonathan,' Engels said. 'Mandela's visit to the British Parliament is our best chance of totalling him. We cannot let anything stand in the way of this opportunity, including Statton. When and where he is taken out of the game is irrelevant, just so long as it happens.'

'It will happen,' Rhodes said simply. 'One way or another.'

'In that case, I propose we instruct Brannagan to start planning to assassinate Mandela in London next month.' He paused and then added: 'All those in favour, please show.'

There was a moment's silence after which Engels said: 'Thank you, gentlemen. That is agreed unanimously. So, Jonathan, it's over to you and our Irish friend to get the Brit out of our hair.'

Paul touched my arm. 'They are out to get you, man.'

'That's the story of my life. In my line of work there's always someone, somewhere out to get you.'

'Well, you'd better watch your bloody back.'

'I'll be going home in a couple of days.'

'A lot can happen in two days.'

'Don't worry. I'll be careful during the rest of my stay in SA,' I assured him, before settling back to listen to the rest of the meeting. It consisted of a lengthy discussion about what would happen once Mandela was out of the way and how the Broederbond and PAC planned to overthrow the current Nationalist government.

It all sounded a bit far-fetched to me, but then so had the suggestion, mooted only a couple of years before, that the Soviet Union was about to break up and the Berlin Wall would fall. I had been wrong then and I could be wrong again.

Two hours later Engels closed the meeting with a warning: 'Gentlemen, we are now at a crucial stage in our plans. Once we are rid of Mandela, I am confident we will succeed.' He paused, before adding: 'But, gentlemen, we cannot be complacent. It is important our discussions here today do not go beyond these four walls. There have been too many leaks already. If we discover any more traitors they will be dealt with immediately.'

Alleluia to that, I said to myself as I thought again about the Phoenix Group's "contact" who had told them about the impending visit by Mandela to London. There was no doubt in my mind as to the identity of that person.

The time was fast approaching when the Rt. Hon. Douglas Campbell MP would have to be dealt with. There was only one person who could do that. Me.

Claremont, Cape Town

That night as I drifted off to sleep with Freddie laying in the crook of my arm I felt more content with my personal life than I had for some time. I was confident we could work things out.

I was confident also that I could keep one step ahead of

Brannagan and prevent him from killing both Mandela and me.

What I forgot was that the first rule of being a good field agent is over confidence makes you complacent.

The second rule is that complacency can get you killed.

Chapter 33

Cape Town, Sunday May 6th

For the past few days Freddie had been ferrying me round in her Mini Cooper, so it felt strange to be behind the wheel of my car again. I drove up the ramp from the underground car-park into a morning in which the sun shone down from a brilliant blue sky.

'Keep your eyes open for that Porsche you saw at the petrol station last week,' I told Freddie as the steel security shutter came down behind us.

'Do you mean the green sports car?'

'Yeah.'

'How do you know it was a Porsche?'

'Just an educated guess.'

'I don't believe you,' she said. 'So, what's the truth?' I had forgotten how sharp she was.

'OK. The truth is I thought I saw a racing-green Porsche following me a few days before you spotted it.'

'Following you?' She sounded alarmed. 'Are you joshing me?'

'No,' I said and went on to explain about Brannagan and Jonathan Rhodes.

'Why didn't you tell me there are okes trying to kill you?'

'Because I didn't want to worry you.'

'What makes you think I'd worry if somebody killed you?'

'Because you love me.'

'There is that.' She gave me a half smile and then frowned. 'But now I *am* worried.'

'There's no need. I can look after myself.'

'If you're so confident of that, why did you mention it?'

'Because it's better to be safe than sorry and four eyes are better than two.' Although my response was double clichéd, it was none-the-less true. Freddie didn't complain about the clichés, but she did spend the rest of our journey into the city centre staring out of the back window.

Despite my earlier bravado, I felt uneasy and kept track of what was going on behind us by checking my rear-view mirror every few minutes. I looked down at my hands. My knuckles were white with tension where I was clutching the steering wheel so tightly.

With an effort I forced myself to loosen my grip. I glanced over at Freddie, but she was still looking at the road behind us and hadn't noticed how tense I was.

It was Sunday Morning and I was surprised at the volume of traffic heading into the centre of Cape Town. We were in a long line of cars as we made our way through the southern suburbs.

When we arrived at our destination, several cars followed us into the car-park that nestled into the base of Table Mountain, which soared above us into a clear cobalt-blue sky. None of the cars was a racing-green Porsche. I began to relax.

Most of the bays in the car-park were already taken. It looked as if it was going to be a good trading day for the city's retailers. Eventually I found a bay at the end of the car-park furthest away from the entrance. I locked the car and we made our way to the city shopping area.

If I'm honest, shopping has never been one of my favourite pastimes. I suppose it's a man thing, but on this occasion, I suffered in silence. I took solace in the knowledge that Freddie was dragging me in and out of shops because she was looking for suitable shoes and clothes to wear when she joined me in London. It was a sacrifice worth making.

We spent four hours shopping and eventually left the city shopping area laden with carrier bags displaying the company logos of several designer retail chains.

By then, we were ready for lunch, so we headed for the quay-side. We ended up in a waterfront restaurant, eating a seafood risotto washed down with a fantastic chardonnay from Paarl.

It was mid-afternoon before we left the restaurant and the earlier clear blue sky had been replaced by a cover of lowering, leaden-grey clouds. As we made our way back to the car-park, it started spitting with rain.

Luckily the car-park was quite close and we reached it before the rain got any heavier. As we walked through the entrance Freddie stopped suddenly and swore.

'What is it?' I asked.

'I left my handbag in the restaurant. I'll have to go back.'

By now the rain had turned into a steady drizzle. 'Don't worry,' I said. 'You head for the car and I'll do it.' I handed her the car keys and the three carrier bags I was carrying. She was already carrying two bags herself. 'Can you manage all the bags?'

Her look of scorn said it all.

'OK, I won't be long,' I told her, before turning on my heel and heading back to the restaurant at a trot.

By the time I arrived at the restaurant the rain was pelting down and I was soaked to the skin. Luckily Freddie's handbag was still where she had left it on the floor under the table at which we had eaten. I opened it and quickly checked that her purse and apartment keys were still there. They were. Satisfied, I headed back to the car-park.

When I arrived, I found the car-park almost empty. My hire-car was in the far end bay, but despite the driving rain I could see Freddie was sitting in the driver's seat.

She saw me and grinned. She pointed at me and then herself in an obvious signal that she was coming to pick me up. I waved my acknowledgement, but carried on walking towards her.

Seconds later there was a flash of light and my car exploded with a blast that lifted me from my feet. I landed on my back and my head slammed against the tarmac surface with a force that stunned me.

Somehow I managed to stagger to my feet, with my head throbbing and a red mist blurring my vision. Despite my pain and the driving rain, I saw that the hire-car had been consumed by a fireball that sent a pall of black smoke into the air, blotting out the stark and brooding Table Mountain.

That's when I lost consciousness and collapsed in a heap on the ground.

Chapter 34

Rupert Disraeli-Astor stared at me with a look of concern. It was not a sentiment my boss often displayed. He rarely did sympathy. His usual good-natured and urbane façade disguised a somewhat insensitive martinet. I suppose active military service does that to some men.

'I'm surprised to see you in the office today, Statton. I thought you would take the rest of the week off. What happened to you in Cape Town must have been quite a shock.'

'I'll survive.'

He tapped a sheet of paper that lay in front of him on his desk. 'But Doctor Wyatt's report says you could be suffering from concussion.'

'Wyatt is a quack. He's just covering his arse in case I drop dead next to the coffee vending machine.'

'We don't have a coffee vending machine.'

'That's alright then, because I'm not going to drop dead.'

'I was sorry to hear about your lady friend.'

'As you once said yourself, sir, shit happens. Now it's time for me to see that the next pile of crap falls on Brannagan, but I won't get him sitting at home feeling sorry for myself. That's why I'm back at work.'

'Are you sure it was Brannagan who blew up your car?'

'You've read the transcript of the Phoenix Group meeting. What do you think?'

'It certainly looks that way,' he agreed. 'So what are you going to do?'

'Well, my first step is to visit the Palace of Westminster this afternoon and have a good look round the buildings.'

'Do you really think the Phoenix Group plans to kill Nelson Mandela next week when he visits Parliament?'

'That's what was decided at their meeting and we have to assume they intend going ahead with their plan. Or rather, they will have instructed Brannagan to do their dirty work for them. I intend to be ready for the bastard, so I want to work out all the likely places from where he can strike.'

He stared at me in silence for a few moments and then said: 'You have another reason for visiting Parliament, don't you?'

I was surprised he read my mind so well. 'Yes. I want to have a chat with your mate Douglas Campbell.'

'That's what I feared.'

'His time is up.'

'That sounds rather drastic.'

'I mean as an informer. I want to make sure Campbell passes no more information to the Phoenix Group.'

'Okay, but remember we have no real proof of Dougie's guilt. So, no violence.'

'Fret not, boss. There will be no violence. I just want to give him the Gypsy's warning.'

'That's what worries me. In my experience, some Gypsies can be belligerent, antagonistic and ruthless.' He stared at me. 'Now, who does that sound like?'

I didn't respond.

He continue to look at me steadily. 'Very well, Statton. Do whatever you have to do, but be careful. The department doesn't need any political aggravation right now.'

'Don't worry, I'll be very careful. The visit by Mandela is my best chance of getting Brannagan and I don't want him being frightened off.'

'Special Branch has been tasked with providing security for Mandela's visit to Parliament,' he said. 'What makes you think Brannagan will actually get within striking distance of him?'

'Because I've seen how he operates. Even if by some miracle Special Branch don't cock up, like they did at Wembley, Brannagan will find a way of getting at Mandela. He might be a psychopath, but he's a very proficient psychopath.'

'In that case be on your guard. You might be the most irritating, sarcastic, insubordinate, argumentative employee with whom I have ever come into contact, but, I still hope you kill Brannagan before he kills you.'

'I didn't know you cared so much about me.'

'I don't, but you're a damn fine field agent and it would be very difficult finding somebody to replace you.'

'Thanks.'

'And your death would mean a lot of form filling and you know how much I hate paperwork,' he added with a smile.

I smiled back. 'By the way, have you told Campbell I survived the bomb blast in Cape Town?'

He shook his head. 'I've told nobody. Why do you ask?'

'Because, if Campbell is involved in the Phoenix Group, he will have heard about the explosion and will think I'm dead. It will be interesting to see the look on his face when I walk into his office. It could tell me a great deal about him.'

I stood up. My head started throbbing again, but I hid the pain. I headed for the door but he stopped me in my tracks.

'That chap from the American embassy contacted me again.'

'Bob Foster?'

'Yes, that's him.'

'When was that?'

'Last Friday.'

'What did he want?'

He wanted to know whether you were back from South Africa. I told him I was expecting you back this week.'

'Did he say anything more?'

'Only that he'd like a catch up meeting with you. I said you would contact him.'

'Thanks, I'll ring him and arrange a meeting, but not until I've seen Campbell.'

When I left Disraeli-Astor's office I was stopped by Colleen Masters, who hadn't been at her desk when I arrived earlier that morning.

'Hi, David. How are you? I was so worried about you.'

'Worried about what?' I said warily.

'The D-G told me about your car being blown up. I was so sorry to hear about your friend.'

Suddenly my headache got a whole lot worse. 'He told me he hadn't told anybody.'

'But I'm not just anybody. I'm his PA. I have to know everything in order to do my job properly.'

'I guess.' I tried to keep any sound of my irritation from my voice. It wasn't Colleen's fault that her boss couldn't keep his mouth shut. 'Does anybody else know what happened in South Africa?'

'I don't know about the boss, but I've told nobody.'

'Not even Poppy?'

'Not even Poppy.' She looked at me with a worried look on her face. 'Are you alright, David?'

'I'm fine,' I insisted. 'I only arrived back from South Africa first thing this morning and I have a bit of a headache.'

'You look sad. Is it because of your friend?'

With her woman's intuition she had put her finger on exactly what was wrong with me.

'Would you like to talk about it?'

'Not now, Colleen,' I said gently, but I suddenly realised that I did want to talk about Freddie to somebody. Anybody.

'What about the weekend? We could go back to that place in Kent where we stayed before.'

'The Wife of Bath.'

'That's the one.' She must have seen the way I hesitated because she added: 'No strings attached.'

I was touched by her understanding and it reminded me why I had started to fall in love with her. However, that was before I met Freddie again but still... 'I'd like that,' I said. 'Can I leave you to book a room? I'm going to be busy over the next couple of days.'

'Not a problem. Secretaries are good at booking hotel rooms.' She grinned at me and for some reason that raised my spirits. However, it didn't do much for my headache, which still nagged at me like a rotten tooth.

When I reached the Section Two offices only my secretary, Poppy Fotheringay-Evans, was to be seen. She was sitting at her desk typing, but looked up when I entered.

'Welcome back, boss.'

'Where is everybody?' I asked.

'We are two thirds of everybody. The other third has popped to the lavvy.'

'I take it you mean Melissa?'

'Correct. I'm typing up some notes for her. How was your trip to South Africa?'

'Interesting,' I replied cautiously. I wanted to see whether Colleen had told Poppy what had happened to me in Cape Town, but it appeared not, because she didn't follow up with another question or comment. I was pleased Colleen had told me the truth.

'How's your love life? When I left London you were on a dirty weekend with Roger the Dodger.'

'The ex-Roger the Dodger,' she said.

'Ex? You haven't killed him?'

'Don't be silly,' she laughed. 'I dumped him.'

'Not before time. What happened?'

'He was a pervert. He wanted me to go to bed with him and his friend Martin.' She gave a theatrical shudder and then, as if I couldn't work it out for myself, she added melodramatically: 'At the same time. The nerve of the man.'

'So you're single again?' I should have known better.

'Certainly not!' She sounded shocked that I should think such a thing. 'Martin and I have a thing going.'

'What? Roger's three-in-a-bed pal?'

'Yes.'

'Out of interest. Is this Martin married?'

'No, he's separated,' she replied.

'Separated? That means he *is* married.'

'He's going to get a divorce.'

'Of course he is.' I headed for my office. 'Please ask Melissa to pop into my office when she gets back from the ladies room and if she happens to be carrying a cup of coffee when she arrives, both of you will get a gold star for effort.'

'I'll make one straight away.'

'Thanks, but don't let the water boil,' I shouted to her as I sat down at my desk. 'It burns the coffee beans.'

'We only have instant coffee,' she shouted back.

'I know. I was rather hoping you'd take the hint and arrange a decent percolator for the office like the one the D-G has.'

I sat down at my desk and stared at my in-tray. It was full to over flowing, no doubt with paperwork accumulated since Des Hobbins was transferred back to the D-G's team. He could have taken the bumf with him; after all, most of it had been sent for my boss's attention anyway.

I pulled the first bulky looking document from the tray and was about to start reading it when Melissa walked in carrying a thin file in one hand and a cup of steaming coffee in the other.

I pointed at the coffee. 'Did Poppy have a lobotomy whilst I was away, or has a change of boyfriend improved her memory?'

Melissa laughed. 'It might be the latter,' she whispered as she put the cup of coffee on my desk. 'She's been spending a lot of her spare time in bed and they say that sleep helps your brain.'

'I don't suppose Miss Fotheringay-Evans has been doing much sleeping,' I said. 'How was your trip to Thailand? When did you get back?'

'Last Saturday. Hazel and I had a fantastic time.'

'Hazel?' I asked.

'Yeah, she's my latest girlfriend. What about you, how was your trip to South Africa.'

'Nothing very exciting,' I said quietly and then changed the subject. 'How are you getting on with researching members of the Phoenix Group?'

'Slowly. As you know I left it with Clive while I was away and he didn't get on very well. He spent several days tracking down information about the Indian guy and then discovered it was the wrong Patel.'

'There are millions of Patels in the world,' I pointed out.

'I know that, but Clive obviously didn't.'

'So where is our Master Flack?'

'Personnel contacted me on Monday and told me the department has been hit by a flu bug and the German desk was short-handed. The D-G decided Clive's time would be better spent helping there, than at the library. I didn't mind. I got more done working on my own, because I didn't have to hold his hand all the time.'

'I don't know where they get them from. There must be a factory somewhere that turns university graduates into idiots.'

She arched a newly painted eyebrow at me.

'Present company excepted.'

'I should hope so. Anyway, I've done quite a bit since Monday morning, including digging out information on the correct Sunil Patel. Poppy is typing it up for me now.'

'So the information isn't in there?' I pointed at the file she still held in her hand.

'No, this is a note on that private detective you asked me to check up on,' she explained, handing the file to me.

'Excellent,' I said, although in truth I had forgotten all about Justin Bloom. I opened the file and scanned the single sheet of A4 paper it contained. I was surprised at what I read. The detective had been married three times and had shared seven children amongst his various wives. 'And there was me thinking that Bloom was homosexual.'

'What made you think that?'

'Only that his mannerisms made him look effeminate.'

'Just goes to show that you shouldn't judge a person by their appearance. Anyway, just because he was married and had children doesn't mean that he wasn't gay.'

'That's true, as history has shown.'

'Is his sexuality relevant to the case?'

'I'm not sure,' I answered truthfully. I explained that Bloom had sex just before he was killed and that I suspected the detective had been killed by the person he had listed as BO in his appointments diary. 'I don't know who that person is, but I thought it might be Brendan O'Leary.'

'He was on the Phoenix Group list you gave Timmy and me to research.'

'Yes. I asked Timmy to check O'Leary first, but he was murdered before he could report back to me. Do you know if he found anything?'

'Not much, I'm afraid. The only notes Timmy left me gave only the most basic information about O'Leary.'

'How basic?'

'That he is a citizen of the Irish Republic; he is Chairman and major shareholder of the Five Continents Travel Limited; he is married; and has a daughter.'

'And that's it?'

'Yup. That's it. I haven't had a chance to dig any deeper.'

'OK, see what more you can find out about him. It would be good to either confirm that he was the BO in Bloom's desk diary, or eliminate him as a possibility.'

'I'll do my best. However, I'm not sure how you will be able to eliminate O'Leary until you find out whether he and Bloom were in a gay relationship. Your problem is the only people who know the truth are him and Bloom who, I would remind you, just happens to be dead.'

'That's true. However, I have no other clue who BO is.'

Melissa looked at me silently, perhaps hoping for divine inspiration, if she was, it didn't come. 'What did you want to see me about?' She asked.

'Des Hobbins.'

'What about him?'

'He was my designated deputy, but now he's been drafted back into the D-G's squad.'

'I know, Des wasn't happy about it. He told me he liked working in Section Two.'

'Que sera, sera.'

'What will be, will be.'

'Exactly.'

'So?'

'I'm going to need a new deputy. Would you like the job?'

'Me?'

'Yes.'

'But what about Colonel Disraeli-Astor?'

'He already has a job, if being D-G classifies as work.'

'I meant what would he say?'

'He would say congratulations, Melissa.'

'He wouldn't mind you promoting a woman as your deputy?'

'No,' I assured her.

'What about a young woman.'

'No, Melissa.'

'What about a young woman who's a lesbian?'

'I'm not sure it's in the job description, but I'm sure we could overcome that little technicality. However, you might have to promise not to try to seduce the Prime Minister.'

'I think I can do that,' she said with a grin. 'Even though Maggie is my favourite female role model.'

'In that case the job is yours.' I stared at her in silence for a few moments. 'Why are you crying?' I asked.

'Because I'm happy.'

'But I thought you had your heart set on a diplomatic career in the Foreign Office?'

'I've changed my mind. I've really loved working in the department during the last few months.' She dabbed her eyes with a paper handkerchief. 'Anyway, they're a bunch of toffee nosed snobs in the FO. No room for working-class lesbos like me over there!'

I held out my hand to her. 'You'll do,' I said with a grin.

The Houses of Parliament, London

The Speaker of the House of Commons has a grace and favour residence in the Palace of Westminster. It is situated just behind the Clock Tower in which Big Ben, the most recognisable bell in the world, peels out the time every quarter of an hour.

The Speaker's house is on two floors, with offices and reception rooms located on the same principal floor level as the debating chamber, in which he presides. His living accommodation is above on the first floor, although technically, it is the second floor. Such is the charm and historic idiosyncratic nature of the building.

Access to the Speaker's residence is via New Palace Yard and was less than a five minute walk from the DFCO offices. I had no problem getting through the police manned security gates at the Cromwell Green entrance in St Margaret's Street. I used my special parliamentary security pass, which was one of the privileges offered to those of us who worked for the British Secret Service.

Unlike other members of the Civil Service and parliamentary staff, my pass allowed me entry into every part of the Palace of Westminster, including those areas that were usually accessible only by Members of Parliament or Peers.

I made my way through Speaker's Court to the lift that took me up to Parliament's principal floor, where I found myself in a corridor that led me to the Speaker's Office. It was situated at the end of an even longer corridor that ran the length of the building all the way to the Lord Chancellor's suite of offices.

The Speaker's Secretary was waiting for me when I walked into his office. 'Good morning, Mister Statton,' he said in a friendly way that belied the fact we had never met before. I was impressed he had taken the trouble to check up on my identity in advance of my arrival.

'Mister Speaker is waiting for you in his study,' he added, with a slight emphasis on the word "waiting" that made me glance at my watch. With an irrational sense of relief I saw I was a couple of minutes early for my 11.30am meeting.

Bernard Weatherill was sitting behind a grand Queen Anne desk, but, ever the gentleman, he stood up when he saw me. He came round the desk to greet me with an outstretched hand and a shy smile on his good-natured face.

'I am delighted to meet you, Mister Statton,' he said as we shook hands. He sounded sincere, which I suppose is the sign of an accomplished politician. He escorted me to one of the easy chairs that stood in front of an ornate fireplace.

As I sat down there was a knock on the door and a man came in. He wore a court suit, with knee-breeches, white stockings and shiny black shoes. From his hip hung a silver-hilted sword.

'I have asked the Serjeant at Arms to join us,' Speaker Weatherill explained. 'I thought he could brief you on what preparations are being made for the visit to the Palace of Westminster next week of Nelson Mandela.'

Sir Alan Urwick offered me his hand. He had the firm, dry handshake of somebody who knows his own mind. Here was a man who was no pushover. 'I understand you have some concerns about Mister Mandela's visit,' he said as he took his seat.

'Yes, Sir Alan. We have reason to believe there might be an attempt on his life.'

'Then my staff must be extra vigilant mustn't they?' He gave me a tight smile. 'Which is why we welcome any help you can give us.' He added this last part with little enthusiasm. The ex-diplomat was renowned as somebody who hated outside interference.

I tried to reassure him. 'I'm not here to interfere, sir. I just want to observe and advise when necessary. I'll try to keep you involved in any action I might need to take, and will do my best to not tread on your toes.'

'My dear chap, *that* is exactly what I wanted to hear. I do suffer terribly from chilblains.'

Bernard Weatherill watched this interchange and had noted the nuances. 'Perhaps you would like to brief Mister Statton about your plan of action, Sir Alan.'

'Of course, Mister Speaker. Where shall I begin?' Sir Alan directed this question at me.

'For a start it would be helpful if I knew exactly where Mister Mandela's address to both Houses of Parliament will take place. Don't such events usually take place in Westminster Hall, or the Royal Gallery?'

The Serjeant at Arms nodded his head. 'That is certainly true for visiting heads of state, but of course Nelson Mandela does not yet fall into that category so he will not be accorded that privilege. Instead, the event will take place in the Grand Committee Room.'

'That's located in Westminster Hall, isn't it?'

'Yes.' It was Speaker Weatherill who answered my question. 'It is up a flight of steps, next to the Jubilee Room.'

'Members of the public have access to Westminster Hall. Has that been taken into consideration?' I asked the Serjeant at Arms.

'It certainly has,' he assured me.

'How will Mandela be protected as he makes his way to the Grand Committee Room and who will be guarding him?'

'Special Branch, will be overseeing security during Mandela's visit to London and, as such, I will be working closely with Scotland Yard,' Sir Alan said. 'However, I have the final say here in the Palace of Westminster.'

'I'm sure you do, Sir Alan,' I said diplomatically.

The Serjeant at Arms smiled. 'We have agreed that Mister Mandela will arrive by car accompanied by an armed police motorcycle escort. He will be driven through Carriage Gates into New Palace Yard, when my part of the plan will kick in. Members of the police SO17 squad and parliamentary doorkeepers will take over his protection and escort him straight into Westminster Hall and up to the Grand Committee Room.'

'What about any members of the public who are in Westminster Hall at the time?'

'There will be no members of the public present. Access will be restricted for a short period before Mister Mandela arrives and again just before he leaves.'

Bernard Weatherill took up the explanation: 'When Mister Mandela has finished his speech, the Serjeant at Arms will escort him out of Westminster Hall. They will go, past the Members' Entrance, along the Colonnade and through Speaker's Court to the Speaker's House. There, he will have tea with the Prime Minister, the Leader of the Opposition and me.'

I nodded my satisfaction. On the face of it I could find no fault with the plan so far. 'What happens after tea?'

'A car will be waiting in Speaker's Court,' Sir Alan explained. 'I will take Mister Mandela down in the lift and hand him over to Special Branch officers who will ensure he gets safely off the parliamentary estate.'

'Thank you, Sir Alan,' I said.

The Serjeant at Arms looked at his watch and stood up. 'I'm afraid I must dash. I have a dress rehearsal in Westminster Hall for next week's visit.' He straightened his sword and marched out of the study.

Bernard Weatherill stared at the door as his colleague closed it behind him. 'Sir Alan does not need much of an excuse to dress up,' he said quietly with a wry smile.

'You don't approve?'

'Everyone to his own, I suppose. I have to wear a wig and gown when I preside over debates in the Chamber. It is expected of me, but I cannot wait to change back into a normal suit. I enjoy my role as Speaker, but I hate the formality.'

'Perhaps it will change, sir.'

'You might be right, Mister Statton. However, I fear it won't be in my political lifetime. It is a shame, because all the frippery and arcane procedures sit ill with my roots. I think at heart I am something of a Puritan.'

He reached into his waistcoat pocket and took something out. He held out his hand. A silver thimble nestled in his palm. 'My mother gave this to me when I first joined the family firm as an apprentice tailor,' he explained.

'When eventually, I became a Member of Parliament she urged me to keep the thimble in my pocket and look at it every day to remind me of my background. She said it was important to remain humble, no matter how important I became.'

He stared fondly at the thimble, then he looked at me and smiled. 'When I die, Mister Statton, I would like inscribed on my tombstone: "He always kept his word." In my book that is the best possible epitaph any politician can have.'

He stood up to show me out of his study.

'I think such an epitaph would suit you, sir.'

'It is very kind of you to say so, Mister Statton,' he said with a modest smile as he took me through to the outer office where his secretary and train-bearer sat at their desks.

I shook Speaker Wetherill's hand and headed out of the office and walked a few paces down the library corridor to where a telephone stood on a wall stand. I picked up the receiver and rang an internal number. A man answered the phone. I recognised his voice, so I put down the receiver without speaking.

I made my way back towards the Speaker's office, but before I reached it, I turned left and headed back along the main corridor.

Instead of returning to the lift down to Speaker's Court, I carried on until I reached a passage that was situated opposite the entrance to the House of Commons debating chamber.

Ahead of me was yet another lift and to my right, a door to the Table Office. This is where staff assist MPs in tabling parliamentary questions and early day motions. It was to a door on my left that I headed. It led to a flight of stairs that took me down to the lower ministerial corridor, where a number of junior ministers had their offices.

It didn't take me long to find the office I wanted. I pushed open the door without knocking, went in and kicked it closed behind me with my heel. Douglas Campbell was sitting at his desk. He looked up with a startled expression on his face, which turned to one of concern when he saw me turn the key to lock the door.

I walked over and stood at his side. Without warning, I swept a pile of papers from his desk onto the floor.

He half rose to his feet. 'What the hell do you think you're doing?' He asked angrily, any fear he might have felt forgotten.

I pushed him none too gently back into his seat. 'What do you think I'm doing?'

'You're trying to intimidate me.'

'Were you born perceptive? Or is it a talent you acquired when you became a Member of Parliament?'

'Get out of my office. You don't frighten me.'

'You ought to be frightened. I could make life very difficult for you if I wanted to.'

'I don't know who the hell you think you are, but your threats won't work,' he said defiantly.

'You don't remember me, do you Dougie?'

He shook his head. 'No. Have we met before?'

'Yes. Think hard.'

He stared at my face intently through narrowed eyes. He frowned in concentration and then I saw his eyes open wider as he recognised me. 'You're Disraeli-Astor's man.'

'That's right. I'm Disraeli-Astor's man. I'm the poor bastard you've been trying to get killed.'

'I don't know what you're talking about.'

'I'm talking about you passing on my every move to Reg-the-sledge.'

'I don't recollect that name.'

'Funnily enough, that's what he said about you, Dougie. Perhaps you know him better as Sir Reginald Wren.'

Campbell looked up at me and shrugged, as if somehow my words confirmed his claim about not knowing Wren.

'But here's the strange thing,' I went on. 'When I told Reg you'd been feeding him information, he didn't deny it.'

Campbell had been looking up at me, but now his eyes slipped away. He stared down at his desk top.

'I also know you've been having sex with his girlfriend.'

'His girlfriend?'

'That's right, a feisty young thing called Misty Olafson.'

'That's nonsense. I have never heard of anyone of that name, and I am certainly not having a sexual relationship with Wren's girlfriend. I'm a happily married man.'

'Of course you are, Dougie,' I said softly. I took a photograph from the inside pocket of my jacket and laid it on the desk. 'And I'm sure the wife to whom you are so happily married would be very interested to see what you are doing with that young woman.' I tapped the photo.

Campbell stared at the photo of him being straddled by the naked, blonde-haired Misty Olafson. Blood drained from his face. 'How did you get this?' He slumped back in his chair.

'I think you probably know where the photo came from, but how I got hold of it is irrelevant. All that matters is I have a number of equally incriminating photographs, all of excellent quality. I'm sure both your wife, and the Tory Chief Whip, would be interested to receive copies of them.'

I pushed the photo out of the way and sat down on the edge of his desk. 'Now, Dougie, let's start again. Do you know Sir Reginald Wren?'

'Yes,' he admitted.

'And have you been passing information to him?'

'I had no choice,' he said quietly. 'Wren was blackmailing me. He said he would send the photographs to my wife.'

'Listen, Dougie, don't expect sympathy from me. We all have to make difficult choices in life. Nobody forces us to make them. For instance: it was your choice to accept Wren's hospitality on his yacht. It was your choice to snort coke. It was your choice to screw his girlfriend and it was your choice to betray your wife. Choices, Dougie, all choices.'

'I didn't know…' he started.

'Shut up. I haven't finished,' I interrupted him. 'It was your choice to become involved with the Phoenix Group and it was your choice to tell Wren that General Urinoff was about to spill the beans about his colleagues and him…'

'But…'

I banged the top of his desk. 'I said shut up. It was your choice to tell Wren I was going to Belfast after Brannagan and it was your choice to tell Wren about my trip to South Africa.'

'But that's not true,' Campbell snapped. He looked at me through narrowed eyes.

'What's not true?'

'Look, I admit passing on some low level information to Wren and I did promise to try to delay any investigation into the Phoenix Group. However, I never told him about the Russian defector, or your trips to Belfast and South Africa. I swear that's the truth. You have to believe me.'

I stared at him in silence. 'You've made it very difficult for me to believe you, Dougie,' I said eventually. 'After all, you denied knowing Misty Olafson? That photo proves you weren't telling the truth. If you lied once, you can lie again.'

'I was telling the truth. I promise,' Campbell pleaded. 'I didn't know the girl's surname was Olafson and had no idea her first name was Misty. Wren introduced her to me simply as Bridget. That's what I called her.'

I believed him. There was something in his eyes that convinced me he was telling the truth. I patted his shoulder in a friendly way. 'I'll tell you what I'm going to do, Dougie.' I picked up the photograph and waved it in his face.

'What? What are you going to do?'

'I'm going to give you the benefit of the doubt.'

He looked at me suspiciously. 'What does that mean?'

'It means the photographs will get lost somewhere in the department's filing system.' I slipped the photo into my pocket.

'Thank you.'

'Don't thank me, because you're not out of the mire just yet.' I slid off his desk and stood up.

He viewed me with wide eyes.

'Dougie, I want you to listen to me very carefully and remember what I say?'

He nodded.

'The photographs we have in our possession will remain unseen by your wife.'

He let out a small sigh of relief at my words.

'However, I want to give you an assurance, Dougie, and it's this.' I paused to add weight to my words. 'Should I suspect you have passed more information to Wren, talked to him, or communicated with him in any way, copies of the photos will be passed to your wife, the Chief Whip and the News of the World. Is that understood?'

'Yes.'

'In addition, should Wren learn of our plans from any other source, I will blame you. Should any more of my colleagues in the department be attacked, I will blame you. Should I be followed whilst going about my business, I will blame you. Should any of my staff or me have an unfortunate accident, I will blame you. Should I catch a cold, I will blame you. In any of those circumstances all bets are off. Do I make myself clear?'

'But that's not fair,' Campbell protested. 'I have no control over what anybody else might do to you, or what ills might befall your colleagues.'

'Do I make myself clear?' I repeated.

'Yes,' he said dejectedly.

'Then we understand each other.' I headed for the door and unlocked it.

As I made my way to Star Chamber Court, I mulled over Campbell's claim that he hadn't told Wren about either Urinoff or my trip to Belfast and South Africa. If he was telling the truth, then somebody else had tipped off the Phoenix Group. But who?

That question worried me a lot, but it wasn't the only thing. For a start, there was the level of security at the Palace of Westminster. During the couple of hours I spent in the House of Commons, not once was I stopped, or asked to produce my pass.

Then there was the niggle in my brain about something Campbell had said. Something significant. Something I was missing. I just couldn't put my finger on what it was.

I shrugged and told myself the missing piece of information would come to me sometime, probably in the middle of a restless night's sleep.

I hoped that when the lightbulb in my mind finally did flicker into life, it would not be too late to read the plot that Fate had written for me.

Chapter 35

When I arrived at the US Embassy it soon became apparent that this was to be no ordinary visit. My previous meetings with Bob Fletcher had taken place in a small room hidden away on the ground floor.

On this occasion I was escorted to a conference room on the top floor, in the centre of which stood a long shiny table surrounded by chairs. At the head of the table sat the US Ambassador.

'Good morning, Mister Statton,' Henry Catto Jnr said as I was shown into the room. He spoke with a Texan accent that reminded me of the chairman of the Phoenix Group, John Derwent Engels.

'Good morning, Mister Ambassador.' I sat down on one of the chairs closest to the door.

'You know my military attaché, of course?' The Ambassador waved a hand towards Bob Fletcher.

'Yes,' I nodded a greeting to Fletcher. There was another man sitting next to him who I recognised immediately. It was CIA agent Hank Graham.

'Hi, Dave,' Hank greeted me with a wide smile. 'Long time no see.'

'Eight years to be precise.'

'You're looking better than the last time we met, pal.'

'That's hardly surprising. I seem to recall I was bleeding like a stuck pig and was in agony.'

'Don't be a pussy,' Hank said with a laugh. 'You weren't that badly hurt.'

'That's easy to say when the blood is pumping out of somebody else's arm,' I replied.

'Come on, Dave, it was only a flesh wound. The situation could have been much worse.' He smiled at me.

I smiled back. 'That's for sure. If you hadn't turned up when you did, I'd have ended up as fish food.'

Hank shot me a warning look. There were things about that night on the beach in Melkbosstrand we both knew must remain strictly between him and me. I understood why.

Hank had turned up on the beach just as CIA deputy director,

Gavin Rogers II, was about to kill me. Hank saved my life by shooting his boss in the back, but this was something that could never be revealed.

Rogers was a traitor working for the Soviet Union, but, so well had he covered his tracks, Hank would have found it impossible to prove his boss's guilt to the US Authorities.

So he decided the best thing would be for Rogers to simply disappear. I helped him dispose of his colleague's body by burning it in the cab of a truck. The CIA never found out what happened to its deputy director.

'I understand from Bob Foster that the Firm never did find Gavin Rogers.' I gave Hank a discreet wink.

'We never saw him again,' he said. 'What about you?'

'The same. The last I saw of him he was heading down the beach towards the sub that collected Zamyatin,' I repeated the lie I had told Fletcher. 'He probably hitched a lift back to Mother Russia.'

'I guess so,' Hank said, then changed the subject. 'I heard you were involved in a spot more bother in South Africa last week. Was it bad?'

'You could say that. Somebody tried to blow me up.'

'What happened?'

So I told him everything that had happened to me in Cape Town, ending up with my car being blown up with Freddie inside.

'I'm sorry to hear that, pal,' Hank said softly. 'I saw her with you a couple of times back in Eighty-Two. She looked a cute kid.'

'She was. That's why I'm going to get the bastard who killed her.'

Henry Cato had listened to this exchange in silence. 'I would also like to extend my condolences, Mister Statton,' he said. 'I know what it feels like to lose a loved one.' He paused as if remembering. 'It is unlikely anything will ever fully ease the pain you are currently experiencing. However, avenging the death of your friend might help. As a start, you can stop Brannagan from killing Nelson Mandela.'

'Don't worry, Mister Ambassador. That's what I'm going to do. Freddie was one of Mandela's biggest fans and would want me to save him.'

'Of course, if the Irishman dies in the process,' Cato shrugged, 'then so be it.'

'Oh, he's going to die alright, sir.'

411

Catto must have caught the emotion in my voice because he allowed me a moment to recover before asking: 'Are you sure Brannagan intends to assassinate Nelson Mandela when he's in London?'

'That's what was agreed at the Phoenix Group meeting in Noordhoek, and I have no reason to think the plans have changed.'

'Was there anything else said at that meeting we should know about?' Bob Fletcher asked. It was the first time he had spoken.

'Yes, there was one thing. Engels admitted he hired Brannagan to murder your CIA colleague.'

'He did that?' Fletcher leaned towards me. 'Do you have any proof?'

I smiled at him and took two cassette tapes from my pocket and slid them across the table to him. 'I thought you might be interested in this recording of the meeting. The first tape is the one you want.'

'This might make our task easier, sir' Fletcher said to Catto.

'Can we use the tapes in evidence?' The Ambassador asked.

'Probably not in a court of law,' Fletcher admitted. 'However, we don't intend this case to reach court.'

The Ambassador looked at me sharply, as if wondering whether I had heard this interchange.

'It's not a problem, sir. We're all big boys in this room,' I told him. 'I know exactly what Bob means.'

'This is not something that sits comfortably with me, Mister Statton, but President Bush has decided the best way of dealing with the threat to our national interest posed by the Phoenix Group is to adopt the Hydra approach.'

'Which is?'

'As you probably know Hydra was a multi headed serpent that was raised by Hera to kill Hercules,' Catto explained.

I nodded my acknowledgement of this fact.

'As his second task Hercules was sent to kill Hydra, which he did by cutting off all its heads. That's what the President proposes should happen to the Phoenix Group. He wants to decapitate the group's leading members: Engels, Rhodes, O'Leary, Sevier and Sir Reginald Wren.'

'What do you mean by decapitate?'

The Ambassador looked uncomfortable again. 'The President's preference would be for them to be put in prison for a long time.

412

However, as in the case of Engels, it is unlikely we would be able to mount a successful prosecution, even with the tapes you gave Bob.'

'But they are still useful,' Fletcher insisted waving one of the tapes in the air. 'The President has demanded proof before sanctioning direct CIA involvement in any move against the Phoenix Group. Hopefully, these will provide him with what he needs.'

'So, what will you do next?'

'That is to be decided, but trust me, one way or another we will nail Engels, even if we have to utilise help from somewhere outside of American jurisdiction.'

'Extraordinary Rendition?' I asked, referring to the top-secret CIA programme that was designed to ensure terror suspects were interrogated in countries that have less onerous human rights regulations than the USA. It helped if the local news media had little inclination to ask embarrassing questions.

'I don't know what you're talking about, pal.' Fletcher grinned.

I turned to the Ambassador. 'The President's strategy is all very well, sir. However, as I remember the Hydra story, for every head the serpent lost, it grew two more. Won't other members of the Phoenix Group simply step in and take the places of the leaders that have been displaced?'

Catto looked at Fletcher. 'Bob perhaps you would like to deal with that one?'

'Of course, sir.' Fletcher turned to me. 'We have already thought about that possibility. So, the plan is to take out all five targets at the same time. Our assessment is that such co-ordinated decapitation action will frighten off the other members of the group. If we are wrong, then they too will be eliminated.'

'When will this action happen?'

'Within the next two weeks. We have already been in touch with our friends in France and South Africa. They have agreed to work with us to ensure action is taken at the same time.'

'Good luck with that.' I said.

'Don't be a cynic,' Fletcher said. 'We have faith in our allies. For instance, the South Africans have assured us they can deal with Rhodes. Despite his influence in their country, they're confident they will be able to neutralise him.' He smiled at me knowingly. 'They're good at that sort of thing. They don't have the same squeamishness about due process that we do in the States.'

413

'Tell me about it. I've seen at first hand the way the South African National Intelligence Agency works. What about Engels?'

'I told you earlier. We will deal with him ourselves.'

'I thought President Bush wanted to keep his hands clean?'

'Things have changed.'

'You mean he now realises there is political kudos to be won being seen to be tough?'

Fletcher smiled, but said nothing.

'What are the French going to do about Maurice Sevier?'

'We forwarded certain information about his international financial affairs to the French tax authorities. They were delighted to receive it and are preparing charges against him of tax evasion and tax avoidance. Monsieur Sevier now faces a lengthy spell in Fresnes Prison.'

'That just leaves O'Leary and Wren.' I pointed out.

'That's where you come in. They are Brits, so we hoped you might be able to take them out.'

'Nothing would give me greater pleasure than to take out Sir Reginald,' I said. 'But O'Leary is a different matter. He's a citizen of the Republic of Ireland.'

'But that's the next best thing to being a Brit. aint it?' Fletcher asked. I could see he was serious.

'No. Think the US and Canada,' I said. 'You might have a common language and the same border, but what would Ottawa say if the CIA deliberately killed one of its citizens?'

'They wouldn't be best pleased,' the Ambassador acknowledged. 'They are very sensitive about their national sovereignty.'

'Exactly. Well the same applies to Ireland. Messing with somebody from Eire would be a nightmare for Britain. It would cause havoc in Northern Ireland and be the best possible recruiting sergeant for the IRA.' It was my turn to pause as I considered how difficult it might be to get the Irish Taoiseach to offer his support, considering the internal pressure he was under. 'However, I will set the diplomatic wheels moving and see whether we can get Charles Haughey onside.'

'I understand the difficulties your government might face, Mister Statton,' Henry Catto broke into my thoughts. 'I can assure you that President Bush will do all he can to help persuade the Irish to play ball. As you know, he has some influence in Dublin.'

'That would be helpful, sir. However, currently my top priority is to keep Nelson Mandela safe when he arrives in Britain.'

'We can certainly help you with that,' Catto said. 'As you recall, the President promised your Prime Minister he would offer all the resources of the CIA to help protect Mister Mandela.' He looked at me with a sincerity that only a diplomat can muster.

'Thank you, Mister Ambassador, but I'm not sure we need all their resources.' I smiled. 'However, a little help won't go amiss.'

'I anticipated that might be the case, which is why I spoke with your Director-General last night. I suggested Agent Graham be seconded to the Department for Covert Operations to work alongside you over the next few days.'

'And what did my Director-General say?'

'He thought it was a good idea, but said it was your call.' Catto looked at me expectantly.

This was a turn up for the books. The idea of Disraeli-Astor leaving any important decision to me left me temporarily nonplussed. I looked across the table at Hank, who winked at me.

'In that case I would welcome Agent Graham's help,' I said.

'Excellent! He will work with you for as long as you need him and Bob Fletcher will continue to be your liaison officer at the embassy. If you need more help, just let him know.'

'Thank you, sir. I have a meeting with the head of the Metropolitan Police Special Branch this afternoon. Hopefully, after the meeting I'll have a better idea of what help, if any, we'll need.'

'Are you cool with me tagging along to your meeting at the Yard, Dave,' Hank asked.

'Yeah. It will be good working with you again.'

New Scotland Yard, Westminster

'**Who** did you say we're seeing, Dave?' Hank asked as we sat waiting in the reception area of New Scotland Yard.

'Assistant Deputy Commissioner Kevin Neal.'

'Assistant Deputy Commissioner,' he repeated slowly. 'That's an impressive title.'

'Don't worry, Hank. Kev doesn't let it go to his head. He's one of the good guys.'

'One of your friends?'

'In a way. His dad Billy and I go back a long way.'

415

'Billy Neal?'

'That's right.'

'Why does that name ring a bell?'

'Because you've come across Billy before.'

'When was that?'

'Back in Eighty-Two.'

Hank frowned and shook his head. 'I'm getting old, pal. You'll have to punch my card for me.'

'Do you remember when you came to pick me up from that pub down by the River Medway?'

He nodded. 'Yeah. I remember it well. It was the day Joe Welensky slugged you on that bridge.'

'Tried to slug me,' I corrected him. 'I ducked and he hit one of the bridge's metal girders instead.'

Hank smiled mirthlessly. 'Joe was a jerk.'

'On that we are agreed.'

'So what about it?'

'Do you remember Alexei Urinoff was on a motor cruiser moored alongside the pub?'

'Yeah. He was attacked by two young punks. A guy from the pub sorted out the trouble.'

'That was Billy Neal.'

'I remember now. I went back to the pub a couple of days later and he introduced himself. He was one cool dude. He knew how to handle himself.'

'That's because he was a professional boxer before he moved into the pub business.'

'So, your pal's old man was a bruiser?'

'Yeah.'

'He don't have a privileged background then?'

'Far from it. Billy's from the East End of London and Kevin grew up on a tough council estate.'

'That's like one of our housing projects. Right?'

'Close enough.'

'And now he's an Assistant Deputy Commissioner?'

'He's in charge of Special Branch.'

'Impressive.'

'Yeah. Billy is very proud of him.'

'I'm not surprised. His boy has done well for himself coming from that sort of background.'

Just then a young uniformed police woman came into reception and made her way over to where we were sitting.

'Mister Statton?' She asked Hank. There was no smile of greeting.

He shook his head and slung a thumb at me as we both stood up. 'I suppose I should feel insulted,' he complained sotto voce. 'It's the first time I've been mistaken for a goddam limey.'

'I'm Statton,' I told the girl. 'Ignore my Yank friend. He's still fighting the American War of Independence.'

There was a tightening in the face muscles of the police woman that an optimist might have interpreted as half a smile, but not me. I'm one of life's confirmed pessimists.

'Please follow me.' She turned on her heel and led us out of the reception area towards the lift that would take us up to Kevin's office. 'The ADC is waiting for you,' she added with a reproachful tone in her voice.

I was about to point out that Hank and I had been waiting in reception for almost twenty minutes, but she beat me to it.

'And he apologises he made you wait,' she added in the same frosty voice as she led us along the corridor to her boss's door.

Kevin must have heard our footsteps approaching because he opened the door himself and ushered us into his office.

'Sorry to keep you waiting, gentlemen,' he said.

'Not a problem, Kev.' I held out my hand.

'I was sorry to hear about what happened to you in South Africa, Dave,' he said as he shook my hand.

'News travels fast.'

'Sir Peter bumped into the D-G at a cocktail party on Tuesday evening. He said your car was blown up.'

I was not impressed. So much for Disraeli-Astor's assurance that he had told nobody about what happened in Cape Town. First Colleen Masters found out and then the Metropolitan Police Commissioner, Sir Peter Imbert. I wondered how many other people my boss had told.

'I understand one of your friends was killed in the explosion.'

I nodded, but said nothing, not trusting my voice to not betray the pain of a loss I had fought so hard to keep submerged, but which now had been dredged up twice that day already.

'A good friend?

I nodded again but I couldn't deceive Kevin. We had been friends for a long time and he was far too astute a cop to not detect how I felt. 'How you coping, Dave?' He asked.

'Life goes on,' I said and then abruptly changed the subject by introducing him to Hank. We settled down in the comfortable armchairs that were arranged round a low coffee table at one end of the room. 'So what happened to your predecessor as head of Special Branch?' I asked.

'ADC Hughes is now heading up the Met's traffic section.'

'I bet that went down like a lead balloon.'

'He wasn't best pleased.'

'What happened?'

'The Home Secretary was unhappy about what happened at the Mandela concert. He put pressure on Sir Peter to sack Hughes.'

'How did Douglas Hurd find out what happened at the concert? I didn't mention it in my report?'

'I have no idea,' Kevin said with a smile that betrayed him. Plainly he knew exactly how the Home Secretary had found out.

'But the Commissioner didn't sack Hughes?'

'Of course not. ADCs don't get fired, they just get moved to less onerous duties.'

'Like counting traffic cones.'

'Something like that.' Kevin's smile widened into a grin. 'So what can I do for you, Dave?'

'You're obviously aware that Nelson Mandela is addressing both Houses of Parliament next week?'

'Of course. As head of Special Branch, I'm in charge of security for his visit. What about it?'

'The Phoenix Group intends to assassinate Mandela during his visit to Parliament.' I gave him the same briefing about my trip to Cape Town that I had given at the US Embassy earlier that day.

'Have you told the Serjeant at Arms?' Kevin asked.

'Yes, I visited Parliament on Wednesday and had a meeting with the Speaker and Sir Alan Urwick, who briefed me on his plans for security during Mandela's visit.'

'His plans?'

'He didn't say that in so many words, but I got the message.'

'That's typical of Sir Alan.' He didn't seem impressed.

'I take it the plan was yours?'

'For diplomacy sake, let's say it was a joint effort.' He offered me a slightly forced smile. 'Did you get the chance to have a look round while you were there?'

'Yeah.'

'What do you think?'

'I think that as long as everybody sticks to your plan, and there are no major cock-ups like the one at the concert, then everything should turn out just fine.'

'Any chance I can get to hear about this plan and have a look round the joint?' Hank asked, speaking for the first time. Only an American could refer to the Palace of Westminster as a joint.

'Hank has been seconded to the department,' I explained to Kevin. 'He'll be working with me on the Phoenix Group business.' I looked at the policeman thoughtfully for a few moments and then asked: 'Are you planning to visit Parliament any time soon, Kev?'

'I'll be going there on Monday. Why do you ask?'

'Can Hank tag along?'

'Not a problem,' the policeman said.

'Excellent! Somebody from the department will need to liaise with you regularly and we're running short of bodies in Section Two so Hank has volunteered. Haven't you, Hank?'

'I surely have,' the big American said with a genial smile.

'Perhaps you could show Hank round Parliament and at the same time brief him on the plan to protect Mandela.'

'That's fine with me,' Kevin said.

'Thanks. Well there's no time like the present. If I leave Hank with you, perhaps you can introduce him to the guys who will be protecting Mandela and let him hang out with them for a while?'

'That makes sense,' Kevin agreed.

'Okay with you, Hank?'

'I'm cool,' he said.

So was I. Much as I liked the American, and owed my life to him, he was still a CIA agent and having him breathing down my neck all the time was not a prospect I relished. I reckoned that by getting Hank to spend some time at Scotland Yard, it would keep him out of my hair.

DFCO offices, Westminster, London

I was back in my office by 1pm. No sooner had I arrived than my phone rang. 'Statton,' I responded.

'David?'

'You sound surprised,' I said.

'Sorry, it didn't sound like you.'

'No need to apologise, Colleen. How are you?'

'I'm very worried about you. You've been through a traumatic time.'

'Nothing I can't handle.'

'That's a typical man's response and it's utter bullshit!'

'You might be right.'

'I know I'm right and I know what you need.'

'What?'

'Something to relieve your tension and help you forget what you've been through.'

'What would you suggest?'

'Sex and lots of it. I've booked a room at the Wife of Bath for tonight and tomorrow. How does that sound for starters?'

Despite some misgivings, I accepted her offer. 'It sounds great. 'I'll pick you up at seven-thirty.'

'I'm packed and raring to go.'

'Is that why you rang me, Colleen?'

'No.'

'So?'

'Dizz wants to see you immediately.'

'What about?'

'I've no idea,' she said in an irritated voice that spoke volumes. She really had no idea what Disraeli-Astor wanted to see me about and it rankled with her.

'OK, tell him I'm coming.'

'Don't you think you should leave that for later, darling?' Colleen asked in a suggestive whisper.

'You know what I meant,' I said with a laugh, but she had already hung up.

When I reached the D-G's office it was to be greeted with the aroma of coffee. I had been given cups at both the US embassy and Scotland Yard, but they did not compare with the Blue Mountain that Disraeli-Astor bought from his little place in the village.

'Help yourself.' He pointed at the cafetière that stood on the side table.

He didn't need to invite me twice. I poured myself a cup of coffee and sat down opposite him.

'Did you get to see Dougie?' He asked.

'Yes.'

'When?'

'What do you mean, when?'

'When did you see Dougie?' He tried to sound patient but his exasperation was obvious.

'Wednesday.'

'Where did you see him?'

'In his office at the House of Commons.'

'How was he when you left him?'

'By the time I had finished with him he would have sooner had his balls cut off than pass any more information to Wren.'

'So, you didn't go to Dougie's home?'

'No.'

'At what time on Wednesday did you meet him?'

'I didn't check my watch.'

'Give me a rough idea.'

'Early afternoon. I had an eleven-thirty meeting with the Speaker and the Serjeant at Arms and went to Campbell's office after that. Why all the questions?'

'Because last night Dougie was found dead in his London apartment. He was shot in the back of the head with a nine-mill bullet. Execution style.'

'And you think I did it?'

'It did cross my mind.'

'I carry a Smith and Wesson point four-four Magnum.' I took my pistol from its shoulder-holster and showed it to him. 'Campbell wouldn't have much of a head left if I'd shot him with this.'

'Oh, do put that thing away. Firearms are very dangerous in the wrong hands.'

'This one is in the right hands,' I pointed out, but slipped the pistol back into its holster.

He studied my face carefully, trying to glean something from my immobile features. He failed. 'That is only one weapon,' he said eventually. 'I wouldn't put it past you to have another handgun hidden away somewhere. You could have used that one.'

'I only have my Smith and Wesson,' I lied. As it happens, I did have squirrelled away in a safety deposit box in Hounslow the pistol I had taken from the IRA thug I wounded in Londonderry. Nobody but me knew about it and I had no intention of letting Disraeli-Astor into my secret. That weapon, along with the ammunition, false passport, credit cards and travellers' cheques that were stored with it, were my get out of jail free card.

'Listen, I gave your mate Campbell an ear bashing, but that's the only bashing he got from me. He was alive and well when I left his office,' I insisted. 'Who found him?'

'His wife, Katie. She usually stays at their constituency home in Hampshire whilst Dougie is in London, but she came up yesterday because she was worried about him. She had not heard from him for a couple of days and was unable to contact him on any of his phones.'

'You said Campbell was killed with a nine-mill bullet, does that mean an autopsy has already been carried out?'

'Yes.'

'That was damn quick.'

'When a minister of the Crown is found murdered, it concentrates the minds of even the bureaucrats in the Home Office, particularly when the victim is one of their own.'

'I take your point. What else did the autopsy reveal?'

'Two things of significance. The first was that Dougie had been dead for twenty-four hours.'

'And the second piece of information?'

'It appears that he had sex shortly before he was killed.'

'Let me see. Setting aside Dougie's sexual exploits, it's clear he was murdered on Wednesday. Yes?'

'Yes.'

'So that's why you gave me the third degree?'

'I was simply considering all the options,' he said defensively.

'Well, in the process of considering all those options did you ask the pathologist to compare the bullet that killed Campbell with the one that killed Justin Bloom?'

He looked at me silently and then shook his head. 'No,' he said, before picking up the phone and speaking rapidly into it.

'Well, considering that Bloom had sex before he was shot,' I said once he put down the receiver, 'did you not consider it might be worth checking whether they were killed with the same gun?'

'You're angry.'

'Of course I'm bloody angry. How would you feel if you were accused of being a murderer?'

'I didn't accuse you of being a murderer,' he protested.

'As good as.'

'Well you did kill that Irishman in Belfast recently.'

'That was not murder. I shot him in self-defence.'

'That doesn't make him any less dead, and you do have a record of letting your temper get the better of you.'

I wanted to shout at him right then, but instead I said nothing and we sat in an uncomfortable silence for a few moments as I let my anger subside.

'I'm sorry,' he said, which did ease the tension somewhat. 'Help yourself to another cup of coffee and then tell me what happened when you met Dougie Campbell.'

'OK, but first answer me one question: What made you think I might have killed him?'

'Revenge.'

'Revenge?'

'Yes. You thought Dougie was indirectly responsible for the death of your lady friend in South Africa. Meeting him might have pushed you over the edge.'

'There would have been a certain logic in that argument,' I agreed. 'Except for one thing.'

'Which is?'

'I don't think Campbell was responsible for Freddie's death, because I don't think he was the one who told the Phoenix Group I was in South Africa.'

'But I thought...'

'That I suspected Campbell?'

'Yes.'

'I did, but I changed my mind after talking to him.' I then told him about my meeting with Campbell.

'You mean it wasn't Dougie who told Wren you were in Cape Town?'

'No.' I sipped some coffee, which really was quite delicious.

'If Dougie didn't betray you, who did?'

'Obviously somebody who knew I was going to South Africa.' I paused 'In fact, it could have been you, sir.'

He exploded. 'That, Statton, is a malicious accusation and is close to insubordination!' He banged his fist on the desk so hard his empty coffee cup rattled in its saucer. 'I would never do such a thing.' His face flushed red with anger.

I looked at him steadily. 'It's not nice being accused of something you didn't do, is it?'

The anger slowly drained from his face. 'Touché. You're right. Nobody likes to be wrongly accused of something like that.'

'Don't worry, boss, I know it wasn't you.'

'That's reassuring.'

'However, somebody leaked my travel arrangements to the Phoenix Group. Whoever that person is, was responsible for Freddie's death. I intend to track them down and ensure they receive the punishment they deserve.'

Disraeli-Astor refilled both our coffee cups. 'Good man. Now, what's happening with this American chappie whose been dumped on us?'

'His name is Hank Graham,' I reminded him. 'And it was you who agreed with the CIA that he could join Section Two.'

'Only on a temporary secondment and I made it quite clear that you had the final say.'

'That's what the American Ambassador told me.' I drank some coffee, savouring its rich taste. 'Out of interest what would have happened if I had said no?'

'Ah! That might have made life difficult for us. It might have provoked a minor diplomatic incident.'

'I see. So, I really had no choice.'

'In a manner of speaking.'

'Which means no.'

Disraeli-Astor shrugged but said nothing.

'Look, I have no problem working with the CIA, particularly Hank Graham, but do we really want such a close and cosy relationship with our American cousins?'

'No, we do not. However, it wasn't our decision. We were pushed into a corner by Downing Street.' He didn't look happy about the situation. 'When the US Ambassador contacted me, he had already spoken with the PM.'

'Why am I not surprised? Henry Catto might come over as a laid-back Texan cowboy, but he's one tricky son-of-a-gun.'

'I certainly cannot disagree with you on that point, but, in you, I suspect he's met his match in deviousness. Which is why I had every faith that you would find a diplomatic solution to our little problem. Did you?'

'Yes.'

He smiled. 'So, what have you arranged for Hank the Yank?'

'I have made him Section Two's link with Special Branch and placed him into the temporary care of Assistant Deputy Commissioner Neal.'

'How temporary?'

'Long enough to ensure he doesn't get in my way.'

'Did Neal agree to that arrangement?'

'Oh yes, I had already sorted it out with him before taking Hank to Scotland Yard.'

'See what I mean, Statton? You're a devious sod.'

'I'll take that as a compliment, boss.'

Before he could respond, his phone rang. He picked it up and listened. 'Lambeth Road,' he silently mouthed to me. It was a short call during which he did little more than grunt a couple of times. 'Thanks,' he managed at least that one word before returning the receiver to its cradle. He stared at me.

'Let me guess. The bullets that killed Douglas Campbell and Justin Bloom came from the same gun?'

'Yes,' he said simply.

The Blue Oyster Club, Soho, London

'It's not a good time, David' Manny Silver insisted. 'Today and tomorrow are my busiest nights. I can't afford to be away from the club then.'

'How about Sunday night?' I asked.

Manny shook his head. 'I'll still lose money,' he insisted.

'You were OK the last time you did a job for me,' I pointed out. 'That was at a weekend.'

He shrugged. 'I'll still lose money.'

'Don't worry, I'll pay you the same exorbitant fee as last time. That should cover any losses and just think how much money you would lose if the police decided to undertake a licensing check on you tomorrow night.'

Manny looked at me with his sad Jewish eyes. 'Friends do not make such threats, David.'

'That's very true, Manny. Friends go out of their way to help each other instead.'

Manny held his hands up in defeat. 'So, Sunday it is. Remind me what it is you want me to do.'

'It's simple. I want you to break into Sir Reginald Wren's gaff, open his safe, remove the Gluck pistol, take it outside, fire one bullet into a ball of Plasticine and return the Gluck to the safe.'

'Oy Vey! Simple he says! What if the mark turns up whilst I am performing this simple task?'

'Don't worry. I'll arrange that Wren is kept occupied.'

'And where will I get a ball of Plasticine?'

'A toyshop. Try Woolworths.'

He shook his head in disgust, but offered no more objections.

'I'll collect the bullet from you on Monday morning,' I said. 'Now is there a telephone I can use?'

I rang Kevin Neal's direct line. Luckily he was in the office and answered the phone himself. I explained what I wanted.

'OK, Dave, I'll pick Wren up on Sunday afternoon,' he agreed. 'But I'll only be able to hold him for twenty-four hours unless you can come up with evidence implicating him in a crime.'

'Twenty-four hours will be ample time. Just as long as he's not at home Sunday night. If there's a problem, let me know immediately.'

'There will be no problem,' Kevin assured me.

I said a silent prayer that he was right.

The Wife of Bath, Wye, Kent

Colleen was right about one thing: sex did help relieve my tension.

We went to bed as soon as we arrived at the hotel. Our love making was frantic, intense and satisfying. When I reached my climax, I let out a stifled scream as the frustration, anger and anguish that had been submerged deep within me for so many days exploded from my body.

Satiated we collapsed in a heap of sweat soaked limbs. I rolled off her, but she pulled me back, clinging to me as if I was about to leave her. Perhaps mentally I was, because I was suddenly haunted by ghosts from the past.

Although Colleen was right about sex easing my tension, she was wrong to believe that it would help me forget what I had been through. It didn't.

I could never forget Freddie.

I could never forget the good times we'd had together. I could never forget how much I loved her. I could never forget the plans we'd made for the future and I could never forget the way in which she died.

'Did you love her a lot?' Colleen said softly, as if reading my mind. 'Your South African girlfriend.'

'Her name was Freddie and yes I loved her very much.'

'I'd like to know about her. What was she like?'

So I told her about our short life together, then we lay in silence for a while, each with our own thoughts. I felt Colleen shiver. I thought she was cold, but then I realised she was crying.

What I didn't know at the time was that Colleen was being haunted by her own ghosts. 'I'm so sorry, David,' she sobbed and hugged me.

'Sorry for what?'

'I'm sorry Freddie was killed and that you have been hurt.'

'I appreciate your concern, but there's no reason for you to get upset. It wasn't your fault.'

'But I am upset,' she sniffled.

I hugged her tighter. I was genuinely touched.

'And you think that your friend was killed by the same person who killed Timmy?'

'Yes.'

'I wish I could turn back the clock and take away your hurt.'

'Sadly, nobody can do that, Colleen. Not you, not me, not even God, if there is such an entity. Time is its own master.'

'I suppose you're right,' she said miserably. 'But it doesn't make me feel any better. I just wish I could do something to help.'

'You can help by being my friend.'

She reached up and touched my face. 'I'd like that.' I know I can never replace Freddie, but I want to make things right for you.'

'That won't be easy. Even at the best of times I'm not the easiest of people to get on with, but right now I'm impossible. My emotions are a mess. In addition, I can't promise to pay you much attention at the moment because my whole focus is fixed on getting Shaun Brannagan.'

'I understand. What can I do to help?'

'Just be patient with me. I'm hoping time is the great healer. People say it is, but I have my doubts.'

'I'll be patient,' she assured me. 'You never know. Perhaps someday you'll be able to forgive and forget.' She yawned and snuggled deeper into my arms.

'I will never forgive, or forget,' I whispered, but she was already asleep.

Chapter 36

The Blue Oyster Club, Soho, London, Monday, May 14th

When I arrived at the Blue Oyster Club, Manny Silver was sitting at a table nursing a mug of black coffee and a cigarette. He looked up when I walked in and viewed me with those sad eyes of his. He didn't look happy.

'That's the last time I do a job for you,' he muttered as he invited me to join him at the table.

'And a good morning to you too, Manny.' I sat down.

He waved and a young man appeared from out of nowhere carrying a mug. The youth wore fashionably tight leather trousers and a bright orange shirt decorated with blue parrots. He had long curly blonde hair, vivid blue eyes and a pouting mouth.

'Thank you, Dimitri,' Manny said and his look of sadness deepened as he watched the boy disappear back into the gloom.

'White coffee with one sugar,' Manny said.

'You have a good memory.'

'It's a knack you need in my game.'

'Why's that?'

'To help remember who you can trust,' he said morosely.

'So, what makes you such a bundle of fun today?'

Manny stared up at the small skylight window that was the only source of natural light in the room and through which a shaft of bright sunshine picked out the row of bottles on the shelf behind the bar. He puffed on his cigarette and the smoke swirled up into the sunlight.

'It's my nephew, Dimitri.'

'What about him?'

'He's such a sweet boy.'

'I'm sure he is, but you've had lots of *nephews* like him over the years, Manny.'

He shrugged as he stubbed out his cigarette and lit another in one smooth action. 'You know how it is. Dimitri is still only a teenager and that makes it difficult for men like me, even in these so-called days of sexual enlightenment.'

'So what about Dimitri?'

'He's leaving me.'

'Leaving you?'

'Yes, he's been offered a job with a new uncle.'

'Doesn't he like being with you?'

'Yes, but he likes money and power more.' He shook his head as if the capricious nature of youth was beyond him.

'Where's he going?'

'He's been offered a position with a Member of Parliament.

'Which one?'

'Some important bloke who works for Mrs T. I think Dimitri said he's her PSP.'

'That would be her PPS. He's called a Permanent Private Secretary.'

'Well I call him a mamzer.'

'His name is Sir Peter Morrison. His father was Lord Margadale, so technically he's not a bastard.'

'Well, he is in my eyes. Enticing my Dimitri away from me like that.'

'So how did it go last night?' I asked, moving him away from the subject of his love rival.

'Not good.' Manny looked even more morose, if that was possible. 'I'm getting too old for this burglary lark, particularly when I'm given duff info about the gaff where I'm supposed to be doing a peter.'

'What was the problem?'

'You told me the gaff would be empty.'

'It should have been. I had the Met pick Wren up and hold him for questioning.'

'They might well have done, because he wasn't there, but that bird of his turned up when I was in the middle of the job.'

'Misty?'

'If that's the shiksa's name.'

'Was it the blonde girl he was with in your club the night I was here?'

'Yeah.'

'That's Misty all right. What happened?'

Manny drained his mug and waved it in the air. Dimitri appeared immediately with a coffee pot in his hand and headed for our table. He looked at me and silently raised the coffee pot. I shook my head.

Manny opened a new pack of cigarettes while the youth refilled his mug. He took out a cigarette and laid the new carton on the table next to the recently emptied packet. He lit the cigarette and waited for the youngster to disappear again, before starting his story.

'It was easy enough to break into the gaff because the burglar alarm wasn't on.'

'Didn't you find that odd?'

He shrugged and looked embarrassed. 'Everything looked kosher so I didn't think nothing of it. Anyway, I went upstairs to the study where the mark's peter is hid behind some fancy portrait. Opening it was a piece of piss because I already knew the combination lock number from my last visit.

'I took the pistol out and checked it was fully loaded then went downstairs to the kitchen where I took a tea towel from a drawer. I made my way out the backdoor to the rear garden. I wrapped the towel round the pistol to deaden the sound of the shot as I fired a slug into a ball of Plasticine. It worked like a dream, by the way.

'I went back upstairs and put the pistol back in the peter.' He paused just long enough to light a cigarette and take a long contemplative drag on it and blow smoke out into an increasingly hazy atmosphere. 'So far, so good,' he said eventually.

'But?' I prompted.

'That's when it started to go tits-up. Just as I was about to leave I heard footsteps on the stairs. I dived behind the curtains. I'm standing there like a right schmuck when the bedroom door opens and somebody walks in.

'I peeked through a crack in the curtains for a butcher's and see it was Wren's bird. She walks straight over to the picture, opens the peter and takes out the pistol.' He paused theatrically. 'Then she looks straight at where I was hiding,' he went on. 'I thought she was going to shoot me. I swear I almost shit myself.'

Manny took another long drag on his cigarette then expelled the smoke with a loud sigh.

'She obviously didn't shoot you, because you're still here.'

'Obviously,' Manny said crossly, perhaps because I had spoilt the build up to the climax to his story. 'She put the gun in her handbag and went back downstairs. I thought she was probably taking it to Wren.'

'Probably,' I agreed, although how Misty thought she could

431

smuggle the pistol into a police cell was anybody's guess. 'So everything was alright in the end then?' I said. '*And* you managed to return home without soiling your underpants.'

'It's all very well taking the piss out of me,' Manny complained, 'but you weren't there.'

'Where's the bullet?' I asked.

'You really do have some chutzpah,' he countered with a shake of his head. 'What about showing me the dosh first?'

I pulled an envelope from the pocket of my jacket and passed it to him. He made a point of counting the notes carefully.

'Where's the bullet, Manny,' I repeated quietly.

He picked up the empty cigarette packet from the table and flipped open the top. 'Hold out your hand.'

I did as I was told and watched as he tipped the packet upside down. A small plastic bag containing a spent bullet dropped from the box into the palm of my hand.

'I guessed you'd want me to keep the slug as clean as possible before forensics get hold of it,' he almost smiled. 'I thought you might want this too.' He took a used brass cartridge case from his pocket and handed it to me. 'It was the one I shot. Before you ask; just in case Wren knew how many slugs there were in the pistol, I found a box of spares in the peter. I used a spare to replace that one.' He pointed at the empty case in my hand.

'Manny, that is why I like doing business with you,' I said.

The Metropolitan Police Forensic Science Laboratory, Lambeth Road, London

As I made my way by taxi to Lambeth Road, I mulled over the telephone conversation I had just had with Kevin Neal. It seems that when Wren was given the opportunity to make a phone call on his arrest, he didn't contact his solicitor, he rang Misty Olafson.

However, that didn't prevent Wren from getting immediate legal representation, because within an hour of his phone call to Misty, a solicitor had turned up at Canon Row Police Station demanding to see his client.

The station commander had managed to hang on to Wren for several hours, but was eventually forced to release him in the early hours of Monday morning, shortly after Manny's successful visit to his home.

It was surely no coincidence that Misty had visited Wren's home at about the same time to collect his gun for him, but for what purpose? That was a question for which I had no answer.

There was still something nagging at the back of my mind. Instinct told me I was missing something important, but I hadn't been able to nudge it forward by the time I arrived at the Met Police Forensic Lab.

I had already arranged to meet the forensic scientist who had identified the similarity between the bullets that killed Justin Bloom and Douglas Campbell. Dr Paul Maguire was waiting for me in reception when I arrived.

'You made good time,' he said.

'The afternoon rush hour traffic was lighter than usual,' I explained as he led me through to the cloak room attached to the small laboratory that specialised in ballistic crime.

'Can I ask you to get into these scrubs?' Maguire passed me a green top and trousers. 'We like to keep the lab as clean as possible for obvious reasons.' He slipped on his own overalls.

'No problem,' I replied as I followed suit.

'Unfortunately, we're going to have to mess up our hair wearing one of these hats.' He handed me a plastic cap and smiled as he saw me look at the bald dome of his head. 'Rules is rules. Hair or no hair.'

I tried to slip the cap over my head, but found it difficult to tuck my hair underneath. I needed a haircut, but Maguire didn't seem to notice the tufts of hair that stuck out from beneath the cap.

'And these.' He handed me a pair of surgical gloves, put on a pair himself and then led me into the lab towards a long workbench on which stood an array of microscopes.

He picked up two small plastic containers with red lids. He showed them to me. They had identical labels, except one had printed on it the name Bloom and the other read Campbell. 'I understand you want to talk to me about these little babies.'

'Yeah. First up; how can you be so certain the bullets came from the same weapon?'

He tapped the side of his head. 'Experience and half a brain.'

I pointed to the workbench. 'And having access to the right equipment presumably?'

'And the right equipment,' he agreed. 'Would you like me to

show you?' He didn't give me a chance to answer, instead he set up a strange looking piece of equipment.

He took the spent bullet from the Bloom container and put the small lump of lead onto a glass slide.

'It looks like a double microscope.'

'It's called a comparison microscope,' Maguire explained. 'It's actually two microscopes that are connected by this single optical device.' He tapped the top of the machine. 'It provides me with a split view that allows me to see two separate specimens at the same time.' He placed the bullet from the Campbell container on a second slide.

'Would you like to look?' He asked as he moved aside to make way so that I could sit on the stool that stood in front of the bench. I looked through the eyepiece of the microscope.

He carried on talking. 'There are two aspects in any identification process. The first thing we do is identify the type of weapon that has fired the bullet. We do that by using three main pieces of information. The first are the lumps and bumps we find on the lead that are created by the rifling in the weapon's barrel. Can you see them?'

'Clearly,' I told him.

'The second is the calibre of the bullet, from which we can calculate the diameter of the barrel. Those are nine-millimetre Parabellum. And the third bit of information is the spiral marks on the bullet that tell us the twist of the rifling in the barrel.'

'I can see those marks,' I confirmed. 'I take it the twist is important?'

'Oh, yes. For a start the barrel of most pistols has a right-handed twist, but those manufactured by Colt are always left-handed.'

'And these bullets?'

'They are not from a Colt.'

'They're right-handed?'

'Yes.'

'That leaves an awful lot of options.' I stood up and moved away from the bench.

'It does, there are loads of nine-mill hand guns on the market, but those bullets are slightly different, which makes them somewhat unique. I'm pretty certain they were fired by a Glock 17 semi-automatic pistol.'

My heart missed a beat at that information. 'How certain is pretty certain?'

Maguire laughed. 'I'd sooner bet on my opinion than a horse running in the Grand National. The rifle in the barrel of most handguns is made using a broaching machine, which cuts into the metal with teeth, however, with a Glock the process is different.

'A slowly revolving mandrel is forced through the barrel. This method not only provides a better seal inside the barrel, which in turn makes better use of the gases when the gun is fired, but also reduces the amount of marking on the bullet, which increases the accuracy.'

'The markings on those bullets looked pretty similar,' I said. 'Do bullets that are fired from any one hand gun have the same markings?'

'Mainly.'

'Mainly?' I queried.

'In forensic science the conclusions made during an examination depend to a large extent on the training and expertise of the scientist involved. For instance, when comparing bullets found at a murder scene with those fired from a known weapon, we look for striations that line up. Once we find one match we look for more matches.

'There is no pre-determined number of consecutive matches that prove the bullets are the same, which is why I always caveat my evidence by making clear that I had found only sufficient agreement between the samples used. That does not make it a certainty.'

'Would you have more confidence in making such a declaration if there was no court case involved?'

'For sure,' Maguire said. 'But I would need an exemplar to make such a decision.'

'An exemplar?'

'Yes, a known sample from the weapon in question.'

'Like this one?' I took from my pocket the plastic bag containing the bullet that had come from Wren's gun and handed it to Maguire.

'Is that from the suspected murder weapon?'

'Yes. It came from a Glock 17.'

He looked at me and grinned. 'So, I was right,' he said, with more than a hint of triumph.

'Only if the bullets match.'

Maguire removed from the comparison microscope the bullet that killed Douglas Campbell and returned it to its plastic storage container. Carefully, he took the Glock bullet from its plastic bag and placed it on the test slide and lined it up with the first bullet.

He sat down on his stool and peered through the eyepiece of the microscope in silence for several minutes and then said: 'We have a match. Those bullets came from the same weapon. I'd stake my life on it.' He stood up. 'Would you like to look?'

'No thanks. I'll take your word for it.'

'Is there a name you want me to store the bullet under?'

'Yeah. Reg-the-sledge.'

'Is that some kind of joke?' He asked.

'I wish it was,' I replied with feeling.

Shepherd's Bush, London

Following our trip to Kent I had spent the previous night at Colleen's flat, so hadn't been home since Thursday. When I eventually arrived at my apartment, it was to be greeted by three days' mail.

I flicked through the envelopes and rooted out the junk mail. Most of it was advertising products and services I didn't want. One leaflet offered me cut-price insurance and another promised me the chance to win thousands of pounds in exchange for an annual subscription to a magazine that's only usually found in the waiting rooms of doctors and dentists.

I threw all the unwanted rubbish in the waste bin. What envelopes remained I added to the small pile of unopened mail that had been on the kitchen table since my return from South Africa. Most of the envelopes looked as if they contained bills and I decided they could wait another couple of days to be opened.

However, amongst the envelopes I found a note from Alf, the old man who lived in the flat underneath mine and acted as unofficial, and unpaid, concierge for the block. Alf knew everything that went on in the building.

The note was written in the neat, but spidery scrawl of an octogenarian.

> *Dear Mr Stratton*
> *One of your lady friends come calling this morning. I told her you were out and suggested she come back tonight. I hope that was in order?*
> *Yours sincerely*
> *Alf (downstairs)*

I took off my coat, poured myself a whisky and considered the note. I wondered momentarily whether Alf was confused and had mixed me up with one of the other tenants. I quickly dismissed that idea out of hand.

My neighbour was closer to 90 than 80 and was increasingly crippled with arthritis. However, although he was old and infirm, he was still mentally alert. I was certain Alf would not confuse me with somebody else. If he thought a woman had visited me, then it was only a question of who she was. I thought about that for a while, but nobody sprang to mind

I wandered over to the window and looked out onto a street scene that was slowly disappearing as dusk threw a veil of darkness over Shepherd's Bush.

My road was deserted except for a dozen parked cars and a battered skip that was half-full of builder's rubble. It had come from the grand old house a few doors away that was being converted into more flats. I didn't recognise any of the cars, except for my battered old Rover 2000 and an almost new Nissan Micra, which belonged to Alf.

Because of our close proximity to the BBC Television Centre and the Loftus Road home of Queen's Park Rangers Football Club, it was not unusual to see luxury cars parked in the area. However, I had never before seen a Rolls-Royce Corniche convertible parked in my street.

Now there was a Roller parked in front of the skip. As far as I could see the car was empty, but there could have been a chauffeur asleep in the driver's seat for all I knew.

I made my way back to the kitchen to see what I could find to cook for my supper. The fridge was empty except for some cheese coated with mould, a few rotting vegetables and half a bottle of curdled milk.

I threw them all in the waste bin with the junk mail and looked in the kitchen cupboards. I found a tinned steak and kidney pie and some baked beans. I was hungry and after a weekend of fancy food this simple fare was suddenly very appealing.

I turned on the oven, opened the pie and put it in. I was in the middle of opening the tin of beans when my doorbell rang. I made my way down the hallway, unlocked the door and half opened it, leaving the security chain in place.

Misty Olafson peered at me through the crack. 'I need your help, Mister Statton.' Her eyes were full of unshed tears. She carried a large black leather handbag, which she clutched to her chest like it was a newly born baby. 'Can I come in?'

I slipped the chain off its hasp and opened the door to let her in. I ushered her along the hallway to the lounge, where she plonked herself down on the settee and put her handbag on the floor next to her feet.

'What's the problem?' I asked.

'It's him.'

'Who's "him"?'

'Reggie.'

'What about Reggie?'

'Can I have a drink?'

'I don't have much.' This was an understatement. I didn't even have milk for tea or coffee.

'What do you have?'

'Whisky, water, or whisky and water.'

'Whisky and water will be fine.' She paused and smiled wanly. 'Without the water.'

I poured a neat whisky and handed it to her. I freshened up my own drink at the same time and then sat down in the armchair opposite her. 'What's the problem with Reggie?'

'He has killed people.'

'That, my dear, is like saying the earth is round. I know all about your boyfriend's past.'

'I'm not talking about his past. I'm talking about the here and now. A couple of weeks ago Reggie killed a private detective called Justin Bloom and last week he killed a government minister called Douglas Campbell.'

'How did he kill them?'

'He shot them with a gun.'

'Well, he could hardly shoot them with a knife.'

She looked at me with narrowed eyes and gave me her hungry lion look. 'You know what I mean,' she snapped.

'Why did Reggie shoot them?'

'Bloom found out he was involved with a group that's planning to murder Nelson Mandela and tried to put the squeeze on him. Reggie doesn't take kindly to being blackmailed.'

'What about Douglas Campbell?'

'Somehow he discovered what happened to Bloom. Reggie was frightened Campbell might grass him up, so he decided to shut him up.'

'So why have you come to me?'

'Because you work for the Government.'

I stared at her without comment.

'You can't deny it. I was with Reggie in the *Blue Oyster* when you told him you were with the Department for Covert Operations.'

'That still doesn't explain why you're here.'

She clasped her glass tightly and her eyes welled up again. 'Reggie is going to kill me.'

'Why would he do that?'

'Because I found out about Bloom and Campbell.' She made the murder of the two men sound as if she had discovered a new toiletry brand. She sipped her whisky and then added quietly: 'He's going to kill you too.'

'Is that so?'

She glared at me. 'You don't believe me!'

'Does it show?' As it happens, I did believe her, but I saw no reason to let her know that.

'You have to believe me.' Her voice rose in frustration.

'I don't *have* to do anything,' I said. 'However, I'm prepared to give you a chance to convince me you're telling the truth.'

'Thank you.'

'There's no need to thank me. Just tell me what makes you think your boyfriend is going to kill me.'

'Because he told me.'

'When was this?'

At first, she appeared not to answer me. 'Reggie was arrested by the police last night,' she said instead.

'On what charge?' I pretended ignorance about Wren being picked up by Special Branch.

'I don't know. He never told me. He just rang me at my flat and told me to contact his solicitor and then go around to his place. He asked me to pick up his car and the gun from his safe and take them to him.'

'At the police station?'

439

'No, he told me to meet him in the café opposite the nick.'

'I see. What happened?'

'It was awful.' Her voice quivered as she spoke. 'As soon as I handed the gun to him he jumped up and started screaming at me. He grabbed me by the hair and accused me of grassing him up.' She paused and took another sip of her whisky. This seemed to settle her. 'I've felt frightened of Reggie before, but this time his anger was the real deal. He was like a madman. He pointed the gun at me and said he was going to kill me and then come after you.'

'What did you do?'

'I kicked him in the balls and ran out of the café as fast as I could. I jumped into his car and drove round for a while before coming here.'

'What make of car is it?' I knew instinctively the answer.

'A Rolls-Royce.'

'Reggie won't be happy you took his roller.'

'Fuck Reggie!' She swore angrily and then finished off her whisky with one gulp. 'I need another drink.' She held her glass out.

'How did you know where to find me?' I poured a single measure of whisky into her glass.

'Justin was tailing you and I was with him when he followed you home.'

'Why was he following me?'

'Reggie hired him because he was worried about you and wanted to keep a track on what you were up to.'

'So why were you with Bloom? Couldn't he follow me on his own?'

'He did work alone most of the time, but occasionally he asked me to join him. For instance, when he followed you to the theatre, he thought it would look better to have somebody with him.'

'How did Bloom know I was going to the theatre?'

'He didn't say. Perhaps he bugged your phone.'

I thought about that possibility for a few moments. If Bloom had infiltrated the department's internal phone system then it was a major security lapse. I decided to mention it to Disraeli-Astor.

'How long was Bloom following me?'

'For two or three weeks, until Reggie killed him.'

I looked at her silently and then asked: 'Where's he now?'

'I don't know. Perhaps he's at the hospital having his balls rubbed by a nurse.' She knocked back her drink in one go and silently held out her glass. She looked at me with eyes that dared me to refuse her request.

I didn't. I stood up, took her glass and poured more whisky into it.

'I don't know what to do. I can't go home because Reggie might be there. He has a key and will kill me if he sees me.'

'There are hotels.' I handed her glass back to her.

'I wouldn't feel any safer in a hotel. Reggie would still get to me. He has spies everywhere in London.'

'What about a women's refuge? I think there's one in Hammersmith. It's not far away. You would be safe there. They are geared up to protect vulnerable women.'

She looked at me as if I was mad. 'Do I look like somebody who would be happy living in a refuge with a bunch of losers?'

'Needs must.'

'I'll never be that needy,' she snapped. She seemed to have forgotten how frightened she was.

'I was just trying to be helpful.'

'You could help by letting me stay here.'

'I'm not sure that's a good idea.'

'Why?'

'No doubt Bloom told Reggie where I lived.'

'Of course.'

'Well he might guess you came to me for help. If he finds you here, he'll think you betrayed him and kill you for sure.'

'But he'll kill me anyway,' she insisted. 'And at least if he found me here I'd have you to protect me, wouldn't I?'

This was becoming a difficult situation. She was backing me into a corner. She probably guessed I could never send her away with the threat of death hanging over her head. 'I only have one bedroom,' I said eventually.

'I don't mind sleeping on the sofa.' Tears welled in her eyes again.

I still couldn't work out whether she was in genuine distress or a damned fine actress. I decided there was only one way to find out. 'The sofa is not very comfortable,' I pointed out.

'Fuck comfort, at least I'll be safe.'

'You can have my bed,' I offered.

Misty smiled with relief. She stood up and walked over to my armchair. Without warning she plonked herself down on my lap and put her arms around me. 'Thank you, David. You're very sweet.'

She reached up and ran her fingers through my hair. As she moved, her right breast pressed against my chest. I felt her hard nipple through my shirt and realised she was bra-less. It was not the worst feeling I'd ever experienced.

'Can I call you David?'

'You just did.'

Misty laughed and hugged me. 'We could always share the bed,' she whispered in my ear. She lowered her hand to my groin and started to massage me.

This was an unexpected turn of events and it wasn't one I particularly welcomed. There was something about Misty that was disconcerting. She was surrounded by an aura of danger I had sensed first when I saw her with Wren at Manny's club. I didn't trust her and had no idea what she was up to, but I decided to play along with her game. If it was a game.

'Are you sure?' I asked.

'Is this your answer?' She kissed me passionately on the lips and increased the tempo of her massaging hand.

I felt myself becoming aroused.

Misty must have felt it also, because she slipped off my lap and pulled me to my feet. She led me over to the settee, pushed me down on my back, pulled down the zip on my trousers and released me from my underpants.

She hoisted her skirt above her hips and I saw she was wearing no briefs. Then, before I could pull away, she sat astride me, guided me into her and started moving up and down with an urgency that was almost animal like in its baseness. Her eyes were closed and there was a look of deep concentration on her face as she took as much pleasure as possible from what she was doing.

There was no passion in the act and it was plain Misty had no concern for my feelings. She was using me as a sex toy. I felt disgusted and my own arousal began to wane. I went to pull myself away, but I was too late. As I moved Misty climaxed and let out a cry of ecstasy.

She opened her eyes and when she looked down at me, it was with Scandinavian blue eyes that were filled with a strange mixture of lust, power, hatred and madness.

That's when the thing that had been niggling away at the back of my mind leapt forward with a force that jolted me. It was something Douglas Campbell had said during our conversation in his Commons office.

'*I didn't know Misty was the girl's name,*' Campbell had told me. '*Wren introduced her to me as Bridget. That's what I called her. I never knew her surname.*'

But I did know Misty's real name. It was Bridget Olafson. Suddenly everything fell into place. She was the BO who had an appointment with Justin Bloom on the day he died. She was the person who had sex with both Bloom and Campbell before she killed them.

This realisation raised another alarming certainty in my mind. I was in big trouble. If murdering her victims after having sex with them was how Misty got her kicks, then it was my turn next.

Misty must have recognised the sudden understanding in my eyes, because she slipped off me and delved into her handbag.

I read somewhere that a man is at his most vulnerable during and after sex. I can now testify to the truth of that statement, because my recent experience certainly slowed down my reactions.

I was left temporarily paralysed as Misty pulled a pistol out from her handbag. She stood there, half naked, with her legs apart and her skirt still hitched round her waist. Even if I hadn't recognised the gun, I would have guessed it was a Glock 17 pointing at my chest.

But my paralysis quickly passed and my training kicked in. I twisted off the settee and knocked Misty to the floor with my right leg just as she pulled the trigger. The stray bullet hit my television's screen, which exploded in a shower of glass, shredding the Yucca plant that stood in a terracotta pot next to it.

Misty leapt to her feet with a scream and pointed the gun at me again. As I stared at her, the hem of her skirt slipped down to cover the top of her legs. This sudden movement seemed to put her off. She glanced down and this gave me the time needed to move. I rolled away as she looked back up and fired. This bullet blew a hole in the large red rug I had bought from Camden Market, the wooden floor boards underneath it, and maybe Alf's ceiling for all I knew.

She snarled and jumped towards me, presumably to get closer so she didn't miss with her third shot. It was a bad mistake. She now stood on my damaged rug, where, only seconds before, I had been lying. She hesitated as she carefully aimed at my head. This was her second mistake. I twisted away, grabbing the rug with both hands as I moved.

I tugged with all my strength and the rug was literally pulled from under Misty's feet. She fell backwards across the settee, still clutching the pistol in one hand.

I jumped up and grabbed her. I pulled her to her feet and held her tightly in a bear hug. She wriggled and squirmed like an eel and, despite the vice-like grip I had on her arms, she somehow manoeuvred herself into a position that allowed her to raise the gun. I felt its muzzle press into my stomach.

As she fumbled for the trigger, I used my left arm to lift her bodily from the ground and at the same time reach between our bodies. With my right hand, I twisted her arm, pushing the Glock away from me just as she fired.

There was a muffled bang and Misty cried out in surprise as the bullet punctured her abdomen and drove up through her body towards her diaphragm, ripping through her internal organs as it went. Then, as the pain finally set in, she cried out again, this time in agony. Blood trickled from her mouth as she went limp. She was dead before I lowered her onto my already ruined red rug.

I searched through her handbag and found the keys to the Rolls-Royce plus a set of house keys. I guessed one would be to Wren's front door. I hoped I was right because a plan was already forming in my mind.

I went through to the kitchen, which was full of the smell of cooking. That's when I remembered I had put a pie in the oven. I turned it off and put on a pair of the disposable latex gloves I kept in a drawer. I cleaned the Glock thoroughly, dropped it into a freezer bag and returned to the lounge.

I threw Misty's handbag onto her body and rolled them both up in the rug. I put on my coat and slipped the bagged gun into a pocket. I picked up Misty's body and carried it out of my apartment and down the stairs. When I reached the hall I paused and listened.

I could hear Alf's television blaring out. It sounded as if he was watching Panorama, which I knew was one of his favourite programmes. He was almost totally deaf, so it was very unlikely he would have heard the shots above the sound of the television. He would certainly not hear my footsteps as I made my way quickly towards the communal entrance and let myself out.

Night had fallen completely by the time I stepped outside and it was almost totally dark. The street lights were still not working, despite numerous complaints to the council by local residents.

Nobody saw me carry Misty to the Rolls-Royce, still wrapped in the rug. I dumped her body and handbag in the boot. I opened the driver's door, slid behind the wheel and started the big V8 engine.

I headed towards Belgravia, driving slowly and obeying all the road signs, not even taking a chance of driving through an amber traffic light, as I might otherwise have done. I didn't want any keen traffic cop pulling me over and demanding to look in the boot. I reached my destination without incident.

When I arrived outside Wren's house, I saw the lights were on. It looked as if he was at home. That was good. There was a large black fob on the car's key ring, which I worked out was a remote control for the electric garage-door that was under the house. I pressed a button on the fob and the door swung up and over. I reversed slowly into the garage and the door automatically closed behind me.

There was a side-door in the garage and when I turned the handle I found it was unlocked. It seemed I didn't need Misty's bunch of keys after all. I pushed the door open and found myself in a utility room full of sinks, washing machines and retractable clothes lines. The sinks were dry, the machines were empty and there were no clothes hanging on the lines. Wren, and the late Bridget Olafson, did not seem very domesticated.

There was a door on the other side of the utility room. I opened it and stepped into a hallway connecting the front door with a wide flight of stairs leading up to the first floor and, beyond, a door I guessed led to the kitchen.

Somewhere above me I could hear Dave Brubeck playing *Take Five*. I wondered whether it was a vinyl recording or one of the new compact discs. I decided a man of Wren's age would be playing the former, although he could easily afford the latter.

Opposite me across the hall was another door. I opened it and found it led into a large lounge full of expensive looking furniture. At one end of the lounge was a long settee, across which lay a beautiful silk throw with Chinese scenes on it. The last time I had seen something similar it was on display in a smart West End shop with a

£3000 price tag on it. Reggie certainly knew how to live the good life.

I grabbed the throw and made my way quickly back to the garage where I laid it on the ground. I lifted Misty's body from the boot, removed the blood-stained rug and hid it in the dark shadows under a workbench, which was fitted to one side of the garage.

I wrapped Misty's body in the very expensive Oriental shroud, carried it back to the lounge and positioned it on the settee. I pulled the throw aside so that Misty's face was visible. She looked as if she was sleeping.

I returned to the garage and used the car phone in the Rolls-Royce to ring Manny Silver and Kevin Neal. Then I made my way back to the hall and started up the stairs, grateful to Dave Brubeck for covering my approach.

When I reached the landing at the top of the stairs a floorboard creaked loudly. A burglar's nightmare. The volume of the music was turned down and Wren's voice called out from behind a door at the end of the landing: 'You took a long time, Bridget. I suppose you screwed Statton's brains out before you shot him.'

I walked along the landing, treading softly.

'Come and tell me all about it, babe. You know how it turns me on to hear what you get up to with other men. I bet the bastard died with a smile on his face.'

I pushed open the door and found myself in Wren's study. The wall opposite me was taken up with book laden shelves. To my left was displayed an array of framed pictures, one of which was a large oil painting of a seated and smiling Sir Reginald Wren wearing the insignia of a Knight Batchelor. The wall to my right was covered from floor to ceiling with curtains.

Wren was sitting in a winged armchair, in front of one of the book shelves, at the far end of the room. He was smoking a cigar and had a large balloon glass of cognac and a half-full decanter in easy reach on a low Queen Anne table that stood alongside his chair.

On the other side of the chair was an expensive looking brushed steel music system, the top part of which was a record player. A black LP was still playing, filling the room with the sound of Dave Brubeck. On the front of the player, in small, discreet letters was the name *Bang and Olufsen*. This reminded me of my recent encounter with Misty and a macabre thought sprang to mind... Bang! And

Olafson was dead.

Life is full of such ironies.

'There were no smiles from me, Reggie,' I said as I stepped into the room. 'And as you can see I'm certainly not dead.' To give him his due, he showed no sign of surprise or alarm.

Instead, he stared across at me and then casually drew deeply on his cigar before blowing smoke rings in the air above his head. 'What the fuck do you want, Statton?' He asked, expelling the last of the smoke from his mouth as he spoke.

'I've brought something for you.' I walked over to him, bent down and turned off the record player.

'What the hell...' he started, but stopped when he saw me take the freezer bag from my pocket and remove the Glock 17 from it. I still wore my disposable latex gloves but Wren didn't seem to notice. He just looked at me in silence. I held the gun by its barrel and handed it to him.

Wren took the Glock and stared down at it. He weighed the weapon in his hand, clasping and unclasping the grip as if deciding what to do with it next.

'Don't even think about it, Reggie. Mine's bigger than yours.'

He looked up and found he was staring down the barrel of my Smith & Wesson Magnum.

'Size isn't everything,' he said with a wry smile.

I had to hand it to him, it takes a real cool character to joke at such a time. Either that or he was as insane as his girlfriend. That was a distinct possibility.

'You might change your mind after my point four-four bullet tears your heart into a dozen pieces. Actually, I'd love you to make a move, because it would give me an excuse to show you what I mean. I still owe you for the death of my deputy.'

'I had nothing to do with his death. It was the Irishman.'

'Yeah, but your friends and you hired him. In my eyes that makes you an accessory before the fact. You are as guilty as he is. So, go ahead and try to pull that trigger and see what happens.'

Wren must have realised I was serious, because he very slowly and gently laid the Glock down on the table next to the decanter and picked up his cognac glass.

He took a sip before asking: 'Where did you get it from?' He nodded towards the Glock.

'Where do you think?'

'I suppose you got it from that bitch, Bridget, but how?

'She gave it to me.' I picked up the Glock and slipped it back in my pocket.

'I don't believe you.'

'What you believe is immaterial. The important thing is I have the gun and you don't.'

'OK, so why did she give it to you?'

'That too is immaterial. All you need know is that she turned up on my doorstep claiming you were going to kill her.'

'Why would I kill her?'

'Only you know that. Her version was that you wanted her dead because she found out you killed Bloom and Campbell.'

'She's lying.'

'In that case, she's a very convincing liar.'

'I can vouch for that,' he said bitterly.

'Your girlfriend also claimed you were going to kill me.'

He didn't try to deny threatening to kill me, instead he simply asked: 'Where is she?'

'The last time I saw her she was sitting in an interview room at Canon Row Police Station singing like a canary.'

'The double-crossing whore!'

'I think we can certainly agree on that.'

'Look, Statton, it was Bridget who killed them two geezers, not me.'

'That's something you will have to argue about with her in court. It's not me you need to convince, it will be a jury. However, that might be difficult because both men were killed with your gun.'

'That's rubbish! The gun belongs to Bridget.'

'Then why was *her* gun kept in *your* safe?'

'I don't know what you're talking about.'

'Of course, you don't, Reggie.' I pointed to his portrait on the wall. 'The next thing you'll tell me, is that you don't have a safe over there, in which there are spare cartridges for the gun you claim belongs to your girlfriend.'

Wren looked stunned.

'In addition, your safe contains compromising photographs of the Right Honourable Douglas Campbell MP having sex with your girlfriend; a bag of cocaine; and ten thousand pounds in cash.

448

There's also a passport in the name of Ernest Thompson which just happens to have your photograph in it. That might take some explaining away.'

I looked at him for a reaction and could see he was still dumbstruck. Keeping my pistol pointed at him, I wandered over to the wall on which the pictures were displayed and tugged on one side of his portrait. It swung open on hinges to reveal a safe. I spun the combination lock, using the code that Manny gave me when I rang him earlier. The safe opened with a click.

'See what I mean?' I reached into the safe and one by one took out the bundles of £20 notes and placed them on a coffee table that stood on the floor next to the wall. I also took out the false passport.

'Who gave you the code to my safe?'

'Do you really have to ask? How many people know it?'

'The bitch!' He swore angrily.

'If you say so.' I smiled.

Somehow Wren managed to bring his anger under control and regain his earlier composure. He stared at the money for a few seconds and then turned away, puffing nonchalantly on his cigar.

I closed the door with a clang that drew Wren's attention again. I spun the combination wheel so that the safe was locked, and then put the portrait back into position.

Wren saw that the cash and false passport was still on the coffee table and his eyes narrowed.

'You're in big trouble, Reggie. We've got you bang to rights. Your only hope is that you get some do-gooder, liberal judge, who believes even thugs like you are redeemable, so only sends you down for a twenty-year stretch.'

Wren took another sip of his cognac and continued to puff on his cigar. He stared at me silently. He was waiting.

'Of course, there might be another option,' I said quietly.

'Which is?'

'This ten grand goes in my pocket and you get to use this.' I picked up the forged passport and tossed it to him.

'Just like that?' He asked suspiciously. 'No conditions?'

'Don't be silly, Reg. Everything in life is conditional.'

'I thought that might be the case.' He relaxed a little. Knowing I was imposing conditions seemed to reassure him I was making a serious offer. 'OK. What's the deal?'

449

'It's very simple. We're going to head to your bedroom where you will pack a suitcase. We will then go downstairs to the garage where you will get into your very nice, very comfortable, very expensive Rolls-Royce.'

'It's not in the garage. Bridget took it.'

'I returned it to you for her. She didn't want to see you.'

'I bet she didn't. The cow.'

I took the car keys from my pocket and threw them to him, where they joined the passport that was already sitting in his lap. 'You will drive straight to Heathrow, you will not stop on the way, and you will not go to your bank to collect money, not even two hundred pounds. If you do, you will go straight to jail.'

'I suppose you think that's funny?'

I didn't respond, instead I continued: 'When you get to Heathrow you will catch a flight out of Britain. I don't care where you go, as long as you are outside the jurisdiction of Europol and the FBI. That leaves you plenty of alternatives. Is that understood?'

'Yes.'

'Do you have your credit cards handy?'

'Yes.' He looked over at the bundles of cash. 'And I take it you will keep all the money.'

'Of course.'

'I thought so,' he said with a sneer. 'At the end of the day, Statton, you're just the same as all the other, two-bit, corrupt cops whose palms I've been greasing over the years.'

'You're wrong there, Reggie. I'm not the same. I have far more expensive tastes than the bent plods you've dealt with in the past. Ten grand is nowhere near enough for me.'

'How much do you want?'

I pointed at the pile of bank notes. 'In addition to that, I want a cheque for ninety thousand pounds, which you will write before we leave this room.'

'You must be joking.'

'I never joke about money, Reggie. That's my price.'

'But a hundred grand!'

'How much is your freedom worth?'

He took only a few seconds to consider that question. 'OK, it's a deal.'

'Excellent. Now, where's your cheque book?'

450

'In the drawer of that desk over there.'

'Get it,' I said.

Later, I watched as Wren packed his suitcase. He worked in a slow, precise way that was at odds with his hard man image.

'You're taking too long.' I walked over and grabbed a couple of suits from his wardrobe and threw them in his case.

'Oi! What's your game?' He asked crossly. 'I like to fold my things properly.'

'Don't worry, I've folded suits before. I'll fold these while you grab some more clothes,'

He glared at me, but made no more objections as I carefully folded the suits with one hand. My other hand was still holding the Smith & Wesson and it was trained on him as he turned his back on me and delved into his wardrobe again. He returned with an armful of neatly folded shirts and stared down at my handiwork.

'Satisfied?' I asked.

'I suppose,' he grunted grudgingly and placed the shirts carefully on top of the suits.

'OK, that's enough.' I closed the lid of the case. 'We haven't got all night and I want you on a plane as soon as possible.'

He shrugged and picked up the suitcase. We made our way downstairs. He didn't bother to turn any of the lights off, but then I don't suppose you worry much about electricity bills when you're a multi-millionaire.

I escorted him through the utility room to the garage and watched as he put his suitcase in the car's boot. Finished he got in the car, with me still pointing my pistol at him.

'Don't come back,' I told him, 'or you will regret it.'

He threw me one last hate filled look, but said nothing. I left him at the wheel of his car and made my way back to the hall where I quickly flicked the light on and off three times. It was the signal for which Kevin Neil was waiting.

I stood in silence and listened to the Rolls-Royce engine start up and then heard a metallic squeal as the garage door opened. Almost immediately the strident sound of sirens filled the air as police cars converged on the front of the garage.

I made my way down the hall to the kitchen and out of the backdoor into the garden, before disappearing into the dark night.

Chapter 37

Colonel Disraeli-Astor stared at the stack of £20 notes on his desk. 'Can this money be used in evidence against Wren?'

'No way!' I gave an emphatic shake of my head. 'If we handed it over to the prosecution, I would be forced to admit my involvement in Wren's capture and arrest. Such publicity is the last thing the department needs.'

'And I suppose the same goes for this?' He picked up from his desk the £90,000 cheque Wren had written.

'Even more so. It has my name on it.' I took the cheque from him and tore it into small pieces. I dropped them into the large glass ashtray that sat on his desk, and was only used when he smoked the occasional cigar he was unable to enjoy at home because his wife disapproved.

Astor took a box of matches from the top drawer of his desk. Slowly and deliberately he set light to the little pile of paper. 'What about the police?' He asked as we watched the remnants of the cheque be consumed by bright yellow flames. 'Won't they report your involvement?'

'Don't worry, I won't be mentioned. I've squared things with ADC Kevin Neal. His story will be that Wren was captured after outstanding detective work by Special Branch officers following an anonymous tip-off.'

'Can you trust him?'

'Yeah. As things stand, the Met can take all the credit. It would make no sense for Kevin to involve me, because it's the management of such outstanding detective work that turns Assistant Deputy Commissioners into Commissioners. Who in their right mind would jeopardise that prospect?'

'What about Wren? He knows you were involved.'

'That's true. In fact, Wren's brief is already squealing about his client being set up by the British Secret Service. However, the Met are playing a straight bat and denying our involvement.'

'Will the murder charge against Wren stick?'

'Yeah. He has zero chance of getting off, unless the police, or prosecution brief screw up big time.'

'What about the woman?'

'Bridget Olafson you mean?'

'Yes. Wren claims she killed the detective and Dougie.'

'And he'll continue claiming his girlfriend was the killer, but it won't stick.'

'I thought you said it *was* her and she also tried to shoot you?'

'Oh, it was Bridget alright. She got her kicks from screwing and then killing men,' I replied.

'I still can't believe a woman would do such a thing.'

'There have been many female murderers through the ages.'

'I know that. I meant the other thing.' He paused. 'You know... getting sexual satisfaction out of killing somebody.'

'Olafson wasn't the first woman to get her kicks that way. Just think Myra Hindley. She and Ian Brady got it off killing youngsters.'

Disraeli-Astor blushed. He had a naïve belief in the innocence of women and really was a prude when it came to all matters sexual, which is why I hadn't told him what Bridget did before trying to shoot me.

'So, if the woman did kill Bloom and Dougie, what makes you so sure Wren won't be believed?'

'Because the evidence does not back up his claim.

'Explain.'

'Just consider the facts. One: The woman was found dead in Wren's lounge. Two: Forensics will prove she was shot with the same pistol that killed Bloom and Campbell. That evidence alone will scupper Wren. Even if the defence could somehow prove that Bridget Olafson killed Bloom and Campbell, which is very unlikely, she certainly can't have killed herself.'

'I can see that,' he conceded.

'But there is more,' I said. 'Three: Wren was caught in his car leaving the scene of the crime. 'Four: He was carrying a false passport, which even the most incompetent CPS lawyer would be able to convince a jury was proof he was fleeing the country.

'And five: and perhaps the most damning evidence against Wren, is that he had a suitcase in the boot of his car, in which the police found the pistol that killed all three people. Finally, six: The only person's fingerprints on that gun were Wren's.'

'Did you put the gun in his suitcase?'

'Of course.'

'How did you do that?'

'Sleight of hand,' I replied with a smile. I explained how I tricked Wren into putting his prints on the Glock 17 and then slipped it into his suitcase when I was packing his suits.

'Very smart. Remind me to check my pockets before you leave. So why was the detective fellow killed?'

'I suspect Bloom put the squeeze on Wren. He was probably after more money. That was a stupid thing to do, because Reg-the-sledge doesn't take kindly to being threatened. Talking of Bloom, I asked the Olafson woman how he knew my movements.'

'What did she say?'

'She suggested he might have bugged my telephone line. I think we should get the department's phone system checked out.'

'I'll have the technical wonks look into it,' he said and made a note on the pad that was on his desk. 'Now what about Dougie? Why was he killed?'

'I think it was because he told Wren he would no longer feed him information. He immediately became superfluous to requirements, but was a danger to the Phoenix Group because of what he knew. The only way to ensure his silence was to kill him.'

'Are they really that ruthless?'

'You'd better believe it, boss.'

He nodded sagely, as if I was only telling him what he already knew. 'Which leads us nicely to Mandela's visit. What's the latest on the security arrangements?'

'There's not much more to report. I'm meeting ADC Neal and Hank Graham at the Commons tomorrow. We're going over the final arrangements with the Serjeant at Arms and then I will be going back to Parliament on Thursday to keep an eye on things.'

'Is everything in hand?'

'I think so, but don't expect me to put that in writing. There are far too many fingers in this particular security pie for me to give any guarantee of success.'

He didn't respond to this comment - he didn't like hearing bad news - instead he sat staring at the bundles of £20 notes.

'What are we going to do with this bloody money?'

'We could give it to charity,' I suggested.

He pondered on that for a few moments. 'Or we could give it to

Timmy's mother,' he said eventually.

This was a different side to the usually ultra-bureaucratic Rupert Disraeli-Astor and he went up in my estimation. 'Good idea, boss.' I wondered what his reaction would have been if I had made that suggestion.

He pushed the cash towards me. 'Do it discreetly. I don't want it coming back to bite us in the backside.'

'Leave it to me. I'll sort out something.'

He stared at me.

'What is it?' I asked.

'I think you should sort out a haircut first. You look like a bloody hippie.'

My boss would never change. You can take an officer out of the army, but you can never take the army out of an officer.

Chapter 38

Houses of Parliament, Westminster, Thursday, May 17th

I stood on the green in New Palace Yard and watched as a convoy of three long, black limousines drove slowly through Carriage Gates accompanied by police motorcycles.

The cars were armour-plated, with bullet proof glass windows, and belonged to the US Embassy. However, the motorcycle outriders were courtesy of the Metropolitan Police and were protected only by leathers and crash helmets.

As the vehicles made their way slowly towards the entrance to the Palace of Westminster used by MPs, where the police escort peeled off. They headed back towards Carriage Gates, where they parked up to await the return journey to the South African Embassy, where Nelson Mandela was staying.

It was a lovely day. The afternoon sun, which beat down from a clear blue sky, glinted on the gold crown that sat atop the sculpture in the middle of the Jubilee Fountain.

I watched as the convoy drew up outside the public entrance to Westminster Hall. Plain clothes Special Branch policemen clambered out of the first and third car, joining armed uniformed officers who stood on either side of the huge wooden double-doors.

Nelson Mandela climbed out of the middle car, escorted by two men, one of whom was Kevin Neil, wearing the dress uniform of a senior officer in the Metropolitan Police. The second man was Hank Graham, who wore a sharp dark suit, white button-down shirt, sober club tie, dark glasses, shiny black shoes and an air of casual competence.

The ANC leader stood on the pavement and studied the impressive Gothic architecture of the Palace of Westminster. For the first time I appreciated his stature: he had the straight-backed bearing of a warrior and an air of authority, a reminder that he was descended from the Thembu Royal Family.

The African towered over ADC Neil, who stood in front of him, and matched inch for inch Hank Graham, who was over six feet tall and who was positioned behind Mandela to guard his back.

The CIA agent stood with his left hand in his trouser pocket and his right held nonchalantly across his chest. He looked relaxed, but I knew that at the first sign of trouble he would be able quickly to draw his weapon from the shoulder-holster that his loose-fitting jacket concealed.

I scanned the area, looking for early tell-tale signs of any potential attack. The entrance to Westminster Hall seemed to present little threat. There were no possible ambush positions that I could see and it was well protected by armed police, supplemented by parliamentary doorkeepers.

The doorkeepers were unarmed, but highly trained and well-practiced in handling difficult situations as part of their responsibility of policing the Commons, to which cops are barred, because police officers are technically servants of the Monarch.

On the other side of New Palace Yard, was an arched colonnade that linked Star Chamber Court to the Clock Tower. This seemed a more likely place from which to launch an attack.

I studied the small groups of parliamentary staff that had congregated on the pathway in the colonnade to see Mandela's arrival. They were being kept at a safe distance from Westminster Hall by armed police.

Above the colonnade were scores of office windows on three floors. These too were a concern, because they offered a possible opportunity for a sniper. However, it took only a quick scan to reassure me the windows were all closed and there was no sign of life behind them.

To my left was a grassy bank on top of which was a wall and high railings. This was also a position, from which a sniper would have a clear line of fire. However, this threat was nullified by the armed policemen who lined the pavement on Bridge Street.

Satisfied there was no imminent threat to the ANC leader I looked back towards Westminster Hall in time to see him being ushered by Hank and Kevin through double-doors held open by two ramrod-straight doorkeepers.

The doorkeepers were dressed in their uniform, consisting of a black long-tailed coat, white bow tie, and silver-gilt waist badge of office. Beneath the badge hung a figure of Mercury, which symbolises one of their important historic roles, which is to act as messengers between the House of Commons and the Monarch.

I let out a sigh of relief. The first stage of Mandela's visit had been safely navigated without any hint of trouble. However, this was no time for complacency; the most dangerous part of the exercise was still to come.

When Mandela eventually made his way from Westminster Hall to Speaker's House he would be exposed for much longer than the few seconds it had taken him to be escorted from his car into the hall. That would be the critical period.

I wandered over to Speaker's Court to check out the route that would be taken. Usually there are cars parked in the small quadrangle, but today it was empty. To protect against car bombs all three entrances in the quadrangle had been sealed with heavy concrete barriers. In one corner scaffolding had been erected as part of the rolling programme of repair work taking place across the Parliamentary estate. There were platforms made from sturdy planks on three levels of the scaffold.

There was nobody working on the scaffold tower, because work had been suspended for the afternoon on the orders of the Serjeant at Arms. However, there was a ladder leading to each level, attached to the scaffolding by heavy ropes. Although it was unlikely anybody would be able to climb up the ladders to target Mandela, I wasn't prepared to leave anything to chance.

A handful of workmen in helmets and yellow Day-Glo jackets were standing with the staff still waiting patiently in the colonnade in the hope of catching a glimpse Mandela when he made his way to Speaker's House.

I went over and showed my identity card to one of the workmen. I asked him to remove the ladder that reached from the ground level to the first platform and find somewhere to store it away. Surprisingly, the man agreed without too many grumbles.

As he worked, I used my time to assess yet again likely fields of fire and possible hiding places. I looked also for tell-tale signs that might hint of a potential attack. There were windows in the buildings surrounding Speaker's Court, but like those overlooking New Palace Yard, none were open and there was no sign of life.

Although I could see nothing suspicious or threatening, I sensed Mandela was in danger. I had always acted on instinct and now my intuition told me Shaun Brannagan was somewhere on the parliamentary estate. That made me very nervous.

However, there was no evidence of the Irishman's presence and I had nothing tangible on which to base my unease. That worried me even more. I hated the unknown. If knowledge is power; too often, ignorance is a disaster waiting to happen.

I watched as the workman made his way across the quadrangle towards Star Chamber Court, with the ladder on his shoulder. He disappeared round the corner, no doubt in search of somewhere to store it.

Shrugging aside my disquiet, I made my way back to New Palace Yard. As I entered Westminster Hall, I looked around the cavernous building for potential dangers. There were no obvious places in which Brannagan could hide.

Even if the Irishman had somehow secreted himself in Westminster Hall, there were armed police positioned at strategic points, including inside the main entrance and at the top of the steps leading to St Stephen's Hall and Central Lobby.

I was confident Nelson Mandela would be safe and well protected whilst he was within the confines of Westminster Hall. However, I was still worried about what would happen once the ANC leader left the building and headed for his tea appointment with the Speaker. I was convinced if Brannagan was going to strike, that's when it would be, but I had no idea exactly where, or what form it would take.

In the northwest corner of Westminster Hall there is a flight of stairs that leads to the Jubilee Room and the Grand Committee Room. It was in the latter room that Mandela was now addressing members from both Houses of Parliament.

I mounted the stairs and headed towards one of the doors leading to the Grand Committee Room. My way was barred by two more uniformed policemen, bearing the same carbines as their colleagues in the main hall and with the same hard eyes.

One of the policemen stood in front of the door, whilst his colleague blocked a narrow corridor that led through to the Jubilee Room and a second entrance to the Grand Committee Room.

I showed them my pass and the cop nodded, at which signal a doorkeeper opened the door. Immediately I heard Mandela's loud, mellifluous voice speaking from the far end of the room.

The African was standing behind a lectern reading his speech.

'We have waited too long for our freedom. We can no longer wait. Now is the time to intensify the struggle on all fronts. To relax our efforts now would be a mistake which generations to come will not be able to forgive…'

He looked up as I stepped into the room. He smiled as he recognised me, but carried on talking. He seemed to know the script off by heart and I guessed he had used the speech before.

People sitting in the rows of chairs in front of me looked over their shoulders to see who had entered, but most of the audience ignored me.

The handful of plain clothed Special Branch officers who were dotted round the room studied me with watchful eyes. One of them made a point of letting me see him edge a hand towards the open front of his jacket, beneath which hung a shoulder-holster full of Glock 26.

The cops only relaxed when they saw me make my way silently over to join Kevin Neal and Hank Graham, who had positioned themselves strategically at the far end of the back-wall, near the second entrance into the room.

'How are things outside?' Kevin Neal whispered.

'I've had a good look round, but found nothing,' I replied in an equally hushed voice.

'You don't look convinced,' Hank Graham chipped in quietly. He knew me too well.

'I'm not,' I admitted. 'I think Brannagan is here.'

'In the Palace of Westminster?' Kevin asked.

I nodded.

'Where?'

'I don't know.'

'What makes you think he's here, Dave,' Hank asked.

'Nothing more than old fashioned gut instinct.'

'Gut instinct is good enough for me,' the American said.

'How long is the main man going to be?' I nodded towards where Mandela was still speaking.

Kevin looked at his watch. 'Not long,' he said. 'He's due to have tea with the Speaker at four.'

I leaned towards Hank. 'What do you think of the security?' I asked, continuing the whispered exchange.

'It's real tight,' he assured me. 'Your Special Branch boys aint done badly for limeys.'

'OK, I'm going back outside to keep my eyes open until you

bring Mandela out. Just be careful.'

'Don't worry, we're cool. You just look after your own butt.'

'Hank's right,' Kevin added. 'We have everything under control.'

'I know that's meant to reassure me, Kev,' I said as I eased past him and headed for the door, 'but I think you'll find the captain of the Titanic used the same words and look what happened to him.'

When I arrived outside the sun was lower in the sky and already casting longer shadows across the buildings as it edged slowly away from its zenith. Each of the windows that looked down on the New Palace Yard from above the colonnade reflected its own mini yellow orb, making me squint as I looked up at them.

I was about to make my way up the steps leading to the Jubilee Fountain when I saw a small group of people on the top step. In the middle was a tall man who I recognised as a Member of Parliament.

He was Frederick Peyton-Blaine, a renowned publicity seeking chancer who spent most of his time being interviewed on television, discussing whatever subject happened to be topical that day. He was the original talking head; all opinions and no principles. He was everything I disliked in politicians.

The MP was flanked by a number of his constituents who seemed pleased to be with him. I suppose there is no accounting for taste. They were being photographed by a young woman, who I assumed was a member of Peyton-Blaine's staff.

I spoke to one of the armed policemen who was guarding the entrance to Westminster Hall and asked why he had allowed the group to get so close to the building's entrance.

'It's a real breach of security,' I complained.

'I did try to stop them,' said the cop. 'But the tall bloke with them is an MP.'

'I know who he is, but that doesn't make the group any less a security risk?'

'I'm sorry, sir. However, the MP insisted he had a right to take constituents up onto the green. He said nobody could stop him.'

There was a young doorkeeper standing next to the policeman who nodded his agreement. 'Technically he's right, sir,' he said. 'MPs and their guests have unrestricted access to New Palace Yard.'

'I appreciate that,' I said. 'However, I would have thought special restrictions would have been put in place today because of Mister Mandela's visit.'

461

'That's what I thought too,' the doorkeeper said. 'Which is why I contacted the Serjeant at Arms to check. He said it would be okay for Mister Peyton-Blaine and his constituents to have their photo taken on the steps, as long as they didn't take too long.'

My heart sank. Sir Alan Urwick's reaction reinforced my already low expectations about security on the parliamentary estate. The idea that the right of an MP to have his photograph taken with constituents should take precedence over the safety of a visiting statesman seemed to sum up the perverse priorities of the House authorities.

The problem was that administration of Parliament was stuck in the 1890's. In the last hundred years the world had moved on, but unfortunately security in the Palace of Westminster, organised by the Serjeant of Arms and Black Rod, had not moved with it.

'Is everything OK, sir?' The doorkeeper asked nervously.

'Don't worry, son. You did the right thing checking with the Serjeant at Arms. Leave it to me.'

I climbed the steps and joined the group. I showed my Met warrant card to the MP. 'Excuse me, sir,' I said politely. 'Could I have a word in private?' I pointed towards the fountain, which was several feet from where his group stood.

'No you cannot. Can't you see that I'm having my photograph taken with my constituents? You'll have to wait until we've finished.' He spoke in a loud voice, with a broad Yorkshire accent.

'I'm sorry, sir, but what I have to say can't wait. It's very important.'

'So are my constituents. They've come all the way down from Sheffield to see me.'

'I'm sure they have, sir, but I must insist. This is police business.' I still had my warrant card in my hand and I waved it at him again.

He took it from me and studied it carefully. 'Very well,' he said resentfully as he handed the card back to me. 'What is it?'

'I really do think it would be better if we had a private chat, sir,' I insisted.

He sighed heavily and shook his head in exasperation, but he excused himself from the group and followed me over to the fountain. 'Well?' He asked grumpily when we arrived.

'No doubt you are aware that Nelson Mandela is currently addressing both Houses of Parliament in Westminster Hall?'

'That is not exactly true, Inspector...?' He raised an eyebrow in query, as if he couldn't remember my name, despite having just spent a long time staring at it on my warrant card. I suppose it was his way of putting me in my place. 'Ah, yes... Stratton.' I noticed his Yorkshire accent had softened.

'Statton,' I corrected him.

'I apologise,' he said with a politician's lack of sincerity.

'And you are?' I played him at his own game.

'Fred Blaine. I am a Member of Parliament.'

'Ah, yes. I remember you now, but I thought your name was *Frederick Peyton*-Blaine?'

'I prefer the shorter version,' he said. 'An aristocratic background and a double-barrelled name might be acceptable to voters in the Home Counties, but it does not help one get elected in South Yorkshire.'

'I suppose not.' It is rare for an MP to admit being cynical and shameless. I almost admired his honest admission of only adopting the cloak of the common man to progress his political career. Almost but not quite. 'What's not true?' I asked.

'What you said about Mandela is not true. He is not actually addressing Parliament. It is only an informal meeting with representatives from the Commons and the Lords, who were invited by the Speaker.'

From his dismissive tone, I guessed Blaine had not been included on the invitation list and was not happy about it.

'And frankly, Inspector Stratton, I do not approve of terrorists being invited to address Parliament.'

'It's Statton,' I reminded him, although I guessed he was deliberately getting my name wrong. Either that, or he was a complete idiot. 'Whether Mister Mandela is a terrorist, is not something on which I am qualified to comment, sir. My only concern is that he is currently talking to members of Parliament in Westminster Hall...'

'The meeting is in the Grand Committee Room actually,' the MP interrupted me in a patronising tone that made clear he thought it was me who was the idiot.

'Thank you for pointing that out, sir.' I felt my anger rise but I kept any irritation out of my voice. 'However, where Mister Mandela is speaking is irrelevant. The important thing is that he is a guest in our country and the Prime Minister has asked us to keep him safe.'

'I hardly think you are in a position to lecture me on Government policy, Inspector,' he intoned pompously. 'Of course, the man must be kept safe.'

'I am pleased you agree, sir.' I managed to keep my tone civil although he was really starting to irritate me. 'With that in mind, you will understand that maintaining a proper safety regime on the parliamentary estate is critical.'

'That goes without saying,' he said.

'It does indeed. The problem is that the presence of your constituents is compromising that safety regime.'

'Nonsense. My constituents are a threat to nobody. *They* are not terrorists. They pose no threat to Mandela.'

'I'm not worried about them threatening Mister Mandela,' I explained. 'I am more concerned about *their* safety.'

'I don't understand,' he said and for the first time he had lost some of his self-assurance.

'In that case let me make it clear to you, sir,' I said quietly. 'Very shortly Mister Mandela will be escorted out of Westminster Hall. When that happens anybody in the vicinity who is not known to his bodyguard is likely to be considered a potential attacker and could be shot if they so much as twitched the wrong digit.'

'That's outrageous. They cannot simply shoot people, just like that,' Blaine protested.

'I can assure you, sir, nobody will be shot on purpose. However, accidents do happen, particularly when there is cross-fire. They and you might be caught in that cross-fire.'

'Are you threatening me, Inspector?'

'Absolutely not, sir. I'm just trying to be helpful. If an unfortunate incident did happen, it would be you who would have to explain to the media why you allowed one of your constituents to be shot, despite having been warned in advance of the danger.'

That got to him. MPs hate negative publicity. Blaine glared at me, but returned to his constituents with a fixed smile on his face. He ushered them down the steps and then made his point by taking his time to lead them across New Palace Yard.

When Blaine and his group reached the colonnade, they joined the other sightseers clustered on the pavement.

I took the group's place at the top of the steps. My position provided me with the best possible panoramic view of the surrounding area. I waited for Mandela and his security detail to emerge from Westminster Hall. I glanced at my watch and saw it was five minutes to four o'clock. They would be appearing soon.

The young doorkeeper left his position alongside the armed policemen on duty outside the entrance to the hall and came up the steps to join me. He was tall and well-built. He peered shyly at me through horn rimmed spectacles.

'I don't know how you managed to persuade Mister Blaine to move,' he said, 'but I'm grateful for your help. I was really worried about their presence.'

'So was I, son.'

'What did you say to him?'

I was about to reply when Mandela came out of Westminster Hall surrounded by a mixture of uniformed and plain clothed cops. The only distinguishing feature they shared was their size. Those boys were all big. Hank Graham was with them and he was bigger than most. He saw me and gave a tight smile.

Mandela stopped on the pavement to chat to the policemen who were guarding the entrance. Hank looked over at me and gave me a resigned smile. This was not in the plan.

Suddenly I saw a movement in front of me. The sunlight that was reflecting on one of the windows opposite, changed shape momentarily. I pulled my .44 Magnum from my shoulder-holster.

I stared up at the building but at first saw nothing. Then I realised it was a small window on the second floor that had caught my eye. Where before it was closed, now it had been opened upwards by a few inches.

As I studied the opening I saw something metallic poking out. It didn't take a degree in weapon design to recognise the barrel of a rifle and it was pointing at Mandela and his entourage.

'Down!' I screamed at Hank Graham.

I saw the American grab Mandela and bundle him to the ground just as the muffled sound of a single rifle shot rent the air. Even from my position at the top of the steps I heard the dull thud as a bullet struck home.

I didn't wait to check who the bullet had hit. Instead, I aimed at the window and fired a shot that drilled a hole in the window with a crack that echoed round New Palace Yard.

'Where's that window?' I shouted at the young doorkeeper.

'The reporters' offices,' he replied without hesitation.

'How do I get there?'

'Come on, I'll show you.' The youngster was already running down the steps.

I followed him, taking the steps two at a time. Out of the corner of my eye I saw that one of the policemen who had been guarding Mandela was sitting on the ground clutching his chest.

Once we reached the road, the doorkeeper ran towards the colonnade. The youngster was quick and I was already half a dozen yards behind him. I heard running footsteps behind me. Glancing over my shoulder, I saw Hank Graham. Like me he carried a pistol in his hand.

'This way,' the doorkeeper shouted as he reached the colonnade and disappeared through the short arched tunnel that led to the Star Chamber.

There was a loud clatter and when we reached the tunnel I saw on my left a heavy door. It was half open and sprawled across the floor of a small lift lobby was the young doorkeeper.

His leg was tangled in the rungs of the wooden ladder that the workman had stored against the wall of the lobby, opposite the lift door. Unfortunately, the ladder was too long and the bottom of it had protruded across the entrance.

The doorkeeper was lying in front of the lift, with blood running from a gash in his head. His left arm was twisted under his body at an unnatural angle. He had lost his spectacles and his face was as white as a sheet. He winced as he tried to sit up.

'Up those stairs,' he managed to say through gritted teeth. He pointed to the corner behind the lift with his good hand. 'Second floor. Door on your left. Up steps. Toilet.'

I stepped over the ladder and headed up the winding staircase with Hank close behind me. On the second floor landing we were confronted by double-doors. They led to offices and the library through which reporters gain entry to the Lower Reporters' Gallery, which looks down onto the debating chamber of the House of Commons. The library was deserted.

To our right were a handful of steps that led up to a lavatory door. We went up the steps and I pressed my ear against the door. I listened, but could hear nothing.

466

'Cover me,' I whispered as I twisted the handle and pushed open the door. With my weapon held in the classic two-handed stance, I pressed myself against the wall and edged gingerly into the room. It was empty. I checked the cubicles and found they were empty as well.

The lavatory had only one window, which was at the far end of the side wall. It had been raised several inches. I walked over and looked out. New Palace Yard was now deserted except for armed policemen who guarded Carriage Gates. I hoped all the other exits on the parliamentary estate were covered as well. I didn't want the gunman to escape.

There was a hole in the lower pane of glass and surrounding it were splatters of blood. There was more blood on the back wall and a few drips on the floor.

'There's more here, Dave.' Hank pointed at the floor by the door. 'You must have hit him.'

I re-joined him. 'It was Brannagan,' I said.

'How can you be so sure?'

'It was him,' I said with certainty.

'So where'd he go? Is there another way out?'

'Yeah,' I replied. 'There is a lift and stairs at the end of the corridor where the reporters have their offices, and there are more stairs at the other end of the library.' I pointed behind him. 'They lead down to the Hansard offices on the floor below.'

'Hansard?' Hank queried.

'It's the official record of every day's proceedings in Parliament, word for word.'

'Bet that's a gripping read.'

'You'd better believe it.'

'OK. I'll go check those stairs out. You take the corridor.' With that he went down the toilet steps in one leap and ran across the reporters' library and disappeared through the door at the end.

I opened the door to the reporters' corridor and walked cautiously through with my .44 Magnum at the ready. I headed for the fire-door at the far end, checking all the offices on the way.

The offices were as deserted as the library. I guessed the reporters were either in the Reporters Gallery, or had been in Westminster Hall listening to Nelson Mandela and had probably been detained after the shooting. If so, they would not be happy. They would be champing at the bit to phone through their report on the afternoon's events.

There was no sign of Brannagan.

When I reached the fire-door, I found it was locked. There was also an *Out-of-Order* sign on the lift. No doubt the lack of an alternative escape route in the event of a fire would have sent the parliamentary health and safety officer into a fit. However, I was grateful the security guard tasked with unlocking the fire-door had been so tardy. At least I knew Brannagan hadn't escaped via this corridor.

I made my way back to the library just in time to see Hank emerge from the door at the end. He shook his head. So, the Irishman was still somewhere in the vicinity.

I made my way down the steps to the doors that led to the Lower Reporters Gallery, looking for any sign of Brannagan.

There were three spots of blood in a line across the floor. I looked up and saw Hank was halfway across the library on his way to join me. I held up my left hand to stop him and indicated with my gun that I was going through the door. He nodded his understanding.

I pushed open the door and made my way into the stepped gallery, where several reporters were sitting listening and taking notes of the proceedings in the debating chamber below. They would have no idea what had just happened in New Palace Yard.

It was silent in the gallery and I could hear clearly the voices of the Members of Parliament who were speaking. In the Public Gallery were a number of people concentrating on what was being said in the chamber below.

Nobody noticed me as I walked silently along the back of the gallery, checking out the reporters.

The clock on the wall opposite showed the time at four-thirteen. Less than a quarter of an hour had passed since the attempt to assassinate Mandela, but it seemed much longer.

I studied carefully the people in the Lower Reporters Gallery and it soon became clear none of them was Brannagan. Having satisfied myself the Irishman was not hiding amongst the reporters, I made my way to the far exit and pushed open the door.

It was as if time had stood still. The library was still deserted and Hank was standing in the same alert position. Behind him was a row of telephone booths with wooden folding doors. Each booth

468

contained a fitted stool and a shelf on which stood an ancient black Bakelite phone. Above the shelf was a much smaller shelf into which was sunk a brass ashtray.

The door to one of the booths opened silently and Shaun Brannagan stepped out. He was pressing his right hand against the front of a white shirt that was stained red. I could see clearly the scar on the back of his hand. Blood dribbled from where his missing finger would have been and dripped down onto the scuffed toe caps of his shoes. His face was gaunt and pain was etched across his pallid features. I felt no sympathy. He deserved all he got.

Behind the Irishman I could see a Kalashnikov AK47 propped against the side wall of the booth from which he had just emerged. He didn't need the rifle, because in his left hand he held a semi-automatic pistol and it was pointing at Hank Graham's back.

Hank had no idea he was in danger. He was still looking at the door through which I had entered the Lower Reporters' Gallery only minutes before. He hadn't noticed I had come out of the other entrance. Nor had Brannagan.

'I'm here, Shaun,' I said quietly.

The Irishman turned to face me. His eyes blazed with hatred when he recognised me. 'You!'

'Yes, me.' I pointed my .44 Magnum at him.

'You did this to me?' He removed his hand from the front of his shirt. He held it up to show me a blood covered palm. He looked as if he was swearing an oath.

'No, this did.' I raised the Magnum until it was level with his eyes.

If Brannagan saw my weapon he didn't acknowledge it. Instead he pointed his own pistol at me. His aim was steady, despite his obvious pain and the weakness caused by loss of blood. But he didn't pull the trigger immediately, instead he grinned malevolently at me and hissed: 'I've been looking forward to killing you. So I have,' he said.

'You tried once before,' I reminded him.

'Aye. So I did.'

'And you failed.'

'Aye, but at least I killed your little, half-caste whore, which was the next best thing. I only wish I'd had a chance to shag the slut before she died.'

469

I closed my ears to that last comment. I realised that I was dealing with a monster. I had to keep a level head if I was going to defeat him. 'I hope killing an innocent young woman made you feel proud of yourself, Brannagan.'

'Oh, it did. In fact I took great delight in killing her. And now it's your turn to die, Statton! Die you prod bastard...'

But those few moments of self-indulgence were Brannagan's downfall. Those micro-seconds of delay allowed me to fire my pistol first. The Smith & Wesson's heavy .44 Parabellum bullet hit him in the centre of his forehead and his head disintegrated in an explosion that covered the telephone booths with blood and bone.

Hank Graham had witnessed our conversation. Now he walked over and stared down at the dead Irishman. He prised the pistol from Brannagan's hand. He looked at it sombrely. 'Thanks, pal,' he said simply.

'No problem. Look upon it as repayment for saving my life that time in South Africa.'

Chapter 39

Disraeli-Astor glanced up at me as I entered his office. I had been summoned to report on the previous day's events. He looked pleased with himself. 'I have been on the phone all afternoon,' he said.

'Well done! You get top marks for agility and endurance.'

'Don't be facetious, Statton. I have just been talking to Fraser's mother. She sounds rather agreeable.'

'Your coffee is agreeable too. Can I have some?' I pointed towards the tray that stood on his desk.

'Help yourself and top my cup up at the same time.'

'What did Mrs Fraser have to say for herself?' I asked.

'It was a confusing conversation.'

'I know the feeling,' I said as I poured our coffees. 'Sometimes, I get confused when I talk to you.'

'I was the one who was confused, not her,' he said huffily.

'Why were you confused?' I added cream to my cup and showed him the jug.

He shook his head. 'I'm trying to watch my waistline. My wife says I drink too much cream.'

'A dash won't kill you.'

'Oh, go on then. Just a little. A couple of spoonful's will be enough.'

'You said you were confused?' I prompted as I used a teaspoon to put cream in his coffee.

'Yes, she was burbling on about Fraser winning the lottery and something about a lost ticket.'

'Ah, yes! That would be the one I found when I cleared out Timmy's desk drawers.'

'You found a lottery ticket in Fraser's desk?'

'Not just any ticket. It was a winning ticket.'

He looked at me suspiciously. 'A winning ticket?'

'Are you going to query everything I say?' I asked. 'Yes, it was a winning ticket.'

'What did you do with it?'

'I claimed the money, paid it into my bank account and then sent a cheque to the solicitor who is acting as the executor of Timmy's estate.'

'When did all this take place?'

'On Wednesday.'

'I see,' he said and I could see from his expression that the penny had finally dropped. 'Let me guess. The amount Fraser won was ten thousand pounds?'

'You must be psychic, boss,' I responded straight faced.

He sipped his coffee and looked at me over the rim of his cup. 'Damned fine work, Statton,' he said eventually. That was praise indeed. 'So that explains why Mrs Fraser asked me to thank you for sorting out her son's lost ticket for her.'

'It was the least I could do. How's she doing?'

'It seems she was struggling financially after Fraser's death, but the lottery money will help her get back on her feet. She's going to use it to start up a beauty salon with her daughter.'

'That would have pleased Timmy,' I said.

'I know. It's a shame he is not here to see it,' he said sadly. We sat in silence for a few moments and then he added: 'But, at least you got the bastard who killed him.'

'Yes. That will be some consolation to his mum.' I remembered the plea Mrs Fraser made to me at his funeral.

'So, tell me exactly what happened yesterday.'

'We were very lucky.' I explained how close Nelson Mandela came to being assassinated.

When I had finished he said: 'What I don't understand, is how Brannagan got into the Palace of Westminster in the first place. Security in Parliament must be pretty ropey.'

'That underestimates the usefulness of rope, boss.'

'Is security really that bad?'

'The most charitable way of describing the arrangements would be to say that they are inconsistent.'

'They are rubbish?'

'Exactly. The police are excellent and check everybody who goes through the gates, but they have to let in anybody who has a parliamentary pass. Once inside, pass holders can go pretty well where they like without being checked.'

'How easy is it to get a parliamentary pass?'

'All applications for a pass are subject to security checks, but, as

Brannagan proved, the system is full of holes.'

'But people can't get on-site without a pass?'

'No.'

'What about members of the public?'

'They have to go through security and are issued a temporary pass. However, they only have access to certain areas, such as Central Lobby.'

'Do we know how Brannagan gained access?'

'Yes. He was carrying a pass accrediting him as a political reporter for the Irish Times. Special Branch believe it was a forgery.'

'What about his weapons? How did he get them in?'

'Nobody will ever be sure, but you can take your pick from a range of options. For instance, he could have concealed them in a bag and thrown it over the railings in Bridge Street in the middle of the night and collected it first thing in the morning.'

'Surely that would risk the bag being seen by somebody before it was collected.'

'Yes it would, which is why it is more likely his bag was smuggled through the Carriage Gates in the back of one of the many service vehicles that come and go all the time.'

'Don't the police check them?'

'Up to a point, but it's impossible to check everything that's carried in every van. For instance, think of the clutter that can be found in the back of a builder's van, or one being used by a telephone engineer.'

'I see what you mean.' He looked thoughtfully out of his window. 'You were right,' he said eventually. 'We were lucky.'

'Bloody lucky.'

He finished his coffee and put his cup gently down on its saucer. 'I had another couple of phone conversations this afternoon. The first was with the American Ambassador.'

'What did he want?'

'It appears the Yank who was chairman of the Phoenix Group has disappeared.'

'His name is John Engels,' I reminded him.

'That's the chappie.'

'The disappearance of Engels doesn't come as a surprise. He's probably on a one way trip courtesy of Uncle Sam.'

'Where to?'

473

'A CIA black-site somewhere.'

'Do black-sites really exist? I thought the State Department denied they used secret foreign prisons?'

I stared at him and then said: 'Come on, boss, don't be so naïve. The Yanks would say that wouldn't they?'

'So they do exist?'

'Of course they do.'

'How can you be so sure?'

'Because I visited one a couple of years ago.'

'What was it like?'

'It was in the Moroccan Sahara; it wasn't on the country's tourism map; and it was certainly no holiday camp. Trust me, if Engels is being held by the CIA in a similar black-site, then he won't be surfacing for some time.'

'That's comforting.'

'Not for Engels, it aint,' I said. 'What else did the Ambassador have to say?'

'He updated me on another Phoenix Group leader.'

'Which one?'

'The Frenchman.'

'Maurice Sevier?'

'Yes.'

'Has he disappeared too?'

'No, far from it. His Paris flat was raided by the Sûreté last weekend. He was arrested for tax evasion and child pornography.'

'Child pornography?'

'Yes, they found thousands of pornographic images on his computer. He denied all knowledge of them, but the Sûreté arrested him anyway.'

I was impressed. That was a real belt and braces job by the CIA. 'Where's he being held?'

'He's currently in La Santé Prison awaiting trial.'

I knew the prison well. It is one of the most dangerous prisons in the world. 'Is that so?'

'You know it?'

'Yeah. It's not a good place to be. However, I expect he's being held in the wing used for Western European prisoners. That won't be too bad.'

'The Ambassador told me Sevier is being held in B block. Does that mean anything to you?'

'B block? Are you sure?'

'Yes, that's definitely what he said. Why?'

'That's where prisoners from Africa are kept. It's the roughest, toughest wing in the prison. The inmates will hate having somebody like Sevier in their midst. He won't last five minutes.'

'Do you think that is what the French Authorities are hoping?'

'Very likely,' I replied. 'They'll be more than happy if Sevier meets a fatal accident in prison and isn't able to appear in front of a judge.' I reached for the coffee pot. It was empty.

'I'm sorry,' he apologised. 'I'd get Colleen to make another pot, but she went home early today.'

I noticed he didn't offer to make more coffee himself.

'She said something about visiting her father,' he explained.

'Her father?'

'That's what she said. You look surprised.'

'I am. If she's visiting her old man, he must have made the most miraculous recovery since the resurrection of Jesus Christ.'

'What do you mean?'

'Colleen told me her father was dead.'

He frowned. 'Perhaps I got it wrong, or perhaps you misunderstood what she said.'

'Perhaps I did,' I agreed. 'So no more coffee then?'

'No, but I still have some Cognac left. Can I tempt you?'

'Does the sun set in the evening?'

He smiled, got to his feet and headed for his drinks cabinet.

'So three of the Hydra's heads have been decapitated,' I said as I watched him pour a measure of Courvoisier into a glass. He held the bottle to eye level to check how much was left, and finding it almost empty he drained the rest into my glass and dumped the bottle into the waste bin.

'Hydra's heads?' He put a generous measure of single malt whisky into a glass for himself.

'Yes, I told you about it. Catto used it as an analogy for taking out the leaders of the Phoenix Group.'

'Of course you did.' He handed me a glass. 'Hydra's heads.'

'Well three of them have now been chopped off,' I repeated.

'Four,' he said. 'The third phone conversation I had this afternoon was with the South African Ambassador.'

'They're like London busses. You don't see an ambassador for ages and then two come along one after the other.'

'I hadn't thought of that.' He stroked his scar. 'I'm always getting caught out by buses not sticking to the timetable.'

At first I thought he was joking and then realised he was serious. Sometimes I despair. 'So what did Hendrick Meyer want to talk about?'

'Jonathan Rhodes.'

'Have they arrested him?'

'No, although the police did attempt to arrest him.'

'What do you mean "attempt"? Did he escape?'

'Again no. Although when the police swooped on his home he tried to escape.'

'But he failed?'

'In a manner of speaking.'

'What does that mean?'

'Rhodes drove his car straight at a police road-block that had been set up at the end of his drive.'

'What happened?'

'He was killed before he hit the road block.'

'How did he die?'

'The police used a couple of armoured vehicles to make the road-block. As soon as it became clear Rhodes intended to ram them, they opened fire.'

'What sort of armoured vehicles were they?'

'Olifants.'

'Are you telling me that Rhodes was going to ram his car into two fifty ton tanks?' I asked incredulously.

'That's what the Ambassador told me. He said Rhodes was killed instantly.'

'I'm not surprised. An Olifant fires a 105 millimetre shell!'

'I know what calibre shell an Olifant fires.' He sounded piqued. 'I was in the Army. I know the specification of the arms, equipment and armoured vehicles used by the armed forces of every country in the world.'

He stared at me. Perhaps he was tempting me to contradict him, but I stayed silent. It was a big boast, but I was fresh out of contradictions.

'The Olifant is the South African version of the British

Centurion,' he went on, once he realised I was not going to challenge his knowledge. 'I've seen the damage one of those shells can do. There wouldn't have been much left of the car or driver.'

'That's why the South African security forces used a tank to kill Rhodes, rather than just putting a bullet through his head.'

He looked puzzled.

'An intact dead body would have been subject to a post-mortem. The pathologist might have asked questions about the presence of a bullet in Rhodes' brain,' I explained. 'As you rightly pointed out, a shell from a tank would have left very little body to examine and so no incriminating evidence.'

'I see.'

'So it's four down and only Mister O'Leary to go.'

'I have discussed O'Leary with the PM. Under normal circumstances it would be up to the Irish to deal with him.'

'Are these considered to be normal circumstances?'

'No, they are far from normal. Which is why Mrs Thatcher wants you to deal with O'Leary.' He gave me the look and then added: 'But do it discreetly, Statton. We don't need a diplomatic row with the Irish Republic just now.'

'I'm the epitome of discretion. Like the South Africans, I won't leave any incriminating evidence behind.' I paused and held my glass up in a toast. I smiled at him knowingly. 'I have a mate in the Second Royal Tank Regiment who owes me a favour. A shell from a Challenger should do the trick.'

He didn't raise his own glass, instead he looked at me through narrowed eyes. He was trying to work out if I was joking, or whether I was really ruthless enough to use a tank to kill Brendan O'Leary.

It worried me that my boss doubted me this way. He should have known I was ruthless enough for anything.

'What's this about finding a lottery ticket in Timmy's desk?' My secretary asked as soon as I walked into the office. She was just putting on her coat. 'I didn't know he did the lottery.'

'You don't know everything, Poppy.'

'I know most of what goes on in this place,' she said archly. 'Like who is having it off with whom.'

'Are you by any chance the illegitimate child of a Stasi officer?'

'What do you mean?' She looked puzzled. 'What's a stasi?'

'It doesn't matter.' I pointed at her. 'Why have you got your coat on?'

'I'm going home.'

'It's only half past four.'

'But it's Friday and I've finished all my work.'

'How do you know? I might want to dictate a letter.'

'You're far too nice to be a dictator,' she riposted immediately.

I refused to laugh at her joke. 'Your problem, Miss Fotheringay-Evans, is that you take me for granted. Someday I will surprise you and give you a written warning for your insubordination.'

'Well, at least I will know in advance. You get me to type all your letters for you.'

'I still know how to write longhand, young lady,' I said sternly. It was difficult. 'Now tell me, how did you know about Timmy's lottery ticket?'

'His mum told me. She rang to thank you this morning. I got chatting to her and she explained about what you did. You weren't here so I put her through to Rupert.'

'I was here this afternoon before my meeting with the Director-General,' I pointed out. 'Why didn't you tell me then that Mrs Fraser rang?'

'I'm sorry, I forgot.' She didn't sound at all contrite.

'Where's Melissa? Has she gone home early too?'

'No she's at the Manor Square Hotel in Kensington. She rang whilst you were upstairs with Rupert and asked me to tell you to meet her there as soon as possible. She said she'd wait for you in the car-park.'

'How long has she been there?'

'She didn't say,' she replied. 'A hotel liaison with Melissa. How intriguing. Is there romance in the air?'

'Don't be silly, Poppy. There is no "liaison", as you put it, and there is certainly no romance. I have no idea what Melissa wants, but I assure you any meeting between us will be strictly business.'

'Is that because she's a dyke?'

'As far as I know, a dyke is something into which a little Dutch boy once stuck his finger?'

'I think you'll find Melissa would prefer a little Dutch girl's finger in her.' She made an obscene movement of her own finger.

'Melissa's sexuality is her own affair,' I said as I headed for the door. 'All that matters to the Department is that she is intelligent, competent, punctual and hard-working. In fact, you could take some lessons from her.'

'I might not have the same qualities as little-miss-perfect,' she called after me, 'but at least I know the difference between a dick and a dildo.'

I shook my head in despair. How on earth Poppy Fotheringay-Evans had got through seven years at the genteel Cheltenham Ladies' College, without being expelled, was quite beyond me.

The Manor Square Hotel, Kensington, London.

Although the Manor Square Hotel was technically in Kensington, it was located on the Royal borough's border with Shepherd's Bush, not far from where I lived. I knew the hotel well. It was a seedy, downmarket hotel that was raided regularly by the local vice squad.

I drove into the hotel's car-park and parked in a bay that was adjacent to one of the new British Telecom telephone booths. It was ultra-modern, with a wide gap at the bottom of its sides that let a draught into the booth, even when there was only a slight breeze, and a plate glass door with BT stamped on it.

Me? I preferred the old-fashioned, iconic red boxes with the gold crown on the front, which were a perfect shelter from the elements and had served me well for decades.

The door of the telephone booth opened and Melissa came out. She looked cold and miserable. 'I thought you were never coming,' she complained as she opened the passenger door and slid onto the seat.

'I came as soon as I could.'

'I rang Poppy almost three hours ago,' she moaned. 'I've been waiting in that damn telephone box ever since, with nothing to do except read the business cards posted there.'

'I bet that kept you busy. I expect there were dozens.'

'Yeah. Most of them gave the telephone numbers of escorts and masseurs.'

'I hope you weren't tempted to ring for a quick massage.'

'It's no joking matter, boss. It was bloody freezing in that telephone box and I've probably caught a cold waiting for you.' She looked at me and pouted. 'You still haven't told me why you were late. I suppose Poppy forgot to give you my message.'

'I was in a meeting with the Director-General. Poppy gave me your message when I got back to the office.'

'I told her it was urgent. She could have interrupted your meeting.'

'That's true, but we are talking about Poppy here.'

'That girl is an airhead,' Melissa said angrily, forgetting she was younger than Poppy. She pulled a tissue from her bag and blew her nose loudly.

'You sound agitated.'

'I *am* bloody agitated.' She pointed at the hotel. 'That place is not only a dump, but it's a knocking-shop. While I was waiting in the phone booth, I was approached twice by strange looking men asking me how much I charged.'

'Well, the guests that stay at the Manor do have a reputation for using their rooms to satisfy the needs of strange looking men.'

'You live close to here don't you?' Her tone suggested that she thought the state of the hotel, and the peccadilloes of its guests and their clients, was my fault.

'Yes, but it's not a hotel I have ever used. Now, why are we here, Melissa?'

'I thought you would want to know that Brendan O'Leary is staying at the hotel,' she said.

'O'Leary is staying here?' I was surprised. When she called the Manor Square Hotel a dump, she was not exaggerating. I had members of the Phoenix Group down as people who would stay at places like the Ritz or Claridge's. 'Are you sure?'

'I'm sure.'

I sensed there was more. 'Is O'Leary with somebody?'

'Yeah.'

'Who?'

'Colleen.'

'Colleen Masters?' I could not disguise my surprise.

'Yeah.'

'How do you know?'

'I followed her.'

I stared out of the window. Something started nibbling at my brain. A man approached the telephone booth and opened the door.

'There's another pervert,' Melissa hissed.

I watched as the man took one of the cards from the display

inside the phone booth and dialled a number.

'See?' She asked.

I saw. It was life, and life goes on.

'I think you'd better tell me everything, Melissa.' I hoped my voice did not betray my doubts.

'Remember you asked me to dig into O'Leary's background?'

I nodded in reply.

'Well, I did.'

'And what did you find?' I wasn't sure I wanted to know.

'I discovered his wife is dead. She left him to bring up an only child on his own.'

'It happens.'

'I know, but that child was a daughter called Colleen.'

'Colleen is a common Irish name,' I pointed out.

'I know. That was my first reaction. Which is why I went to the Personnel Department and pulled Colleen's employment records. Masters is her married name.'

'I know. She told me.'

'But did you know that her maiden name was O'Leary?'

'No, I didn't. Perhaps it's a coincidence.'

Melissa shook her head. 'On the application form Colleen put Brendan O'Leary down as her next-of-kin.'

That's when I was forced to accept the truth. It all began to make sense.

Whoever had been passing information about me to the Phoenix Group, was somebody who was party to my movements. The only person who knew every move I made during the Mandela operation was Disraeli-Astor.

Colleen had openly boasted she knew everything that her boss knew. My heart sank.

'While you've been working on the Mandela visit over the past couple of days, I thought it would be a good idea to keep an eye on Colleen. Today I followed her to this hotel.'

'How do you know O'Leary is here as well?'

'It was a guess, so I checked.'

'How did you do that?'

'I went to reception and asked which room Mister O'Leary was staying in. I pretended I was a member of his staff and said I had to deliver an urgent message to him. I don't think the receptionist

481

believed me, but he gave me his room number anyway.'

'He probably thought you were a call girl. As you pointed out earlier, it happens all the time in this area.'

She bristled. 'Do I look like a call-girl?'

'Who can tell? I'm sure not all prostitutes dress in short skirts, skimpy tops and high heels. It takes all sorts. Some men might get turned on by torn denim jeans, baggy sweatshirts, leather jackets and Doc Martens boots.' I looked at her straight faced. 'Particularly the strange looking ones.'

She glanced down at her clothes and then grinned at me.

'So why are you dressed in your old clothes?' I asked.

'They're not old. I bought them last weekend.'

'From a jumble sale I assume?'

'Very funny. No, from a very smart shop in the West End. It's the grunge look.'

'I don't know about grunge, but whoever sold you jeans with holes in must have had a grudge against you?'

'You wouldn't understand, boss. It's called fashion.'

'Fashion? So what about that thing you have on your head?'

'It's an *alpaca chullo*.' She flicked at the hat's hanging ear muffs with her fingers. 'It's from Bolivia.'

'The hat might go down a wow in Sucre, but why are you wearing it in Shepherds Bush?'

'I thought it might stop Colleen recognising me.'

'Did she see you?'

'No. I was very careful.'

'So the hat didn't help?'

'You're teasing me.'

'You guessed.'

'I bet the mandarins at the Foreign Office wouldn't take the mick out of me like you,' she said with a pout that didn't quite work.

'That's true. Senior bureaucrats are not renowned for their sense of humour.'

'But I bet the FO Permanent Secretary knows what an *alpaca chullo* is,' she said with a grin.

'Of course, he does. It was such knowledge that made the British Empire great.' I stared out of the window again, this time at the shabby building that was the Manor Square Hotel. 'How do you know O'Leary and Colleen are still inside?'

'Because I've been watching the entrance.' She pointed towards the glass doors that were accessible from the car-park. 'Colleen did leave the hotel about half an hour ago. I followed her to a supermarket round the corner where she bought some cigarettes, then she went straight back to the hotel and has not appeared again.'

'O'Leary could have left whilst you were following Colleen to the supermarket?'

'That did cross my mind, but decided it was unlikely. As far as I remember, Colleen doesn't smoke.'

'She doesn't,' I confirmed.

'So, I assumed the cigarettes were for her father. Logically, it would mean he's still in his room.'

I continued to stare at the hotel. It made sense. 'Which room is O'Leary staying in?'

'Room 210. It's a suite on the second floor.'

'How do you know it's a suite?'

'I went up to the second floor and checked the location of Room 210. It's on the corner of the building.' She pointed at the hotel. 'As you can see the room has two windows on this side and there is one on the other side. So it must be quite large, which would make it a suite.'

'Clever girl!'

She grinned at me again. 'To be honest, I found a floor plan displayed in the corridor which showed that each of the corner rooms on the second floor is a suite!'

'Sneaky girl!'

'What do we do now?' She asked.

'We do nothing. I'll deal with it on my own.'

'Won't you need back-up?'

I pulled my .44 Magnum from its holster and checked it was fully loaded. 'This is all the back-up I need,' I said and hoped I was right. 'You get yourself off home.'

'OK. If you're sure you don't need me, I will go. I'm going out to dinner tonight and I need to change.' She got out of the car and strode off in the direction of Shepherd's Bush Station.

Two minutes later I entered the hotel and slipped past the receptionist without being seen. I made my way silently up the stairs to the second floor. Room 210 was at the end of the corridor, just as Melissa had reported.

I knocked on the door and heard footsteps on the other side. There was a click as a key was turned, then the door swung open.

Colleen didn't seem surprised to see me. 'I thought it might be you,' she said in a flat voice. 'Sixth sense I suppose.' Her face was pale and she wore no makeup. She had been crying.

'How did you find me?'

'Melissa worked it out and followed you here.'

'Clever girl.'

'Yeah. That's what I told her.'

'I suppose you'd better come in.'

She closed the door behind me and led me into a shabby lounge area. She walked over and sat down on a settee. In one corner of the room two pink suitcases stood on the threadbare carpet.

'Going somewhere?'

'That was the plan.' She picked distractedly at the frayed and faded floral cover of the settee. 'But it doesn't look as if I'll be going anywhere now.'

I didn't sit down in the armchair opposite the settee, instead I stood looking down at her. 'Where's your father?'

She looked up at me with eyes that were red and moist. 'In the bedroom.' She pointed towards a door on the other side of the room. It was slightly ajar.

I walked over and pushed the door open fully. Brendan O'Leary was lying on the bed with his eyes closed. He was fully clothed in a blazer, open necked blue shirt, smartly pressed navy slacks and highly polished black leather loafers. I could see that his black socks were decorated with tiny green shamrocks.

I pressed my finger against the side of his neck, but could detect no pulse. I'm no pathologist, but the Irishman was still warm so it seemed pretty obvious he hadn't been dead long. There was no visible bruising, or sign of any wounds, and no other indication of the cause of death. He just looked as if he was in a deep asleep.

'What happened?' I asked when I returned to the lounge.

'I popped out to get dad some ciggies,' she pointed to a packet of 20 cigarettes that lay unopened on the coffee table in front of her. 'I was only gone a few minutes and when I got back I found him dead on the bed. I think it was a heart attack.'

'Smoking has that effect on some people,' I said.

'Dad has suffered from heart problems for years. I warned him about the danger of cigarettes to his health. He gave up smoking after he had a heart attack last year. However, he's been under so much stress recently that he started again.'

'Why was he under stress?'

'His company is on the brink of bankruptcy. That's why he's been reduced to staying in this dump.' She waved her hand in the air. 'He always used to stay at the Dorchester.'

'I'm sure having to use cheap hotels like the rest of us plebs must have been very stressful for him,' I said.

'That's very unfair, David.' She glared at me angrily, her pale cheeks flushed red.

'Perhaps you could explain your concept of fairness to Timmy Fisher's mum,' I said coldly. 'What was fair about your father getting Brannagan to murder her son in cold blood?'

The dash of colour drained from her face immediately and her eyes dropped to the floor.

'And while you're at it, perhaps you could explain to her why you tipped off your father that Timmy was on his way to visit Brannagan in Slough.'

She started to cry again. 'I didn't know Timmy would be killed,' she sobbed. 'You have to believe me.'

'That might be difficult.'

'I thought the Irishman would flee the country when he found out Timmy was on his way to check out his flat. That's the truth.'

'Is that so? And to which country exactly did you think Brannagan would flee when you told your father I was in Cape Town? You must have known he would follow me there.'

She said nothing for a while, instead she stared down at her hands as she clasped and unclasped them in agitation. Finally she looked up at me. Misery was etched across her tear stained face.

'Dad promised me there would be no more killing. He told me that Brannagan was following you to South Africa to find out what you were up to.'

'And you believed that?'

'Yes.'

'Are you really that stupid, Colleen?'

'What do you mean?'

'Why would your father get Brannagan to follow me all the way to Cape Town when all he had to do was ask you what I was up to?

He must have known you were aware of my every move.'

Colleen looked towards the bedroom. 'Oh, daddy. You lied to me,' she murmured. 'How could you do that to me?'

She turned to me. Tears still streamed down her face, dripping onto her starched white blouse, leaving wet patches through which I could see her pink brassiere. 'I didn't think,' she said softly. 'I was stupid.'

'Exactly. And your stupidity got somebody killed, but sadly for your father, and his Phoenix Group pals, it wasn't me.'

'Jesus, David. I'm so sorry about what happened to your girlfriend.' She wailed and let out a loud sob that made her body shudder. 'I didn't know that crazy man was going to blow up your car with her inside it.'

'But he did, Colleen. Didn't he?'

'Yes. And it's something I will have to live with for the rest of my life. Freddie, Timmy and the Russian are dead because of me. I killed them all.'

'How were you responsible for the Russian's death?' I asked.

'When I read the transcript of Urinoff's second interview, and saw he was going to reveal the names of the Phoenix Group members, I told my dad where he was. He told me they had somebody who would be able to get into the safe-house and steal the Russian's brief case. He didn't tell me Urinoff would be killed.'

She looked at me with tears streaming down her face. 'I killed them all!' She wailed and then started sobbing again.

The last woman I heard sobbing like that was Bridget Olafson. On that occasion she had been play-acting. Colleen was different. I could tell she was genuinely upset and despite my anger I felt sorry for her.

'No. You didn't kill them, Colleen,' I said quietly. 'It was Shaun Brannagan who did that, and now he's dead too.'

'That doesn't make me feel any better. I really liked Timmy.'

'Were you at his funeral?' I was pretty certain she was the woman in the bottle-green coat and veil whose bearing had struck a chord with me at Timmy's funeral.

She nodded silently. 'I wanted to pay my last respects to him and try to atone for what I did.'

'And?'

'It didn't help. I still have nightmares about Timmy's death.'

I said nothing, but remembered hearing her talk in her sleep the first time we stayed at the Wife of Bath. I didn't think anything of it at the time, but I suppose it was her guilt coming to the surface.

'I've found it difficult to live with myself,' she went on. 'I wanted so much to turn back the clock and start again.'

'So why did you continue to pass information to your dad after Timmy died? You not only betrayed Timmy, but you betrayed the department and…'

'I don't care about the department,' she interjected, 'but Timmy was different.'

'And you betrayed me,' I finished my sentence.

She nodded her head and tears dropped from her face onto the cellophane wrapping of the packet of cigarettes. 'That's my greatest regret, David.'

'So why did you do it, Colleen?'

She sat for a long time saying nothing, as if trying to put together an answer that would rationalise her deceit. 'I was trying to help my dad,' she said eventually. 'He's all I have.' She looked towards the bedroom again and corrected herself: 'All I had.'

'Why did your father need your help? I'd have thought he could look after himself.'

'At one time that was true. In fact, he used to be the strongest person I've ever known. He was able to look after us both, without any help from anybody, but recently he lost some of his confidence.'

'What happened?'

'I'm not really sure. Dad was a proud man who kept his problems to himself.' She paused. 'But a few months ago he admitted to me that his tour company was struggling. A major part of his business was based on guided tours to South Africa and it was being hit by political uncertainty in the country.

'He told me he was frightened the trips would dry up completely if the ANC took over the country. Losing the South African safari business would have tipped his company over the edge. The Phoenix Group's plan was his last hope, which is why he joined it and why I agreed to help him. What else could I do?'

'You could have persuaded him to sell up and retire.'

'I tried that, but he wouldn't listen. As I told you, he was a proud man and he refused to admit that his company was beyond saving. However, this year has been tough and he became increasingly stressed.'

She stared at the bedroom door again and dabbed at her eyes with a tissue.

'And things got worse over the past couple of days. Dad saw the Phoenix Group plan disintegrate before his eyes. That's when he realised his last hope of saving his company had gone and I finally managed to convince him we should go to Ireland.

'I have property in County Cork that was left to me by my grandpa. It was gifted to me in trust and is not tied up with dad's travel company. So, if he was forced to file for bankruptcy, we would still have somewhere to live. That's why my luggage is here. We were booked on an Aer Lingus flight to Dublin this evening.'

Her eyes shifted from the bedroom door to the two suitcases.

'But I think seeing my suitcases, and realising I was prepared to give up my career and go back to Ireland with him, got to him. I think it was a sense of despair that brought on his heart attack.'

I considered her words. Colleen was indirectly responsible for Freddie's death. She knew it and I knew it. I should have been angry and bitter, but, as I looked down at her, the only emotion I felt was pity.

'So what do we do now?' She whispered.

'You have an airline ticket to Dublin in your handbag,' I told her. 'I suggest you use it. Don't come back.'

'What about my dad? I can't just leave him here like that.'

'That's your choice, my dear, but, there's nothing you can do to help him now.'

'What are you going to do?'

'Me? I'm off to the Blue Oyster to listen to some decent jazz and get very drunk.' I made my way to the door, but she called out as I opened it.

'David.'

I turned to face her.

'Whatever you might think. I do love you.'

I looked at her sadly. 'Perhaps you do, Colleen. The trouble is you loved your father more.'

ACKNOWLEDGEMENTS

I would like to thank TAUP UK for providing humble writers like me with an opportunity to see our efforts in print.

In particular I would like to thank James Apps and Peter Apps without whose dedication TAUP would not exist.

Local writers on Sheppey owe them a debt of gratitude for the way in which they help and advise us all.

I would like to thank James and Peter also for all their hard work in editing my manuscript and making it ready for printing.

I would like to thank all those who read my last book, *Operation Seal Island*, and gave it such enthusiastic reviews. Your comments encouraged me to write this follow up.

Writing a book requires dedication, commitment and an understanding wife, who so often loses her husband behind a computer screen. So, a big thank you to Louise for putting up with my constant tapping on the keyboard when she is watching her favourite television programmes!

And, finally, once again I would like to thank YOU for wanting to read *The Mandela Project*. I hope you enjoy it.

Gordon Henderson

Gordon Henderson was born in Brompton Military Hospital in 1948 and is proud to be a true 'Man of Kent'. His early life was spent in the Medway Towns, where he grew up on a council estate in Chatham and went to Fort Luton Secondary Modern School.

Gordon left school at 16 to join Woolworths, where he worked his way up from being a 'stockroom boy' to senior store manager.

After spending some time in South Africa, where he had a restaurant, Gordon had a succession of jobs. They included being a political agent, a senior contracts officer in the Aerospace Industry and an operations manager for an international manufacturing company.

In 2010 he was elected as Member of Parliament for Sittingbourne and Sheppey.

Gordon has written a volume of short stories, *Pigeon Pie*, and two novels, featuring David Statton, *Operation Seal Island* and *The Mandela Project*. He is now working on his next novel in the series, entitled *The Phoenix Papers*.

www.ingramcontent.com/pod-product-compliance
Lightning Source LLC
Chambersburg PA
CBHW071216250626
47163CB00001B/4